Praise for *In Twilight's Shadow*

"Nonstop action, magic-laced suspense, and
some sizzling sexual chemistry fuel
In Twilight's Shadow, [an] inventive
paranormal romance."

—*Chicago Tribune*

"A fresh and dark paranormal romance
that should not be missed."

—*Romance Reviews Today*

"A terrific new story . . . will keep you on the edge
of your seat and reading well into the night."

—*Fresh Fiction*

Tor Books by Patti O'Shea

In the Darkest Night

Patti O'Shea

TOR®
paranormal romance

A TOM DOHERTY ASSOCIATES BOOK
NEW YORK

This is a work of fiction. All of the characters, organizations, and events portrayed in this novel are either products of the author's imagination or are used fictitiously.

IN THE DARKEST NIGHT

A Tor Book
Published by Tom Doherty Associates, LLC
175 Fifth Avenue
New York, NY 10010

www.tor-forge.com

Tor® is a registered trademark of Tom Doherty Associates, LLC.

ISBN 978-0-7653-6170-7

First Edition: April 2010

Printed in the United States of America

0 9 8 7 6 5 4 3 2 1

For my parents for their support as I wrote this story. Also, thanks to everyone on Twitter who helped me with research on both *Edge of Dawn* and this book, with a special shout-out to the Seattle residents who answered my many questions. And a special thank-you to my writing buddy, Melissa Lynn Copeland, who always comes through no matter what I throw at her.

I'd also like to express my appreciation to all the readers who've taken a chance on my stories. Thank you for letting me share them with you. If you'd like more information about my books or to sign up for my sporadic newsletter, please visit www.pattioshea.com.

In the
Darkest
Night

1

CHAPTER

Farran put the last bottle of shampoo on the shelf, broke down the box, and pushed her cart over the grayish linoleum to the toothpaste aisle. One of the wheels emitted a sharp squeak that grated on her nerves, but she gritted her teeth and ignored it. There were three different brands to stock here and that should keep her busy until break time, which was—she glanced at her watch—in exactly nineteen minutes.

She opened the box of Crest gel and began filling the empty spot on the shelf. Until she'd started working here, she'd never owned a watch. The Tàireil were in tune with the Earth, even when it wasn't their dimension, and she'd always had a good idea of what time it was. If she needed to be more precise, there'd always been the clock on her cell phone, but all that had changed. Farran couldn't afford a phone now—not that she had anyone to call—and this discount chain was obsessive about punctuality. The watch had an ugly yellow plastic strap and looked as cheap as it was, but it kept her from getting fired and that was all that mattered.

To her chagrin, she needed this lousy job. It barely paid above minimum wage and didn't offer health insurance, but no one else would hire her. Not after they got a look at her face.

Reaching up with one hand, she touched her right cheek and traced two fingers across the skin. It was smooth, but thick and uneven, and it stood out in stark contrast to the softness of the rest of her face. The scar was hideous—Farran knew it—but she couldn't fix it. She wanted to—oh, how she wanted to—but her magic wasn't strong enough for the task and it wasn't as if she could ask someone to heal it for her.

Finished with the gel, she moved down the row to the next brand of toothpaste and began putting the Colgate on the shelf. The fluorescent lights made the scar even more noticeable, but she couldn't avoid them.

A crash from a couple of rows over made her jerk and Farran drew a deep breath before reaching for more packages and placing them in their spot. Whatever had been knocked over had an orange scent to it and it grew stronger the longer she stood there. She moved faster, wanting to get out of the area before the smell made her gag.

"But, Mom," came a whiney voice in the next aisle, "I'm supposed to text Veronica in fifteen minutes. We have to go home now."

"We'll leave when I have everything on our list."

"I don't know why I had to come anyway or why you wouldn't let me bring my phone. Other kids get to carry their phones with them all the time." The voice became less audible, sounding as if the pair had moved into the main aisle and away from Farran.

This was what her life had come to—listening to complaining teenagers and smelling some putrid orange cleaning product while she stocked shelves for a pittance. It was pathetic.

Farran checked her watch again. Eleven minutes until break. Dragging her feet, she wheeled the cart to the end of the aisle. She felt exposed here, on display, and dipped her head forward, trying to use her hair to hide her cheek. It was longer than she used to wear it, but not long enough to offer the concealment she so desperately wanted.

She focused on her task, doing her best to ignore the shoppers wheeling their gray-plastic carts past where she stood, trying to pretend that she didn't see them look over a second time and stare until they were out of view. Farran wanted to finish this last box *now* and find somewhere less visible to work.

Her hands shook and she inhaled deeply in an attempt to relax. Anxiety strummed through her and she tried to bring that under control, too. Despite her efforts, her breath shuddered out and she moved faster, trying to keep her focus on the job. How likely was it that most people cared about her? It was her imagination, her self-consciousness that made her feel as if she were standing in a spotlight, but that wasn't reality.

The laughter made her muscles go rigid. It wasn't jovial, we're-having-a-good-time laughter. No, this was the nasty kind of laugh she'd heard too often over the last seven months. It was mean-spirited and cruel—like the people who thought that just because she didn't look like them, she was fair game. After all, a freak with a scar on her face couldn't have feelings, right?

She picked the group up in her peripheral vision—two men, three women, all around college age. The blonde was the ringleader, the sneer on her face contemptuous. Farran fumbled with the packages of toothpaste, sending them tumbling to the floor. There was more laughter as she picked them up.

Go away. Please go away.

Her entire body began to shake and she tried to still it, not wanting them to know they had the power to decimate her. There was a gaping wound deep inside her, as if they'd sliced a cavernous gash into her soul and Farran could barely comprehend the casual viciousness.

It was hard, but she made eye contact with them, hoping it would humanize her and they'd leave, but that wasn't what happened. The blonde raised her cell phone and took a picture of Farran's scarred face.

That froze her, and for an instant, she couldn't react, couldn't think. Then it dawned on her. That girl was going to post the picture on the Web—Facebook, MySpace, or maybe some other site—letting other malicious people laugh at her disfigurement. It sucked the breath from her, the physical ache matching the one in her soul.

What did she do? How did she stop this? Did they think she wanted to look like this? That she didn't wish with her whole heart that her appearance was *normal*? Did they think that she was undeserving of being treated with the smallest modicum of kindness because she was different? Or did they believe she had no right to be out in public, repulsing the world with her face?

If Farran had a choice, she would hide. She hated thinking about every place she went, wondering who would be there, how many people would see her or how they'd—

Miss Cold-Cruel-and-Shallow walked away, her entourage following in her wake. Oh, God! That picture. That picture!

Farran wanted to run after them, grab the cell phone, and erase the image, but her feet wouldn't move. She wanted to scream *stop* and threaten the woman with a lawsuit if the picture was used anywhere without permission, but her voice wouldn't work. She wanted to be powerful enough magically that she could successfully use her powers on electronic items, but she wasn't.

The urge to vomit swamped her, and she half hoped she would. Maybe that would relieve the sick, shaky feeling that had settled in her belly, but all her stomach did was roil. The worst thing was the realization that there was nothing she could do to prevent her photo from being plastered wherever that girl chose to put it. Nothing. Her stomach heaved again.

Tears welled, and biting her bottom lip, Farran blinked them back. She wasn't letting some girl make her cry. She wasn't!

Her exhale hitched and Farran swallowed hard. The group was still laughing and before they turned the corner, the blonde looked back over her shoulder and gave a toss of her hair. Then they were gone.

Numbness kept the totality of her devastation at bay, but Farran felt her daze fading with each second that ticked by.

Choking back a sob, she blinked harder. God, she wished she could go back in time. If she could do it over, she'd work slower and stay away from the aisle until after that heartless woman and her friends were gone. Closing her eyes, she balled her hands into fists and whispered, "Just a couple of minutes—that's all I need, please."

Idiot, she berated herself, dropping her chin to her chest. Not even the strong Tàireil had control of time, and her magical power was so weak that she was limited to ordinary spells. And even some of those were tough for her. Farran forced her fingers to relax.

There was nothing she could do—not a damn thing. She was on until closing; she had to get over this and survive the rest of the night. Had to. Farran gathered her courage, her resolve; she needed to return to work before her boss saw her standing idle and fired her.

With one last deep breath, she opened her eyes. And frowned. She was in the middle of the toothpaste row, not on the end by the main aisle. Had she walked backward without being aware of it?

Shaking her head, Farran turned to move the cart back up the aisle to finish stocking, but went still. She'd already shelved all the Colgate, but the box was full. Looking to her left, she expected to see the shelf filled, but it wasn't. She stared at the empty spot and then back at the toothpaste.

A crash a couple of rows over made her jerk and suck in a sharp breath. She detected the slightest hint of orange in the air and that's when it dawned on her—the overpowering scent had been missing. Her hands shook harder and she wrapped them around the handle of the cart.

"But, Mom," came a whiney voice in the next aisle, "I'm supposed to text Veronica in fifteen minutes. We have to go home now."

"We'll leave when I have everything on our list."

"I don't know why I had to come anyway or why you wouldn't let me bring my phone. Other kids get to carry their phones with them all the time."

Farran's eyes went wide. This didn't make sense—nothing made sense. If she didn't know better she'd think she was replaying—

Stupid. She was being stupid. But she looked at her watch anyway. Twelve minutes to her break time.

Twelve minutes!

Her knees buckled and Farran locked them to keep from hitting the floor. This wasn't possible.

Staggering to the back of the store, she pushed through the doors into the employees-only area and leaned against the wall. *It wasn't possible.* This didn't happen. No one traveled through time. No Tàireil, no matter how powerful, had ever been able to do it, and many had tried. There was no way she could have time traveled either.

No way.

Maybe the thing with that group was some kind of precognitive event. Maybe it hadn't happened yet and she'd mentally seen into the future. Never mind that her skills in that area were as nonexistent as most of her other magical abilities; that made more sense than her other idea.

The nauseating orange scent was strong enough to penetrate the stockroom and she swallowed hard. She'd been around talented Tàireil seers and few ever experienced an odor with their visions. Farran had.

She'd seen the store, the rows of toothpaste in front of her. She'd heard the sound of something breaking, the whining teenager. She'd felt the smooth packaging of the toothpaste boxes and the rough cardboard box they'd been contained in. The only sense she hadn't experienced was taste.

What were the odds that she'd suddenly developed prescience?

Slim and none, she knew, but to replay . . . Shaking her head, she ran through the timing of events tonight. If she'd really gone backward a few minutes, that nasty group should be walking by the aisle any second. Of course, if she'd had a view of the future, they'd be passing by any minute, too.

Farran's legs trembled as she forced herself to cross to the door and peer out the yellowed plastic window.

No one was out there.

See? Just some brain stutter or her overactive imagination.

Then Farran saw her, the blond girl who'd taken her picture and the girl's friends. The emotion that shot through Farran was too strong, too violent, too immediate to be caused by some manifestation of her imagination or peek into the future. The scorn, the way they'd treated her had happened. It had really happened.

That meant—

Farran's knees did give out then and she slid down the wall until she sat on the dirty floor. Somehow, some way, she'd replayed a few minutes from her life and she had no idea how or why it had occurred.

Farran zipped up her Polarplus jacket as soon as she stepped outside the store and tipped her face up to the sky. The night was damp and cool, but she let it envelop her. She only wished she had an umbrella.

Her friend—her former friend—Shona would have chuckled and commented on how she could tell Farran wasn't originally from Seattle, that no one here bothered with an umbrella for a little drizzle. Farran would have laughed with her and said something about how it was only good common sense to stay dry. It had become a standing joke in the months they'd been close.

Jamming her hands into her jacket pockets, she started walking. She missed Shona. Farran had never had many friends—she'd never really fit in the Tàireil world and here it was worse—but she and Shona had been as close as sisters. If only Farran hadn't been forced into her father's scheme. If only she could have gotten the dracontias from Shona without her knowing Farran had been behind her loss of the dragon stone. If only.

Farran snorted quietly and slogged along toward the bus stop. There weren't a lot of people around, but the deep blue of her jacket helped her disappear into the darkness and she welcomed that. She wanted to barricade herself in her apartment, to be somewhere that she wouldn't face ridicule.

Her fingers came up and touched her scar, her thumb trailing just above it. That girl, her friends, their cruelty—it had happened. And it hadn't.

Farran couldn't figure it out and she'd thought about it most of the evening. She hadn't come up with any answers, but some things were certain. One minute she'd stood on the end of the toothpaste aisle, staring after her tormenters, and the next minute she'd been midrow. She wasn't able to wield a spell to rewind the clock, that was a given, so who was powerful enough to do such a thing and why had he done it for her?

It wasn't a member of the Gineal. They couldn't alter time any more than the Tàireil could. In fact, both societies shared the theory that it was impossible to time travel or change the flow in any way, that there was some natural law preventing it. Farran had accepted that, but after tonight—

Someone was behind her.

She stiffened, her step hitching before she resumed her pace. Probably a human headed home the same way she was, nothing to worry about, but a shiver coursed through her. Farran moved faster and sensed whoever was back there pick up his speed, too. Not a coincidence, then; he was following her.

The streetlights seemed somehow dimmer and she looked around, hoping enough people were around to deter the guy, but the sidewalks and road were deserted now. The emptiness made the hair at her nape stand on end.

She took her hands from her jacket pockets and pulled some energy from the earth. It was a risk. Because the Gineal could track magic, she'd avoided using her powers as much as possible. But if someone meant to mug her or worse, it would be her only defense.

Needing to know whatever she could about her stalker, Farran opened her senses and probed. Her heart froze for an instant, then pounded wildly. The energy she gathered fell away.

Demon. Oh, God, she had a demon after her!

Farran pulled more energy. She couldn't worry about humans seeing her or about the Gineal tracking her. Not now. She silently recited the incantation to open a transit.

Nothing happened.

Half running, she repeated the spell, this time aloud. The gate wouldn't open.

The demon must have blocked her ability to create a transit. If she were stronger, his containment spell wouldn't work, but she wasn't. She wasn't, damn it. Grimly, Farran considered her odds of surviving a one-on-one fight. Almost zero. He was powerful enough magically that without a miracle, he'd easily beat her. While she could take on any human and win, even a minor demon would level her.

He gained on her and Farran panicked. She knew better, but she ran. There was no way to outdistance him, no place to hide. She kept going anyway, using all the speed she possessed. Her breathing became harsh and ragged, her field of vision tunneled, but she zigzagged wildly along the sidewalk to avoid getting hit. The demon didn't fire at her.

The space between them widened again. Maybe she *could* outrun and elude him. She threw a cloaking spell around herself. Farran couldn't hold it long, but she only needed enough time to get out of his range. She spotted an opening between two buildings up ahead and changed course. He might miss the fact that she turned off.

Even in the dark, she could make out spray-painted Dumpsters and the garbage cans that lined both sides of the alley. Bags of refuse were piled next to doorways and she had to make a sudden sharp jag to avoid a discarded wooden pallet. Farran ran on.

The dark brick building on her left gave way to a second building that was painted white. There were dark blotches of graffiti marring the surface, but she couldn't spot any break between the two structures that she could exit through. On her right, the building was long, continuing back a great distance. She raced on.

Farran checked on the demon. He wasn't at the alley yet. So far her cloak was holding, and since he'd track her on her energy signature, he couldn't know for sure where she was. All she needed to do was get out of here, take a few more random twists and turns, and maybe— just maybe—she really could shake him off.

Hope shattered abruptly as the alley ended at a brick wall. Fighting off the burst of fear, she hurried back the way she'd come, searching for the exit that had to be here. *It had to be!* But she didn't spot an opening.

Oh, God. Oh, God. Oh, God!

Turning down here had been a mistake. A huge mistake. If she were at full strength, she could use a levitation spell, but it would require all her magic and she was low on power already. She didn't have enough left to propel herself over the wall and it was far too high for her to climb.

Despair washed over her, but Farran fought it off. He wasn't getting her this easily.

She tried another transit, but it was still closed to her. Desperately, she examined the buildings around her, looking for an open window, any way inside. No matter where she ended up, it had to be better than where she was now, but the windows were shut tight.

Hurrying down the alley, Farran yanked at a door-knob, but it was locked. She ran to the next and the next, but no one had been careless.

Where was he? She scanned and went still. Too close. The demon was too close. Her only hope now was that her shield was strong enough to conceal her. Quickly, she searched for the best hiding place and chose the deep shadows of a doorway. As he neared, she eased farther back, pressing herself tight against the metal door.

Her breathing was still ragged and she tried to calm down, to inhale and exhale normally. Quietly.

She repeated the incantation to strengthen her cloak, but it didn't do a lot—she'd used up too much of her power. Farran clenched her hands, her nails cutting into her palms as she fought to control her fear.

From her position, she saw him stop at the opening to the alley. The faint light of a nearby streetlight outlined his form, letting her know a little more about what she'd be facing. He was tall, broad-shouldered, but that was all she could tell from his silhouette.

Keep going, please keep going.

As if he heard her, he turned toward her. She wanted to shrink back, but she couldn't get any closer to the door. Farran clenched her fists tighter.

"Why are you running?" he said, holding out both hands in an I'm-harmless gesture. "I only wish to talk to you."

His voice beguiled her, made her want to step out from hiding and go to him if only to hear him speak more. Before she could give in to the impulse, she felt the magic that was compelling her response.

"It must be lonely," he continued, "a Tàireil caught in a world that isn't hers. Forced to live among humans in order to remain hidden from the Gineal."

A shiver went down her spine that had nothing to do with the cold, soggy night. The Gineal were searching for her and everyone knew they killed Tàireil. She'd been forbidden to ever travel to this dimension, and when she was a little girl, her mother had warned her that should she find herself in the vicinity of one of these other magic users, she should hide and cloak herself. Too bad her father's ambitions had led her to a situation where she had no choice except to live in this world.

"Humans," the demon scoffed lightly. "They can't understand a woman like you, not when they're incapable of rising above their own small existence to see what the universe truly is." He strolled forward a couple of paces and Farran stiffened. "Don't you wish for a friend who has power as you do? Someone you can talk to openly without fear of being thought insane? I certainly would in your place."

She did want that. It was hard denying such a large part of who she was and some days it wore on her. Why not befriend him? He hadn't hurt her.

Farran almost fell for it, but she caught herself before she moved. Demons with this one's power didn't mingle with the Tàireil—ever—and she'd seen no indications that anything was different in this dimension. He was playing her, trying to get her into the open the easiest way possible.

"Ah, precious, you disappoint me," he said with mock sorrow and started down the alley.

Farran tried to shrink inside herself, but she wasn't strong enough to make herself invisible and he'd find her—it was only a matter of time. She had to be ready.

After months of rarely using her magic, it was strange to call on it again and again, but now there was no choice. If the demon got his hands on her, she'd be praying for death long before she was granted that mercy.

Trying to be unobtrusive, Farran pulled all the power from the earth that she was capable of holding and kept it ready. He'd feel her draw, but wouldn't be able to pinpoint it closely enough to pick out her exact location and she wasn't going down without a fight.

Afraid to so much as breathe, she waited, measuring the distance between them. She couldn't allow him to get too near, but her shot would have more impact if he was closer. And maybe if she got really lucky, he would give up before he zeroed in on her and walk away. She'd had one miracle happen today, why not two?

The demon sauntered along, casually looking around as if she were only of minor interest to him. It was a ruse. He was alert, aware, almost vibrating with intensity, and it was all focused on finding her. Farran studied the area, weighed her options, and picked a spot. Once he went past the white spray-painted heart about ten feet away, she had to fire.

Energy danced along her skin like a thousand snakes slithering around her body and it added to her unease. His power was old and unmistakable.

Thirty feet to the mark.

Her gulp sounded loud, but the demon didn't react. She was going to die here tonight. What other outcome could there be when she couldn't let him take her alive?

Twenty-five feet.

It wasn't fair. She'd hardly lived. It wasn't as if she'd wanted much. Unlike some, she hadn't desired riches, fame, or power. All Farran had ever dreamed of was to belong somewhere. To be accepted. To have someone care about her.

Twenty feet.

She'd learned a thing or two about combat seven months ago as she'd watched the Gineal troubleshooters battle her brothers. Don't hesitate. Act, don't react.

Fifteen feet.

The demon wasn't giving up. He wasn't going to walk away. She wasn't getting her second miracle. A shudder went through her and his gaze snapped to where she stood. As their eyes met, he smiled. "There you are, precious."

Time had just run out.

2

CHAPTER

Her heart slammed into the wall of her chest, but that was the only part of her that moved—at least until her lungs demanded she breathe. She sucked in air with a wheezy rasp, but she couldn't tear her gaze from his. The dim light didn't hide his confidence, his determination, or his delight. Farran swallowed a plea. She wouldn't beg; it wouldn't change anything.

Act. Do something.

But what?

Remember the Gineal.

Farran dropped the cloak. He could see her, so what was the point of concealing her energy any longer? Using all the magic she could draw, she created a fireball. Her arm shook, but she hurled it at the demon.

Her aim was true, but his protective shield barely glowed. His smile widened.

The troubleshooters had kept firing that night and Farran did as well. Maybe one of her blasts would break through and hurt him. Just enough to allow her to flee.

But shot after shot had no visible effect.

She began to tire and it took more time, more effort to

draw power. Farran choked back her despair. She wasn't giving up.

The demon stopped her latest fireball, and with a flick of his finger, made it disintegrate. "I've been patient, but that's enough." Extending his right hand, he ordered, "Come to me."

Farran shook her head and fired again. He dissolved this shot as easily as the last. She wasn't going to defeat him, that was painfully obvious, and it left her with no choice except to incite him. Demons were overly emotional and all she needed to do was infuriate him for a moment. One full blast should be enough to kill her.

She panted, not so much from exertion as from fear. Farran didn't want to die, but she knew what demons were capable of with their captives. She'd seen the results.

Though her blasts were growing weaker, she continued to aim them at her enemy. She had to anger him. Soon.

Her plan didn't last long. The demon clapped his hands together twice and Farran was unable to move her arms or legs and unable to access the Earth or the universe to pull energy. She fought the spell, trying to break loose, but she was no match for his magic. She'd failed. Again.

"I said enough." He put his hands in the pockets of his jacket. "I tried to allow you to exercise good judgment," he added, sounding like a parent scolding a naughty child, "but you refused. Remember that."

Why? What difference did it make? She didn't ask.

He strolled toward her and Farran had her first good look at him. His brown hair was wet, as if he'd been standing outside in the drizzle for quite some time; there was a small soul patch beneath his lower lip; and he was every bit as tall and strong as she'd feared. She searched his face, hoping for some sign of mercy. The cruel tilt to his lips dashed her final hope.

Squeezing her eyes shut, she waited. What would he do to her? How badly would he hurt her before death saved her?

"It's not that bad, prec—"

The sense of light made her open her eyes. There was another man in the alley now. Farran barely had time to take that in before the demon fired at the newcomer.

There was a . . . flicker in her vision, before she saw the shot miss. She blinked, trying to clear her eyes, then stared at the guy. Farran hesitated to label this male as her rescuer, not when he looked scarier, more dangerous than her attacker.

He was as tall as the demon, maybe taller, and he had long hair. The top was pulled back in some way to keep it out of his eyes, but the rest was unbound, falling past his shoulders and looking as wild as if he hadn't combed it that day. His clothes were dark and something about them seemed odd, but with the poor light, she couldn't figure out why.

In the split second it took to evaluate him, the new guy shot back at the demon, but instead of fire, a bluish glow snaked from each fingertip. Her eyes widened. It wasn't lightning—it looked like bolts of electricity— but she'd never seen something like that shot from anyone's hands before.

What was this man? Not human and likely not Gineal or Tàireil. Another demon?

She didn't have enough magic to fight, but there was enough for her to scan the longhaired guy. His energy signature confused her. It was nothing that she could re-call reading before, yet she felt she should know it.

The two men continued to exchange volleys—the demon shooting fire and the newcomer using more of that strange electricity stuff. With a roar of outrage, her captor whipped up the wind until it whirled like a cyclone. He made the Earth shake, the skies open up, and then he sent the tornado directly toward his adversary. She realized that the demon was scared, and that knowledge terrified her.

Farran fought against the incantation holding her in place with renewed determination. Dark demons like this one weren't easily frightened by anything or anyone, and if this longhaired guy had him this unsettled, she didn't want to be around to find out what happened to her if he won the battle.

Maybe she'd blinked. In the instant when she wasn't looking, the other man managed to evade the demon's elemental weapons.

She struggled harder, but couldn't break free. Stifling a whimper, she quieted. If she was patient and allowed the power to amass, she might be able to accumulate enough to get loose—especially if the demon was pre-occupied and let the spell lapse.

The longhaired man directed an intense barrage toward her captor, matching him power for power, but the demon's shield withstood the attack. He smiled with insouciance and sneered, "You can't hold out much longer, can you, shadow walker?"

Her eyes widened and she audibly gulped, but the men were too busy with each other to pay attention to her. Shadow walker. They were relentless, unstoppable, and didn't give up no matter what until they completed their mission. The only good thing about them was that they rarely ventured from their own dimension. Except one was here in this alley now.

What *would* he do to her if he won?

Farran fought with all her strength to free herself, but damn it, the demon's spell held. She was breathing hard and knew she was close to hyperventilating, but she couldn't calm down, not when all the horrible stories she'd heard about shadow walkers raced through her mind.

The next blast of blue made the demon stagger and Farran bit her lip. Whom did she root for? Who would hurt her the least?

Another shot drove her captor back a couple of steps. Maybe she'd be okay if the newcomer came out on top— Farran had heard that shadow walkers never swerved from their task. If this guy wanted the demon, then he wouldn't care about her. He'd defeat his target and leave. She hoped.

Without warning, the spell holding her prisoner collapsed and Farran could move. Gasping, she wiped her clammy palms on her pants and tried to find an escape route, but there wasn't any, damn it. The back end of the alley was one big obstacle, and to get to the street, she'd have to wade through the middle of a battle. One shot from either male and she'd be dead. That was a risk she wasn't willing to take. Not yet.

Gather power. Now that her connection was restored, she had to collect her strength in case she needed to save herself. Farran drew as much as she could, but as she saw the alley aglow in fire and blue energy, her magic seemed pitiful. It had to be enough, though; it was all she had.

The shadow walker became nearly transparent for an instant. This wasn't a trick of her eyes or the light, but something else. His next blast nearly sent the demon to his knees, but he kept his feet. "I can outlast you," her captor growled.

The longhaired man didn't respond. Instead, he released another volley. This one dropped the demon to the ground, but he didn't stay down long.

Farran twisted her fingers together. She couldn't just stand here, she had to do something, didn't she? From her position behind the demon, she could help the shadow walker, but did she want to? Was she right about his interest being limited to the male he fought with?

Her arm trembled as she raised it and she tried to steady herself. If she shot like this, she'd miss her target. When she had her body under control, Farran watched the shadow walker, and as he released a shot, so did she. It caught the demon in the back.

And did nothing.

It was a waste of power and a mistake she wouldn't make again. She'd infuriated the demon. He didn't turn to her or even so much as glance her direction, but she felt his anger and knew that if he won, she'd made her situation much worse.

Maybe the two men would hurt each other badly enough that they'd forget about her and she wouldn't need to fight anyone. It might happen, but she couldn't count on it. She drew energy.

Her power wasn't fully recharged when the shadow walker vanished. A stab of panic made her throat constrict, but she didn't have time to react before he reappeared. The fight with the demon resumed, but Farran was worried. Why had he left? Why had he come back? And what would happen to her if he disappeared with her captor still standing?

"Not much longer, shadow walker," the demon taunted, but he seemed short of breath and not completely steady.

Farran had her power ready, but this time she held it and waited. If she brought it to bear, it would be in a last-ditch effort to save herself.

The shadow walker disappeared again and it was close to a minute before he returned. Farran had thought him long gone, but the demon had known better—he hadn't abandoned his fighting stance.

Somehow the tone of the battle changed. It wasn't that it hadn't been intense before, but there was a new urgency now, one that unnerved her.

A shot knocked the demon down in the alley, but the shadow walker vanished after releasing it, and by the time he returned, the demon was back on his feet. Farran clenched her hands and watched. Any other Tàireil would be able to do something to help herself, but not her. Her lack of power left her standing uselessly and it wasn't fair. Why should her fate rest in the hands of two men?

The shadow walker let loose with a burst of blue so brilliant, Farran had to turn her head away because closing her eyes wasn't enough. When it faded, she looked back. The demon was prone and unmoving, and the other male was gone.

She waited for him to return, waited for the demon to rise, but neither happened. Was her captor dead?

Her legs trembled as she stepped out from the door-way she'd cowered in, but the world stayed quiet. The shadow walker must have been after the demon, and with his prey dead, he'd left. She said a silent thank-you that he hadn't been interested in her and that he'd felled her attacker.

Farran stopped when she drew even with the demon's body and stared down at him. She had to make sure he was dead. If he wasn't . . . He stirred and she jumped back, sucking in a sharp breath.

Still alive!

Her heart lodged in her throat, she tossed a blast of fire at him using all her magic, and then she ran. Instinct was driving her. If the demon wanted her badly enough, he'd eventually track her down and she'd be in even more trouble then.

There was little chance he'd be as patient the next time he cornered her, not after tonight, and she'd be an easy target. Farran didn't slow as she glanced back over her shoulder; didn't dare. As she took a corner, she slipped and fell. Her palms took the brunt of the impact, but she scrambled to her feet and kept moving, ignoring the sting of her abraded skin. How much longer until she had enough magic accumulated to open a transit?

Getting far away from here was her first problem, but her second was every bit as important—she needed some-one strong enough to protect her from the demon. In this dimension, that meant a Gineal. A sob escaped, but Far-ran stifled the next. She wouldn't cry. It did no good.

Reality was that the enemy of her people might be her only chance to stay alive—provided they didn't kill her themselves.

As much as she feared what they'd do to her, she feared the demon more, and that was the critical fact. She had one hope. The Gineal's Seattle troubleshooter was involved with Shona, and her friend might still care enough to persuade him to help. Or maybe not, but it was a chance she'd have to take.

Her lungs burned and a stitch developed in her side. Farran had no choice except to reduce her speed, and that made her anxious. The demon might be hurt, but he could be after her already, and even if his power was reduced to a mere quarter of normal, she was no match for him.

A few more minutes and she should have enough magic to open a transit. As soon as that happened, she was showing up on Logan Andrews's doorstep and begging for his aid.

Kel surged to his feet, fighting for air. He grabbed the neck of his sweatshirt, yanking it away from his throat, but he still couldn't take a full breath.

The walls were closing in on him. The chanting inside his head was getting louder and he cranked up the stereo until Korn blasted through his house. It didn't help. He could hear the echo of their words, smell the scent of burning herbs. Tonight was going to be a bad one if he couldn't circumvent this. Soon.

Nearly all the lights were on, but Kel moved, snapping on the few that he'd missed. It didn't help. A searing pain started near his left shoulder blade and he rotated it, trying to make it stop. The sensation only intensified.

He dragged both hands through his hair and struggled to control the fear. Kel wasn't letting those bastards win—he'd escaped, damn it. He'd escaped.

Perspiration beaded on his forehead, dampened his hair. And the voices increased in volume.

"No." No, he wasn't going through this, not again. Not today. He couldn't. Four nights in a row was too damn many. He felt as if he were made of glass, as if another tap would shatter him into a million jagged pieces. And maybe this time he wouldn't be able to put himself back together.

Maybe this time he'd stay broken.

Kel shuddered, an icy chill raising goose bumps on his arms. There was a little time left to head this off before he reached the point of no return, but letting anyone see him this close to the edge made his stomach roil.

He paced around his living room again, and with every circuit, the straitjacket tightened around him. Screams reverberated through his head, made his mouth go dry. It wasn't real, but that wouldn't matter—it would feel real once it overtook him. Kel wiped the sweat from his upper lip and clenched his hands, hoping to halt the shaking.

The sole way to prevent the replay was to find some company, and there was only one person he trusted enough to see him like this. Going to his brother created a new set of problems, though. Logan might not ask questions tonight, but he would tomorrow or the next day and he wouldn't allow Kel to slide. Logan already knew too damn much and this would reveal even more.

He shouldn't have waited this long. Too bad he hadn't sought out Logan before reaching this point.

If it was just his brother, it would be easier to give in, but things were different since Logan got engaged. It wasn't only his brother's home anymore, it was Shona's, too. Admitting defeat meant more than one person would see him with his soul bared, his weaknesses exposed. He liked Shona, but he didn't have the same level of comfort with her that he had with Logan. And she'd brought changes that Kel didn't welcome. He grimaced. Be honest—it wasn't so much that he didn't appreciate them as he couldn't deal with it.

Korn gave way to Seether and Kel continued to move. He could feel the cold stone slab against his chest and belly and the heated iron a millimeter away from his back.

God. Please. Not tonight.

Pain lanced through his shoulder, strong enough to drop him to his knees. He groaned and panted harshly, unable to get enough air. Kel heard the laughter, the taunts. The scent of charred flesh bit at his nostrils and he swore he could feel the iron pressing into—

He couldn't do this. He couldn't fucking do this. He'd deal with Logan's questions later. Now, Kel needed salvation.

Fighting his way to his feet, he did the spell to open a transit and crossed to Logan's home. The place was dark and he cursed quietly. He was interrupting. Again. It would embarrass Shona, but he needed his brother even if it meant knocking on the bedroom door. Kel waved a hand to turn on the lights and only then did the emptiness register.

Reaching out with his senses, he scanned the house, but no one was present. Where were they? Logan and Shona weren't supposed to leave for London until Fri— Shit, it *was* Friday, and if he remembered the flight time right, they'd taken off from Sea-Tac about an hour ago.

Kel closed his eyes and wrestled with the upsurge of desperation. He could contact Logan telepathically, ask him to use a transit to come home and he would, no questions asked. The problem was that his brother wouldn't be able to return to the airplane, not when it was traveling at five hundred miles an hour, and it was about eight more hours until it landed at Heathrow. The flashback would be long over by then.

The trembling began in earnest and Kel crossed his arms over his chest, trying to control it. There was no one else he could turn to, not when he was like this. His parents were already worried about him and he'd scare his sisters. Logan had been his last hope. His only hope.

As if that admission was all it took, he could see shadowy forms hovering over him, hear their voices, feel their pleasure at his pain. "Stop!" But Kel could barely hear himself over the roar in his head over the pounding of—

The door. Someone was at the door. He grabbed on to that knowledge like a lifeline.

Lurching forward, Kel staggered into the marble foyer and to the front entrance. He didn't care who was out there. What mattered was the past had receded enough that he was no longer looking into the abyss.

More frantic knocking. He flipped on the porch light, grabbed the knob, and jerked open the door.

He didn't recognize her by appearance—the one time he'd seen her, she'd been messed up pretty bad—but he'd never forget her unusual energy signature or the mental calmness he'd felt while healing her. Farran Monroe. She was Shona's best friend and the Gineal had spent months looking for her.

"You're not Logan," she accused.

Since they were identical twins, Kel didn't see any need to mention they were brothers. Instead he said, "Logan's not here." He couldn't help but be suspicious. She was Tàireil—a darksider—and they were dangerous.

She gave a fast glance over her shoulder before meeting his gaze once more. "When will he be back?"

"Not for a while."

"What does that mean?" she demanded. "Not for a few hours? Not for a few days?"

He wasn't allowing her to pin him down on specifics about his brother. Her magic might be weak—although with her energy pattern it was hard to be completely certain—but she'd conspired with her more powerful family against the Gineal dragon mage. Just because she'd felt enough remorse to protect Shona in the heat of battle didn't mean Farran could be trusted now. "He won't be back tonight."

She appeared panicked. "Shona—"

"Is with Logan." The swell of protectiveness Kel experienced surprised him. Somewhere along the line, Shona had become another sister and that was just great—someone else to look out for when he could barely take care of himself. Of course, *this* little sister had annihilated three strong Tàireil on her own and had Logan to defend her, so it wasn't as if she needed Kel to watch over her, too.

Farran glanced over her shoulder again and Kel narrowed his eyes. What had this darksider frightened? "Why are you here?"

There was an almost imperceptible hesitation before she said, "I need a troubleshooter."

Kel became more alert and his ghosts drifted farther away. For the first time, he noticed the water dripping from her jacket and the dirty wet patch on her pants. A fast scan with his talent picked up scraped palms, an accelerated heartbeat, and quickened respiration. She was agitated, but he didn't know why. Was she afraid of something or anxious because the plan to hurt Shona and Logan was falling apart?

"I'm a troubleshooter." Or close enough. The council had taken away his territory and he wasn't considered active, but he hadn't been permanently relieved of his job. Yet.

Biting her lower lip, Farran started to reach for him, but her fingers hit the magical barrier that surrounded Logan's home and she pulled back quickly. She shook out her hand at her side, probably trying to get rid of the tingling the protective field had caused, and asked, "Will you help me?"

She'd tried to sound matter-of-fact, but Kel had picked up a plaintive note beneath the surface. And he'd discerned something else, a kind of fatalism. It was as if Farran expected him to turn her down. That's what he should do. He should tell her sorry and send her on her way. Or he should contact the council and let them know that she was here. They could assign another troubleshooter to watch over her if the situation warranted it. He was in no condition to help anyone. But . . .

But he could recall the blessed mental calmness he'd felt when he'd put his hands on her to heal her injuries. It had been seven months since he'd touched her, but it was the first—the only—sense of peace he'd had since his capture. He was willing to take the gamble for more of that serenity.

"I'm sorry I bothered you," she said, subdued, and began to turn from the door.

"No!" He couldn't let her walk away, not until he learned how she brought about that odd tranquility. "I'll—"

Before he could figure out what he was going to say, a cracking noise made her gasp and whirl. The blind panic in her eyes had him stepping through the protective barrier and closing the door behind him. Kel was afraid she'd try to run through it and hurt herself if he didn't. A scan turned up nothing, but that didn't mean it was clear—Logan had told him that the Tàireil had found a way to cloak themselves from the Gineal.

Kel stood in front of her, shielding her as best he could. He had two choices: ask Logan to grant Farran permission to enter his house, something Kel didn't want to do since he couldn't trust her motives, or take her to his own home. It was a no-brainer. He opened the transit and ordered, "Move."

Farran didn't have to be told twice, she almost leaped through the glowing gate. Kel paused, did another scan, and followed her.

The music continued to blast through his speakers, but Kel closed the transit before crossing to the stereo and turning it off. She stood there, waiting. Watching him. And he studied her in return.

She was short for a darksider—maybe a little over five and a half feet tall—but that didn't mean she wasn't a threat. Her hair was kind of a caramel shade with just enough red in it to leave him at a loss over what to name that color.

He felt more confident about her eyes—they were the denim blue of frequently washed jeans outlined with a navy ring. With her jacket concealing her, he couldn't get a good look at her body, but her face was classically beautiful. An unwelcome surge of heat welled, but Kel smothered it. It wasn't her—it couldn't be her—he knew better.

Dispassionately, he returned to his perusal. The only things marring her appearance were the small bump on the bridge of her nose and the jagged scar on her right cheek. Kel dismissed it—he'd heal that for her tonight the way he'd meant to take care of it seven months ago.

Her expression was impassive. He looked deeper, beyond the surface, but he couldn't see much and it made him wonder what she was hiding. There was wariness in her gaze, but her only outward sign of unease was how tightly she clasped her hands in front of her. The poise seemed unnatural.

He needed to ask questions, find out if there really was something after her or if she was working against the Gineal once more, but Kel didn't feel any urgency. The shield around his home was impenetrable—the nine councilors had made certain of that—and nothing could enter without his consent. "Take off your jacket and have a seat. Do you want coffee or something warm to drink?"

Farran shook her head.

The words had come out gruffer than he intended, so he didn't blame her for turning down the offer. Frustrated with his inability to put her at ease, Kel looked for something, anything to help. With all the lights on, it was as bright as a movie set in here. Maybe turning off a couple of the lamps would make a difference. He jerked forward to catch the switch behind her and was shocked when she flinched away from him.

Kel froze, afraid to even breathe. Her fear wasn't feigned and that prompted him to find his voice. "I was just going to turn off the overhead light. The switch is on the wall over there." He pointed, only moving his finger, nothing else. "That's all I was doing."

She nodded and Kel lowered his arm carefully before taking a slow, circuitous route around her to the switch. He didn't miss the way she shifted, keeping him in view.

He doused the light, and while it improved things so the room didn't look like a helipad, there was still more than enough illumination to keep Farran from freaking out on him again. At least he hoped so. Logan was the one who was good at dealing with women. Hell, all three of their sisters always ran to him and never to Kel when they needed a big brother. It shouldn't bother him, but it did. He was the oldest, damn it.

Keeping the distance between them, Kel turned to Farran. "Want to explain what has you skittish of me? I've never done anything to hurt you. In fact, I've only tried to help."

"I know. You're the one who healed me that night at the mansion. I remember. Thanks."

She hadn't answered his question. "Why are you afraid?"

"You're Gineal." Farran looked uncomfortable, and her fingers clenched together hard enough to turn her knuckles white. "Your people kill Tàireil."

Kel stared at her, dumbfounded. "You think I'm going to *kill* you?"

"Maybe not you—after all, you did expend a lot energy to heal me that night—but you could send me to your rulers who might sentence me to death." She lifted her chin to meet his gaze squarely.

"If you don't trust the Gineal, then why did you go to Logan for help? Did you think he'd be different than the rest of us?"

Farran shrugged. "He's the Seattle troubleshooter. Who else would I go to in that city? And there's Shona. She might have enough feeling left for me to protect me from retribution."

Retribution? Was she insane? The Gineal didn't run around offing darksiders for sport. In fact, the only Tàireil deaths for which they'd been responsible involved rogues who'd visited this dimension and attacked humans—or the Gineal dragon mage. "If we're such amoral killers, why the hell come to us at all?"

"Because I'd rather die at the hands of the Gineal than be tortured and then murdered by a demon with the darkest energy field I've ever sensed."

Kel dropped his head back and closed his eyes. "Fuck," he muttered. "You're saying you ran into one of the god-demons, aren't you?"

3
CHAPTER

Seth's stomach heaved as he pushed himself to his hands and knees. He swallowed hard, hoping to dispel the need to retch. It was a difficult endeavor when he could smell the odor of rotting garbage and feel filth beneath his fingers. His misery was compounded by the unceasing dampness. It left him chilled and wishing he'd remained in Egypt. Did it never stop drizzling?

His breathing was harsh and his lungs burned as he worked on drawing oxygen. Seth closed his eyes and concentrated on regaining his strength.

Time was short. She'd run and he needed to locate her before she began to think clearly. Once it occurred to her that only the Gineal could shield her, things would become much more difficult for him, and his life posed enough challenge.

He drew another ragged breath and blinked to clear his vision. This woman couldn't be allowed to elude him. She held the key to his prison cell and he wasn't losing this opportunity. He'd miscalculated, however, and hadn't anticipated the arrival of the shadow walker. Foolish mistake. Seth should never have allowed his excitement to cloud his judgment. He knew better.

Another wave of nausea welled and he closed his eyes until it passed. He'd been aware that the Gineal were searching for the woman, though he hadn't understood why. A Tàireil female with weak magic was hardly a threat, but he'd followed her anyway, certain that there must be a reason.

Tonight he'd discovered what it was.

Seth's lips curved. Soon the power he'd lost would be his once more. The thought alone had him fighting to his feet. He swayed precariously, but stayed upright. Good.

Reaching out with his senses, he tried to find the Tàireil woman, but couldn't locate her. If she was in the area, he'd have detected her energy and that could mean only one thing—she'd realized she needed a Gineal troubleshooter. He had to hurry. Even with his full complement of magic, he hadn't been able to breach the fortress around their homes and he had much less power now.

Putting one foot in front of the other, Seth staggered down the alleyway. He called on energy with each step, and before he reached the street, he'd accumulated enough to transport himself to the home of the Gineal's Seattle enforcer.

As he arrived, he spotted her on the front porch talking with a Gineal male. She was still vulnerable. He strode forward, but a wave of dizziness washed over him and Seth lost his balance. To prevent himself from falling, he reached for the tree branch over his head. It didn't break, but it did crack loudly. He swallowed a curse, but his silence came too late. The man opened a transit and the woman went through before Seth could react.

He followed their trail, landing in a wooded area behind a brightly lit residence. As he'd feared, the house was shielded. Frustration threatened to swamp him, but he reined it in. Seth wouldn't allow emotion to cloud his mind, not again.

Leaning against a nearby tree for support, he considered his options. Was there a chance he could catch her unprotected?

Perhaps the bigger question was could he afford to cede so easily? The answer to that was simple—no. He'd wait and watch and perhaps he'd find an opening.

Liberation had nearly been within his grasp. Seth wasn't giving it up, not without a fight. He could be patient.

Kel realized he'd made an assumption. Just because she said the demon had the darkest energy she'd ever felt, that didn't mean he was a god-demon. If Farran was telling the truth—and that was a big *if*—it could be any demon from the dark end of the spectrum. She might not have much experience with their different energies, and only a few god-demons were loose in this dimension anyway. What were the odds that one of them had decided to go to Seattle?

Except that demons had a hard time tracking around water, and the city would be a natural choice if, say, Seth—A.K.A. Set—wanted to hide from the others.

Opening his eyes, Kel ran both hands over his face. He needed to question her, find out if she was telling the truth or if her surviving family had returned and was using her to exact revenge for its defeat. His instincts said she was being honest, but he couldn't believe them, not when she was the first woman who'd caught his interest since his capture.

He looked back at Farran, but she appeared confused. "What?" Kel asked.

"What are god-demons? I've been in this world long enough to pick up how humans speak, but I haven't spent time with the Gineal."

"That's how we refer to the demons who were strong enough to be worshipped as gods in ancient times. You know, like Zeus, Odin, Horus, and Set." He kept his tone neutral with effort, but her ignorance seemed disingenuous.

She nodded. "The deamhaidh. This demon wasn't

that strong. At least he didn't feel as if he was that powerful."

"That would fit," Kel muttered and called forward a file from the basement. He looked through it, needing to refresh his memory. The council issued a monthly magazine to all employees of the Gineal Company. Humans saw nothing but a slick corporate publication, but beneath that facade important details were disseminated to the troubleshooters. It might be the digital age, but the ceannards were in no hurry to embrace it despite being prodded by their enforcers.

"What are you doing?" she asked.

"Trying to find something. Hang on a sec." At last, Kel put his hands on the issue he wanted. He reviewed the details there and the picture that had been embedded in the page.

When he finished, he returned the file folder where it belonged and shifted his attention to Farran. She stood in profile to him, her scarred cheek out of his view, and he knew it was deliberate. Her distrust—and that's what the gesture was—irked the hell out of him. Unable to quell his irritation, Kel growled, "Can you create an image of what the demon looked like?"

"It'll take me a minute," she said, sounding apologetic, but whether it was because of the time factor or because he knew she mistrusted him, Kel couldn't guess. Unsure what to say, he nodded, and she closed her eyes. A furrow formed between her brows as she worked the necessary magic.

At first the image was insubstantial, so faint he couldn't decipher more than a flickering of light. Slowly, the form became more solid until he could clearly see the male figure. Kel jammed his hands into the front pockets of his jeans and cursed. Farran's eyes popped open and the image disappeared. She watched him warily and he swallowed the need to swear again.

"That's Set," he explained. The visual display increased the odds that she was sincere, but it didn't confirm it. Seth had lost enough magic that he was no longer able to change his appearance at will and the Tàireil would have had plenty of time to learn what he looked like.

"It can't be him," Farran argued, showing more animation than she had since he'd opened the door and found her on his brother's doorstep. "I'm good at judging another's magical strength and this demon was only about as powerful as you are."

"It is him. A little over a year and a half ago Seth—that's the name he's going by now—had a run-in with the Gineal." Kel paused and decided she didn't need all the details. "He lost the fight and ended up having most of his powers stripped from him, but before he could be captured, he disappeared."

"How could anyone, even a Gineal troubleshooter, take power from a deamhaidh? They're too strong."

"It's a long story." And one Kel wasn't about to share with an outsider, especially not a darksider who might be working against his people. "You're going to have to trust me on his identity. How did you attract Seth's attention anyhow?"

Farran clenched her fingers at her waist hard enough that Kel saw her knuckles go white. She was pissed at him. Tough.

"I'm not sure," she said, sounding calm. Kel admired that kind of control even as he cataloged it for future reference. "Tonight is the first I've sensed his presence and I didn't do anything differently than any other night."

"Run through what happened."

"Does that mean you're going to help me?"

"I don't know yet."

"When will you know?" she demanded and he felt satisfaction that he'd shaken her poise enough to see some heat.

"Maybe after you tell me what the hell went down tonight and I decide whether or not you're telling the truth. You darksiders don't exactly have the best track record when it comes to honesty and fair play."

Farran's face went red. "You're thinking of my family's egregious actions against Shona."

Kel didn't say anything, only stared at her.

She was quiet for a moment—maybe thinking of her own actions in the plot against Shona—and then Farran said, "I got off work at ten and was walking to the bus stop when I felt someone following me. A probe told me he was a demon and I ran. Unfortunately, I turned down a dead-end alley and was trapped. I did the only thing I could do—hide—but he found me." She swallowed audibly. "That's when things became really strange."

"Strange how?" he prompted into the silence. Farran bit her bottom lip, but didn't speak. Great. At this rate it was going to take all night to get the facts out of her. If his ghosts were still hovering nearby, he wouldn't mind, but they'd been driven off—for the moment. Kel pulled his hands from his pockets, took a few steps away, and leaned his hips against a side table. He might as well get comfortable.

"You're not going to believe it," Farran said at last.

"Try me," he challenged.

Her chin went up. "A shadow walker showed up and attacked the demon." She threw that out like a gauntlet.

"Bullshit." Kel crossed his arms over his chest. He didn't know what she was up to, but the darksider was trying to pull something. "Shadow walkers almost never come to this dimension."

"They rarely visit our dimension either, but one showed up here tonight and he and the demon fought it out in the alley."

He narrowed his eyes. "Why?"

Farran took two steps toward him before she stopped short. She was angry and unable to conceal it. The flush on her cheeks, the fire flaring in her gaze left him feeling satisfied. Kel liked seeing an emotion other than fear from her.

"How the hell should I know?" Farran's voice held as much snap as her eyes. "It wasn't like either one of them stopped shooting at the other to explain to me what was going on between them. All I know was they battled until the demon went down and then the shadow walker disappeared. I checked to see if the demon was dead, he moved, and I fled."

Her story was improbable, but he'd seen the fear in her eyes when she'd turned up on Logan's doorstep and she hadn't faked that. Something had scared her, but was it because she was part of another plot against Shona or was it the demon? "Are you sure he was a shadow walker?"

"No," she said, shaking her head. "His energy was something I'd never felt before and didn't recognize."

"Then how—"

"When the demon taunted him, he called his opponent *shadow walker*," she interrupted. "I assumed that since demons can read energy the same way we do, he knew who he was fighting."

A demon as old and experienced as Seth wouldn't make a mistake in identifying his enemy—if she wasn't lying about that. Kel curled his hands around the edges of the table on either side of his hips and measured her. Farran met his gaze, not flinching under his scrutiny.

He didn't trust her—he couldn't—but Kel wasn't willing to let her walk away either. Not if she could make his nightmares disappear with a touch.

But if what she told him was legit, he might end up fighting a demon. Goose bumps rose on his arms and a cold shiver snaked down his spine. After every clash, he had a period when it seemed as if his flashbacks intensified, and they were bad enough already.

Kel pushed that aside—he'd worry about that later—and ran through what he knew about shadow walkers. It wasn't much. One: they rarely ventured out of their own dimension, wherever that might be. Two: they were relentless, with a Terminator-like dedication to completing their missions. No one wanted a shadow walker on his ass, and if he really existed, that was bad news for the demon, but good news for Farran.

And for Kel. Seth would be taken care of and Kel wouldn't have to go head-to-head with the demon. He could keep Farran in his house and learn why she soothed him.

Farran took a few more steps toward him and there was entreaty on her face. "I know I have no right to ask you or any of the Gineal to protect me, not after what my family tried to do to Shona, but I swear to you that I did the best I could to shield her."

Maybe she had, but he didn't like how she put all the blame on her family and took no responsibility herself. She'd been part of it, and if she'd wanted to, there was a sure way Farran could have guaranteed Shona's safety. "You could have told one of us what was going on."

"Why would any Gineal believe what I said? I'm Tàireil."

"You don't trust us either."

"Your people have been hunting me," she accused.

Kel ground his teeth and gripped the edge of the table harder. Leave it to a darksider to twist things until they bore no resemblance to the facts. "We haven't been *hunting* you. We've been trying to find you because Shona's worried. She wants you safe."

That knocked the fight out of her. "Shona doesn't hate me?"

The hopeful expression on Farran's face, the pleading note that creeped into her voice, and the way she leaned forward as if she didn't want to chance missing whatever he said, had Kel tempering his frustration. "No," he said, and again, his voice came out more gruffly than he intended, "she doesn't hate you. As far as Shona's concerned, you're still her best friend."

Farran turned away from him, but not before Kel saw tears fill her eyes. He started to stand, decided he'd be no more successful with this woman's crying than he was when one of his sisters went off, and settled back against the table. Hell, maybe it was all an act anyway. Darksiders lied.

"How is Shona?" Farran asked. She kept her back to him, but her voice sounded thick.

"Fine," he said, unwilling to give away any information.

"Fine?" She pivoted and stalked over until she was practically toe to toe with him.

There was no sign of the tears and that made Kel more suspicious—shouldn't there be some trace that she'd been upset? "Yeah, she's fine."

"That's the best you can do? Is Shona well? Is she happy?"

"Yes to both," he said and enjoyed the fireworks that exploded in her eyes.

"You're insufferable!"

She made a sharp U-turn and strode away from him. Kel couldn't hear what she was muttering, but he decided that was for the best. He waited until she began to wind down before adding, "If you'd hung around instead of disappearing, you'd know how Shona was doing."

Temper put sparks back in her eyes, but Kel enjoyed watching her when she was angry. Not good. He changed the subject before Farran found her voice. "Back to the topic at hand—do you have any guesses why Seth is interested in you?"

For a moment, he thought she'd light into him anyway, but she banked her irritation. "No, I have no idea."

"A human would be an easier target."

"Maybe be needs someone with magic. If so, I'm the best option. The Gineal protect their own and I have no one here to defend me."

Kel had to admit it made sense. Demons were opportunistic and Farran was without resources in this world—maybe in her own, too, since she'd betrayed her father. The Tàireil didn't believe in forgive and forget, not even with family.

"Does the reason really matter?" she asked.

"Yes." Kel frowned when he realized she'd shifted to hide her cheek from him again. "Why he's after you will influence his actions. It might be easier to anticipate Seth's strategies if we can answer that question."

"Does that mean you're going to help me?"

For a minute, Kel didn't speak. Her hands were clenched at her sides and her expression was resigned. She thought he was going to turn her down and maybe he would. He was in rough shape—he knew it, the Gineal council knew it.

There were only two options open to him: hand Farran over to the ceannards or protect her himself. His decision was going to come down to a single factor—would touching her still make his turmoil disappear? Time to find out. "Come here," Kel ordered, straightening away from the table.

"Why?" She looked as distrustful as she sounded.

"I'm going to finish healing your face the way I meant to seven months ago." It was partial truth.

Farran jerked. "You think my scar is hideous."

"No, I think *you* think your scar is hideous. Personally, I don't give a shit." She didn't move. "You can't mend it, but I can. Are you going to let pride or whatever it is you're battling with right now keep you from getting rid of something you don't want?"

Kel waited, not saying another word. He could guess what she was feeling right now and he let her work through it.

Her first step was hesitant, as if she thought better of it before she completed the stride. She gained confidence on the second. By the time she stopped in front of him, Farran appeared determined and Kel liked that courage.

"I need to put my palm on your cheek," he told her, not wanting her to freak out on him a second time.

"Okay."

Moving slowly, Kel raised his left hand. She closed her eyes, but didn't flinch as he brought it to her face. Healing was natural for him and in seconds he had the energy flowing.

He was in no hurry to finish because once he did,

he'd have to stop touching her. Just as the night she'd been injured, contact with her calmed his mind. Kel didn't know why, but he wasn't letting her leave until he learned how she did it.

As the green light flowing between his palm and her face began to ebb, her eyes opened. Reluctantly, Kel lowered his hand and his disquiet returned as soon as he broke contact. He hated it. No, that wasn't strong enough. He fucking loathed it. If he could change his life, this would be one of the things he got rid of.

She gazed up at him and he nodded, wordlessly telling her he'd been successful. Immediately, she took a step back, but Kel stopped her. "Hold out your hands, palms up."

Without questioning him, she obeyed. It took him seconds to heal the scrapes there. "Done," he told her.

Before he could say another word, Farran raised her fingers to her cheek and trailed them over her skin. She traced the area where the scar had been at least half a dozen times before she froze and lowered her arm to her side. He could only guess that she'd realized how much the gesture revealed.

Kel gave her a moment to collect herself before he said, "I'll show you to one of the spare bedrooms. Tomorrow we can discuss strategy for keeping you safe from the demon."

Farran had been awake long enough to brush her teeth, shower, and dress in the clothes the troubleshooter had conjured for her, but she didn't leave the bathroom. She couldn't. The only mirror she had was in here.

She was unable get as close as she'd like to it. The left side of the counter was snug against the wall of the linen closet, and while she could get nearer on the right before the toilet tank stopped her, the position didn't allow her a clear view of that cheek. Instead, she stood squarely in the center and leaned in as far as she could. Farran tipped her head this way and that, trying to see her face from all angles, but no matter which way she turned, the scar was gone with no indication it had ever existed.

Why, then, didn't she feel any different?

Last night she'd been able to write it off as being exhausted or needing time for it to sink in, but she'd slept for nearly eight hours and nothing had changed. Farran brought her fingers up and ran them over her cheek, stroking the skin.

Smooth. Soft. Supple. The way it had felt before that night when she'd thrown herself in front of Shona. Why couldn't she believe it?

It wasn't as if she hadn't seen magic at work many times in the past. Humans might get stuck on how suddenly the change had happened, but Farran had grown up in the Tàireil world and knew a spell could reverse things instantaneously.

She was twenty-five and she'd only had the scar for seven months. Seven months versus years with an unmarred face. Why did she still feel ugly? Why did she want to hide?

Lowering her arm, Farran straightened and tried to take in her entire appearance—at least as much of it as she could see. The navy Henley shirt was a great match for her coloring and she wondered if the troubleshooter had been lucky or if he'd known it was a good shade for her. No makeup—that made her feel naked—but she hadn't been carrying a purse last night and he hadn't bothered to provide so much as a tube of lip gloss.

Farran put her hands on her hips and considered using her own powers to bring her makeup bag here. It only took a moment, though, to opt against it. The Gineal had said they'd *discuss strategy for keeping her safe from the demon,* but he hadn't said he'd protect her. If he told her she was on her own, she'd regret wasting her meager store of magic on vanity.

Before she could stop it, Farran caressed her cheek again and grimaced over her behavior. She couldn't stay in here all day no matter how tempting that idea was. For one thing, she was hungry, and for another, the troubleshooter would grow impatient with her and come in after her.

Just the idea was enough to prod her along. There was no exit from the bathroom to the hall, so Farran was forced to reenter the guest room she'd used last night. She stopped cold at the sight of the bed—it was made of twisted, gnarled wood, and even in the bright sunlight streaming in the windows, looked like something out of a horror movie—and shaking her head, continued out of the room.

For a moment, Farran paused to listen, but she heard nothing that told her the troubleshooter was up and moving. In a house this size, though, that might not mean much and his bedroom *was* on the opposite end from the room she'd used.

As quietly as she could, she went down the hallway and entered the kitchen. Empty. She released a long, relieved breath. Farran glanced around, noticed the gleaming hardwood floors and gulped. Had she tracked them up with her tennis shoes? Half afraid of what she'd see, she looked behind her, but didn't spot any footprints. Thank goodness.

Everything in the kitchen was polished and perfect—the black stone countertops, the stainless-steel appliances, and even the three pendant lights hanging over the center island were dust free. Knowing how she cooked, Farran put aside the idea of making breakfast. The last thing she wanted was to face a man who was angry at the mess she'd left in her wake.

She spotted a coffeemaker on the counter next to the stone encasement that arched over the stove and headed there to start a pot. That should be safe enough. Farran found a bag of imported coffee in the creamy-taupe cabinets beneath the counters and a collection of mugs in the pear-colored cabinets overhead.

After pushing the button, she leaned against the

counter and looked around some more as she waited. She pegged the style here as French country, but with an incredible amount of elegance and gloss that she found intimidating. Despite that untouchable quality, there was a warmth, a hominess that she had a hard time reconciling with the troubleshooter she'd spoken to last night.

Farran grimaced—the troubleshooter. She knew his surname was Andrews because of his brother, but she had no idea what his given name was and it hadn't occurred to her to ask. If he chose to, he could make her feel incredibly awkward when she did work up the courage to pose the question, but she didn't see any other alternative. It would be far worse to need to address him at some point in the future and have to settle for *hey, you.*

The coffee gurgled to a stop, and after pouring a cup, she wandered over to the kitchen table. It was nestled in a turret of windows and Farran paused to admire the incredible view. The house must be built on the side of a hill because the back looked down into a heavily forested valley. Spectacular. And the fact that there was no signs of any other inhabitants in the vicinity made it even better.

There was a curved deck off the kitchen and Farran debated taking her mug outside—she didn't doubt the protection around his house extended to that area as well—but it looked too cold to stay out for long. Instead, she sat on a chair at the table and turned to stare out the window as she drank her coffee.

Peace settled over her and Farran let it spread through her body, through her soul. Maybe this was why the troubleshooter had chosen this place as his home.

She'd relaxed too soon. Motion had her jerking her head to the left and staring intently, but she didn't see anything. Probably an animal, nothing for her to be concerned about, but with a demon after her, she couldn't afford to let her guard down. Even if the Gineal decided to help her, he'd expect her to remain alert and work with him.

Farran was still peering intently into the forest when she sensed a change in the room behind her and shifted to see what had caused it.

He'd showered—his dark hair was damp—and though he'd pushed it off his face, some of it fell over his eyes. Last night he'd had a couple of days' worth of stubble on his face and he hadn't bothered to shave this morning either. Something about the rough look he sported made her shiver, but it wasn't with fear.

She dropped her gaze to her mug, but it didn't take long before she was peeking from beneath her lashes, watching him as he made his way to the coffeemaker. He was a big man—muscular and a couple of inches over six feet—but he moved with a smoothness that made her think of a top athlete.

But he *was* a Gineal troubleshooter. Not only did they have the strongest powers, but they were physically trained as well. They had to be in order to answer any threat that arose.

Giving up any pretext of interest in her cup, Farran studied him as he filled his own mug and headed toward her. The jeans he had on today were only slightly less faded than the pair he'd worn yesterday, but he'd traded in the ratty sweatshirt for a long-sleeve, burgundy polo shirt.

It set off his eyes. They were the deepest, most intense blue she'd ever seen and Farran had to look away again as he settled across from her at the small table.

"You sleep okay?" His voice sounded drowsy—thicker and rougher than what she'd heard last night.

"Fine, thanks." He drank from his mug and Farran watched him swallow before she raised her own cup. Ask him now, she told herself. He appeared much more mellow than last night. "I don't know your name," she said, and when he stared at her, she realized she'd blurted that out. "I'm sorry."

He put his mug on the table and shrugged. "It's Kellan Andrews, but call me Kel. Everyone does."

Kellan. She rolled that over in her mind and decided it

fit him. Farran nearly said it aloud, but stopped herself in time. If he asked her why she thought that, she'd be unable to articulate her reasons and it was better not to try.

"Hungry?" he asked after he'd finished his coffee.

Farran nodded. She'd skipped dinner last night—too short on money to buy food—and she felt half starved.

He made toaster waffles. Quick, easy, and they didn't leave a mess in his immaculate kitchen. If she knew him better, she might have teased him about his neat streak, but she didn't know him well, she was imposing on him, and she needed his protection.

She matched him waffle for waffle, but he didn't comment, just kept making them until neither of them could eat any more. Farran helped him clean the table, rinsing the dishes while he loaded the dishwasher. It had been a silent meal—she'd been too intent on filling her stomach to converse—and the quiet suddenly seemed awkward. Rude. "I think there's enough coffee left for both of us to have one more cup," she said.

Kel closed the dishwasher. "Yeah, and we can talk while we finish it."

All her muscles pulled tight, but Farran accepted the mug he handed her and returned to the table. She watched him rinse out the coffeepot until a glint caught her eye and she turned to look out the window. A bird flew past and her lips curved before she remembered that she hadn't told Kel about the sense of motion she'd spotted earlier. It might be nothing more than an animal—likely was nothing more than an animal—but if she didn't share that with him, he'd be angry and she wouldn't blame him. It was something he needed to know. Just in case.

When he rejoined her, Farran said, "I forgot to say something earlier, but I saw motion in the woods this morning before you joined me in the kitchen."

He lowered his mug without drinking, started to stand, and then sat again. "Which direction?"

"Over there, to the left." Farran pointed.

"Okay." Kel picked up his cup.

That left her puzzled. She knew enough about Gineal troubleshooters to predict how he'd react and this wasn't what she'd been expecting. "Aren't you going to check it out?"

"Maybe later," he said, voice hard. "It was probably just a deer—there's a lot of them around here—and on the off chance it was Seth, the house is protected. He's not getting in."

"Well, yes, but . . ." She let her words trail off. Farran didn't want to anger him and who was she to tell him how to do his job? If he'd even agreed to take her on as an assignment. She still wasn't sure about that. Grabbing for bravery, she said, "You said we'd discuss strategy this morning, but you didn't say if that was so I could protect myself or because you'd decided to aid me. Are you going to help me?"

"Yeah." Now he did sound mad. "If I wasn't, you wouldn't have spent the night here."

Used to appeasing her father, her brothers, Farran immediately dropped her gaze a fraction and said, "I'm sorry. I simply wasn't clear on what you meant and I didn't dare to make such a huge assumption. I know your—"

She stopped short when his hand covered both of hers. He squeezed her gently and pulled away, but the gesture was enough to leave her speechless.

"Don't ever do that again," he told her. "I'm not your bastard father and I won't hurt you for asking questions."

Her gaze shot back to his and she read the knowledge there. It shamed her, made her face heat, but she fought the desire to look down again. It wasn't her disgrace. It wasn't! "How?"

"I healed you, remember? I know you had injuries that didn't come from the blasts you took. It wasn't just that night either or his fury over Shona merging with the dragon stone. You can't heal yourself at all and no one else bothered to do it for you, did they?"

"My mother did," Farran admitted quietly, "but no one after she died."

"And you were forbidden to call a healer."

It wasn't a question, but she nodded anyway. Kel's face appeared harder than ever and Farran fought the need to shrink into herself. He wasn't mad at her—she knew that in some instinctive way—but angry males made her wary.

"When I worked on you that night, I healed the past stuff that would impact you as you aged," Kel said, voice as hard as his face. "I didn't do anything about the rest. Like your nose. Unless you break it again, it's probably not worth the energy it would take to get rid of a tiny bump."

Farran nodded jerkily and prayed he'd leave it alone. She didn't want to talk about this, not with anyone, but especially not with this stranger. She didn't know him, and while she might be forced to trust him with her life, she didn't trust him with her soul. There was no one in whom she could put that kind of faith, not even Shona.

Her friend had been cherished, cosseted by her parents, pampered and spoiled. They'd worried about her and protected Shona to such a degree that she'd never understand the minefield Farran had learned to negotiate every day of her life until she'd left her father's house. It was more than that, though—her lies had stood like a wall between herself and the woman she'd considered a sister and Farran hadn't dared to breach it.

Clearing her throat, she asked, "Do you have any guesses why Seth is after me? You know more about him than I do."

"I get it—time to talk about something else," Kel said and he sat back, pushing a hand through the top of his hair to move it out of his eyes. He gazed out the window a moment before looking back at her. "No, I don't know, but we need to figure it out."

Relieved that he'd gone along with the change of topic, she took a deep breath and relaxed slightly. "Are you really sure it's him? I can't imagine a deamhaidh caring about me."

"As sure as I can be."

Farran felt her tension ease further. He'd said she could question him, but his lack of reaction reassured her.

"We need to run through the past few days again," he said. "Maybe something happened that means nothing to you, but has some significance for Seth."

"Okay," she agreed without enthusiasm. As if he didn't know enough about her, now he could discover how pathetic her life had been since she'd run off. Not that it made much difference, Farran guessed. Could he find her any more pitiful than he did already? She doubted it.

"You done with your coffee?"

She nodded and he took both cups to the sink and rinsed them out before adding them to the dishwasher. Farran hoped she reached a point when she could trust him. Seriously, any man as anal as this one was needed to be teased about his neatness.

Her amusement disappeared abruptly as the air between the table and the center island shimmered. She remembered that sight. Farran managed to squeak his name—barely. Kel turned at the same time the unsettled space transformed into a male form.

The shadow walker had bypassed all the shields and he was looking directly at her.

4
CHAPTER

Son of—

Training kicked in and Kel fired even as he threw protection spells around himself and Farran. He had no doubt that the intruder had his defenses up and Kel was right—his lightning bolt hit the man squarely in the back, but the shield prevented any damage. It did get his attention off Farran, though.

The guy turned toward him and Kel ducked behind the center island. Crackling blue electrical streams sailed over his head, tearing up the hardwood floor just behind him.

Kel scanned the man's energy signature, but it was one he didn't recognize. This had to be the shadow walker. The long hair and odd clothing matched what Farran had described. Great. He didn't know anything about fighting this guy.

Damn it, he should have gone outside when Farran had told him she'd caught motion out there. It must have been the shadow walker she'd seen lurking in the trees and everything would have been easier if he'd confronted the man outdoors. Much easier. By trying to avoid an altercation, he'd made his job more difficult.

Here there was no room to maneuver and Farran was at greater risk from a ricochet or mistake.

Shifting for a better angle, Kel sent another bolt of lightning at the intruder. Where *was* Farran?

He spun to avoid the shadow walker's shot and searched for her. Under the table. Kel grimaced. It was a lousy position, but there was nothing better. Not within reach. If she made a break for another room, she'd be an easy target, and he wasn't sure he'd be able to distract the enemy long enough to cover her.

Kel eased back to his left, trying to keep the fight as far away from her as he could. It wouldn't be a cakewalk. His kitchen was large, but not big enough to ensure that Farran stayed clear. One stray shot . . .

The shadow walker's next blast connected and Kel felt it even with his protection spell in place. He grit his teeth and rode out the pain, but he didn't stop moving.

This was nothing—he'd survived worse—but sweat beaded above his lip and his muscles quivered.

Drawing extra power from the Earth, Kel let loose with both hands. He mixed fireballs in with the lightning, hoping that a combination would cause more damage, but the shadow walker's shield showed no signs of weakening.

Kel ducked to avoid another volley. He'd barely recovered from the first hit and didn't want another. His microwave exploded, sparks flying as it died a fiery death.

For an instant, the shadow walker stood frozen and their gazes met. He appeared startled, but then determination entered those icy-gray eyes and Kel raised a hand, using a wave of energy to ward off the next electric stream.

Sending another barrage of fireballs toward the enemy, Kel tried to think. He didn't have his brother's flair for unconventional tactics, but something would come to him.

It had to.

The shadow walker deflected some of his shots and one fireball seared the floor damn near the table.

That upped the stakes. He'd promised Farran he'd keep her safe and he was failing. Why hadn't he done some reading on shadow walkers last night? But who the fuck would have guessed they had the ability to bypass the security around his home? Nothing else had ever breached it.

At least the protective shield he'd thrown around himself and Farran was holding. That gave him some breathing room, but he wasn't having any epiphanies on how to beat this guy and Kel wanted the fight finished.

He hit the deck to avoid the sparking energy the shadow walker fired at him. This blast slammed into his cabinets. Wood burst outward like shrapnel and clattered to the floor.

Kel's nerves pulled so tight his stomach hurt, but he couldn't stay down here long. If he didn't keep the intruder engaged, the man might take the opportunity to go after Farran. Damn, though, Kel wanted a minute to control his pounding heart and rapid breathing.

Getting to his feet, he did his best to avoid his enemy's shots. More than one hit and his protection faltered. Kel reinforced it, but with tremors going through his body, it took more power than he wanted to use.

Kel released a series of lightning bolts. The third one made the shadow walker grimace and take a step back. Good. The man's shield was losing strength.

There wasn't time to enjoy the small victory because the next salvo connected and Kel's defense fell. Before he could direct power to it, a second shot hit him dead-on. His legs turned to Jell-O and he hit the floor. Hard.

He clenched his hands as he fought the pain, but the stab of fear was harder to ignore. Taking time to fully recharge his shots was a luxury he couldn't afford—not any longer.

Kel heard Farran squeak and fought his way to his feet. Still weakened, he redoubled his efforts to end the fight, firing a continual flow. His streams of lightning crossed the electric-blue currents of the shadow walker, and when the two met, there were flare-ups that charred the ceiling. What the hell was this guy shooting?

The shadow walker vanished.

It was only for an instant, but it surprised Kel enough to go still. As soon as he reappeared, the enemy let loose with another round and it slammed into Kel. His protection held this time, but it dropped him to his knees.

He struggled not to groan aloud, not to give the man any indication of how badly he hurt. Cold sweat covered him, made him feel clammy, and his stomach heaved.

Shaking, Kel reinforced his shielding spell again and staggered back to his feet. He returned to nonstop shooting, but his mind turned over the fact that the shadow walker had disappeared. That was significant.

The continual firing was a gamble. He could very easily drain himself of magic before he saw any tangible benefit. Or he could be wrong that the vanishing act meant something. It had been only a split second. Maybe stress or pain had made his eyes lie to his brain.

But when the shadow walker had another invisible moment, Kel knew he was on the right track.

The third time the enemy vanished, he stayed gone long enough that one of Kel's shots flew through where the man had been standing and sent slivers of his wood floor exploding toward the table. He saw her recoil. "Farran, did you get hit?"

"I'm okay."

Good thing, because the intruder returned, and if anything, he looked more resolute than he had earlier. So was Kel. "I'm not going to let you hurt her, you bastard."

He had no idea if the shadow walker understood his words or not, but stating his intent made Kel feel stronger.

The tenor of the battle changed, though he couldn't say how. Maybe it was nothing more than the fact that they were both tiring and trying to end it.

They continued to circle each other with the island in

the center. Kel kept up a steady stream of fire, but it lacked the punch he was used to having at his call. His hair was damp with perspiration and his breathing was ragged. He shouldn't be at this level of fatigue this quickly, but then it had been months since he'd been in battle. And even longer since he'd felt the kind of pain he'd experienced this morning.

In the middle of another round of shots, the shadow walker was gone and Kel winced as his blast tore up the doorway into the family room. After a couple of minutes, he said, "You can come out now; he's gone."

"Don't let your guard down," Farran warned, not moving from beneath the table. "This happened last night and he—"

The intruder's return had Farran stopping short and Kel had to dig deep to find enough strength to resume the fight. After another half dozen shots, his enemy disappeared yet again. This time Kel remained on guard, but it stayed quiet. "Do you think he's gone this time?" he asked when nearly five minutes passed.

"I think so." Farran crawled out from beneath the table slowly enough to worry Kel. "At least he didn't come back after this length of time when he fought the demon."

Kel drew a deep breath and hoped she didn't hear how shaky it was. "Did you get hit by anything?"

She shook her head. "A couple of near misses, but nothing connected. What about you?"

"I'll live," he said shortly. And he would. He ached damn near everywhere, but this was nothing. Kel ran through options on where to hole up. The demon was still out there, still a factor, and because the shadow walker had the ability to bypass Gineal security, there was no perfect choice. One thing was clear, though—they couldn't stay in his house.

"Get your jacket."

"Why?"

"We're leaving."

There was a slight pause while she looked at him, then Farran headed down the hall behind the kitchen. While she went off to the right, Kel took the hallway to the left. He pulled open the closet door in the mud room, shrugged into his winter jacket, and grabbed a large knapsack off the shelf. Back in the kitchen, he opened the pantry and began loading the pack with canned goods.

He knew when Farran returned, but she didn't say anything. Kel went to the fridge and added meat and other staples to his bag. When the pack was full, he zipped it, slung it over his shoulders, and grabbed a loaf of bread before rejoining Farran near the center island.

Kel opened a transit. "Come on, we need to get out of here."

"And go where? There's no safe haven, not any longer."

"I know that." The only thing that kept the growl out of his voice was exhaustion. "I'm concealing the energy of the transit. Unless he's within a hundred yards of here, he won't be able to follow us."

"He'll find us."

"Probably," Kel conceded. "Eventually. But it buys us time."

She stared at him without speaking for a moment. "Time to do what?" she finally asked. "Write my will? It's obvious now that the shadow walker is after me and not the demon."

"Yeah, I think so, too." And it raised questions, lots of them. "But I was at a disadvantage in the battle today because I don't know anything about him. I'll be better once I have some idea how to fight."

Farran didn't make a move to cross the transit and Kel bit back a curse. He couldn't fucking hold the concealment spell forever, damn it, not when he'd already burned through most of his magic. As much as he wanted to grab her and toss her through the gate, he didn't dare. Not with her background and not when she was half afraid he'd hurt her, too.

Taking a deep breath, he held out his hand to her. It shook and he knew she saw it. Kel didn't lower his arm. "Trust me to protect you even if you can't believe anything else."

When he'd nearly given up hope, she nodded and took his hand. Kel led her across the transit.

Farran looked around, but nothing helped her identify their location. It was a house, a small one with wooden walls, and they stood in the middle of the living area. To her right was a bank of windows that went from her knees to the peak of the A-frame roof. Drapes were pulled across the lower panes, maybe to keep in what little heat there was, but the glass above was uncovered. To her left was a fireplace with a stone hearth and straight ahead was the kitchen—she could see the sink and pale gold counters.

"Where are we?" she asked and released his hand.

"My family's cabin. It has protection around it like my house did and we won't use any magic while we're here—none—because it's traceable. I know, I know, the shadow walker can get in if he finds us," Kel said before she could tell him that. "It might not stop him, but it'll keep everyone else out while I hit the tasglann."

She understood that word because the Tàireil used it, too, and the most obvious place for the Gineal to have their archives was near their stronghold. He'd said he was going to help her; he wouldn't turn her over to his council, would he? Her heart racing, Farran turned to Kel. "Where exactly is this cabin?"

He crossed to a counter that partially separated the living area from the kitchen and put down the bread before taking off the backpack. After leaning it against the half-wall between two of the stools, he said, "Wisconsin."

That didn't tell her much and she suspected he knew it. Before she could try to pin him down, she shivered.

"Hang on," Kel said. "Let me get the heat turned up. It's only warm enough to keep the pipes from freezing." He started down the hall. "Why don't you open the drapes and get some light in here. That'll help."

Farran doubted it, but she would like a better view of her surroundings—maybe that would tell her how close they were to Gineal headquarters. She started with the largest set of windows. There was a deck that went around the house, and beyond that a small lake that still had ice on it. The ground was mostly brown grass, but there were a few scattered patches of snow. It didn't tell her if they were in southern Wisconsin.

Pulling the drapes on the smaller window to her right revealed a tiny copse of trees close to the house. Since they were directly off the deck, they blocked the view, and she didn't get any additional information.

Finally, she headed to the eat-in part of the kitchen and drew open the thermal drapes over the patio door. To her left Farran saw a dirt driveway came down a short, but fairly steep hill to the cabin. Directly in front of her was a lot of brown grass covering gentle hills, and farther away, more trees. To her right, she had another angle of the lake.

There were no other houses in sight and it appeared as if they were in a remote area. Another shiver went through her that had nothing to do with the cold.

She had to trust the troubleshooter—there was no one else—but it wasn't that easy. Most men weren't like her family, not even among the Tàireil. She understood that, but because of the situation, she was at Kel's mercy. He could kill her and no one would know. No one would care. Farran took a deep breath, released her grip on the drapery cord, and reminded herself of how shocked he'd looked when she'd flinched from him last night. Her father was never surprised when she recoiled from him. She was taking Kel's reaction as good sign, but his council . . .

How much distance was there between her and Chicago? The Gineal would monitor the area around their stronghold much more often and much more thoroughly than anywhere else. Because her magic was weak, it would be harder for them to find her, but not impossible, especially not if she was within their buffer zone.

When she heard the heat come on, Farran left the sliding door and walked deeper into the kitchen. She needed a moment to collect herself before facing Kel again. Uncomfortable with the idea of checking out the cabinets, she went to the gold refrigerator and peeked inside. Except for a box of baking soda and a couple of cans of pop, it was empty. And warm. She spotted the plug lying across the back of the counter next to it.

The sound of a door opening yanked Farran from her perusal. She pivoted and hurried out of the kitchen, afraid that Kel was abandoning her. As she rounded the breakfast bar, she found him halfway out the back of the house.

To her embarrassment, he must have read the panic on her face because he said, "I'm just getting some wood off the deck. A fire will warm things up quicker."

She shuddered as cold air blew into the cabin and was glad he'd told her to get her jacket—she just wished she owned a warmer one. Kel carried in the first armload of wood, put it next to the fireplace, and made a second trip outside. He was taking care of her while she stood around. Again.

It shamed her to recall how he'd battled the shadow walker while she'd cowered under the table. This was the second time in two days that she'd tried to stay out of the way while two males went at it. The first time she hadn't believed it was her fight. Today, though, it clearly involved her. For a brief moment, as her body vibrated from the residual magic flying through the room, she'd nearly felt strong enough to join in. Nearly. Fate's little joke since she was nothing like the Gineal woman who had fought beside Kel the night he'd battled her family.

She watched him kneel in front of the fireplace and check it out, she assumed to make sure it was working okay and wouldn't send the cabin up in flames. Kel had been losing the fight with the shadow walker. His shielding had wavered, she'd felt it, but he'd kept hers at full strength. That counted for something.

Not just something, a lot.

No one would have blamed him if he'd let her protection fail and took care of himself, but he hadn't. And what had she done to help him? Nothing. Not a damn thing. It was her torment to be magically weak, to be forced to rely on others for things any Tàireil could do easily, but somehow it was much worse to be useless when someone needed her.

Farran dropped her chin to her chest. Kel hadn't condemned her, hadn't looked at her with scorn or derision, but he didn't have to. She despised herself.

"Get the matches, will you?" he asked, glancing over his shoulder. "They're in the kitchen cabinet closest to the table."

With a nod, she went to find them. They were on the bottom shelf, easily within her reach, and she returned to hand them to Kel. Their fingers brushed as Farran gave him the box and her skin tingled where they'd touched. It took all her control to not jerk away, but as soon as he had the matches, she eased back.

He lit a partially wadded up piece of newspaper and held it inside the fireplace until it nearly burned down to where he gripped it, then used it to light the balls of newspaper under the grate. Once the small fire was going, Kel positioned the screen and stood, watching it burn. Farran studied him, trying to figure out why she reacted so strongly to this man.

Maybe it was because of the shaggy hair and the stubble, but he looked rough and dangerous. That alone should send her scurrying the other direction. In the past, the males she'd been interested in had all had a certain softness to them and she'd been the one in control.

It hadn't taken five minutes in his presence to realize that Kellan Andrews wouldn't let her run the show.

She didn't want to be attracted to him. Not only was he Gineal and hard-edged, but her entire life was in turmoil right now. The shadow walker and demon were only part of it. Farran brought her fingers to her face and brushed the tips over her cheek. It was only when she felt smooth skin that she realized what she'd done. She laced her fingers at her waist.

Kel had his own ghosts—she'd seen them in his eyes last night. Any woman who got attached to him was facing heartache and Farran wasn't going there. She'd been hurt enough to last a lifetime. If she became involved, it would be with someone easy.

His gaze connected with hers and Farran fought the need to shiver again. The intensity she saw was both arousing and frightening at the same time. She had to look away.

There was nothing easy about Kel. He was complicated, likely carrying wounds that ran deeper than her own, and he sure didn't have a sense of peace around him. She wanted calmness and serenity almost as much as she wanted to belong somewhere.

She could feel his eyes on her and Farran gathered up her courage to face him again. He was staring. "What?" she asked.

"Just trying to figure out why there's a storm blowing around you. A demon and a shadow walker. What the hell did you do to attract their interest?"

Farran shook her head. "I wish I knew."

"So do I." Detouring around her, he bent to grab the backpack and hauled it around the counter into the kitchen.

She trailed behind him. He put the pack on the counter, plugged in the refrigerator, and began unloading food. Slipping her hands into her jacket pockets, she watched him for a moment, then asked, "Do you have any guesses at all about the shadow walker? I know you said you're unfamiliar with them, but you must have learned something. You're a troubleshooter."

He finished emptying the pack, shut the cabinet door, and turned to her. "I think training on them lasted all of about five minutes." Kel leaned against the counter and crossed his arms over his chest. "There are other beings much more likely to show up in our world, and that's what we concentrated on."

"What about reading on your own?"

"The odds were against my ever needing the information and I studied things that were more—" With a grimace, Kel stopped short. "Hell."

"What? Did you think of something?"

"No, but after all the shit I gave my brother because he didn't know anything about the dragon mage, it's humbling to find myself using the same excuse that he threw at me. Good thing he's not around or I'd never hear the end of it."

There was a slight tilt to his lips as he said that and Farran didn't understand. The idea of giving her brothers ammunition to use against her wouldn't leave her amused. More like shaking in her shoes. "You're going to the library and learning more, right?"

"*We're* going to the library."

Farran's blood went ice cold and she fisted her hands inside her pockets. "No, I'm not going. You don't need me."

"I don't, but I can't leave you here alone, not when the shadow walker could show up at any time."

"You concealed the use of the transit." She heard the desperation in her voice, but if he dragged her to the library, it would be as good as turning her over to his council.

"Do you want to be on your own when he shows up?"

There was nothing derogatory in his tone, but Farran had no doubt he was remembering her curled under the table as the battle raged. No, she definitely didn't want to face the shadow walker alone, but the alternative was every bit as bad. "I can't go to your tasglann," she said quietly. "The librarians will report my presence to your rulers and they'll take me from you."

"That is a problem."

Farran wasn't sure how to read his laconic delivery. "You can call the books to you. There's no need to physically go there."

"I could, but that will leave a trail of magic right to the cabin and I'm not going to do that."

"Why couldn't you go to the library, get the books, and bring them here? That would only take you a couple of minutes—not that large a risk." Did he want to get rid of her? If so, why not simply hand her over to the council and be done with it?

Kel straightened away from the counter and closed the ground between them. Farran's first instinct was to back away, to maintain that distance, but she forced herself to hold steady. He didn't stop until he was directly in front of her.

"Because the longer you stay in one place, the easier it will be for the shadow walker to track you down." He stuck his hands in the front pockets of his jeans. "This is the last house with protection around it that I have access to, and if we're forced to leave here, that opens you to attack from the demon."

It made sense, but she still didn't like it. Farran shook her head, denying his logic.

"Think about it," Kel said and the intensity in his voice would have had her backing up quickly if his hands weren't safely tucked in his pockets. "You've got multiple threats. If it was only the shadow walker, I'd say fuck it and bring the books here, but there's the demon. Seth might not have all the power he once possessed, but he's still dangerous. He's not going to give up and fade away, not from what our reports on him have said."

"The shadow walker could track us to the library."

"He could, but he'd have to be brazen to try to grab

you there, especially when there's a group of troubleshooters on guard at all times."

Hesitantly, afraid of how he'd take it, Farran pulled her hand from her jacket and rested it on his forearm. "The tasglann is part of the Gineal stronghold; I'm no more welcome there than the shadow walker would be."

For a moment, he simply stared at her. "I'll leave the choice up to you." The knot in her stomach eased. He was going to be reasonable. "You can either do things my way or I'll return you to Seattle and you can look for someone else to protect you."

5
CHAPTER

Kel splashed water on his face and grabbed a towel as he straightened. He felt vulnerable clean shaven, but he looked less disreputable and that was what he wanted.

With a grimace, he draped the damp towel over the bar and took one last look in the mirror over the sink. Shaving had probably been unnecessary. If things went according to plan, no one would be aware of their presence anyway.

He opened the door, shut off the light, and left the bathroom. A brief glance to his right showed the bedroom door was still closed, but then he hadn't expected her to reappear until she had no other choice. Not as pissed off as she'd been when she'd stalked out of the room an hour ago.

The aroma of coffee had him moving again. Farran thought that he planned to palm her off on the council. Or maybe she believed he was a moron for assuming he could get her into the library without someone turning her in to the ceannards.

The odds were against that happening. Kel knew the tasglann. Not only did he spend huge amounts of time there studying, but when he'd first come out of troubleshooter training, he'd been assigned to guard it and the accumulated knowledge stored there. If he played his cards right, and if things hadn't changed dramatically since he'd been nineteen, they should be able to stroll inside without anyone knowing about it.

The council and their chief headquarters were housed in a skyscraper in downtown Chicago, while the tasglann was on a huge tract of land outside of the city along with the rest of the central Gineal buildings. It had been designed to look like an office complex to outsiders, and while it was guarded, it wasn't as closely protected as the seat of their government was.

Why should it be? Although there'd been a few incidents—the most recent a couple of years ago—the library, healing temple, and the rest had rarely been attacked in the entire history of his people.

Kel got down a mug, poured himself a cup of coffee, and wandered over to the windows. The sky was a silver-gray and light flurries wafted around in the air. His parents had bought the cabin when he'd been a kid and his family had come here year-round, but rarely in the winter. He had only good memories of this place—fishing on the lake with his dad, sailing with his brother, hiking with his little sisters to see the horses on a nearby farm. His lips curved as he remembered the awestruck expressions on the girls' faces. Maybe he should have come to Wisconsin to heal rather than riding things out at home.

After taking a sip of coffee, Kel settled at the table and wrapped both hands around the mug. Maybe he should pass Farran off to someone who wasn't as fucked up as he was and just hide out for a while. Immediately, he dismissed the thought. This was his job, his plan.

He'd carefully thought through his idea to get Farran in the library, had it all worked out in his head. There was a lot of space between the buildings on the Gineal campus and a lot of trees—so much of both that one structure wasn't visible from another. That meant he only had to worry about the troubleshooters guarding the tasglann.

From his days assigned to watch over the library and the dìonachd who worked there, Kel knew standard practice was to monitor who entered and left via a transit, but they didn't watch the doors. There was a protective spell cast around the building that prevented anyone who wasn't Gineal from entering and the troubleshooters who were assigned to the tasglann were kids fresh from their apprenticeships. If he couldn't outthink some hormonal teenager, then he didn't deserve to get his territory back.

Farran would point out that she wasn't Gineal. He knew that, but he'd read a report issued by some of their scholars awhile back that pretty much proved the Gineal and Tàireil had been one people before their worlds had split off to separate dimensional paths. Maybe enough time had passed that their DNA wasn't identical any longer, but Kel bet she was close enough genetically to pass through the incantation.

If he was wrong . . . well, looking reliable couldn't be a bad thing.

The plan wasn't foolproof, of course. The tasglann was huge and Kel knew which sections of the building were rarely used, but that didn't mean a dìonachd wouldn't happen to need a title shelved in one of those areas. It was a risk they had to take.

He would have explained all this to Farran—if she'd bothered to ask. She hadn't. Instead, she'd immediately assumed the worst of him.

Normally, he wouldn't give a damn, but in this situation he couldn't afford her skepticism. If . . . no, make that *when* . . . the shadow walker found them, Kel might have to give Farran orders.

She'd been knocked around, probably by her father, and it might not be easy for her to put her faith in any man. Kel couldn't blame her for that, but if he told her to do something, he needed her to obey him without question even if what he told her was counterintuitive. The only way she'd do that was if she trusted him. Really trusted him. Getting her safely into the library might be a start to building that bond. But getting inside was about more than that. He needed information. Badly.

Kel got up, topped off his mug, and went searching for a notebook. He located one in the cabinet next to the fireplace. On his way back to the table, he checked the remnants of the fire. It appeared to be out, but he'd take another look before they left.

Finding a pen that worked was more difficult, but he finally dug one out of a kitchen drawer near the front door. Back at the table, he drew a line down the center of the paper and wrote *shadow walker* on one side, *demon* on the other. It was simple to fill in what he knew about Seth since he'd had a well-documented confrontation with two troubleshooters, a former troubleshooter, and one apprentice. The librarians had also been assigned to research all the god-demons, and while the data was incomplete, it gave Kel a baseline to work with.

The other side of the page was more difficult. The shadow walker appeared to want Farran, but neither of them knew why. Shadow walkers weren't believed to live in this dimension, but where they came from was unknown. Shadow walkers—at least one of them—were able to bypass Gineal security, but how he'd done that was unknown.

And then there was the man's arsenal. Kel scowled as he recalled the fight. He thought the energy the shadow walker had used was electrical in nature, but he wasn't certain of that. What he did know was that even with a protection spell in place, he'd felt every blast that connected.

Partial facts, suppositions, and a million question marks—that was all he had. Great.

Kel tossed down the pen and reached for his coffee. He knew so little about his adversary that it was laughable. And potentially dangerous. At least he had a plan of action for when they went to the library—get a general overview of who the hell he was facing and go deeper from there.

He glanced at the clock on the microwave. A few more minutes and he'd have to roust Farran. Kel had weighed his options and decided that showing up at the tasglann during lunch offered them the least risk. There might be a few dìonachd around, but odds were they'd be in a backroom on break. As for the troubleshooters, Kel figured only one on duty at noon and the kid would probably be bored. For damn sure he had been when it had been his turn to cover the meal period.

Pushing back from the table, Kel poured the rest of the coffee into his cup, shut off the machine, and rinsed out the pot. He'd probably been the most impatient of the group assigned to the tasglann—nineteen and so fucking arrogant that he couldn't believe he hadn't immediately been given a territory to take care of after training.

With a snort, Kel wandered over to the window with his mug and stared out at the island in the center of the lake. There'd been six of them there who had finished their apprenticeships at about the same time, and in shortly over two years, all of them had left the tasglann for their own territories. Busy territories.

Ryne Frasier had been the first of them to go and Kel had been fine with that. They'd all known at least in some peripheral way how powerful she was and it had been good for her to get out after the truth about her mentor had been revealed.

Logan had been the next to get a territory. Jealousy had been there, but Kel had been happy for his brother. The two of them had never been all that competitive with each other anyway.

It had been much tougher for Kel to deal with who'd been the third troubleshooter to leave the library. The council had assigned Los Angeles, one of the most active territories, to Sinclair Duncan. That had irked the hell out of Kel. Not only had he wanted the city for himself, but Duncan was a prick and Kel had never liked him. In retrospect, it probably had been for the best, but it sure hadn't felt that way at the time.

Logan would have been fine in L.A. and Kel allowed himself a brief stab of envy. His brother had a way of doing his job and not letting any of it eat at him. Kel wished he had that kind of focus, that ability to compartmentalize—but he didn't.

He shook his head, the irony not lost on him. Everyone thought Logan was great—the good twin—warm, friendly, a sociable guy. And he was, but not when he was in battle. When he was fighting, Logan was ice cold, emotionless, and he felt no sympathy for his enemy, no empathy.

"No mercy," Kel said softly. Logan's motto and one Kel wished he could adopt himself.

It wasn't that easy. Despite his rep as being a standoffish asshole, Kel's big problem was that he felt too damn much and felt it too intensely. Healers had a strong degree of empathy, they had to, but he had more. It was so powerful that at times it was nearly like mind reading, and if he wasn't careful, he could feel his enemy's pain. It was a bitch. He'd give nearly anything to do his job without worrying about his mental shield slipping.

Right. Like that would ever happen.

Kel shuddered as a stray memory surfaced, and ruthlessly, he quashed it. He wasn't going there. Not now, not if he wanted to be able to function today.

You think too damn much. How many times had Logan told him that? And maybe that was part of the problem. Kel spent far too much energy analyzing everything and it never seemed to help. He couldn't control the uncontrollable, he couldn't undo the past, and no amount of examination would change those truths.

Pivoting sharply from the window, Kel put his cup in the kitchen sink and checked the clock. Close enough. He headed around the counter and down the hall to get Farran.

* * *

As soon as she crossed the transit, Farran shrank into her jacket, letting the collar hide her cheek. Two things occurred to her almost simultaneously—no one was in the vicinity and her face wasn't scarred anymore. She looked around more carefully, but there were no people in sight of the asphalt path they were on. To her surprise, the tasglann wasn't in view either; all she saw were trees. She looked at Kel for an explanation.

"We need to head that way," he said, pointing to the left.

Farran nodded, but she stayed put. She'd expected the transit to open directly into the library and it stunned her that he'd chosen to put them outside. Of course, this wasn't the only time he'd knocked her off balance today. She still couldn't get over how different Kel looked without the stubble. Younger. More approachable. Sexier.

Tucking her hands into her pockets, Farran glanced away. He might be helping her, but she couldn't forget he was Gineal. The enemy. She couldn't even be sure that he really *was* on her side. Not when he'd threatened to abandon her if she didn't come here.

"It's going to be fine," Kel said. "Trust me."

"That's not easy to do."

"Yeah, I know. C'mon, it's cold out here. Let's get moving."

He headed off without a backward glance, but then he didn't need to check on her—she had no other options and he was aware of it. Slowly, Farran followed him.

The paved path wound its way through the trees and zigzagged up a hill. Kel waited for her at the top, but Farran took her time. As she reached his side, she saw what must be the Gineal tasglann laid out in front of her. She'd expected marble, columns, arches, and maybe a dome—something that would make her catch her breath in wonder. This wasn't impressive at all.

It looked like a million other large office buildings—

five stories high, very few windows, and a brick facade. No one looking at it would understand what it housed. And then Farran got it. Humans wouldn't glance twice at this place and that's what the Gineal wanted. Hide in plain sight.

Farran felt Kel's eyes on her and she turned her head to meet his gaze. "Even after living in this world for nine months, I still sometimes forget how different things are here."

"You were expecting a cathedral," he said, understanding what she was commenting on as easily as if she'd told him.

"Or something comparable."

"The front has more glass and an atrium lobby." Kel paused, then admitted, "But it isn't much more elaborate than this."

She wanted to ask more questions, keep him talking, anything to delay the inevitable, but before she could form words, Kel headed toward the building. Farran hesitated and then trailed in his wake. He was opening the door when she felt a magical wall blocking her and stopped short.

"Come on," Kel said.

"I can't. The barrier's in my way." He had to know that.

Kel let the door close and returned to where she'd come to a halt. He stood on the other side of the force field, facing her. "You can cross it, I promise."

Farran shook her head.

"I thought you were gutsier than this."

He what? "Me?"

"Yeah, you. You are the one who risked her own life to protect Shona, aren't you? And weren't you the one who warned Logan that your brothers were closing ground even though it led to your being considered a traitor? Or am I thinking of someone else?"

Her hands fisted at her sides. "Goading me isn't going to work," Farran told him.

"If you don't like it, stop acting like such a baby. We both know you're tougher than what you've been showing me."

He was trying to get her mad enough to make her storm across the barrier, but despite her knowledge of what he was up to, she wanted to prove to him that she wasn't always a coward. "Don't."

"Don't what?" he drawled. "Don't hold a mirror up so you can see your actions?"

A picture of herself hiding under the table while he fought on her behalf flitted through Farran's mind. Damn him. She took a shuddery breath and considered the shield. The Gineal wouldn't make it strong enough to fry someone, not when it might lead to a human getting hurt or killed, and that meant the odds were it would simply be unpleasant when she tried to cross. Once she gave it a shot and failed, he'd have to concede.

Bracing herself, Farran inched forward. She half expected Kel to make more obnoxious remarks to get her moving faster, but he stayed quiet. As she neared the edge of the field, her eyes closed—she couldn't help it—but she kept easing toward him, waiting for the zap she knew she was going to get at any second.

It didn't come when she expected and Farran guessed she'd misjudged the boundary. But when she kept moving and nothing happened, she opened her eyes to gauge the situation.

"Welcome to the Gineal tasglann," Kel said.

"I'm past the barrier." That was obvious, but she couldn't believe it.

"Yep. I told you to trust me." And more quietly, he added, "And I said you were tough enough to take the risk."

"No one likes people who say, *I told you so.*"

One side of his lips quirked up, but it wasn't quite a smile. "Ready for your next challenge?" Kel asked as he crossed to the building and opened the door.

Farran scowled at him. "Has anyone ever told you that you're annoying?"

"Why do you think I get called the evil twin? Let's move, sunshine."

Gritting her teeth, she walked past him and into the library. Here was all the majesty Farran had expected to see at the tasglann. Ornate, polished bookcases rose from the floor to the top of the ten-foot ceilings and each one was filled with book after book—all sizes, all colors. The floor wasn't marble, but gleaming hardwood and spectacularly beautiful. She could sense another barrier between her and the shelves, but this was to protect the fragile paper, not to keep her out.

Kel closed the door and stood at her side, his shoulder brushing hers. Farran didn't like the shiver of awareness that went through her, but she refused to show her discomfiture by sidling away from him.

We're going up to the fourth floor. Stay quiet and follow me.

The telepathic message had her stiffening, but she nodded. That was one question answered about the Gineal. She'd wondered if they had the same kind of mind-speak capabilities that the Tàireil possessed. Now she knew.

She dutifully followed him through a maze of twists and turns, so many that she wasn't sure she'd be able to find her way out again without him. And everywhere she looked were bookcases, every single one as full as possible. The knowledge amassed here, the history of spellcasting and of other facets of magic had to be incredible. Farran envied the Gineal this library. In her world, grimoires stayed in families, and their tasglann, while beautiful in appearance, had nothing like the sheer volume of references contained in this unassuming building.

As she came around the corner of one bookshelf, Farran skidded to a halt and sucked in an awed breath. Before she could think better of it, she went to the railing and looked out. Above her was another floor, below her were three floors, and as far as the eye could see were books.

It was beautiful. Stunning. Down the middle of the main floor were tables with chairs for those researching to sit and study. The bookcases were built into elaborately carved columns that circled the center of each story and the dark wood shone every bit as brilliantly as the floor. My God, she thought, there had to be more books here in this one building than in her entire world.

She was still paralyzed in wonder when Kel's arm went around her waist. Farran stiffened, but while his hold was firm, it didn't hurt. He turned, taking her away from the railing and then released her. Before she could protest, he sent, *Do you want to be spotted by the Gineal? Damn it, why didn't you just shout out a* hello, we're here *and be done with it?*

Sorry. I wasn't thinking. I just— Wow.

Kel reached for her hand and twined their fingers before continuing. That was one sure way, she guessed, to make sure she didn't wander off again, but it left Farran too aware of him. The warmth of his palm against hers was enough to speed up her heart rate and she hated that. Why this man?

She mulled over possible answers as he continued to thread them through the bookcases, but Farran didn't like anything she came up with.

He tugged her into a small room and closed the door behind them. Kel released her the instant they were inside. "Study room," he explained, maybe reading the question on her face. "The tasglann has them scattered throughout the building. This one is in a section that doesn't attract a lot of traffic, so if we keep our voices down, it should be all right to talk here."

"Okay." Farran took a look around. In the center of the room, there was a table with four chairs, on one side was a credenza, and on the other were two stuffed chairs like the kind people put in their living rooms with a large table between them. The lighting came from a source she couldn't see and was bright enough to make reading easy, but not so bright that it would cause a glare. The walls themselves were an off-white and one had a painting of a sunflower done in an almost impressionistic style. Comfortable, but conducive to study.

"Do you read the old language of the Tàireil?" Kel asked.

"Yes," she said, not sure why he cared. "It's actually fairly close to what we still use."

"Good, then you can help me research." He pulled out a chair at the table, went around to the other side, and sat down. Books started appearing and she knew he was responsible for calling them forward.

Farran took the seat he'd designated as hers and reached for one of the nearby volumes, unsure why he thought knowledge of her people's tongue would help her with this task. "What kind of information are you interested in?"

"Everything. I know next to nothing about shadow walkers. I'm looking for general overview stuff first, then we'll drill down from there if something looks interesting."

She put her hand over the book, curled her fingers to the area where she felt the words for shadow walker, and opened it. Starting a few pages before the mention, Farran began reading. Nearly every word she saw was understandable to her and it made her wonder how closely the Gineal and Tàireil had been connected in the past.

Almost as soon as the question arose, she pushed it aside. What once was didn't count now; all that mattered was that the Gineal had repeatedly acted against the Tàireil. She couldn't afford to forget that.

With a shrug, she scanned for the next instance of *neach-faileas* and did the same thing, continuing on until she reached the end. Farran didn't find anything more than vague references, and put the book aside. As she reached for the next one on the stack, she noticed that Kel was watching her. Her hand started to go to her cheek, but she caught herself in time and lowered it. "What?" she asked.

"How are you doing that?"

"What do you mean?"

"You're finding references without having to skim through the entire volume looking for them."

She considered him for a moment, but he was serious. "You call the books forward by seeking out ones with the right word or phrase, right?"

"Yeah, but I can't do that within a book. Can I?"

With a shrug, Farran said, "I don't know if you can or not, but I sense where the words are that I'm looking for and open it there."

Kel looked thoughtful. "Send me how you're doing it."

It wasn't merely a telepathic passing of information. This would be closer contact than that, and if she was unscrupulous, she could do some prying before he could block her out again. Maybe Kel felt he could risk it because he was strong, but he still had to trust her—at least a little—to allow this.

Almost afraid to believe he meant it, Farran made the connection to him and transmitted without words how she did it. She didn't abuse his faith in her, she didn't linger over the union, and after she pulled back, she didn't comment about the roiling emotions she'd felt inside him or the fortress she'd sensed. Looking into his brilliant blue eyes, she saw awareness there—he knew she'd picked up something despite his efforts to shield himself. "Does how I do it make sense?" she asked.

Some of Kel's tension eased. "Yeah," he said thickly, "I got it. This should help get through this pile faster."

He bent his head to the book in front of him and Farran stared a few seconds longer before doing the same with her own volume. It took awhile, though, for her astonishment to pass. Kel Andrews was more than a cold, lethal enemy of her people. He was also a man with vulnerabilities and his own troubles. She'd picked up ghosts in his eyes last night, but hadn't understood how deeply they haunted him. Now she had a better idea and it shifted her attitude toward him.

This man wasn't only a Gineal warrior any longer. Now she thought of him as an ally as well, and that would make it harder for her to hold him at arm's length.

6
CHAPTER

Kel closed the book he was looking through, and leaning back in his chair, scrubbed his hands over his face. He was tired, he was hungry, and he was frustrated. By now he'd expected to be deep into the research, but he was still trying to find more than vague references to the shadow walkers.

An encyclopedia listing all beings and a little about them would be a big help, but none of the councils had ever assigned the librarians to work on that. Some dìonachd had tried to do it on their own, but it had been as a hobby and nothing had ever been finished. In fact, there were about half a dozen incomplete versions stored in the tasglann and he'd called all those attempts forward. None of them had included anything about shadow walkers.

The lack of information was odd; the Gineal recorded everything and the library was filled with journals and personal papers as well as an incredible number of books because of that. It was part of the reason why some troubleshooters weren't excited about research—the amount of data available was overwhelming. Add in that nothing had been input into a computer system and only a fraction had been cataloged in ledgers and it became that much more difficult. But Kel was good at investigating; he knew where and how to find things. They should have basic knowledge on the shadow walkers by now.

Stretching his arms over his head to ease the stiffness, he tried to figure out why they were coming up empty. Someone had to know something and that person must have written it down. That's what his people did.

His stomach growled and Farran glanced at him briefly before returning to the book she held. It would be time to leave soon. Maybe it was smarter to stay and work deep into the night. The library became nearly deserted after about eight or nine o'clock and they'd have less to worry about if they left then, but Kel wasn't hanging around that late.

When they walked out of here, he wanted enough light to see if any enemy was coming his way. Yeah, he could use his other senses to scan, but he preferred to have visual references.

And he didn't want to fight at night.

He hated the dark. Kel unclenched his fists and jaw. If anyone ever discovered that he slept with a lamp on— or tried to sleep—he'd never hear the end of it, but he needed the light.

Just the thought of being outside after dark made him twitchy and Kel checked his watch. Maybe they should leave now to be safe. The library should be quiet enough since it was after five and there was still time before he had to worry about sunset.

Besides, they could take books with them to the cabin. He didn't want to call them to their hideout on the off chance that the trail could be followed, but if they carried the research, the texts would be hidden with the same spell that he used to conceal the transit's energy. They should be fine.

Yeah, he decided, that's what they'd do. Kel began magically returning the books they were done with to the shelves. Farran closed the volume she held and watched him.

"Are we finished here? Did you find the information you wanted?" she asked.

Kel shook his head. "No." He was going to drop it there, but realized if he wanted to foster a sense of trust with her, he was going to have to offer information when he could. "We need to leave before it gets dark. If we both carry an armload, we should be able to take enough books back with us to get a few more hours' worth of work in tonight."

"Okay." She slid a pile across the table to him. "I went through these already."

With a nod, he returned those as well. When he was done, Kel stood and began to divvy up the remaining tomes.

"You know," Farran said slowly, "it seems strange how little detail there is on the shadow walkers. Plenty of references, but no real substance. Is that normal in the Gineal library?"

"No, but there have been so few encounters over the millennia that it might make locating the firsthand observations difficult." But they'd gone through enough references that they should have found something more than the vague facts he'd seen. If nothing else there should be an account from someone who knew someone who'd fought a shadow walker, but even hearsay had been strangely absent.

Farran rolled her shoulders, working out her own kinks, and then looked at him. "Do you think the shadow walkers are powerful enough to eliminate information about themselves when someone wrote about them? The one after me *was* strong enough to come in past your house's protection."

Kel went still. "Yeah, but to do something like that . . ."

"Nearly impossible."

He moved the smaller pile of books over to her side of the table. "It's more likely that we haven't gotten lucky yet."

"You're probably right," she agreed.

But he wondered. Thanks to Farran showing him her method of searching text, they'd gone through at least ten times the number of books he'd expected to cover. What she did was a simple thing and Kel couldn't believe he'd never thought of it, but the amount of ground they'd covered made the absence of facts more puzzling. If he'd come up with even one additional detail, he'd dismiss the idea of shadow walker manipulation out of hand, but what the hell did their *unusual powers* encompass anyway?

"We'll go out the same way we came in," he said, picking up his stack of books. "Stick close and don't wander off this time."

Ignoring her frown, Kel went to the door and extended his senses, searching for the locations of anyone still in the library. It wasn't an easy thing to do. Many of the books had magic cast over them and it interfered with the flow of the energy patterns, but when he was confident the coast was clear, he opened the door.

His route through the tasglann was circuitous, but it improved their odds of remaining undetected. Yeah, paranoid, but Kel had learned to err on the side of caution.

As they traveled among the stacks, he glanced over his shoulder now and then to make sure Farran was still back there. She scowled every time she noticed and that amused him. He didn't think she'd forget their situation a second time, but this was another risk he wasn't going to take.

Kel remained careful when they reached the exit, but a scan showed it was safe. He cast a basic protection spell around Farran and himself, opened the door, and stepped outside. Only when he was absolutely certain it was clear did he move aside and let her join him.

The sun was low in the sky, but there was plenty of daylight and Kel didn't pick up anyone in the immediate vicinity. As soon as they were far enough away from the building, he'd open a transit and they'd be safely back at the cabin.

She was quiet as they headed down the path away from the library, but then Farran never seemed to say a lot. It wouldn't bother him except Kel couldn't help but wonder if her silence was because of him. From everything he'd heard about her, she wasn't someone who was reticent. At least she hadn't been. Life had a way of changing people, though. He should know.

That soured his mood and Kel picked up his pace. There was no way to outrun his thoughts—he'd learned that—but if he was busy, sometimes they'd fade.

A blast hit his shield.

Kel dropped the books and whirled to face the threat. Simultaneously, he pulled his arm back to fire and worked to reinforce the barriers that surrounded them.

He didn't finish quickly enough.

The demon's second shot dropped him to the ground. Kel struggled to remain conscious, but he felt the dark rolling in on him and he couldn't stop it. Farran. She needed him. He couldn't leave her to the demon. He couldn't.

Kel remained careful when they reached the library's exit, but a scan showed it was safe. He cast a basic protection spell around Farran and himself, opened the door, and stepped outside. Only when he was absolutely certain it was clear did he move aside and let her join him.

The sun was low in the sky, but there was plenty of daylight and Kel didn't pick up anyone in the immediate vicinity. As soon as they were far enough away from the building, he'd open a transit and they'd be safely back at the cabin.

Farran was quiet as they headed down the path away from the library, but then she never seemed to say a lot. It wouldn't bother him except—

He stopped short. Hadn't they already walked past here? And hadn't they been surprised by Seth farther down the trail? Or was his mind playing tricks on him again? Deciding to puzzle through this later, Kel went with his gut. He strengthened their protection spells and opened a transit.

"Go," he told Farran when she hesitated. She crossed. Kel started to follow her, but something made him stop and visually sweep the area ahead—past the place where he thought he remembered being attacked. His gaze locked with the demon's and Seth looked furious. If they'd been a little farther along the path, they would have been at point-blank range.

Not waiting any longer, Kel used the gate, closing it immediately when he was inside the cabin.

The late winter landscape gave Seth few choices for concealment and he was at a greater distance from the lodge than he'd prefer. The stand of trees to its rear would have put him considerably closer, but with no foliage it left him too exposed. Once, he wouldn't have worried overmuch—he simply would have used magic to make up for barrenness—but those days were gone.

Instead, he'd been forced to settle on another copse that was perhaps four hundred yards from the structure. He was near enough to monitor when they left, but couldn't see much beyond the lighted windows of the weathered wooden structure.

It maddened him, but Seth was growing accustomed to the frustrations and inconveniences. That didn't mean that he accepted them. He would not concede.

If he did, he'd spend the rest of his life looking over his shoulder, wondering when Horus or his allies would strike. That was only part of it, however. Seth had known great power for thousands and thousands of years. To settle for a fraction of what he formerly was capable of would be like a human who'd never driven anything save a Lamborghini suddenly being forced to use a Geo Metro. They were both cars, but what could be done with one was a far cry from what could be accomplished with the other.

The cold made him shiver and he used magic to keep himself warm. It cost him more power than he wanted to spend, but he refused to stand here and freeze. Seth remembered when adjusting his body temperature had required nothing more than a brief thought, but pushed it aside. He needed to focus on what was, not on the past.

Seth watched someone cross in front of the windows, but from this distance, he couldn't tell if the silhouette was male or female. It mattered not. With the protection in place around the lodge, he had no hope of reaching her as long as she remained inside.

So close.

He worked to unclench his jaw. Today was a setback, not a defeat, and it was something for which he should have been prepared. Foolish of him not to be.

And he'd learned something—the Tàireil woman had no idea what she was able to do. He could turn that to his advantage.

The looming question, however, was did the Gineal warrior know, or had his council kept this secret from their foot soldier? It was a certainty that they had the information. Why else would they seek out the woman with such persistence? That didn't mean they'd felt the need to tell any of their troubleshooters.

Seth mulled it over for a few moments and decided they had not shared the real reason they wanted the Tàireil. If he was aware, the Gineal would have immediately turned her over instead of trying to protect her himself. That was to his benefit—if the troubleshooter hadn't learned the truth after what the woman had done this evening.

And if her actions hadn't alerted the shadow walkers of her location. They were the real threat, not the Gineal. Seth could outmaneuver any troubleshooter even if his magic was merely equal to theirs, but shadow walkers were a more serious hurdle. One instance they might be able to dismiss, but two? No, they'd be coming after her with all throttles open. They were too close to risk beginning their sentence anew.

Waving a hand, Seth conjured a stool, and after ensuring that it was well balanced, sat down and gave some thought to the shadow walkers. The troubleshooter had shielded his transit, and the only reason Seth had been able to follow it was because he'd been within range of the energy. There had been no shadow walker in the vicinity either time. He knew that unequivocally.

Seth leaned forward and rested both forearms on his knees. If he was right, that meant they were unaware of the lodge and that gave him a small edge. Very small, but he'd take whatever he had. Unfortunately, unless the pair left the structure, there was no possibility of his taking action here.

What would the shadow walkers do? They could be unpredictable, but Seth felt confident about a couple of things.

They'd strike quickly. The Tàireil woman hadn't crossed the line as of yet, but she'd skated close and the shadow walkers couldn't risk waiting.

Outside the library then—if the duo went back there—but he thought they would because both had been carrying an armload of books tonight. He needed a plan, some method that would allow him to turn the shadow walker's attack to his benefit. The male had defeated him in their previous encounter, but Seth would be better prepared this time. He had to be.

He couldn't allow his ticket out of purgatory to slip from his fingers again no matter what action he needed to take.

Farran found something soothing about washing dishes by hand. She'd never done it before—even the cheap apartment she'd called home the past few months had a dishwasher—but the cabin didn't have that amenity. The only thing that kept her from relaxing was Kel. He stood beside her, taking the dishes from her and drying them before placing them back into the cabinets.

He was wired, pulled so taut that he was practically vibrating from it, and that put her on edge. Not because she was scared of him—she wasn't—but she was afraid *for* him. And Farran couldn't say why she felt that way.

She'd asked him a couple of times if he was all right and Kel had tersely assured her that he was fine. It was clear that he was far from okay, but she knew he'd never tell her the truth and she decided to let it go. The quiet was unnerving, but maybe she could keep his mind off whatever was eating him and ease her own nerves with some inconsequential conversation. Farran searched for a topic.

"I thought cabins were more rustic than this. You know, no central heat, no indoor bathroom, and no microwave. Do I have it wrong?"

Kel was quiet as he dried a glass and it wasn't until he put it away that he said, "No, you're not wrong, but my mom doesn't like roughing it and we've had this place since I was little. Can you imagine bringing five kids here without running water?"

"No." She rinsed another glass and handed it to him. "There are only two bedrooms; where did all of you sleep?"

He sighed, but he answered her. "The room you claimed is the one my three sisters use, my parents have the other, and Logan and I camped out in the great room." Kel gestured over his shoulder with his thumb. "The two love seats pull out into beds. It doesn't work as well now that we're all adults, but with our schedules it's rare that everyone's here at the same time anyhow."

Farran nodded to show she heard him. This explained why there was a bunk bed along with the single bed in the room she'd chosen. She reached for a plate and ran the soapy rag over the surface. "Have your parents considered adding on?"

"They've thought about razing the entire cabin and starting from scratch. They're worried about having room for all the grandchildren." Their hands brushed as he took the dish from her. "And I guess with Logan getting engaged, it's only a matter of time now."

His scowl made her heart stop. "You don't like Shona?"

"I like her just fine."

"You don't like babies?"

Kel turned that glower on her. "I don't have anything against babies either."

"Then what is your problem?" she demanded.

"Drop it."

He pivoted, prepared to walk away, and Farran reached out, snagging the waistband at the back of his jeans with her wet hand. Kel froze and looked over his shoulder at her. That's when she realized her fingers were beneath the band of his briefs, too, and that she'd dripped water down his butt—enough to leave wet streaks on the seat of his pants.

Her cheeks heated and Farran nearly apologized, but she quashed that instinct. "You're not going anywhere until you tell me why the thought of Logan and Shona getting married makes you frown so fiercely. She's my best friend and I'm not letting you ruin things for her."

"You think I'd come between her and Logan?"

"I don't know. Would you?"

"No." Kel said that with so much conviction that she believed him. "I love my brother and Shona makes him happy. Even if I didn't like her, that would be enough for me."

"Then why—"

Before she could finish the question, he reached back and gently freed himself from her grip. "I have trouble with change; that's all you need to know."

There was more to it than that, but Farran nodded and

let it go. As long as Kel wasn't going to cause trouble for Shona, it was none of her business. Besides, if she pushed him on this, he might think that gave him the right to pry into her life and he already knew too much.

And her plan had backfired. Instead of conversation helping him wind down, she'd managed to make him tighten up even further. Farran went to the stove, grabbed the pan, and brought it back to the sink. Since he was already keyed up, might as well ask her next question. "Are you going to open the transit inside the library when we return?"

"I can't. All travel in to and out of the tasglann is monitored closely. We'll both be in a shitload of trouble if you're detected, and even as green as those kids guarding the library are, they'll pick you up instantly."

"And Tàireil are the enemy."

"Yes."

Farran looked around, but there were no more dishes to be washed. She wrung out the rag and wiped down the counters and table as Kel dried the pan. He'd cooked tonight, something that surprised her. She doubted her father or her brothers could have found their home's kitchen on a dare and would be helpless if they did locate it, but the troubleshooter had put together a delicious meal without her assistance. Granted, it had been simple, but the mere fact that he could do it softened her toward him. Just a little.

Kel opened the sink, let the water drain out, and leaning his hips against the counter, watched her work. It made her uneasy and Farran stopped what she was doing. "What?"

"We need to talk about what happened earlier."

"About you spotting the demon after I crossed the transit?"

Shaking his head, Kel said, "No, the part where I have two memories of events—one where I saw the demon after you left and the other where I was attacked by him and went down."

"I can't explain that."

"But you know something." She started to deny it, but before she could get a word out, he said, "Don't bullshit me. If you want me to protect you, I expect you to be honest."

"You can't keep throwing that in my face every time you want to get your way."

"Yes, I can. I'm the one doing you the favor, remember?"

Farran swallowed hard. That was true and he didn't have to help her. She was also aware of how much she needed him on her side. "I have two memories as well," she confessed reluctantly. "The same ones you have, although I didn't see the demon before I crossed the transit to the cabin."

"I'd wondered if I was losing what's left of my mind," he said with a slight tilt to his lips. "This has happened to you before, hasn't it?"

She wanted to deny it, but Farran couldn't take the chance that Kel would figure out she was lying and wash his hands of her. Her fingers tightened around the dishrag. "Once, but it had nothing to do with this situation."

"Why don't you tell me about it and let me be the judge?"

Her cheeks went hot and it was all she could do to continue meeting his gaze. Not only was she embarrassed, but she was ashamed, and that was stupid. If anyone should feel shame, it was the blond woman with the camera phone, but logic had nothing to do with it. Farran felt as if the fault were hers in some way.

Biting her lower lip, she drew in a deep breath and struggled to find her courage. Kel thought she was tough, but he was wrong. She wasn't. The idea, though, of disillusioning him prodded her to start talking about what had happened. Farran wasn't brave enough to keep looking him in the eye, but she decided that fixing her gaze just past his shoulder wasn't too cowardly. Maybe.

The job she'd had was mortifying enough, but she couldn't avoid telling him what she'd been doing. When she got to the part with the picture, Farran heard her voice wobble and clamped down on her emotions. She told the rest of the first version quickly, wanting it over immediately.

"That bitch," Kel growled and his vehemence startled Farran enough to swing her gaze back to him. He appeared furious. "I hope you threw a spell on her that made her outward appearance match the inner one."

"I, uh, I'm not that powerful, but it didn't occur to me anyway. I thought you protected humans."

He straightened away from the counter. "Making her face as ugly as her heart is simply truth in advertising, not something I'd feel any need to protect her from."

As Farran stared at Kel, his blue eyes blazing in anger for what she'd gone through, a warm feeling started in the center of her chest and spread outward. She hadn't expected this reaction from him, but she liked the way he sprang to her defense even though there wasn't a physical threat involved.

She wanted to thank Kel, but her throat was too thick to squeeze the words out. Farran settled for smiling at him. It trembled, but she hoped he read into it all she couldn't say. She was twenty-five years old and never, not once, had any male supported her. It meant everything to her.

"If that's the first version of events," he asked after a moment, "what was the second?"

Clearing her throat to get rid of the lump, Farran continued her story, telling him how she'd ended up in the back room, how the time on her watch had gone backward, and how she'd missed the blond woman the second time.

Kel nodded. "Interesting. When did this happen?"

"Last night."

His gaze sharpened as it bored into her. "Last night?

And you think this has no bearing on the situation you're in now?"

"It doesn't!" she insisted. "This happened hours before the demon or shadow walker showed up and it's not as if I caused it to occur. It was some weird fluke, that's all."

"Once is a fluke, twice is a pattern. And remember, neither Seth or the shadow walker appeared to have any interest in you until after that incident. You might not have caused it, but I don't believe in coincidence."

"I don't either, but it can't be anything else."

Without a word, Kel crossed to where she stood by the table, took the dishrag from her hands, and tossed it into the sink before pulling out a chair at the table for her. He took a seat to her left and reached for the pad of paper and pen on the island counter behind him. "Let's run through this again, step by step. Everything you remember, no matter how small you think it is. Something's going on here and we need to get to the bottom of it."

Farran couldn't sleep. They hadn't gotten to the bottom of anything even though Kel had insisted they review every detail again and again. When that hadn't yielded results, he'd switched to what had happened today. Even with his observations, they hadn't been able to come up with any answers.

Kel had wanted to keep on replaying events, but she'd insisted she needed to go to bed. For all the good it had done her.

She snuggled the blankets up to her chin and wondered what his sisters would think of his generosity with their clothes. Everything she had on belonged to someone else, but he was adamant about not using any magic that might lead the shadow walker to this place and there'd been no other choice.

She still couldn't get over Kel. Even as he kept pushing her tonight, trying to dredge up every little fact she might have forgotten, she hadn't been able to get mad at him. He'd been on *her* side when it came to that picture. Hers! Every time she thought about it that warmth began to creep through her again.

He wouldn't understand why it meant so much to her. From everything he'd said, it seemed that Kel had a close-knit, loving family. She didn't.

It wasn't that she'd been constantly beaten—she hadn't been. Mostly, she'd been ignored. Hammond Monroe, her father, had shown absolutely no interest in her, and growing up, she'd only seen him sporadically. She pulled her hand out from beneath the blanket and rubbed her finger over the bridge of her nose. As strange as it sounded, at least when he hit her, she felt as if she was real and not invisible.

Her mother had died when she was six, and from that day on, no one had really seemed to notice her presence. Even the humans assigned to care for her had been impersonal about it.

When she'd been old enough, her father had noticed her briefly as he'd tried to marry her off in some political arrangement. Unfortunately—or perhaps fortunately— no Tàireil had been interested in uniting with someone as weak magically as she was. Power was genetic and no one wanted to risk having children who weren't strong.

After that failed attempt, she'd been given permission to move off the family estate. The world had opened up for her then and Farran had begun to make a place for herself in the Tàireil dimension. Until her father had summoned her.

He'd never told her how he'd learned she was the dragon mage or how he'd discovered that Shona had the dragon stone, but it didn't matter. All that mattered was what had happened next. Farran had finally felt as if she meant something to her father and the dragon mage was not weak. At last she'd be respected.

Lacing her fingers behind her head, she stared up at the knotty-pine ceiling. As in the great room, the upper triangular-shaped windows in the bedroom were uncovered, and in the moonlight, she could see the exposed beams clearly.

All her plans had gone to hell, though, when she'd discovered how much she liked Shona. Farran's motivation had changed. She'd gone from wanting the dragon stone to please her father and to have her own strong powers, to trying to get that stone before her father or brothers hurt Shona to acquire it.

In the end, she'd failed miserably on all counts. It had been Logan who'd defended Shona and Farran had been used as a hostage. She could still taste the blood in her mouth from the backhand she'd taken when her father had learned Shona had melded with the dragon stone. That had only been the start of it, and every time Farran had lost consciousness, her father had revived her. He'd wanted her to feel every whit of her punishment.

And after she'd taken the blasts meant for Shona, Farran had waited for death. Instead, Kel had come and healed her. She hadn't known who he was then, only that he was Gineal and that he had a gentle touch, a special way with energy.

You're a fool if you believe anyone except a human would have any interest in you.

Her father's words after another one of his potential alliances had fallen through because the man in question didn't want to be shackled to her. Something Farran better recall if she started getting romantic thoughts about Kel. Yes, he'd healed her, he'd agreed to protect her, and he'd sided with her against the camera phone woman, but that didn't mean he had any interest in a nearly magicless member of the Tàireil.

And she was just being stupid because someone had shown her kindness. Farran had to be smarter than this. She had to remember that—

Kel called out and every muscle in Farran's body went rigid. Had the shadow walker found them?

She thought about crawling under the bed, but how

could she cower again? Especially when Kel believed she was tough and thought she was worthy of being treated with respect.

He shouted again, but the words were so slurred, Farran couldn't make them out. What she didn't hear, though, were any sounds of battle. Slowly, she pushed back the blankets, got to her feet, and tiptoed to the door. She sensed nothing out there and as quietly as possible, she opened it.

Still nothing. The house remained dark except for a sliver of light coming from beneath Kel's bedroom door.

Farran nearly returned to bed, but he yelled again. She had to check on him, make sure he was okay even if he would be angry at her for overreacting. Her hand shook as she put it on the knob and opened his door.

He stood next to the dresser on the right, clawing at the wall. "Kel!"

For an instant, he started to turn toward her and Farran saw that he was sleepwalking. Then something else, some figment maybe, caught his attention and he swiveled the other direction.

Farran gasped, her hand coming up to cover her mouth. On his left shoulder blade, he had a brand burned into his skin. It was Tàireil and seared in not only with molten metal, but with magic as well so that it could never be removed, not even by someone with power. It was how the human serfs were marked as property.

What made it worse was that she recognized that brand. It belonged to her family.

7

CHAPTER

Kel turned on the overhead lights in the hall and his bedroom before returning to the great room to shut things down for the night. All the drapes were drawn, but he felt exposed and he couldn't help but wonder who was out there. Not the shadow walker—he'd be inside if he knew where they were—but maybe Seth. It made sense. The demon had been close enough to follow the transit's energy even with Kel shielding it.

He scanned the area outside the cabin, but came up empty. That didn't mean the demon wasn't out there— Seth would know how to cloak himself—and Kel wasn't able to dismiss the sense of being watched.

Paranoia?

The thought made him uncomfortable, but he couldn't shrug it off—especially when the bout he'd avoided yesterday seemed to be roaring down on him tonight like an A380 on takeoff. He'd been walking the razor's edge all evening and trying to conceal it from Farran, but he wasn't sure how successful he'd been, not when she'd looked at him oddly a few times.

With Farran down for the night, though, he didn't have to worry about hiding anything. His lips curved thinking of her sleeping in a Scooby-Doo nightshirt. She hadn't wanted to wear any of his sisters' things, but after a brief discussion, she'd conceded. All three of them had grown taller than Farran was, but they'd left some of their old clothes behind, and while they were juvenile for her, they looked as if they'd fit.

Toiletries had been taken care of, too. His parents kept extras of everything here just in case someone forgot to bring some necessary item—and with five kids, sure enough at least one of them had always missed something when they'd packed.

Memories of his family crowded into this tiny cabin lightened Kel's heart. They'd squabbled and bickered and probably made his parents insane long before they'd ever arrived here, but the car trips were something he looked back on with fondness. And after he'd left home at twelve to begin training as a troubleshooter, those summer vacations had meant even more.

Thinking about training destroyed his pleasure and he moved. Kel checked the stove—it was off—and made a circuit of the doors even though the magical protection around the cabin meant that was unnecessary. It was a way to stall, an excuse not to have to closet himself in the bedroom.

Finally, though, Kel had nothing else to do except turn off the lights and head to bed. He paused in the hallway and looked at the closed door to the room Farran was using, but it was dark and quiet. No respite there.

Reluctantly, he switched off the hall light and entered the bedroom, closing the door behind him. Even with the overhead fixture on, it wasn't bright enough. Kel turned on the lamps on either side of the queen-size bed. It was better, but the room was small. Confining. Taking a full breath became difficult.

It felt as if he stood at the edge of an abyss and one wrong turn would send him tumbling into the darkness. For a moment, he teetered there, wondering what would happen if he let it swallow him, and then Kel pushed it aside. He wasn't giving in this easily. They hadn't defeated him while he'd been held captive and he was damned if he'd let those bastards win at this late date.

He paced, trying to work off the tension that had been building since early this evening, but it was only four strides from one end of the room to the other. Four strides.

It was black, not even the slightest amount of light penetrating his cell. Kel counted off each step, trying to learn the dimensions of his prison. Four feet long. Touching the earthen wall, he positioned himself and counted off the width. Another four feet. It was square, then and . . .

Kel shook his head and the bedroom of the cabin came back into focus. He couldn't go through this again. Not now. Not while he was guarding someone. Couldn't his mind give him a fucking break for a few days?

As if in answer to the question, his left shoulder blade began to burn and Kel shrugged, trying to get rid of the sensation. It didn't help. The weight of his shirt seemed to make the searing worse, and when tugging at the material didn't improve the situation, he whipped it off and tossed it onto the dresser.

The relief was short lived.

Excruciating pain ripped through his body and Kel jerked, barely stifling a bellow. *God, no. Make it stop.*

But he wasn't surprised when it didn't. It didn't matter how he begged or pleaded or railed, it kept coming. That's just the way it was. He should be inured by now, able to ride it out without feeling as if it were happening all over again.

Should be, but wasn't.

The scent of burning herbs made sweat bead on his brow and Kel shuddered. As the chanting increased in volume, the pine walls receded.

He was naked and strapped down on a marble slab—an altar maybe, but Kel couldn't see enough to be certain. They'd placed him on his belly, and not only were his arms and legs manacled, he also had a restraint

*around his neck. His power was drained, his body was
lethargic, but his mind still worked. Still analyzed.*

*They'd positioned him with his head toward the fire. It
was contained in a bowl and fed with magic until it was
white hot. As he watched, the tall man—the leader—
pulled an iron out. The metal glowed red in the darkened
chamber.*

*Both men were robed, hoods hiding their faces from
his view, but Kel knew their energy, and when the time
was right, he'd hunt them down. Kill them.*

*His captors chanted together, the raised branding
iron held aloft. Afraid of what would happen next, Kel
strained at his tethers. He couldn't break free. They
closed the spell and turned to him. Unable to stop himself, Kel tensed, and as the metal pressed into his skin,
he screamed.*

Kel jolted back to the present. He was gasping for air,
breathing as hard as if he'd sprinted all out for a mile,
and sweat had dampened his hair, his chest, his face.
Had he cried out for real or only in his mind?

It was difficult to hear with his heart pounding, his
blood thrumming loudly, but he thought the house was
quiet. Maybe he'd stayed silent and Farran hadn't heard
anything.

Tremors wracked his body and Kel dropped onto the
edge of the bed. Breathing deeply, he tried to regain
control. That damn brand. He hated it. He wanted it off.
And he was stuck with it. No one had been able to remove it and they'd tried. Every healer from apprentice
to master had worked on it. Even the nine council members had combined their magic and tried to get it off his
body and they couldn't.

Branded for life.

Maybe that was why he couldn't shake this—he had
a permanent memento of his time in hell. Kel couldn't
see it unless he twisted to check it out in a mirror, but he
always knew it was there.

And he was lucid. He took a shuddery breath. This

wasn't usual. Normally once he was plunged into the past, he stayed there and reality was a long time returning. Could it be Farran's presence? His internal maelstrom calmed when he touched her, but could her proximity be enough to ease the severity of his flashbacks?

It seemed difficult to believe and there could be other reasons—there were enough variables at play—but the idea was tantalizing. If she could stave off the worst of his hell . . .

Something crawled on his back.

Kel jumped to his feet, trying to knock it off. It stayed put. He felt something on his shin and he looked down to see what it was, but he couldn't make out anything in the pitch blackness that surrounded him.

More little legs whispered over his skin and he undulated in an attempt to get them off. But Kel couldn't dislodge them, damn it. Spiders. He shuddered. God, he loathed the things and his captors knew it. They'd pulled that from his mind and used it against him.

There could be hundreds of them in here with him. Thousands. Hundreds of thousands.

Kel thrashed, but it seemed that for every one that fell off, two more took its place. He choked back the whimper. Damn it, he was a troubleshooter and troubleshooters didn't fall apart. They sure as hell didn't snivel like babies over a spider or two.

But this wasn't just a couple of spiders. There was a horde of them. They were in his hair, on his face, and no matter what he did, he couldn't get rid of them.

He couldn't get rid of them!

It was instinct to try and escape, but he didn't get far before he ran into the earthen wall. Four feet, damn it. Four fucking feet and he was trapped.

And still they crawled on him.

What if there were poisonous spiders in here with him? What if he was bitten by one of them? Those bastards wouldn't heal him, and without his powers, he couldn't heal himself. He had to get out of here. Kel clawed at the walls of his cell, trying to dig his way to freedom. Earth would yield. It had to yield.

But no matter how hard he tore at the wall, it wouldn't give way. Had they reinforced it with magic?

The spiders covered his body and Kel kept his eyes and mouth closed. Now he moaned, unable to prevent the sound from escaping. He alternated between thrashing to dislodge the bugs and digging at the earth, but neither seemed to get him anywhere.

How long could this go on? How long before they grew tired of their games and just killed him?

They might have the upper hand now, but he was a troubleshooter, damn it, and troubleshooters never gave up. Chanting that like a mantra, he kept scraping at the wall. He couldn't stop another groan, but he firmed his jaw and dug for freedom. He was getting out of here and he was getting even.

I'm coming for you, you bastards. Watch your backs.

He heard his name and the voice was soft, feminine. Kel felt pulled toward her, but a spider dropped from above, brushing his cheek and he turned away. She was a mirage, another way to torment him.

Kel went still as he felt a gentle caress on his shoulder. She skated her fingers over the brand on his back, and for the first time since they'd marked him, he felt the pain ebb. But was this real? Was *she* real? Or was this some new game they were inflicting on him? Did they want him to reach for her so they could yank away her presence?

No matter how hard it was to resist, Kel wouldn't give them that satisfaction. He wouldn't let them know how hungry he was for a kind touch.

But the longer she stroked him, the more difficult it was for him to hold strong and at last Kel had no choice except to turn to her. She didn't vanish. Putting his hands at her waist, he drew her against his body and covered her mouth with his. There was desperation in his kiss, in the way he held her, but he needed her. His salvation.

She returned his kiss tentatively at first, but soon she

was meeting his frenzy with her own. That was all he cared about. Kel didn't give a damn who she was or what she looked like, the only thing that mattered was her willingness.

Her tongue dueled with his and he took, unable to curb his selfishness. Next time. Next time he'd make sure she found pleasure, too; this time he needed the reprieve too much. The escape. Even if it was only temporary, this was a sanctuary from the torture he'd endured hour upon hour.

Kel wanted to cup her breasts, to bare her to his gaze, but he couldn't let go of her long enough to do any of that. Through the haze filling his mind, he spotted a bed and he shifted, bringing her down on the mattress and covering her with his body. He worked his thigh between her legs and pushed rhythmically into her, rubbing his hard-on against her stomach.

Reaching between their bodies, he opened the button on his jeans, and between strokes, worked at the zipper. "Hard and fast," he rasped, not taking his mouth from her lips. "Make it up to you."

He tried to pull back far enough to push down his pants and briefs, but she clutched at his hips, keeping him close. "Kel," she moaned.

"I know, baby. Let me—" He thrust again. "—get my pants down." *And your panties off.* But he didn't have enough breath to add the last part because she arched into him, pressing herself firmly into his thigh. They both shuddered.

"Kel."

This time his name penetrated the fog in his brain, but it was momentary. He needed to get off, wanted to get off, wanted to forget, and she was the key. Kel shifted, centering himself between her thighs. He managed to push his jeans out of the way, but his briefs and her panties remained between them. This wasn't going to be enough, not for long, but she held him tightly and he was hesitant to break the connection.

He could feel how wet she was and Kel groaned. It was going to be so damn good. If he could ever get inside her.

She gasped, then said, "Kellan."

It was part plea, part demand, and the use of his full name cleared his head for an instant. Just long enough for Kel to realize it was Farran beneath him. Her face was flushed with arousal, but there was a vulnerability beneath the heat that made him stop midmotion.

Her eyes opened and met his. Kel could take her. She was willing and aroused enough that even with his hair trigger, he could probably make her come. His body liked that idea, surging slightly at the thought.

But his damn empathy kicked in and he felt her fragility. Having sex with him meant something to her, but to him, it was nothing more than a release, a way to forget his past for a few moments. She'd used his name more than once, telling him that she was aware of who she was in bed with. Kel hadn't known, hadn't cared who she was. He would have responded the same way to any female body.

The right thing was obvious, but still he hesitated. That wasn't what he wanted to do—he wanted to lose himself in her. Farran undulated beneath him and Kel put his weight down on her, pinning her hips so she couldn't do it again.

"Kel?"

"Hang on," he gritted out. Hang on while his conscience battled his body for dominance. Hang on while he tried to remember all the reasons why he shouldn't go full speed ahead, damn the consequences. Hang on while he waited for some sign that he wouldn't mess up her life by being this selfish. That sign didn't come, though.

What did spring into mind was that this woman was his soon-to-be sister-in-law's best friend. That Farran would probably stay in this dimension, probably be invited to holiday things because of Shona, and Kel would see her on and off for years.

Females shared things with their best friends and Shona would be angry, give him the cold shoulder. That would drive a wedge between him and Logan because his brother would naturally side with the woman he was going to marry. The idea of losing the closeness he had with his twin was like a slap.

Kel rolled off Farran and got to his feet, hitching up his jeans as he moved.

"Why?" she asked quietly.

In the mirror over the dresser, Kel could see her reach up and touch her cheek, the one that had been scarred, and that cooled his arousal. He turned to face her—she deserved that much—and said, "Because all I wanted was some no-strings-attached sex and you were looking for more."

Farran blushed. The nightshirt had ridden high on her thighs and she pushed it back down before sitting up. "I know you don't love me. I don't love you either."

"I didn't say you loved me, but . . . I don't know, it's like you're looking for a connection and I can't give you that."

She stood and walked toward the doorway. Instead of leaving, though, she asked, "Why did you start then? If you knew I came with strings, why tease both of us like this?"

Kel crossed his arms over his chest and went for brutal honesty. "You woke me from a nightmare and I didn't know who you were. All I cared about was forgetting for a little while and getting off was a good way to do it."

"But I said your name." She knew exactly what had done it.

"More than once." He grimaced. "I didn't catch on the first couple of times, but the third one did it."

Farran nodded, the motion jerky. "Thank you."

"What?" What the hell was she thanking him for? She should be kicking his ass for being such a bastard.

"Thank you for stopping. You didn't have to and I

wouldn't have blamed you if you hadn't." Her voice was soft, but strong and she impressed him.

"It's—"

She held up a hand, cutting him off. "It's not nothing, not for either one of us, so don't try lying to me. Or yourself."

Her smile made him as uneasy as her words and something about this conversation suddenly started feeling way too serious. He decided to lighten it up. "Maybe I just couldn't keep an erection with Scooby-Doo grinning up at me. You ever think of that?"

As he'd hoped, that made her laugh. "Do you think I'm blind? You're still at least half hard."

"More like three-quarters," he muttered, but quietly enough that he was sure she couldn't hear him. "Are things going to be awkward between us tomorrow?"

"Probably, but we'll both get over it."

He nodded. "Yeah, I guess we will." What choice did they have since they were stuck together for a while. Kel waited for her to leave—either with or without a good night—but she didn't move. This wasn't good. His muscles began to tense.

"Kel?"

Oh, shit. He'd been raised with three sisters, he knew that tone meant trouble. "Well, good night," he said, hoping to avoid whatever path she was headed down.

Farran ignored the hint. "How'd you end up with a Tàireil brand on your shoulder?"

He went taut so fast, his body jerked. "Leave it alone."

"But—"

"Damn it, Farran, I said leave it the fuck alone!"

She recoiled, but he couldn't worry about that now—he had his own problems. The mark was burning him again.

Kel expected her to scurry off, but she didn't. Instead, she looked him squarely in the eye and said, "No matter how hard you run, you can't escape yourself. You know that, right?"

Only then did she turn, walk out of the room, and shut the door behind her.

Farran closed the book she was reading and reached for the next one on the stack. After another day spent locked in the study room at the Gineal library, they knew nothing more about the shadow walkers than they had before they'd started this hunt. It was frustrating, and being cloistered with a man who'd had a scowl on his face since showing up for breakfast didn't make things any easier.

Awkward. Yes, that was a good word for how things had been between them today. From the looks of him, Kel hadn't slept last night after she'd left his room, and the furrows he had etched between his brows indicated that it wouldn't take much to ignite his temper.

That should worry her—she knew what an angry man could do—but she wasn't scared of Kel. She hadn't even known him forty-eight hours yet and that was too quick to really be able to trust someone, but she knew he'd never raise a hand to her.

It wasn't because he'd stopped before having sex with her last night. What gave her confidence in him was when she'd asked about the brand. To say he was furious was understating it. And when she'd pushed, he'd become more enraged than she'd ever seen anyone in her life— and that included her father—but Kel hadn't moved from in front of the dresser and he hadn't stormed over and grabbed her.

And he hadn't called her names or belittled her either. He'd just told her to leave it alone and thrown in an expletive or two. She could live with that.

It would make him grumpy to hear it, but Farran had come to the realization that despite his gruffness, Kel was sweet. Imagining his reaction if she shared that with him had her smiling. He'd tell her she was crazy, that the Tàireil world had warped her if she thought he was sweet, but she was right.

She noticed it in the little things, like the fact that he'd referred to what had nearly happened between them as sex. He could have called it fucking because that's what he'd meant, but he hadn't. It wasn't because he was opposed to using that word either, so what reason was there to pick a kinder term other than sparing her feelings?

And then there was the way he'd reacted when she'd come up on him last night. In retrospect, touching him while he was lost in a nightmare had been stupid. Wouldn't his first instinct be to lash out, believing her to be a threat? But Kel hadn't done that; instead he'd gathered her against him and kissed her.

Or how about the fact that he'd agreed to help her so quickly when she'd turned up on his brother's doorstep? Or that Kel had fought a shadow walker for her while she'd hid under the table? Or that he'd worried about her having something to wear that would fit and had gone through his sisters' clothes, looking for things? He'd even been concerned that her jacket wasn't warm enough and had dug up one that belonged to his mom for her to wear because it was filled with down. And that had happened *this morning* when he'd looked surly enough to take on a grizzly—and win.

Yes, despite all the crustiness on the surface, Kellan Andrews was definitely sweet.

"I don't like that grin," he complained.

"Too bad."

He growled, but her smile simply widened. Kel muttered something that sounded like *women* and shut the book he had in front of him. "You didn't find anything, did you?" he asked.

That leached her good humor. "No, and you haven't either."

"Not a thing," he confirmed.

"It makes you wonder, doesn't it?"

"About your crazy idea that the shadow walkers were able to alter Gineal books?"

She nodded. Kel leaned back in his seat and pushed a

hand through the top of his hair. The stubble was back on his chin, but that went with the gruff-and-tough image he liked to present to the world.

"Let's just say," he said quietly, "that I'm willing to consider it more seriously than I was yesterday. I've done some calculating and we've gone through more than three hundred books that reference shadow walkers and none of them has added one detail to our base of knowledge. That's not normal."

"Luck of the draw?" Farran suggested, playing devil's advocate.

"That's what I thought yesterday, but we've been through too many volumes to write it off that easily."

"There could be other possible explanations."

"Yep," he agreed, "and that will be our job tonight—brainstorming possible reasons for the dearth of info."

"You mean we aren't going to haul half the tasglann home with us again?" she teased and then froze. She really did trust him at a deep, instinctive level; this was proof of that. Farran never gave anyone little pokes until she felt safe. Maybe to most people what she said wasn't a big deal, but for someone who'd never known when she'd step on a landmine, it was huge.

"No, we'll leave the books here tonight." Kel sounded distracted, not even a bit grouchy, and the last watchful part of her relaxed. "You know what else is strange?" he asked.

"What?"

"None of the Gineal seem to realize that there's a shortage of information. Troubleshooter training is intense. We're given incredible amounts of knowledge, and after our apprenticeship is over, we're supposed to continue our studies. Wouldn't someone somewhere at some time wonder why there was so little here about shadow walkers?"

"Maybe no one needed to read about them."

Kel sighed. "Yeah, that might have a lot to do with it. You've seen the numbers of books here—there's no way to study every topic, and we usually choose the subjects we're most likely to need to know."

He shrugged and checked his watch. "I'm going to return the books, then we can leave. It's late enough that the tasglann should be pretty quiet."

Farran laced her fingers in her lap and wished she could help. This time, it wasn't her weak magic that was the issue, it was the fact she was Tàireil. If she shelved a book, the next person who used it could pick up a trace of her power, and then she imagined, all hell would break loose. Her people were the enemy and the powers that be would want to know how one had gotten into their *guarded* library. Whether it happened tomorrow or ten years from now didn't matter, Kel would be in serious trouble when his involvement came to light.

"Ready?" he asked, pulling her from her thoughts.

With a nod, she got to her feet and followed him. His caution was every bit as thorough as it had been yesterday and it took awhile to wend their way through the shelves.

"How long are you going to wait to open the transit?" she asked when they were outside. Although he had strong protection around both of them, this was when they were the most vulnerable and they couldn't risk another surprise encounter with the demon.

"Not too far, but we have to be out of range of the guards. Come on, let's move, sunshine."

She moved. Farran didn't want anything to happen to Kel, but their luck was worse than it had been yesterday.

As they went around a bend to the bottom of the hill, two shadow walkers materialized in front of them.

8
CHAPTER

Kel blocked their shots and cursed. His senses sharpened, exhaustion forgotten as adrenaline surged through his body. How the hell was everyone keying in on them here?

He didn't have more than a split second before the pair of shadow walkers fired again. That damn electric-blue energy was insidious. He'd managed to sweep most of it aside, but a snakelike tentacle slipped around his magic and hit his barrier. He was prepared for the pain this time, but he had to grit his teeth to hold back the groan. That shit hurt.

Pulling all the power he could from the Earth, Kel let loose with ropes of fire. They hadn't tried to flank them and that made it easier to fight and defend against them.

Damn, though, he wished Farran wasn't with him. If he was alone, Kel would try an actual physical attack. That might get him nowhere, but he wanted to know if they were able to shield against that, too, or if they were only able to stop magic. But Farran *was* here and that meant he kept her behind him. He couldn't try any low-percentage maneuvers.

As he continued shooting, Kel debated and eliminated

options. No opening a transit and escaping as they'd done yesterday. He didn't think the shadow walkers had found the cabin—not yet—and he wanted to keep it that way. Once they discovered it, he and Farran lost the last protected location he had access to without involving another Gineal.

Scoping out the area turned up no good options for cover. The closest stand of trees was too far off to reach safely and—

A knife appeared in his grasp. It surprised Kel so much that he nearly dropped it, but reflex made his fingers tighten. Farran. This had to be her doing.

Firing with his free hand, he glanced down at the other. Who the fuck fought with something like this? The blade widened toward the haft, spreading outward in different directions and each edge was sharpened and lethal. Even the base of the hilt had a small curved razor attached—one wrong move and he'd carve himself up. A zap yanked his gaze away from the weapon and Kel returned the darksiders' volley.

His attention fragmented when Farran came up beside him holding the same knife. "Get back, damn it!"

"Magic isn't working too well. I thought a physical assault—" She ducked behind him as more crackling blue stuff headed at them.

Kel started to move his right hand, realized he still had the blade, and hurled it at the enemy. The male shadow walker blasted it and the steel atomized, the particles flaring briefly before disappearing.

"Why'd you do that?" Farran asked. "It's a great weapon; the maighistirs use it and they're our best warriors."

Clenching his jaw, he rode out the next hit. "Because I have no training with it, and without that, I'm more likely to hurt myself than those bastards." And because he couldn't leave her undefended and there was no way in hell he'd allow her to attack with him. "Now get rid of that thing before you slice up your own body or mine."

His field lit up like Times Square, but nothing penetrated. Damn, he better concentrate on the actual battle and quit arguing with her.

Borrowing one of his brother's favorite tactics, Kel cast a spell to protect his and Farran's hearing and began to amp up the air, pressurizing it into a tight ball. When it reached critical mass, he released it.

It exploded on impact. The concussion was loud enough to shake the ground. For an instant, the enemy looked startled and confused, but it wasn't the devastating blow he'd hoped for.

He quickly fired off a couple of bolts of lightning, but their shields remained strong.

Kel assessed his attackers, something he should have done earlier. Male and a female—and the man wasn't the same guy that he'd faced before. That concerned him. Where was shadow walker number one? Out of the picture or showing up later as part of a second attack wave? The last thing they needed was him popping up behind them and pinning them in the middle.

Then there was the demon to consider. Was Seth hanging around, ready to spring if he had the opportunity? It was a distinct possibility, he decided grimly.

Retreat? Kel considered that, but they were far enough away from the library that he didn't think they'd make it. And even if he and Farran were able to reach it, the shadow walkers could follow them inside. There was no safety there.

While the dynamic duo was still regrouping, Kel raised the wind and added ice particles to it. He sent it whirling toward them, raising the speed until every pellet would burn.

If the ice penetrated their protective shields.

For about ten seconds it looked like a good idea, then before he could counter it, the shadow walkers turned the storm back on him. Kel quickly reinforced the field he had around himself and Farran, but he wasn't quite fast enough and the sting made him flinch before he neutralized it.

"You okay?" he called to her as the storm now raged harmlessly around them.

"Yes. Is there something I can do to help?"

"Just stay out of the way."

From within the tornado of ice, Kel collected his power and blasted out with balls of fire.

The frozen crystals around them disappeared and so did the shadow walkers. After the last fight, that wasn't a surprise, but it made him uneasy. He did a fast spell to put a wall of protective magic at Farran's back as a second line of defense in case they were planning to hit them from behind.

The enemy returned in seconds and they separated, putting enough distance between them to make each one a distinct target. So much for what little advantage he'd had.

Two streams of blue shit pounded into his shield and Kel's knees buckled. He locked them before he went down.

Residual tremors rippled through him, but it didn't throw off his aim. He smacked the woman with a bolt of lightning that had her doing that vanishing act again.

Before Kel could reload and turn his direction, the man connected with a shot of his own. Kel's eyes rolled back, but he breathed deeply until it passed. By the time he rode out the worst of the pain, both shadow walkers were present and firing at him.

Electricity and water? Maybe he could short out their shots before they reached him. He sent a wall of water toward them as the next round headed his direction.

"Oh, fu—!" Kel turned, grabbed Farran, and dove for the ground, covering her with his body. He reinforced their shields.

Instead of making the shadow walkers' energy fizzle,

the water broke into droplets and carried the power out like shrapnel off a mortar. Kel flinched as the rain came down on his back, but luckily it had blown out most of its force in the air before landing on him. "That was a huge mistake. Remind me never to do that again," he muttered against her ear.

"I can't keep hiding behind you. Maybe I can do something."

"Like what? I'm barely making a dent and I'm for damn sure more powerful than you are."

"I know, but—"

"Intermission's over," Kel interrupted as the water drops tapered off. He used his body to shield Farran as they got to their feet and he took a few more hits that almost put him back on the grass.

Grimly, he sized up his attackers. Which one did he focus on? Which one did he have the best chance of taking down? As he studied both their expressions, he chose the male. Gender had nothing to do with power and there was something in the woman's face that suggested she had an attitude problem. That chip on her shoulder might make it tougher to defeat her.

Because he'd always been most comfortable with it, Kel fell back on fire. The ropes he slung at the shadow walker connected again and again, but before he could take advantage of it, the woman came to her partner's aid, swiping at Kel until he had to shoot at her in self-defense.

He'd been hoping they'd act more as individuals.

The wall he'd been holding at Farran's back faltered and he let it fall. He was running through his power fast. Because he'd been supercharging his shots, it wasn't going to take much longer before he was low enough for things to get critical.

Squaring his shoulders, he took aim at the male shadow walker and let loose.

Farran cried out and Kel realized the female had circled around and was aiming at her. He shifted, trying to cut down her angle, but then it was the man moving trying to get at Farran.

It was their new strategy—shoot at Farran—and it put Kel in a bad situation. They'd stopped standing there politely and firing; the duo was in constant motion now and they were only interested in him because he blocked access to their target.

"You better start blasting whatever you can," Kel said over his shoulder. "I'm running low on magic and I can't cover both of them at the same time."

To her credit, she immediately started shooting around him, but her fire was weak. Of course, since it wasn't sundown yet, he was lucky she could do even this small thing. The Tàireil didn't have much use of their power during daylight hours. Still, he needed her to be troubleshooter strong, and by the time her ammo hit the shadow walkers' shields, it was too mild to do anything.

This wasn't good. Did he summon some of the troubleshooters guarding the library?

Kel balked at the thought, but he might have no other choice. But would those arrogant kids arrive in time to do any good or have any better luck than he was having?

Another shot hit Farran. She didn't cry out, but he felt how much she hurt.

He started to reinforce their shields when he noticed a newcomer. Shit. Shadow walker number one had decided to be here for the kill.

Farran was still trembling when Kel froze. She shook off the pain and followed his gaze. Off to their right was the first shadow walker, the one who had attacked in Kel's kitchen. She choked back a gasp.

Kel had said his magic was low and she was next to useless. What did they do now?

Before she could ask, the female shadow walker said, "Rhyden." The tone wasn't one of welcome and his reply was no friendlier, although Farran didn't know what he said since the language was unfamiliar to her. What was going on here?

"Kel?" she whispered.

"I don't know either," he said softly, "but stay behind me."

She edged nearer until her nose was nearly in his shoulder. The conversation continued between the three and it was more heated than earlier. "Do you think Rhyden is his name or a greeting?"

"Could have been a warning." Kel didn't take his eyes from their attackers. "You know, like, *this is our kill, hands off.*"

After a minute more of raised voices, she asked, "Shouldn't we be getting out of here?"

"And go where? As close as they are they can follow a transit even if I cloak it and no protective wall keeps them out. Do we run? And then what? Hope they don't shoot us in the back before we make the library?"

"We can't just stand here."

"Yeah, I know, but I haven't come up with a better idea yet. Besides, I'm hoping—"

The original shadow walker, Rhyden, let loose with a shot of blue fire. It forked, hitting both the man and woman that Kel had been battling.

"Bingo!" Kel muttered.

He rejoined the fight, shooting at the pair of shadow walkers, and timing his shots to work with the first, the one she thought of as Rhyden. Maybe he wasn't fighting the other two to help them, but Kel was using the opening anyway.

And a funny thing happened. Rhyden glanced their way and then engaged the pair differently, doing it in a manner that seemed to give Kel more openings and better firing angles.

Kel immediately took advantage of it. Maybe it was a case of my enemy's enemy is my friend, but the men were definitely working together against the couple. It amazed her, but Kel didn't seem to spend even a second questioning it.

Farran couldn't see much of the battle, not without going up on her toes to peer over Kel's shoulder, and she cursed. Not only did she get ripped off genetically when it came to magic, but she'd also been short-changed in the height department. For a human woman, she was above average, but she wasn't as tall as most Tàireil females and it irritated her.

Especially when she wanted to know what was going on.

All she got were flashes and a sense of motion at times. She heard someone cry out and went back on her toes. Kel, damn it, chose that moment to shift and fire and it left her dizzy. She dropped back on her heels.

The light-headed feeling didn't pass. Instead, it intensified, her equilibrium so far off she feared she'd have to grab Kel to keep from falling.

She couldn't do that. It would distract him, leave him vulnerable. Maybe long enough for him to get hurt.

The world swayed around her as she closed her eyes and breathed deeply. *Come on, body,* Farran coaxed. *Get it together and toughen up. You can't do this to me now.* It couldn't because her weak powers already made her useless and her getting all faint and acting like a sissy in the middle of battle would make her worse than that. She'd be a burden.

Okay, a bigger burden than she already was.

The weaving sensation slowed, then stopped. Farran took another deep breath and opened her eyes. The world stayed steady and she let herself relax.

And that's when she noticed there were pinpricks of light in every color sparking around the area. They flashed and glinted and some of them seemed to seep into her body, where they continued to dance. It was an odd feeling, but one she enjoyed once she grew accustomed to it.

A burst of blue from one of the shadow walkers

headed toward her, but instead of ducking, Farran held up her palm to stop it. The shot zagged to her left, but that probably had more to do with the shield Kel had around them than anything she'd done—yet it was nice to think she could actually prevent an attack from landing.

Since it did no harm, Farran mirrored her motions to Kel's, imagining that she was firing with him. Dreaming that she was powerful enough to do something more than wait to be saved.

Kel had told her she was tough. He'd even cited examples, but Farran knew it wasn't true. She'd only done what she'd had to do to protect her friend. That's what people did, right? They took care of those who were important to them.

She wanted to be tough. Not biker-chick tough or claw-up-the-corporate-ladder tough—she wanted to be able to take care of herself. If someone started firing at her, she wanted to be able to stave off the assault, not go running for a troubleshooter. Hell, she wanted to *be* a troubleshooter, to belong to their cadre.

Farran remembered looking out the window the night her father had tried to get the dragon stone from Shona and watching the Gineal woman fight beside the others. She'd been an equal, not someone who was in the way.

"Damn it, Farran, pay attention," Kel growled. "You're supposed to stay with me."

"I have been." She checked her position and she was behind him as ordered.

"Like hell. You were completely open with only the shield between you and the shadow walkers until I moved and put myself in front of you again."

"Sorry." She did have to watch. He'd warned her that his magic was low and the protective field he'd put around her hadn't been reinforced for a while. Kel was counting on her to do this small thing to keep them both safe. Farran ignored the dancing lights and how they filled her to keep her eyes on him.

It wasn't much longer before she heard Kel whisper, "Okay. Okay, what next?"

She went up on her toes again and saw that the two shadow walkers were gone, leaving Rhyden to their right. Kel didn't fire, but his hand was back, ready if he needed to.

"They must not be returning," she murmured after a few minutes.

"They're not the ones I'm worried about right now."

Then Rhyden held up his hands in the universal gesture of surrender. He said something, but again it was in that other language, the one they didn't understand.

"Sorry," Kel called, "I don't know what you're saying."

Rhyden frowned, nodded, and tried again. This sounded like a different dialect of some sort, but it was no more intelligible to her than the first.

Kel replied in the Gineal language, but the shadow walker looked blank. "I'd try Spanish," Kel said, "but it's been a few too many years since college."

With a shrug, Rhyden spoke, sounding . . . apologetic maybe? Was that possible when he'd attacked them just the day before? Before she could decide for certain, he flickered out, returned for a moment, and then vanished.

Arm still poised, ready to fire, Kel waited.

"Do you think he'll come back and attack us?"

"Probably not. He had an opportunity and didn't engage, but that doesn't mean I'm going to take any chances." Kel looked around and added, "Plus, we have the demon to worry about. The Attila triplets might be gone, but Seth could be out there, waiting to catch me off guard."

"Attila triplets?"

Looking over his shoulder, Kel threw her a quick grin. "They were all dressed like extras from that movie *Attila*."

"I've never seen it."

"After this mess is over, we can rent it." He gave another look around and Farran figured he was scanning with more than his eyes. "Come on, let's get out of here while the getting's good."

Kel opened a transit and she stepped through to the cabin with him right behind her.

"Well, sunshine," he drawled when the gate was closed. "You must have really pissed someone off. You have a demon and three shadow walkers on your ass."

"Two shadow walkers. Rhyden fought with you today."

Shaking his head, Kel warned, "Don't read too much into that. There are all kinds of reasons for him to have shifted allegiances for an afternoon. Maybe the two we faced are the Hatfields to his McCoys and he shot at them and not at us because of a lifelong blood feud. The next time he shows up, you could be in his sights again."

Farran was familiar with blood feuds and she nodded. "I understand, but we've got a problem."

Kel scowled, crossed his arms over his chest, and sat on the arm to one of the love seats. "Yeah, we do. More than one."

She waved that off. "I'm talking about how fast you went through your magic when you fought the two shadow walkers. They were beating you—us," she quickly amended, not wanting Kel to think she was blaming him. "If Rhyden hadn't shown up when he did, they probably would have won in a few more minutes."

"I know that." He wasn't angry or defensive. Instead, Kel sounded serious. "You had a shot of their electrical blue stuff hit you, right?"

"Yes, it hurt."

"It shouldn't have. With the shield, neither one of us should have felt the blasts connect—at least not until the field weakened. That's some powerful juice they're tossing around and it does more than cause pain. It erodes the well of magic." His frown deepened. "I didn't notice it at first, not until my power level really dropped, but those bastards can siphon it off."

Walking a couple of steps over to the counter area,

Farran pulled out a bar stool, turned it to face Kel, and took a seat. "That means they're a lot stronger than we are, doesn't it?"

Kel shrugged. "Maybe in some ways—that one did get inside my house—but I don't think the magic draining was deliberate. I was observing them and they didn't use what they stole from me, they just let it seep back into the Earth."

"Maybe they couldn't use it," Farran said slowly. "Their power felt different from yours, did you notice that, too?"

"Yeah, I noticed." He shook his head. "They don't draw from the Earth or the universe like we do, but I couldn't figure out where they were pulling from. If I could come up with that answer, I might be more effective fighting them."

"More research," she said. That meant they'd keep making trips to the library and continue to be vulnerable as they walked far enough from the tasglann for Kel to open a transit.

"I know, but you keep forgetting we're just as susceptible to attack inside the cabin or the library. You might feel safer, but it's an illusion."

It didn't surprise her that Kel had known her thoughts about that. "Seth—"

"I can hold my own with the demon," Kel said and there was a touch of impatience in his tone. Maybe because he hadn't held his own yesterday. Farran didn't think he'd be that unprepared again, but there were no guarantees that they wouldn't be caught unaware in the future and no one could be on guard night and day.

"But he's one less threat if we're inside a protected building."

"I know that." He rubbed a hand over his chin and sighed. "You're losing focus. Seth is a side issue. The main threat is the shadow walkers."

That raised her ire—she had *not* lost focus. The problem was that Kel was too zeroed in on the shadow walkers. He hadn't been there when Seth had hunted her in that alley. He hadn't seen how the demon had held out his hand and bade her come to him. He hadn't heard the tone in Seth's voice when he'd called her *precious*. But Farran took a deep breath and saved her arguments. From the flatness of Kel's expression, she knew he wasn't in the right frame of mind to listen to her.

"That's it?" he asked. "No ranting at me?"

She clenched her hands into fists and shook her head.

"Good." Kel got to his feet. "I'm going to crash then for a couple of hours."

As she watched him go, Farran noticed how unsteady he was and her heart double-clutched. Just how close had Kel been this evening to running through his magic entirely?

9
CHAPTER

Kel sat slumped forward in his cell. His back felt as if it were on fire and it was hurting him more than anything ever had. He was aware enough to know that his fever was dangerously high and that the brand was probably infected, but he had no magic to heal himself with.

He'd lapsed in and out of consciousness and he didn't know how long he'd stay awake this time. Not when he was already out of it enough that he felt Logan's presence in the cell with him.

For an instant, it was so real, Kel reached out, his fingers brushing the base of the earthen wall, but it didn't last. In the next instant, Logan was jerked away so hard and fast that Kel knew it was his addled mind playing tricks on him. The movement exacerbated his pain and he hissed out a breath.

"It hurts, Mom," he whispered. So much. So damn much.

But it wasn't his mom he saw. It was Ryne Frasier. Troubleshooters don't cry.

She'd never cried, no matter how bad things were, and he wasn't going to let some girl outdo him. It was a good thing, though, that his fever was high enough to burn the moisture out of his body or he might have embarrassed himself.

He thought about surrendering, about letting the pain swallow him and take him away. It would end then. The torture, the torment, the excruciating agony.

Troubleshooters don't give up.

Yeah, Ryne had never given up and Kel wouldn't either. But it would be easier if he did.

Who told you being a troubleshooter was easy?

"Dad?"

It's a responsibility, Kellan. It's not about glory and adulation, it's about protecting the Gineal. There will be times you achieve your missions with no effort. You'll be tempted to let that go to your head, to let your ego run free, but you must rein it in, because if you don't, you'll find yourself in trouble later on.

"You were right, but now what, Dad? How do I get out of this one?" But his dad was gone and Kel was alone in his cell again.

Ego, yeah, that had cost him, and his empathy, too. He'd been certain the latter made him almost infallible— he was damn good at reading people, seeing the things they didn't want him to know. Their secret hearts were open to him and that was the place where the unadorned truth lived.

Even Logan. It made his brother insane trying to figure out how Kel knew things he hadn't wanted to share. It didn't matter how many times Kel explained it, Logan didn't have enough empathic ability to understand what Kel was telling him.

Lucky bastard.

Kel would trade all his empathy, all his healing talent, for his twin's ability to shut off his emotions and ruthlessly battle the enemy. Logan didn't feel remorse or guilt after fighting. And he'd never felt another's pain while he died. Never replayed that moment again and again while he laid in bed at night praying for sleep.

It was a curse. To be restrained on that marble slab and

feel the sheer joy his captors experienced as they tortured him. To realize that kind of depravity existed. Thrived.

This would be easier for Logan to bear. Much easier.

Evil twin. You'd wish this on your brother?

"No, never. I'd kill to keep Logan safe." But they just laughed at him. They didn't understand. His brother meant everything to him. His best friend, the only person who really understood him; they'd been together since their cells had divided. He'd die to keep Logan safe. He wasn't evil. He wasn't.

Kel screamed as a bucket of liquid was thrown over his back. Troubleshooters don't cry. Troubleshooters don't cry.

But excruciating didn't begin to cover it. Whatever it was ate at the skin around the brand, ripping fire into every line, every laceration.

"So you wish your brother was here instead of you." The cowled face was near his and Kel realized he was on the marble slab again, their altar.

"No," he tried to say, but his throat was so thick, the word wasn't understandable.

"Yes, we heard you. We'd enjoy meeting him. Perhaps when we're done with you . . ."

"No!"

Kel bolted upright. His heart thundered and sweat covered his body. Had he screamed for real? Had he yelled? But Farran wasn't running so maybe not.

Swinging his legs over the side of the bed, Kel leaned forward and dropped his head into his hands. Fuck. Fuck!

Between having no sleep the night before and nearly using all his magic today, he'd thought he'd be too exhausted to dream. He'd been wrong. Way wrong.

It wasn't real. Most of what had transpired in his dream hadn't happened while he'd been in captivity. Some of it—like the conversation with his dad—had taken place years earlier. Other things hadn't occurred at all. For sure he hadn't been that mentally lucid while he'd been recovering from the branding. That part of his imprisonment remained one big fever-induced blur and maybe it was better that way.

He reached for his jeans, and even though his body was trembling so hard he could barely manage to get his legs in, he pulled them on and got to his feet. Kel had to get out of this room, had to get away from his thoughts, his memories, his own damn mind.

No matter how hard you run, you can't escape yourself. You know that, right?

Maybe Farran had been right, but he didn't care. He wanted to try. If he could, he'd put on his tennis shoes right now and run. He'd run until he'd burned the past out of his brain, until it evaporated into nothingness and he could sleep again. Until he could spend time with his family without feeling as if he didn't belong with them anymore. He'd run until he was unable to move another step.

But he couldn't. Farran needed to be protected even inside the cabin. He grabbed an old sweatshirt out of one of the dresser drawers and yanked it on. His hands continued to tremble, but he couldn't stay in here another second. The walls were closing in on him and it was accelerating his breathing again. No choice—he had to go out into the living area.

Kel just hoped he looked normal enough to keep Farran from asking questions.

The great room had two love seats, two chairs, and one enormous square coffee table. Farran discovered that the chairs swiveled and she sat in the one closest to the windows with the lights out, watching the moon rise over the lake. Kel had been asleep for over an hour now, and while she was hungry, she didn't feel like cooking anything for herself.

There was a grouping of trees on the island in the middle of the water—the number was too small to refer to them as a copse—and with their foliage gone, they lent a stark beauty to the night sky. Off some distance beyond that, she saw a pair of headlights cut through the dark and wondered where the road went and if she'd ever get to see more than the inside of the cabin.

She wanted to think about that, about what the closest town looked like, or where the nearest house was. That was better than spending time on what had her brain spinning, but no matter how hard she tried to repress it, the topic refused to go away.

You must have really pissed someone off.

In a better life, she'd be able to tell Kel unequivocally that she'd never infuriated anyone enough to have her killed. In a better life, she'd be able to tell him that she'd never met someone who would think of hurting another person. In a better life, she wouldn't have to confess that the man who was enraged enough to want her dead was her father.

But had he sicced Seth and the shadow walkers on her?

She had no problem picturing her father negotiating with a demon. If it suited his needs, he wasn't above making a deal with anyone, no matter how low he had to sink. She could also see him wanting to get even for her betrayal of him and the family. He'd earned a nickname in their world—The Hammer—and it wasn't because he liked to build things.

He was cold-blooded and icy in his dealings. Farran had seen him go to extremes to wreak vengeance over nothing more than an unintentional slight and she'd also seen him shrug off more egregious sins because it didn't fit his agenda to get even.

It was always about the bottom line with her father, about how it all played into the results he wanted to achieve.

Meeting with a former god-demon, asking Seth to kill his daughter? Unfortunately, Farran had no trouble visualizing that at all. She raised her fingers and touched her cheek, before moving to the bump on the bridge of her nose.

The part that stopped her was the shadow walkers.

They almost never appeared in the Tàireil world. She could count on one hand the number of sightings reported in the last hundred years and still have fingers left over. If her father was behind these attacks, how had he contacted them? How had he convinced them to go along with his quest for revenge?

Her father spoke a lot of different languages, but did he know the one they used? Why would he when the shadow walkers didn't come to their dimension?

Farran had question after question and no answers. Maybe she should bring this up with Kel, see what he thought, but it was hard. He came from a family that was obviously close. She'd heard the affection in his voice when he talked about his parents, about his siblings. It was bad enough that he knew her father had hurt her, but to share that he might hate her enough to have her killed? It was mortifying.

Worthless. She'd heard that word almost every time she'd seen her father. That wasn't often, thank goodness. He'd truly had no interest in her except on rare occasions, but when she did encounter him, she was always denigrated. And sometimes hit.

She lowered her fingers from her nose and folded them in her lap. At times she'd wondered if things would have been better if her mother had lived. She'd shielded Farran from a lot, and when she hadn't been able to protect her, she'd healed her daughter. And in darker moments, she wondered how her mother had died. She'd been a relatively young woman and healthy—what were the chances that a fall alone would be enough to end her life?

Had her father killed her mother?

Sometimes the uncertainty haunted her. She didn't know. Maybe that was the worst part—the fact that it was possible.

While the Gineal world was far from perfect, overall Farran preferred it to her own dimension. Here, her father wouldn't be able to act with impunity. Maybe it simply would have driven him to be more covert. But on the other hand, if there were consequences for his behavior, maybe he wouldn't have done some of the things he had. And maybe her mom would still be alive.

Farran heard Kel moving around and used her fingers to blot the moisture from her eyes. She didn't want him asking questions—it was too shameful. No, the shame wasn't hers, she understood that, but the man was her father. Half her DNA came from him.

The bedroom door opened and she braced herself for Kel to flip on the lights. He didn't. Instead he settled in the love seat beside her. Because of their positions—her looking toward the lake and him looking toward the fireplace—there was an intimacy in how close their faces were to each other. Farran dropped her gaze and hoped he couldn't see her turmoil.

But when he didn't say anything, didn't ask her why she was sitting in the dark, Farran turned her head. He was expressionless and she was about to dismiss his silence when she realized she needed to look deeper. She knew him better than that—Kel felt things.

It was only then she picked up the small signs—the tightness of his jaw, the fine lines at the corner of his eye, the flatness of his lips. Before she could think better of it, she rested her hand over his on the arm of the couch.

He tensed and she waited for him to tug away. Waited for him to say something . . . if not cutting, brusque at least. Kel did neither thing; instead he turned his arm and laced his fingers with hers. And still staring straight ahead, he held on to her firmly, as if he was afraid she'd pull loose if he didn't.

That made her study him a little closer. In the dark, it was impossible to be sure, but he appeared pale. Another nightmare—she'd bet on it, although she had no reason to believe that.

She didn't wish bad dreams on anyone, but it made her realize she could talk to Kel—if that's what she decided she wanted to do. He might have grown up with a family that actually cared about him and valued him, but he hadn't made it through life unscathed.

"Have you ever wondered what you did to deserve your burdens?" Farran asked quietly.

Kel snorted, but didn't answer.

"I do. All the time. The thing is that I haven't done anything that horrible, so then I wonder what kind of person I was in my past lives. There must be some reason for everything I've had to go through."

"Maybe not. Sometimes the universe just sucks."

His voice was rough, thick, and Farran knew she'd been right. He'd had another nightmare. "I don't like random," she said. "If I'm going to suffer, I want to think I deserve it even if it is for something from a life I have no memory of."

For a moment, he squeezed her hand, offering sympathy. "You're thinking of your father."

"And my brothers." She couldn't think of her father without her brothers becoming part of the equation. They'd been his henchmen—some more willing than others—but none had stood up to him. None had defended her.

"Um, yeah. I'm sorry for your loss."

Kel sounded so stiff and uncomfortable that Farran nearly laughed, but her heart was too heavy for humor. "Don't worry about it. I rarely, spent time with any of my brothers and didn't mourn Jal, Lathan, or Derril's deaths. If I did grieve over something, it was that they'd never been the family I'd wished they'd been."

"That's pretty sad commentary on their lives."

"On mine, too." Farran tried to free her hand, but Kel hung on. "Maybe if I'd made more effort . . ." She shook her head. "It wouldn't have made any difference. My father's influence was profound. Roderick—he's my oldest brother, the one that escaped back to the Tàireil dimension—Roderick is my father's soul twin. They're exactly alike."

"The others?"

"Jal was mean—scary mean. Here, he'd likely be labeled as criminally insane or something and institutionalized, but in my world he ran loose with only my father to rein in his most monstrous behavior." Farran looked at Kel and confessed, "My father only brought him to heel when it jeopardized his plans or authority. That wasn't often and his actions with humans, some of his atrocities . . ."

She was quiet for a long moment, trying to recall something charitable she could say about the youngest of her four brothers. Nothing came to mind. "Lathan and Derril weren't as bad. They were followers, not strong enough to break away or stand up to my other brothers and most definitely not to our father, but not evil if left to their own devices."

"What about your mother? Before she died, what was she like?" Kel asked.

Farran looked down at their linked hands and thought about what to say. "I was so young when I lost her. I remember her shielding me when my father was angry and her healing me when she wasn't able to stop him from getting to me. I say that as if it happened all the time and it really didn't. Mostly my father left me to my human nanny or my mother, but I guess I remember his appearances in my life so vividly because they always brought pain of one kind or another."

As the quiet lengthened, Kel prompted, "What are some of the other things you remember about her?"

"Her patience. She never became short with me no matter how many questions I asked. Her willingness to talk to me and read to me and play with me."

"Those are good memories to have."

"Yes, I know, but I was sitting here tonight, wondering how she died." Farran braced herself, then lifted her head until her gaze locked with his. "Wondering if my father either killed her himself or hired someone else to do it. That says a lot about what kind of family I have, doesn't it?"

She'd actually managed to shock Kel into silence, at least momentarily. "Your mother was murdered?" he asked.

"I don't know. At six, things like that aren't said in front of you, but she died in a fall. She hated heights and she avoided them whenever possible. I just can't help wondering. I mean if he hit me, why wouldn't he hit her, too?"

"You think maybe he hit her too hard and tried to cover it up?"

"Maybe. Or maybe he just grew tired of her and decided it would be good to be a widower."

Kel reached over with his other hand and held hers in both of his. "I'm sorry."

"Me, too." Farran grimaced. "You can see why I envied Shona and her perfect family. Mine's horrible."

"Shona's family isn't perfect."

"No, of course not. There is no such thing as perfect; I know that. But it was a damn sight better than mine."

"Yeah," he said gently, "but almost anyone's is better than yours. Shona has her own family issues to deal with right now, though. She can tell you all about them after we get this situation with Seth and the shadow walkers wrapped up."

Farran had to look away and it took her a few minutes to regain control. "Your council isn't going to let me near the dragon mage. I'm Tàireil."

Kel huffed out a long breath. "Why do you keep thinking the Gineal have it in for your people?"

"Maybe because you keep killing us!" She tried to jerk her hand away, but Kel held on.

"Bullshit. The Gineal avoid your dimension whenever possible—your turf—so it's not like we go over there cruising for someone to attack. Have we killed Tàireil? Hell, yeah, because whenever *your* people come to *our* world, they can't keep their hands off the humans. We protect humans here."

"I know that, but—"

"But what? The last Tàireil that were taken out by the Gineal were your brothers. Those would be three of the four men who were trying their damnedest to kill Shona. The one before that had a troubleshooter sent after him because he was attacking three human women. He's the one who decided to fight it out rather than leave peaceably. You want me to keep citing cases?"

"No, but if this is true, why have the Gineal been ceaselessly hunting me?"

"I told you, Shona was—is—worried about you. She made the council promise that we'd find you, so she could make sure you were okay. You might not think Shona's desires mean a lot, but you'd be wrong. She's the dragon mage and that carries quite a bit of status with it." Kel scowled. "And if you'd been conscious to see her in action that night, you'd know why. That's one Gineal no one wants to piss off."

Farran couldn't help but smile thinking about Shona, who was probably as sweet and nonthreatening as they came, scaring anyone into doing her bidding.

Still, she could believe the status part of being dragon mage. In the Tàireil world, the mage became empress and that had been enough for her father to finally discover a use for Farran. Unfortunately for him, Shona had found the stone first.

But she put that aside and came back to the part she had trouble believing. "I'm supposed to trust your council?"

"You can, you know. Even if they wanted to punish you for some strange reason, Shona won't let them hurt you and I won't either."

He was sincere, Farran could see that clearly. After basically knowing her for two days, Kel was willing not just to fight shadow walkers and demons, he was volunteering to take on his council, too. For her.

Amazing. And all this time—all her life—she'd had no idea men like him really existed.

10
CHAPTER

Kel didn't want to sleep even though he needed it. His magic wouldn't return to normal levels until he'd had time to rest. If he had to fight tomorrow while he was fatigued, he'd burn through his stores faster—something he couldn't risk when the shadow walkers could siphon off small slivers of his power. But it didn't matter, not tonight. He couldn't cloister himself in that tiny room again.

He had all the lights on out here, even the one on the stove top. It was a risk. If Farran woke up, she'd see the glow under her door and probably come out to see what the hell was going on. But he hated the dark. Hated it.

Roaming the L that made up the main part of the cabin, Kel ensured the drapes were drawn all the way and the shades down to the bottom of the windows. Seth was out there. Kel could feel it and he was damned if he'd provide a free show. Farran would have to be warned, but he was hesitant to do it because she was already too worried about Seth. No, he couldn't be dismissed, but he was manageable now that Kel knew he was around.

Not that she believed that, but then the demon had scared her more that first night than the shadow walker had and Kel had been careless the day the time phase had happened.

That phase thing, that was weird, and something he should have spent more time thinking about already.

He walked over to the island where the notebook rested, flipped it open to a blank page, and reached for the pen. Both he and Farran had two sets of memories. For him, the one where he opened the transit before he saw Seth was much sharper than the other where the demon shot at him. Kel hadn't asked Farran which she thought was more vivid, but she'd talked about them differently than he did. It was his impression that both were equally clear to her.

Kel jotted that down and put a question mark next to it. When he had a chance, he needed to ask her about it.

Okay, who had done it? He listed anyone and anything that came into his head, then worked on eliminating them. The first name he crossed off was his own. As much as Kel wished otherwise, he didn't have that kind of power, and if he did, this wouldn't have been the first time it manifested.

Seth's name was the next one he drew a line through. The demon wanted Farran, and in the original scenario, Kel was down and she was undefended. It was unlikely that Seth had sabotaged himself, not even accidentally.

Then there was Farran. She was weak, she hadn't lied about that, and it would take someone with an incredible amount of strength to pull it off. Besides, it had been daylight and the darksiders had very little magic while the sun was up. Even if she was the most powerful Tàireil ever born, she wouldn't be able to do this in the late afternoon.

Magical strength had him dismissing some unknown Gineal or Tàireil being behind it. In the case of the darksiders, daylight was a huge factor, but even in the middle of the night, they didn't have enough power to alter time. Neither did his people, even if they combined their powers.

What about a Tàireil or a Gineal who'd turned to dark magic?

Kel had to give that some thought, but after a few minutes, he drew a line through that possibility as well. There were no indications that even the most powerful who'd fallen were able to manipulate time in any way. If they could, he'd know.

That brought him to the shadow walkers. He didn't think they'd done it. If they had that ability, wouldn't they have used it to back up and catch Farran when she was alone? Instead, they'd fought it out with him on the path today, in his kitchen yesterday, and with the demon the night before that. But even with all the arguments against this group being responsible, Kel couldn't eliminate them. He simply didn't know enough to rule them out absolutely.

His final possibility was *weird cosmic anomaly*. But while he couldn't cross this item out either, he doubted it. Not when it had happened twice. Once? Yeah, he'd say it was maybe just some freak thing, but this was Farran's second experience. And that's what stopped him.

She was the only common denominator.

Was something or someone hanging around her that did have the talent to alter time? He hadn't seen or sensed anyone. That didn't mean they weren't there, but few beings of any dimension were able to hide from him. His empathy was too developed.

Unless it was some creature that felt no emotion.

Kel added that to his list, put down the pen, and scrubbed both hands over his face. This hadn't provided any answers, but it had allowed him to think through a few options. And who knew, maybe after he had some sleep, something else would occur to him that made this whole time phase become clear.

That was the problem with this damn situation—nothing about it made sense. There was a piece of the puzzle that he didn't have yet, and it was the one that made everything else fall into place.

He thought about flipping to another new page and making a list of reasons why he wasn't finding any information on the shadow walkers, but Kel was too tired to go there. Maybe tomorrow morning he and Farran could tackle that question together. Tonight . . . Well, tonight he hadn't wanted to bring the conversation back to business.

She'd been in such a pensive mood, sitting in the dark and wondering what her father was capable of. Walking into the great room earlier, Kel had nearly turned on the lights, but her emotions slammed into him as hard as running into a brick wall and it didn't take a genius to figure out she needed the shadows.

Farran didn't appreciate how difficult the dimness was for him, but that was okay, she didn't need to understand. Empathy could be like mind reading sometimes and he knew exactly what triggered this for her—wondering who wanted her dead. God, he couldn't imagine growing up in a family like hers. How the hell had she survived?

It would have been easy for Farran to end up warped like her youngest brother or some spiritless doormat thanks to being knocked around, but instead she was smart, genuine, and gutsy. She'd even worked against her father to protect Shona and that took incredible courage. Yeah, Farran had done most of it subversively, but what other choice was there?

And to this day, she paid a price. Kel sensed that clearly, too. She could never go home again, not unless she wanted to die.

What had she left behind in the Tàireil world? Was there someone important to her back there? A lover?

Kel didn't think so. When she thought about her dimension, her only emotion was tied to her father and brother. In fact, he didn't get a sense of anything that she missed there at all; it was more that she felt as if she didn't belong in this world.

Of course, being born here was no guarantee of anything either. Take him for example. He wasn't sure he fit in either. Not anymore.

That was enough to bring his ghosts back and Kel pivoted away from the counter, pacing the length of the kitchen. His family was worried about him. They wanted him to talk—if not to them, to someone. Logan had come at him from so many different directions, there were times Kel was surprised he didn't become dizzy trying to block all his brother's attempts to help.

But Kel didn't want to discuss what had happened. He didn't want to remember. Hell, he hadn't even told the council every detail, although he wouldn't be surprised if they knew anyway. Monitors with retrocognitive abilities would have been assigned to investigate.

It was possible, though, that they hadn't seen everything. He'd been told that they'd been searching for him while he'd been missing and no one had found him. If the monitors hadn't located him while he was imprisoned, why would they find him in the past?

Or he might just be trying to make himself feel better by taking refuge in denial.

Kel added the living room into his pattern. He hoped no one knew everything that had gone on while he'd been captured, but that's all it was—a hope.

Of course, maybe he should gather his family and confess it all. They'd never look at him the same way again, but hell, maybe it would be worth it if it drove his nightmares away for good. And he wouldn't have to worry about his brother or parents pressing him about his life ever again. Kel could retreat to his house and become a hermit without anyone showing up and trying to drag him out into the world.

He snorted. Yeah, big talk at midnight, but in the cold light of day he never did it and he probably never would. For all their nosiness, Kel loved his family and he didn't want to lose them.

It would kill what was left of his soul to lose them.

Making a few more circuits, he tried to come up with something to think about, anything that wouldn't lead down the road to his own personal hell. It wasn't that easy, though. His ghosts been lingering since his night-mare, and now that they had his attention, they were un-willing to give it up.

"Go away," he muttered, pushing both hands through his hair to get it off his face. "Just go away and let me forget."

He reached the bench by the front door, turned, and started back for the table. It was going to be a bad night—another one. So much for his hope that Farran's proxim-ity was lessening the severity of his memories.

They cut him, slicing his body with fine blades that made shallow lines. He was facedown on the slab, but while this didn't hurt too much, Kel knew there was more coming. But what?

Whatever it was, it couldn't be good. Not when he could feel how gleeful the two darksiders were.

Why his back? Why not his front? Wouldn't the pain be worse there? Or was it because the position in which he was strapped down didn't let him see much of what was going on? Maybe that was it. The psychological as-pects were worse because he couldn't watch. Although if they blindfolded—

Kel forgot all about his questions when they stopped slicing him. He tried not to tense—that would make whatever happened next worse—but he couldn't stop his muscles from locking.

More chanting and it sounded like a spell, although it wasn't one Kel was familiar with and he couldn't tell what its aim was from the words he heard. He attempted to seek refuge in his mind, to mentally leave, but they'd blocked that route with magic the first hour he'd been captured. No matter how hard he tried, Kel couldn't zone out for more than a minute at a time before his conscious-ness was dragged back to his body and he had no choice about it, damn them.

The bastards had perfected their incantations to get the maximum out of their tortures and that told him they'd done this before. Lots of times.

They stopped chanting and Kel waited. His stomach churned with dread, his throat tightened, and breathing became difficult.

Whatever they slathered over him had the consistency of honey, but it didn't hurt much even with his cuts. It felt warm, almost soothing as they covered his entire back area. Kel couldn't help it—he let down his guard.

That's when they did it. They closed the spell.

He screamed and screamed, losing his voice mid-holler. God, God, God, help me! *His eyes closed, rolled back in his head, but he didn't pass out.*

Kel bucked against his restraints, trying to get free. He writhed, seeking relief. And he shook, trying to throw off whatever the fuck they'd put on him. Nothing worked. Nothing.

Sweat dripped from him and Kel trembled. Damn it, that one had snuck up on him. He was leaning on the counter of the island, using it to hold himself up, and his head was nearly down on the yellow Formica, but he didn't have the strength yet to stand up.

As he gasped for air, he tried to beat back the memory, to lock it away where it couldn't torment him further. Damn them. They were dead and they still had this power over him.

He rested his head on his forearm and fought harder. If he didn't stop this now—if he followed the usual pattern—what came next would leave him drained emotionally, physically, and magically. Kel sucked in a harsh breath. How many times had he come to and discovered that he'd blasted holes throughout his house, fighting a foe that was long gone? Fighting a battle that had ended more than a year ago?

Not tonight. God, not tonight. If he used his power here, it might be all the shadow walkers needed to locate them. For damn sure he and Farran would be vulnerable tomorrow and it would take him days to recover enough to be able to fight effectively. Kel just didn't think he could stop what he knew was coming.

Farran. His salvation. He raised his head enough to see her closed bedroom door. What if he went to her, climbed in bed beside her, and asked her to hold him? They didn't have to do anything, he just needed her calming touch.

But even as he told himself that, he knew it wouldn't stop there. Holding her wouldn't be enough, not when he was this close to frantic—not when he hadn't stopped noticing her today and she hadn't called a halt last night. He couldn't count on her to say no tonight either, not even with her awareness that all he wanted was sex.

Logan, Kel reminded himself. Think of losing the closeness with Logan.

It didn't cool his need. If it had only been physical or only emotional, he might be able to pull back, but it was both those things and maybe more.

If Farran knew the score, would she hate him when this situation ended? Would she tell Shona what a prick he was and get his brother's fiancée furious at him? Would Logan really take Farran's side over his own brother's even with his future wife involved?

Kel shuddered and dropped his head again. It didn't matter. Not now. Not when he could feel the black cloud on the horizon. He'd do anything to prevent this next memory from replaying.

Risk anything.

Even his relationship with Logan.

He couldn't repeat this next part. Not again. Not when there was something—no, some*one*—who could save him.

Another shudder swept through him, strong enough to hurt, but Kel had made his decision. Eyes closed, he used his arms to lever himself away from the counter and took a deep breath. Did he hope she turned him down or did he hope she didn't?

Blowing out a slow breath, he opened his eyes again and stiffened in surprise. Farran was standing there and not even the Scooby-Doo nightshirt could keep his body from heating at the sight of her.

* * *

Farran couldn't believe she was spending another night staring at the bedroom ceiling, but she wasn't able to sleep. Maybe it was talking about her father and brothers, but she felt alone and lonely. Not that she'd ever been close to her family, but at least she knew she had bonds of a sort with someone. Here she had nothing. No one.

Shona was a friend, and for a time, Farran had thought of her as a sister, but it wasn't true. They'd only known each other a couple of months and Shona was the dragon mage. The Gineal council definitely wouldn't want her near the other woman.

There was no one else. Kel wasn't a friend; he was barely an acquaintance, and she'd never bothered to get close to any humans—not out of some prejudice, but because she had secrets. A million secrets. She couldn't allow them to know she had powers, of a sort, and how did she explain that she'd grown up in an alternate version of Earth? It was a sure bet that her childhood experiences were very different from anyone born here.

She'd assimilated a lot of this world and the culture of America since she'd crossed over. Farran had the lingo down—most of the time—and a lot of the cultural references, but she didn't have it all. Even if she lived here for another sixty years, she still wouldn't know everything she should. There was a large difference between learning something and living it.

Farran was without roots. For all its faults, the Tàireil world was her home, the place where she'd grown up. And it was the one place she could never go. Not and live. Her father would have her killed the instant he learned she was there.

Loneliness rolled through her, strong enough to make her physically ache, and Farran blinked away the tears. She'd been completely cut off the last seven months. There'd been no one to talk to, no one to hang out with, and no one to give a damn if she died.

By now, her position at work had been filled. Her supervisor had probably only missed her long enough to curse her for being AWOL for her shift, then he'd called someone to cover, and went looking for a replacement.

She was twenty-five years old and she hadn't left so much as a ripple in either world. That was likely the saddest thing she had to face—she was as worthless as her father claimed.

Shifting to get more comfortable, Farran noticed the light shining in under the door. What was Kel still doing awake? She didn't have a clock, but she was in tune with the planet and knew it was late, especially for someone who hadn't slept the previous night.

Kel was alone, too. Even with his family that he seemed to love so much, he was solitary. The temptation was there to go to him, to kiss him and let him take her to bed. Yes, it was only sex, but it was a connection. For a short time she could assuage her loneliness and maybe even feel as if she belonged somewhere. They could help each other and she could live without the pretty words and promises for the chance to ease the constant sense of isolation she had. It would be worth it for that alone.

And it would be good. As aroused as she'd been last night when Kel had kissed her and taken her down to the bed, there was no doubt in her mind that she'd find pleasure in his arms. Another reason to go to him.

He could forget whatever haunted him and she could forget she was completely alone—at least for a little while. They could each have something they wanted.

Farran tossed back the covers and got out of bed. As soon as she eased the bedroom door open, she saw Kel. His arms were resting on the island and his head was down. He needed her and that idea teased her. She'd never been needed before.

Kel must have sensed her because he raised his head and their gazes met. Her body tingled as she saw his eyes go hot. "You should be in bed," he said.

"So should you," Farran countered.

"I'm not tired."

"Liar. You didn't sleep at all last night. How do you think you'll fare against the shadow walkers tomorrow if you're exhausted?"

"I'll be fine."

That was such a blatant falsehood that she didn't bother to call him on it. Instead, she let his desire wash over her. There was a difference between last night and this one. Something inside her that she hadn't realized was tight loosened. He might want nothing more than sex, but no longer did he just want a female body. Tonight he wanted her. Specifically her.

Farran knew this was the moment of truth. She had to decide now whether or not she rounded the counter and went to him or if she returned to the bedroom and forgot her crazy idea. Finding someone just to feel good for a little while wasn't something she did. It was a false boost, one that wouldn't last, but at this moment, it didn't matter. Not when loneliness sat so heavy on her chest, she wasn't sure she'd be able to breathe much longer.

Kel got her all steamed up. It wasn't only his looks, although the man was gorgeous, but also his innate kindness. He wouldn't hurt her tonight and he wouldn't make her feel cheap when they were done. That meant a lot and it was what gave her the courage to take the first step.

He stiffened as she headed toward him, but that was his only reaction. Farran curled her hands into fists at her sides to hide the way they were shaking and kept walking.

She didn't stop until she stood far too close to him. Farran expected him to put space between them, but Kel stayed where he was. Instead, the heat in his eyes increased and she felt waves of desire swamp her. Good. That's what she wanted. Him hot for her and her senses swimming in desire.

Reaching out, she put her hand on his chest over his heart and made a small circle.

"Do you know what you're doing?" Kel asked.

There was more than one way to take that question, but she knew what he was asking. Was she aware that she was inviting a sexual encounter? "I know," she assured him.

"Are you sure?" Are you sure you want to do this, that's what he was wondering this time.

"I am."

"You're making a big mistake."

"My decision."

"Yeah." Kel put his hand over hers on his chest and stopped the motion. "This is your last warning. If you don't leave now, I'm going to take you to bed and do you until both of us have trouble walking in the morning."

"I'm holding you to that," Farran teased.

Something flared in Kel's eyes and she realized that he'd just dropped the leash he usually held on himself. His hands went to her waist. For a moment, he paused, his fingers flexing, and then he tugged her against him. He was already getting hard and Farran gasped as he pressed into her stomach.

He hesitated again. It was nearly imperceptible, but she picked it up and her heart rate spiked. He wasn't going to change his mind, was he?

Farran put her arms around Kel's neck and pulled his lips to hers. She kissed him as hungrily as he'd kissed her last night, trying to show him how much she wanted this. How much she wanted him.

Although he'd said he'd given her his final warning, Kel let her have the lead. The same man who'd told her they were doing things his way or she could find someone else to protect her seemed more than content to let her be the aggressor. At first, it made her anxious, but as she grew accustomed to the role, Farran reveled in it.

She loved kissing Kel, taking it slowly and letting her arousal build. With a soft sigh of pleasure, she ran her tongue across the seam of his lips and he opened for her.

"Get that sweatshirt off," she ordered between kisses. "I want bare skin."

"Yes, ma'am." The corners of Kel's lips were tilted up as he stepped back and yanked his shirt over his head. Without looking, he tossed it toward the counter. She loved his muscles, and even though she'd seen them before, the sight still made her mouth go dry. But as much as she wanted to stare, she wanted to feel him pressed against her even more, and Farran almost dove back into his arms.

He was warm against her palms, and as she kissed him some more, she ran her hands over his back, letting her fingers dip beneath the waistband of his jeans. He liked that. A shiver went through him and Farran delved a little lower.

Kel found the hem of her nightshirt and rucked it up high enough to cup her bottom with both hands. She shuddered and he growled low in his throat. "Damn, you're not wearing anything under there."

She ignored the commentary and ran her mouth over his collarbone, kissing and leaving teasing nips as she moved. His skin held the tang of salt and soap and him. Giving him one last bite, she licked at the spot, soothing the sting she'd caused.

With a groan, he started to lift her garment and Farran froze. No, he couldn't take that off now, not when she was naked underneath. Her plan was to be flat on her back all night.

Breaking away, she said, "Bed."

"Countertop," he argued, voice a rasp.

Farran shook her head. "Bed."

Reluctantly, he took her hand and led her down the hallway. She had to all but run to keep up with his long strides, but she didn't mind. He wanted her that much. No one had ever really wanted her in any way. She'd been an embarrassment, a castoff, a worthless bargaining chip, but she'd never been wanted.

As soon as they entered his bedroom, Farran made sure she faced Kel, hiked her nightshirt up around her waist, and sat on the bed before pulling the shirt over her head. She felt brazen, but she couldn't leave it up to him.

For an eternity, Kel stared and she felt self-conscious until he reached for the snap of his jeans. He was down to his briefs in seconds and then he joined her on the bed.

Lying beside her, his hands roamed as they kissed. Control shifted. It happened gradually, but Farran was aware of it. Kel cupped her breasts, teased her nipples with his thumbs before lowering his head and taking her in his mouth. Her eyes slid shut and she pulled him on top of her.

There was impatience in the way he touched her, but then she wasn't willing to wait either. Farran buried her hands in his hair, stroking him as she held on.

He moved to the undersides of her breasts, nibbling lightly. "I am going to taste every inch of you," Kel promised. "Every inch."

Licking his way down her torso, he kissed each hip bone and then blew gently on her in just the right spot. Her hips arched and Kel took that as an invitation. He parted her and ran his tongue through her folds. Farran almost orgasmed right then, but he was only warming up.

Kel continued to lick her oh so slowly as if she were some treat to be savored. She closed her eyes and her grip on him loosened as she enjoyed what he was doing to her. Her hips moved, trying to hurry him up, but he didn't rush.

Her whimper turned to a groan as his tongue thrust inside her. He stroked in and out until she was rocking with him and then the bastard kissed her inner thigh.

She couldn't find the words to express her frustration so she settled for a moan of annoyance. He made it up to her. Kel returned to where her pleasure was centered and sucked her into his mouth. As he held her there, he licked and slid two fingers inside her.

Trying to tell him how much she loved what he was doing didn't work—she was incoherent—so Farran tightened her hold and pulled him into her firmly. She was close now and she wanted to go over the edge.

Kel must have understood. He didn't stop and then she was coming. Her orgasm seemed to last forever and she went boneless when it was over.

When she regained enough sense to know what was going on, she realized Kel was licking the inside of her knee. She should be doing something for him, but Farran felt so good, she laid there and let him work his way down to her ankle, then back up the inside of her other leg.

It was her own damn fault.

She'd become too tranquil. Too mellow.

"Front side down," he said as he rolled her on her stomach. "One more to go."

It wasn't until she felt him stiffen that she snapped out of her languor. She knew exactly what had happened— he'd seen her tattoo. Farran tried to return to her back, but Kel pressed her down, pinning her in place. "No," she moaned softly.

His hand cupped it and she felt tears gather. Damn it, why hadn't she stayed vigilant? From the start she'd been aware of the need to conceal this from him.

"You're one of them," Kel accused and there was nothing loverlike in his voice. "You're one of those fucking bastards."

11

CHAPTER

Kel all but catapulted himself out of the bed. He'd thought he'd killed all those responsible for his nightmare, but he hadn't realized there were more than two. Grabbing his jeans off the floor, he yanked them on and zipped. He didn't have to worry about his cock getting in the way; he'd lost his erection when he'd seen that damn mark on her.

"Kel—"

"Don't. Don't say a word."

Farran scrambled to her feet and held out her arm. Kel backed away to prevent her from touching him. The walls were closing in and he turned blindly, hoping his instincts were taking him out of the room. They did and he kept moving. He needed to get away from her. Had to get away.

He hit the front door before it dawned on him that he was trapped. There was no possibility he could go outside in his current state, not when Seth was out there.

Frustrated, Kel whirled and stopped abruptly when he realized Farran was behind him. She hadn't bothered to pull on any clothes and his eyes lingered on her bare breasts before he realized what he was doing.

"Kel, please."

"Please what? Please listen to you lie some more? Are the shadow walkers and the demon in on this with you or did you just get lucky when they showed up?"

"In on this? You think I'm part of some plot against you?"

"Or against Logan. It was his house you showed up at." Logan. God. Kel started to shake and he jammed his hands in the pockets of his jeans to hide it from her. They weren't going to touch his brother. He'd kill her or any other darksider that he had to if that's what it took to keep Logan safe. Hell, he'd *die* if that's what it took. That decision was made.

The determination cleared away Kel's confusion and knocked him out of his daze. He had a purpose now, something to keep him from falling into that endless pit of despair, fear, anxiety, and hopelessness. But while those draining emotions were gone, betrayal remained. If she wasn't up to no good, wouldn't she have said something when she'd seen his brand?

Her silence condemned her.

"I swear, I'm not part of any conspiracy against you, your family, or any other Gineal." She took a step forward and he retreated, his back hitting the wood of the door.

"Stop trying to touch me." Kel was relieved his voice came out coldly. Her nipples were hard, damn it, and he couldn't stop sneaking glances even though he knew she was guilty as sin. If he ended up back in hell, he had no one to blame but himself.

"I just want you to listen." She gestured with her hands and it made her jiggle.

"For heaven's sake!" He sidled around her, strode over to the island, snagged his sweatshirt, and tossed it at her. "Put this on."

Farran's cheeks went red and she quickly donned the shirt, but Kel wasn't sure he believed the embarrassment, not when she'd shown no signs of modesty until now. The hem came down to midthigh, more than covering her, but he still didn't want to look in her direction. The disillusionment was nearly more than he could deal with, but that was his own damn fault, too. He never should have forgotten she was Tàireil, not even for a moment.

"Now can we discuss this?" Farran asked.

Damn it, he didn't want to talk. He wanted to open his eyes and discover this had been nothing more than some new nightmare, that he really had been right to believe what she'd told him, to believe what he'd sensed from her. Since that wasn't going to happen, Kel wanted to throw her out and let her fend for herself. And he couldn't.

Not if he ever wanted to sleep again.

He might have accused her of being in collusion with the demon and the shadow walkers, but with a few minutes to cool down and think, Kel knew that wasn't true. There was a threat against her, a significant one, and Farran wasn't strong enough to deal with it. He could tell her to go find some of her cronies, but the bottom line was that he'd promised to protect her and he'd been raised to keep his vows—no matter how much that sucked.

Without a word, he walked out of the kitchen. Kel dropped onto one of the love seats, sprawling out so Farran couldn't sit beside him, put his feet up on the coffee table, and crossed his arms over his chest. It was no surprise when she trailed after him.

Short of leaving the cabin, there was nowhere he could go to get away from her. Even if he decided to risk a confrontation with Seth, Kel had no guarantee that Farran wouldn't follow him and that would be all he needed. Better to let her say her piece and get this over with.

She sat facing him on the coffee table, her hip against his legs, and Kel shifted until they were no longer in contact. Why couldn't she respect his wishes and stop touching him?

And while he was asking himself rhetorical questions, why couldn't he be as big a badass as his brother? Why?

If their positions were reversed, Logan wouldn't be sitting here, waiting for a darksider to find enough courage to speak. Unless Shona was able to convince him otherwise, his brother would have packed up Farran and shipped her to the council. She'd be protected, he'd argue, albeit by someone else, and he'd be keeping his word.

But Kel, patsy that he was, knew how afraid Farran was of the ceannards and he couldn't find it in him to send her off to face them despite the tattoo. Yeah, he was a chump all right, an idiot, a total loser.

His impatience got the better of him. "You want to talk? Fucking talk already or go back to your room. I've had enough of you tonight."

She paled and he nearly apologized, but then decided to hell with it. Maybe if he acted more like a badass, he'd start to become a badass. Besides, if anyone should be saying he was sorry, it was her—not him.

Farran still didn't say anything. Kel sighed pointedly and said, "Go to bed."

"No."

Shrugging to let her know he didn't give a damn, Kel closed his eyes and leaned his head against the back of the love seat. It was worse than looking at her. Now all he could see was that brand. There were multiple parts to it. The circle itself was a little over two inches across and wavy lines came out from the east and the west. The north and south had three straight lines and in the center was another symbol, one that didn't match anything he'd seen before. It was like a backward S and a forward S connected by a long tail in the middle, and at the very bottom of the backward letter, there was a swirl.

Her symbol was much smaller, much more delicately drawn than his. Hers was only maybe an inch across, including the outward protrusions, and his was probably closer to three when those were factored in. But then there was a difference between a brand and a tattoo.

He saw the burning iron coming at him and Kel opened his eyes again. Watching Farran was preferable to another replay of that moment.

His stare had her shifting and looking uncomfortable. "I didn't have a choice about the tattoo," Farran blurted. "It's Tàireil custom to mark newborns." She must have read his skepticism. "There are spells put on the symbol. The first is to ensure that it can never be removed, even by magical means, and the second allows it to grow with the person. It never lost its shape, not when I went from baby to child or from child to adult, and it never will."

"Every darksider gets the same mark? What's the point?"

Farran shook her head. "No, not everyone gets the same figure." She hesitated, then continued. "There are twelve clans among the Tàireil and each has its own symbol. This is the emblem for mine, for the one I was born into."

"So I have your family to thank for my branding."

Kel could sense her exasperation and felt oddly satisfied by that. He didn't like it when she was meek and apologetic.

"One in about every twelve Tàireil have this same tattoo—that's a lot of people. Could it have been a close relative? Yes, it could—you know what my brothers and father are like," she confessed somberly, "but it's just as possible that it's someone I've never met. Or it could be someone who wanted to implicate my family by branding you with our mark. My father leads our clan and it's not as if he's endeared himself to many."

"That would be assuming the Gineal knew about your clan emblems, would use that to assign guilt, and were willing to go to war over what was done to me."

Those were three pretty big assumptions. Kel hadn't known about the clan affiliations, and if he was unaware of it, a lot of other Gineal didn't know either. As for the war part, the council had been satisfied when he'd reported the deaths of the men who'd done this to him and he'd been content with that, too. He hadn't wanted to punish the innocent and there'd been no need to take on the Tàireil world.

Farran nodded. "I know. It's far more likely that members of my clan were responsible, but Kel, that doesn't mean I had anything to do with it or had any idea what was happening."

"Yeah," he admitted grudgingly. He couldn't hold her responsible for what someone she was related to had done. She'd been no more able to control the actions of the men who'd tortured him than she'd been able to control her father or brothers when they'd decided to go after the dragon stone.

As if reading his mind, her gaze dropped to her hands and she confessed, "Not that I could have helped you if I had known. Our society is strongly patriarchal, and not only am I female, I have weak magic—another reason to scorn me."

"And you risked your father's wrath."

Another blush spread over her face. "Yes, although I doubt he knew of your branding. He might have no love for the Gineal, but he respects your powers. It's why he wanted to take the dracontias without any of your people becoming aware of our presence or that Shona was the dragon mage."

The last of his anger drained away and Kel sighed. He should have known better than to go off the deep end. As a troubleshooter, he'd been trained to control his emotions, and since he hadn't done that tonight, he'd reacted without thought. "I'm sorry," he apologized. "I saw that tattoo of yours and went a little crazy. I don't have any excuse for that other than the memories of that situation aren't good ones."

Farran finally lifted her gaze. "I'm not surprised. It would be unlikely that they did anything to dull your pain while the iron was applied. What I don't understand is why you were branded at all."

"I wish to hell I had a clue." His only guess was that it was part of the torture. It hit him on two levels—pain and it was a way to break him down psychologically.

"How did they get you to begin with? And how did they keep hold of you long enough to brand you? It doesn't make sense."

Kel stiffened. "Leave it alone."

"But—"

"It's none of your business."

He sounded tired and that was how he felt. No matter whom he was with, someone always had to ask about things he didn't want to discuss. Some people were curious, some honestly were concerned, but if he wasn't going to talk about this with his family, Kel sure as hell wasn't telling all to a near-stranger—no matter how intimate they'd been.

Icy wind slashed at her and Farran scrunched deeper into her borrowed down jacket. It seemed much colder in downtown Chicago than it had in the suburban area where the library was located. Here, though, they weren't far from Lake Michigan or the river, and with giant skyscrapers on either side, it seemed to create a tunnel for the wind to whip through.

It amazed her how busy the streets were at midmorning on a Monday and the sheer numbers of people out despite the cold had made her gawk—until Kel had asked if she got off the farm much.

The memory had her scrunching up her nose. Her world didn't have huge urban centers or the human population to sustain them and Seattle wasn't as large as Chicago. But maybe she had been a little obvious as she'd marveled at the sights, and Farran had done her best to be more unobtrusive since then.

She just wished she knew why they were here and not

at the tasglann continuing their research. Kel had adjusted his pace to hers, but he wasn't talking and no amount of prodding on her part had gotten him to say anything.

That would worry her except that he'd been quiet since last night. Kel had gotten some sleep—probably not as much as he needed, though he looked better than he had yesterday—but he seemed subdued. The farm comment was the only normal thing he'd said or done today and Farran couldn't help but wonder what had brought this on. He had nightmares, but she didn't think he'd had one last night. Was her tattoo enough to do this to him?

They stopped at a traffic signal and people crowded around them, all talking either to each other or into their cell phones. It made her uncomfortable, and tentatively, she reached out, slipping her hand in Kel's. He stiffened, but he didn't pull away, just looked at her curiously. "Your hand is warm," Farran said, although it wasn't much of an explanation.

He threaded his fingers with hers and kept his hold when the light changed. They gained some space between themselves and the crowd when they crossed the street and that let Farran relax. She had enough empathic ability that people pressing in made her feel as if she were on overload.

Kel didn't seem to share her problem even though she knew he was a stronger empath than she was. "How do you do it?" she asked.

For an instant, he looked confused, then he figured out what she was asking. "I'm not sure. Maybe it's because I grew up near here and I'm a huge Cubs fan. Wrigley Field is pretty much sold out every game day and if I wanted to watch baseball live, I had to get control of being in a crowd. Do you know about baseball?"

Farran nodded. "I saw it on television in Seattle a few times. I don't understand the game, though."

"You don't know what you're missing," he said and Kel sounded much more alive, much more enthusiastic

than he had all day. "We can go to a game and I'll explain—" He stopped short. "Sorry. The season doesn't
start for a couple of weeks yet."

And the odds were good that by then the situation
would be resolved and she'd be back in Seattle looking
for another job. Or if by some odd quirk of fate things
weren't wrapped up, they couldn't risk her being among
a crowd of humans, not when the demon or the shadow
walkers could attack.

"That's okay, I understand." And she did. Kel wasn't
her friend, not really. He was the Gineal troubleshooter
who'd agreed to protect her, but he wasn't promising
more than that.

"Maybe we can catch a preseason game on WGN.
They usually broadcast a few on the weekends."

"It's okay. It's no big deal."

"Everyone should have an appreciation for baseball,"
Kel grumbled, but he didn't suggest they make a date
for this summer to watch a game together.

"Did you go to the games alone?" Farran asked, changing the subject slightly to get them past the awkward
part.

"Usually with my brother. When we were kids, we
had to wait till my dad would take us, but once we
were teenagers, Logan and I would meet there whenever we could."

Meet? Why wouldn't they go together? Then she
knew why they hadn't. "Training. How'd you deal with
being separated?"

For a minute, Kel looked as if he was going to balk at
the question. It had been more personal than anything
he'd been willing to answer, but he surprised her. "It
wasn't easy. Logan and I did everything together from
the time we were born until we started our apprenticeships at twelve. We even shared a bedroom, and suddenly being apart was strange. Maybe a little scary, too."

Or maybe a lot scary for a twelve-year-old boy who
was living away from home for the first time and was

used to always having his twin around. Farran squeezed his hand. "You two must have been opening transits all the time to visit each other."

Kel lifted his brows, shrugged, and said, "Not as much as you think. There was a lot to learn, but we did sneak off in the summers and catch some games together."

Farran tried to imagine Kel as a small boy, but she couldn't do it. All she could see was the man—tall, muscular, and sexy. Her body tingled as she remembered what he'd done with his mouth last night before he'd spotted her tattoo. He had a talent, that was for certain.

They stopped at another intersection and Kel gestured across the street with his free hand. "That's where we're going."

That jerked her out of her sensual memories. Water Tower Place. It looked like some kind of shopping center and Farran glanced at Kel in surprise. He didn't offer an explanation. She had to bite her tongue, but she didn't ask any questions, just followed him when the walk signal appeared. He released her hand, allowing her to enter the revolving door first, but he joined her in the same section. She could feel his heat at her back and the temptation to lean into him nearly overwhelmed her.

Once she was inside, Farran stopped short to stare at the fountain positioned between the up and down escalators and Kel bumped into her. For a moment, she savored the feel of his groin nestled against her rear, then he urged her forward and she lost the contact. It *was* a shopping center and that surprised her.

Before she could ask him what next, a woman moved away from the wall and waved. "Kel!"

He waved back and picked up his pace. Farran had to rush to keep up with him, but she slowed when the woman threw herself in his arms and Kel hugged her. It seemed to Farran that he held on to her a lot longer than he needed to and she drew to a halt a couple of feet away to wait.

Finally, they broke apart and Farran recognized her

as the troubleshooter who'd fought with Kel and Logan the night her father had attempted to get the dragon stone from Shona.

"Hi," the woman said and she made no attempt to hide her curiosity.

"Tris, this is Farran Monroe, Shona's Tàireil friend. Farran, this is my sister Beatris, but if you want to live, you'll call her Tris."

"It's nice to meet you, Farran." Tris held out a hand, and after they shook, she scowled at Kel. "Why do you always introduce me that way?"

"Because I can."

"Do you see what I have to put up with?" Tris asked her. She didn't wait for Farran to answer before turning back to Kel. "Everyone's been worried about you. We've been taking turns calling for two days and getting more frantic every time voice mail picked up. It doesn't help that no one can get inside your house to check on you."

"You didn't try telepathy," he offered blandly.

Tris looked ready to rip into him, but she reined in her temper. "Because you always ignore any mind contact. Where have you been, damn it?"

"Not at home."

A determined expression crossed her face, but before she could try to pin her brother down, an older human couple came up and asked where a store was. Kel shrugged, but his sister turned to help them.

Farran took a moment to study her. Her eyes were blue, though not as dark as the deep blue that Kel had, and her hair was a shade or two lighter than his with blond streaks. She was taller than Farran—maybe by a couple of inches—but that wasn't a surprise, since most Tàireil and Gineal surpassed her height. "Your sister is exceptionally beautiful," she said softly to Kel. "You must have had your hands full scaring off amorous men."

"Logan and I threatened a few lives early and managed to instill enough fear that all it takes now is occasional reminders."

Kel sounded so smug as he spoke that Farran nearly laughed—and she nearly cringed as well. Poor Tris. Two overprotective brothers. Then she rethought that. Lucky Tris. Farran would change places in a heartbeat if it meant she'd have a family that gave a damn what happened to her.

"Bet she loves that," Farran said dryly.

"What she doesn't know keeps Logan and me from losing limbs." But Kel grinned as he said that and Farran forgot everything except staring at the sexy, crooked smile that she rarely saw.

"Sorry," Tris said, rejoining the conversation after the couple left. "Why did you ask me to meet you here?"

"I need your help," Kel said.

Tris's expression didn't change, but Farran had the sense that she'd just become all business. "What do you want me to do?"

She was immediately ready to assist him—no hesitation, no excuses, no questions asked. Farran felt a pang. That would never have happened in her family and she wondered if Kel realized how fortunate he was.

"Can you throw some protection around the area to keep us from being overheard?"

"We should go somewhere more private to talk."

Kel shook his head. "I'm hoping all the human energy conceals us. Not from the Gineal," he explained quickly when he saw the look on Tris's face. "Put up the field and I'll explain."

With a nod, Tris erected the barrier. "Why didn't you do that?"

"Because I think they've identified my power signature—Farran's as well—and are using our magic to home in on us."

"Who's *they*?"

"Shadow walkers." Kel began explaining what had been going on without Tris having to ask and finished by saying, "The damn thing is that we can't find information in any of the books and that's just wrong. The Gineal write everything down."

"No kidding," Tris said, "but I'm still not clear on what you want me to do."

Kel unzipped his jacket before he said, "Farran and I were talking and she suggested that maybe the shadow walkers were able to erase all references to themselves."

"That's far-fetched," Tris said and added a smile for Farran, a way of saying nothing personal.

"Yeah, we both know that, but it seemed just as unlikely that we'd go through hundreds of books and come up with nothing more than what you and I learned as apprentices. You know what our library is like and the mass of information has given troubleshooters fits for generations. But last night, I had another thought."

"What was that?" Farran prompted before Tris did. She almost asked when he'd managed to think about the situation, but restrained herself in time. That was one topic she didn't want to open in front of his sister.

Kel glanced at her and smirked, picking up on exactly what she was remembering. "The shadow walkers would be taking a big chance on erasing individual references to themselves. It's too easy to miss one and that's all it would take. But I started wondering, what if they were able to construct a way to hide the information about themselves in all our books?"

"A spell like that would take massive amounts of energy," Farran said. "No one could pull it off."

Tris shook her head. "It's not a spell, not exactly, but what Kel's suggesting is more outrageous than some shadow walker having enough power to invoke that kind of incantation."

"It's not outrageous, it's logical," Kel disagreed. "If you wanted to make sure all references to yourself remained unseen, you could take a chance and try to catch them, eliminating them one by one, or you could manipulate the energy to hide every mention. Which would you go with?"

"I would—"

"Wait," Farran interrupted. "Explain something to me. Isn't manipulating energy and spellcasting the same thing?"

"No," Kel said. "Spellcasting is a form of energy manipulation, but it's not the only kind. It is the one, though, that the Gineal and Tàireil are most comfortable with and most adept at. Most of us live our entire lives without ever going beyond using spells and rituals, but every now and then someone is born who can do more and he or she can go past magic and into the heart of the energy. Tris is one of them."

That didn't make things clearer for Farran, but she could pick up Kel's growing impatience and decided to save her questions for later. They were in public and there was no guarantee that Seth or the shadow walkers wouldn't find them here even though he'd masked the transit and opened it blocks away from this place.

"What are you suggesting then?" Tris asked. "That they altered the energy around the Gineal or around our books?"

"Does it matter? I want you to go to the tasglann and call out volumes that reference the shadow walkers, but instead of reading them like the rest of us do, I want you to study the energy, and if it's been corrupted, undo it. I need to know everything possible about these people ASAP."

"I'll try, but there's no guarantee that this is what they really did. You know, it is possible that the Gineal haven't had enough encounters with the shadow walkers to write down much about them."

Kel snorted. "Like that's stopped our ancestors before. I know it's a long shot, but it's worth checking out. Will you do this for me?"

"You know I will." Tris looked at the clock on her cell phone. "Why don't we meet back here around five. That will give me time to go through a good number of texts and we can have dinner while I tell you if I've found anything."

"Five? What the hell are we supposed to do in the meantime?" Kel groused.

"Why don't you buy Farran some clothes? Mom's jacket looks as if a bulldozer ran over it and my jeans are about ten years out of date. I think that's how long it's been since I painted my bedroom the teal color that's spattered on the legs."

Kel tried to interrupt, but Tris didn't let him.

"Don't worry," she said, "I won't tell Mom and Dad you're using the cabin. Or the council either. I am right about you neglecting to mention to them that you found Farran, right?"

12

CHAPTER

Seth idly ran his senses over the lodge and snapped upright from his recumbent position. They'd left and he didn't know how long they'd been gone. He muttered an expletive before he regained control of his emotions. The last time he'd run a check had been about an hour ago and that gave him a window, but it still frustrated him.

He'd scanned repeatedly this morning and neither of them had seemed to be in a hurry to do anything. His mistake was in allowing their indolence to lull him.

A closer perusal showed that the Gineal had cloaked the energy of the transit—not a surprise—but because Seth was such a long distance from the lodge, he was unable to overcome the concealment spell and follow anyway. If only he'd been a hundred yards nearer . . . He let that thought trail off. Deal with what was, not what you wish, he reminded himself.

There was no tracking them, but that didn't mean he was out of options. What were the odds that they'd gone to any location save the Gineal library?

After considering that for a moment, Seth decided it was unlikely that they'd headed anywhere else. The question now was did he go immediately or did he delay a few hours? It was too late to catch them on their way to enter the building and he wasn't certain he wanted to sit there for hours waiting.

Of course, what was the alternative? Sit here for hours waiting?

Seth stood and transported himself to the area around the library, but as he'd suspected, there was no sign of his prey. It was going to be a long day. A boring day. If his goal wasn't critically important, he'd go somewhere and have fun, but he couldn't risk not being present when they left.

Damn Maia. This was her fault. *Everything* was her fault. Revenge, though, would have to wait. There was nothing more critical than reclaiming his power. He unclenched his hands finger by finger. Later. He'd deal with her later.

The wind gusted and Seth huddled deeper into his coat. He needed to choose a location that gave him optimum sight lines while shielding him from the elements, but he doubted he'd find such a place. He settled for a clear view of the structure. How much magic could he risk using to stay warm? If he was too low on power, he might lose to the troubleshooter, but he loathed being cold. A small amount should be okay, he decided.

As the hours passed, Seth grew more uncomfortable. If there was anything to take his mind off his misery, it might be easier to wait, but there was nothing. The tedium was making him impatient and he couldn't afford that, not when he'd already miscalculated. Every mistake made his task more difficult and lowered his chances of success.

Seth couldn't let this opportunity slip through his fingers. Not when there might not be another one.

It was early evening, about the time he expected the troubleshooter and the Tàireil woman to leave the library, when Seth spotted a pair of shadow walkers. So they were lying in wait, as well.

Moving slowly in order to avoid discovery, he shifted for a better view. He scowled when he recognized them as the same two who had attacked yesterday. Was the first shadow walker, the one he'd battled in the alley, also present? Seth searched, but detected no sign of him.

This duo hadn't fought yesterday to capture the Tàireil; they'd been shooting to kill, and without the first shadow walker here to assist the Gineal, today they might succeed. That would ruin all of Seth's plans.

The idea of having to help the troubleshooter himself had Seth's mood descending even further, but if that's what it took to protect the Tàireil woman, then that's what he'd do.

No matter how much it galled him.

As the delay lengthened, Seth became more optimistic. Shadow walkers were unable to remain out of their dimension for long, and the more power they had to expend to linger, the faster they'd run out of energy in a fight.

He began to wonder if he could use their presence to his advantage. If they fought the troubleshooter, forced him to burn through his magic, and had to return to their dimension before achieving their objective, Seth could swoop in himself. He'd have to take out the Gineal before he could open a transit, but that might be possible, especially if he was fatigued.

Seth smiled, feeling more cheerful than he had all day.

His good humor didn't last long. The first shadow walker arrived and Seth had no doubt that he'd fight to aid the Gineal the same way he had yesterday. It was impossible to guess his agenda, but he had protected the woman twice—once from Seth and once from his own compatriots—and it was a safe wager that he wouldn't allow Seth to grab her this time either. He scowled and then his lips curved. What if the shadow walkers fought it out among themselves?

He'd lose the advantage of the duo wearing out the

troubleshooter for him, but gain the benefit of the pair forcing the first shadow walker to exhaust his supply of power. The male would have to depart then—likely the other two as well—and that left the Gineal man and Tàireil woman to Seth. Not perfect, but far better than a replay of yesterday's scenario where Seth had wound up empty-handed.

That was decided then. He'd take his chances one on one with the troubleshooter.

With a little magic, Seth made his shot at the first shadow walker appear to come from the other two. That was all it took to ignite a battle.

Ah, it was almost like the old days. How much fun he'd had stirring up the humans and then watching while they rolled out their armies to wage war against each other. When he'd still been revered as a god, Seth had sometimes chosen to show himself to the side most devoted to him in an effort to impel them on to greater feats. Other times, he'd merely taken a front-row seat and enjoyed the spectacle laid out before him.

This fight didn't hold quite the epic scale that the humans had managed, but it was a step forward in his plot and Seth could appreciate it for that alone.

They battled each other full-force, and with that kind of power expenditure, it didn't take much time before all three shadow walkers were appearing and disappearing. It wouldn't be long now, Seth thought gleefully, and once they were gone, the field was wide open for him.

His chortle became a choking noise when the three turned and fired at him. Seth dove out of the way just in time.

From his belly, he released several bolts of lightning and transported himself to a new position. He didn't fool them, however; they knew exactly where he was and fired in unison.

Seth barely suppressed a yelp as a jagged snake of energy connected. They weren't supposed to work together.

He sought a more defensible location and shot at them from there. This time he scored a few direct hits himself and the female shadow walker vanished. There wasn't so much as an instant to enjoy his results.

The two males sought to flank him and Seth leveled all his power at one, driving him back before he disappeared.

A blast hit him squarely between the shoulders and he realized the female had returned, damn her. The pain was excruciating even with his protection in place and Seth struggled to stay on his feet. He couldn't falter.

Digging deep, he found more strength and whirled, leveling a barrage of lightning at her. She faded out again, but now the first shadow walker found a clear angle.

Seth's knees sagged and he locked them to stay upright. They would not defeat him. They would not.

Doggedly, he fought on, but every time one vanished, another would press him and Seth found himself spread thin. It was anyone's guess if he could outlast them, but they were disappearing more and more often and for longer periods. He would emerge victorious. He must.

He grabbed a tree to keep from falling when another energy snake found him. Leaning against the trunk, he fired at the woman. She was vanishing more frequently and would be the first to be forced back to her own world, but then she had expended the most energy before the shadow walkers had realized he was present. If Seth took her out of the picture, his odds improved.

With that goal in mind, he only fired at the males to keep them from positioning themselves, otherwise all this power was aimed at the female.

It worked. She disappeared, and when she didn't return after a couple of minutes, Seth knew he didn't have to worry about her anymore today. He turned his attention to the two males. Which one did he target next? Before he could decide, the first shadow walker connected with multiple streams of his blue energy.

Seth fell.

Survival instincts honed over millennia had him rolling out of the way of another round, and even as he convulsed, he fired. The second male dematerialized and didn't return by the time Seth regained his feet. Another one gone.

He faced the first shadow walker alone and put all his remaining energy behind a bolt of lightning.

Number one vanished.

He'd won. He'd outlasted his enemies. Seth swayed, tried to grab a tree again to stay upright, but missed and landed on the cold ground.

It was a hollow victory, he decided as he laid there, shivering. He was in no condition to take on the troubleshooter or make any attempt to get the Tàireil woman. Damn the shadow walkers, but he couldn't put much vehemence behind his cursing, not when he felt as if a herd of elephants had trampled him.

Seth tried to stand, but all he managed to do was crunch dead leaves beneath his body. He needed to go somewhere warm where he could recover in comfort.

Gathering all his power, Seth transported himself away from the Gineal library. It galled him to retreat, but withdrawing now and fighting another day was smart. Tomorrow he would face the troubleshooter and take the woman.

Tomorrow he'd achieve total victory.

Kel didn't like having his back to the entrance of Water Tower Place, but the bench on which he'd managed to snag a couple of seats faced the fountain, not the doors to the street. They didn't have much room, not with all the other people seated here, but he couldn't find it in him to mind when he had Farran snuggled against his side and his arm around her shoulders.

She was as tired as he was, but they'd had to keep moving. The likeliest scenario was that the shadow walkers were tracking them on magic use, but he wasn't completely sure of that and Kel couldn't risk a battle happening with humans in the area.

They'd shopped, covering miles of ground, but hadn't bought much. There was one oversized shopping bag between his legs, and most everything belonged to Farran, but she'd balked at him spending money on her. He'd managed to talk her into a couple of pairs of jeans, some shirts, lingerie, and a winter jacket, but she'd refused everything else except a few toiletries.

Only one thing in the bag was his—the condoms. The lack of protection hadn't bothered him last night—hell, he'd never even thought about it—but when he'd walked down the aisle in the drugstore and spotted the rubbers, the blood had drained from his face. He wasn't planning on having sex with Farran, but then that hadn't been his intent last night either. With her leaning into his side, Kel was aware of the heat building between them and he figured the purchase had been smart.

"You okay?" he asked, because the silence gave him too much time to remember.

"Yes. I like shopping, but I'm not in any hurry to do it again for a long time. If you wanted to make sure that I never asked you to go with me in the future, you've succeeded."

Farran sounded as if she was smiling and Kel shifted to check it out. Yep, she was. "Then my mission was accomplished," he said, deadpan. Her grin widened and he leaned back, satisfied.

"Thanks again for the clothes," Farran said. "I'll repay you, even if it takes me years to do it."

"You don't owe me anything."

"Yes, I do."

Kel recognized stubbornness when he heard it and gave up the argument. Besides, he understood pride. In her place, he'd probably insist on making good on his debt, too, and it wouldn't matter what anyone told him. Looked like they were both bullheaded.

"Your sister's late. You don't suppose she ran into any trouble, do you?"

"No." God, he hoped not. "Tris can transit right into the tasglann, so she wouldn't be exposed like we were." But the shadow walkers could get inside the library. "And if the worst happened, there are about half a dozen troubleshooters there who could help her." Nineteen-year-old kids without much real experience and facing something that they'd never fought before.

Farran put her hand on his knee and squeezed. "I'm sorry, I shouldn't have started you worrying. It could be that she's still going through books or maybe someone stopped to talk to her. Or you said she was a trouble-shooter, maybe she had a job."

"Yeah," Kel said. "She probably got a call-out and she's not that late yet."

Someone laughed loudly and he felt Farran stiffen. He glanced over in time to see her bring her hand to her cheek. "There's no scar," Kel said softly as he leaned his face toward hers. "And the person who laughed wasn't looking our direction, I promise."

"Sorry. I just— It's just that even though I know it's gone, I feel as if it's there. As if every time someone looks at me, all they can see is how ugly I am."

"You're not ugly. Even with the scar, you weren't ugly."

He felt her skepticism, but before Kel could say more, Tris rushed up to them. "Sorry. I know I'm late."

"You're okay?" he asked, checking her out. She looked fine.

"Yes, I'll explain what held me up over dinner. You're buying."

Kel let his lips curve. Yep, Tris was fine. She even had the restaurant picked out and he trailed behind his sister and Farran as they walked to a pizza place.

They were settled in a corner booth, him and Farran on one side, Tris on the other, but instead of talking about what had happened at the library, they were study-

ing their menus. He'd had to beat his sister to get the
bench with the wall behind him, but Kel had used the
fact he was four inches taller to his advantage. Exposing
his back was not something he was willing to do, not for
any reason.

After the waiter took their order and left, Kel raised
an eyebrow and asked, "Are you that hungry that we had
to order the large stuffed pizza or are you paying me
back for getting the better seat?"

"I'm starved—I didn't eat lunch and I burned a lot of
power. I'll get even on the seating arrangement some
other time."

"So what happened today?"

Tris started to speak and then stopped, leaning back
to let the waiter distribute their beverages. "We might
as well wait until the appetizers come, otherwise we're
going to get interrupted again."

"Just answer one question for me—was I right about
the energy?"

Tris nodded. "Oh, yeah, were you ever. It was the
most incredible thing I've ever had to deal with. I'll tell
you all about it while we wait for the pizza." She turned
to Farran. "What did you buy?"

Kel tuned out the shopping talk and did a second sur-
vey of the restaurant. On one side, the walls and columns
were covered with a red brick facade, but the other walls
were painted a warm red color and covered with pictures
of historic Chicago. There were booths along both walls,
the benches upholstered in black, and the tables were a
rich, dark wood. The best part, though was the level of
lighting—not too dim, but not so bright he felt on display. Leave it to Tris to pick a perfect location for dinner.
He just hoped the food was half as good as their surroundings.

Sipping his Coke, Kel did another sweep, but everyone was human and no one gave a damn about them.
Something inside him relaxed—a little. They'd made it
all day without anyone or anything tracking them down.

When the breaded mushrooms arrived, Kel gave Tris a couple of minutes to eat and then prodded her. "So? What happened?"

"So," his sister said, rubbing her fingers on her napkin, "I went to the library and called a few books forward. I didn't feel anything as I handled them—to be honest, I didn't expect to—and I was about to write the whole thing off when I got the slightest whiff of something."

Tris grabbed another mushroom and Kel reined in his impatience. She'd skipped lunch for him, he could wait.

"Even with this sense that something was there, I couldn't get a handle on it and I didn't understand why."

Kel turned to Farran and explained, "Tris is incredible with any kind of energy puzzle. It's really saying something if she couldn't get a grip on it."

"You did figure it out, didn't you?" Farran asked.

"I did." Tris reached for her lemonade. "It took me all day and that's no lie. I didn't unravel the thing until about fifteen minutes before we were supposed to meet up again."

"That's why you were late," Kel said.

His sister nodded. "I wasn't going to give up until I busted that thing wide open." She grinned. "Even if that meant I had to spend every day at the tasglann for the next six months. That's no exaggeration. At the rate I was going, it might have taken me that long." She helped herself to a few more appetizers and popped one in her mouth.

If it had been his youngest sister, Keavy, who'd said that, Kel would have immediately chalked it up as an embellishment, but not with Tris. She told it like it was—always had.

Of all his siblings, she was the one who worried him most. Logan was a badass, but he was smart and knew when to retreat and regroup. Iona, his middle sister, was bookish, serious, and on her way to a career healing animals. Keavy had a way of charming her way out of trouble, but Tris didn't back down. Ever.

That was his fault—his and Logan's. She was four years younger than they were and they'd been amused watching a toddler try to keep up with them. They'd even egged her on. Those early days had set the tone and she still was trying to outdo them. And she could in some ways—like with energy knots—but Tris kept trying to best them in physical contests where they had the edge.

Logan got bored and would let her win when he was ready to quit, but Kel never did and he never would. If he allowed Tris to win, he was afraid it would give her a false sense of confidence and she already took risks in battle that gave him heart palpitations.

Not that he'd witnessed them firsthand. Kel figured he would probably have a stroke if he'd actually seen some of the stunts he'd heard about, but nothing he'd said to Tris had gotten through to her.

Farran rested her palm on his knee under the table and Kel put his hand over hers to keep her from withdrawing. He'd needed the signal—he hadn't noticed that Tris was talking. "Sorry, what?"

"I said the energy morphed. Every time I got about halfway through the maze, it would shift and I'd have to start all over again. They have some pretty strong and unusual powers, I think, though I couldn't tell you why I got that sense."

"They can cross the protection that the council put into place around my home," Kel said. "Damn straight they're strong and unusual."

Tris waved a hand, dismissing that. "It was ingenious. I think—and I'm still not sure about this—that the energy knot was around not just every book that enters the tasglann, but also around any written record touched by the Gineal. The kind of power something like that would take . . . incredible."

"They put it around the building?" Kel asked.

"No, not around that library specifically. You know we've had more than one throughout the generations. It was more generic than that."

"But how—"

"Kel," Farran interrupted. "Does it really matter how they did it or what the logistics are?"

He scowled. "No, I'm just curious."

But Farran was right, he didn't need to know this now. Once everything was wrapped up, the shadow walkers were defeated, and she was safe, then Kel could pull Tris aside and ask her questions until he understood what the hell she was saying.

"You were able to undo the energy lock permanently?" Kel asked. That was the most important piece of information.

"Probably. I can't be sure because it's so different from anything I've dealt with before, but I'm reasonably confident I took care of it." Tris stopped short when the waiter returned and cleared the empty appetizer dishes from the table to make room for dinner. "Have you ever had Chicago-style pizza before, Farran?"

"No, isn't pizza pizza?"

Kel smiled. "Not a chance, sunshine. No place on Earth makes it as good as Chicago, especially stuffed pizza. You are about to have an epiphany."

They all watched Farran—even the waiter—as she took her first taste. Her eyes closed and look of bliss crossed her face.

"Epiphany," the waiter said with a smile before he left.

Tris picked up her fork. "Welcome to pizza nirvana. You've now been spoiled for the rest of your life."

They ate in silence at first. Kel was hungry, too, and while the appetizers hadn't interested him, the pizza did. When he had the edge off his appetite, he said, "Since it took you all that time to bust the code, you wouldn't have had an opportunity to learn anything about the shadow walkers."

"Not much," Tris agreed, "but I did take a few minutes to glance through one of the books. I learned two things. One, it takes an incredible amount of power for them to leave their world for even short periods. Almost none of them can do it, and the few who can aren't able to stay away long."

"That might explain why they keep disappearing during fights," Farran said. "They ran out of the strength to stay here."

"That's what I'd guess," Kel said.

"Me, too." Tris took a swig of lemonade. "The Gineal who wrote the text didn't come right out and say it, but I had the sense that the shadow walkers who can hop dimensions are their society's version of enforcers."

Which raised the question of why they needed troubleshooters, but Kel was aware that Tris probably didn't have the answer. "What's the second thing you learned?" he asked instead.

Tris put down her fork and leaned forward. "The book said that the shadow walkers live in a dimension that isn't theirs and that they're imprisoned there because of a curse."

13
CHAPTER

As Farran grew more alert, she noticed light seeping in beneath her bedroom door. Again.

She threw back the covers and sat up—then she paused. Did she want to go out there? Would Kel assume she wanted sex when tonight she only meant to check on him? For a moment, she didn't move, waiting for the grogginess to dissipate enough to let her think.

It didn't take long to make a decision. Kel was watching over her, fighting to protect her; the least she could do was make sure he was okay.

All the lights were on in the living area of the cabin and Kel was lying on the love seat near the windows, his legs hanging over one of the arms and his forearm over his forehead. His eyes were wide open and he turned his head, watching her as she entered the great room. Farran stopped next to the coffee table and waited.

Kel stared at her, grimaced, and sat up. "You should be in bed," he said.

Farran took the seat beside him. "So should you. Do you ever sleep?"

"I would if I could."

It was a revealing statement, but she let it go. Kel shut

down when he was questioned and she didn't want him defensive. Instead Farran leaned back and put her feet on the coffee table, crossing them at the ankle. She wore the smiling dog nightshirt with lavender and purple striped fuzzy socks, but it was too cold to be barefoot no matter how ridiculous she looked.

"How do you pass the time when you can't sleep?"

"Any way I can." Kel imitated her position.

They were nearly hip to hip and Farran leaned toward him, wanting his warmth. She half expected Kel to ignore her or maybe even edge away, but as he had at the shopping center, he put his arm around her shoulders and tugged her into his side. With a sigh of contentment, she relaxed against him.

"We never finished our conversation this evening."

"Which one?" she asked. They'd talked about a lot of things today—a surprising amount given how terse Kel could be—but she couldn't think of any topic that had been left open.

"The one about your scar."

Farran stiffened. "We were done talking about that."

Kel ignored her. "Why do you think you're ugly?"

"Why do you think you can grill me when you refuse to answer any questions about what happened to you?"

It was his turn to go rigid. "That's different."

"The only thing that's different is who's under the microscope. You want to keep your silence? Fine, but don't expect me to open a vein for you."

Now he pulled away, got to his feet, and paced around the area. He was grumbling something, but she couldn't hear what he was saying and Farran wasn't sure she cared. It was always all her. Yes, he was doing her a favor—a big one—but he didn't get to take her apart while he kept his own secrets. She crossed her arms over her chest and glared at him as he strode past her.

"You don't want to talk to me," she said, raising her voice so he could hear her, "that's fine. What about your family? It's obvious they love you, that they're concerned about you, but instead of letting them help you in any way, you pull back."

Kel stopped short and pivoted to level a scowl at her. "You don't know that."

She got to her feet and didn't stop until she was toe to toe with him. Farran tipped her face up, meeting his frown with one of her own. "Yes, I do. I'm not an idiot. I have eyes and ears. I heard and saw what was going on today between you and your sister. She was walking on eggshells with you anytime it veered from business. Did you notice how many worried glances she tossed at you? How she kept restraining herself from asking how you were or what you were up to?"

"You're reading too much into that. If she was looking at me funny it was probably because she was curious about what was going on with me and you. We weren't exactly sitting like two strangers on that bench when she showed up."

Her cheeks warmed—just a little. "Tris gave us the thumbs-up in the restroom, just so you know."

Kel looked appalled. "She didn't."

"Oh, yes she did. She said I'm the only person you've let touch you for more than a moment at a time and that it was the first encouraging sign you've given anyone in over a year."

"I'm going to kill her," he growled.

"Ha!" Farran said. "We both know better. You would kill *for* her, but that's a much different thing."

"I think I liked it better when you were leery of me."

"Another lie."

Absolute frustration sailed across his face and then resignation. "Yeah," Kel admitted, as the fight went out of him. He raked both hands through his hair, pushing it off his face and sighed loudly. "It freaked me out when you looked at me like I might hit you or hurt you somehow."

"Because you're incredibly gentle," Farran said quietly. "That's why you're prickly—to protect yourself."

"Don't psychoanalyze me, okay?" There wasn't any

heat in his voice. He stepped around her and returned to the love seat, dropping down onto the cushions.

Exhaustion was etched on his features—she could see it plainly—but Farran didn't think it was the conversation draining him as much as the lack of sleep, the battles, and the shopping marathon. She followed him, sitting beside him again, and this time she snuggled into his side immediately. His arm went around her again and something inside her eased.

"You're not ugly, you know. If you were, it would be a lot easier for me."

Farran sighed, not surprised by his persistence. It didn't matter, though, how many times he brought this up, she didn't have to answer. She could be as private as he was.

"And you only had that scar for seven months," Kel continued. "If you'd had it all your life, I could see why you'd still be having trouble getting past it. Maybe even if you were a human who wasn't used to magic and how quickly things can be healed, I could buy it, but you're not human and you are used to instantaneous healing. So what gives? Why do you feel ugly?"

"Why can't you sleep, Kel? What torments you so much that you need to have every light in the cabin on? How did you end up with a Tàireil brand on your back?"

She felt his muscles grow more tense with every question she tossed at him and Farran guessed it was taking a lot of restraint for Kel not to spring to his feet again. He didn't say anything, neither did she, and the silence lengthened.

When it became too uncomfortable, she said, "The information that Tris told us about the shadow walkers was strange stuff."

"Really strange," Kel said, going along with her.

"And it begs the question that if they are cursed, who or what is powerful enough to imprison them in another dimension? I don't know about you, but it's unsettling to think about."

His arm tightened around her shoulders in a kind of a hug and he said, "That's why I'm ignoring that part of it."

"Repression isn't working for you when—" She cut herself off. "Um, isn't working for you when these super powerful creatures show up."

"Not a real good save," he said dryly.

"It's the middle of the night."

Kel sighed and put his feet back up on the coffee table. "You think if I talk about what happened that it all magically goes away? It doesn't work that way." He sounded as fatigued as he looked. "If that was what it took, I'd be all over it."

"You could have your memories erased magically."

"Maybe the memories, but not the anxiety." Kel laughed, but there was no humor in it. "I'm afraid of the dark. I'm twenty-nine and I turn on every damn light as soon as the sun starts to set. That wouldn't go away and I'd start wondering why, what gave me this phobia? And once I started asking questions, I wouldn't stop. I couldn't stop."

Farran put her hand on his thigh and squeezed, wordlessly offering her support.

"The brand doesn't go away—everyone's tried to remove it and it can't be done. Every time I saw it or felt it, I'd know something happened. It would make me nuts to not remember."

She stroked his leg. "No benefit to it then."

"None." He dropped his head to the back of the couch and stared up at the light fixture. "And our memories make us who we are; it influences how we act and react. Maybe what happened keeps me from making an even bigger mistake in the future."

"What was the original mistake you made?"

Again, his arm tightened around her briefly and it wasn't until he loosened it that he said, "I trusted my empathy too much."

That didn't tell her a lot, but she put it in context with

Kel. He felt too deeply, not only his empathic ability, but he honestly cared about people and wanted to make things better for them. Sure, he'd grouse about it first, growl and snarl, but at the end of the day, he was compassionate and caring. He masked it well. Farran wouldn't be surprised if only his family and a few close friends understood this about him—and maybe not even all of them.

"You're used to taking care of others," Farran said, "and you're not comfortable with anyone fussing over you. Is that why you can't accept anyone wanting to help you now?"

He shrugged.

More to it than that then, Farran decided, but it was something she wasn't going near and he'd cut her off if she tried. "Do you want me to help identify the Tàireil who branded you? If they're known to me, I'll tell you exactly who they are."

"They're dead."

Farran snuck a glance at Kel. The edge in his voice spoke volumes. "Why does that haunt you?" And then she got it. She couldn't believe it didn't occur to her immediately. "You felt them die, that's part of what's bothering you. And," she said as another realization dawned, "you felt what they were feeling while they branded you. They found pleasure in it—"

Kel went rigid and she stopped talking immediately. She was right, but he couldn't go any further. Not tonight and maybe not for a while. Farran circled her fingers on his leg as a sort of apology, not stopping until he began to unclench his muscles.

Turning toward him, she rested her head on his shoulder. She allowed the silence to soothe him, let him unwind and destress before she offered him a piece of herself. "My first memory of my father is from when I was about three," Farran said. "I'd slipped away from my nanny and wandered through the house. I didn't know who he was, but then he'd had nothing to do with me."

It was Kel's turn to stroke her and his fingers glided lightly over her arm.

"His face contorted as soon as he saw me, I remember that clearly. I also recall what he said. He bellowed, *Get this ugly little brat out of here.* My mother had doted on me and his reaction was so far outside my frame of reference that I didn't understand it. In my obliviousness, I wandered closer to him. That was the first time he hit me."

Kel stiffened again and Farran tried to block her emotions. She wanted to shield him from her pain, but she didn't think she was successful.

"He always referred to me as ugly, and when it became obvious how weak my powers were, that was another mark against me. When he found out I was the Tàireil dragon mage, things changed. Some. Suddenly I wasn't useless. I had a purpose—he could use me to rule our world."

"He's a bastard. You shouldn't let him have any power over you." Kel sounded ferocious, but his touch remained tender.

"I know that intellectually, but emotionally? How do I discount all the years of hearing my own father refer to me so disparagingly?"

"Yeah," he conceded reluctantly and drew her nearer.

Farran wrapped her arm around Kel's waist and let herself sink into his warmth. She didn't deserve this, but she wasn't strong enough to turn it away. "I always felt physically ugly—I guess you can only hear something so many times before you start to believe it—and the scar only reinforced that, but I never felt ugly at a soul level until Shona. It wasn't as if my father coerced me into this whole mess; I was eager to please him."

"And you had some kind of respect from him because you were the Tàireil dragon mage," Kel said.

She nodded. "I leapt at the chance to prove my worth and I actively worked against Shona. We knew she always stopped in a shop called The Menagerie and I got a job there, talked to her whenever she came in, invited her for coffee so we could discuss art all with the purpose of taking the dragon stone from her."

"No one can blame you—"

"I do. I blame me. Shona was sweet, younger than her years in a lot of ways because her parents were overprotective, and a genuine friend to me. By this time, I liked her, too, a lot. I thought of her as the sister I wished I'd had. It made me feel . . . dirty to maneuver against her. I was a liar and a would-be thief."

Farran had to stop and take a few minutes to compose herself. She knew Kel was picking up on her feelings again, but she was too agitated to even think about containing them. And he didn't say anything, just hugged her and caressed her arm, letting her have the room she needed. It helped her rein in.

"If I could have backed out, I would have," she continued when she had her self-command, "but if I walked away from the job, my father would have Roderick take over. My oldest brother is as cold as our sire and he would have had Shona killed without turning a hair."

"You protected Shona. You even threw yourself in front of the shots meant for her. Farran, you don't have to beat yourself up over this. Shona doesn't blame you."

"She should."

Kel shook his head, she could feel his chin move against her hair. "You never had a choice. What would your father's reaction have been if you'd told him no when he approached you about stealing the dragon stone?"

Farran bit her lip. She knew how he would have reacted, but that didn't absolve her. "He would have made me see reason."

"A euphemism for he would have beaten the shit out of you until you agreed to go along with his scheme and nothing would have changed. You still would have come here and tried to take the stone, you still would have gotten to know and like Shona, and you still would have risked your life for her. All you did was avoid the pain part of the equation."

"A better person would—"

"Better person my ass," Kel growled. "You protected Shona the best you could, and when that failed, you put yourself in danger to keep her safe. Most people wouldn't have done even a fraction of what you did."

He'd argue with her all night, but Kel was wrong. If she'd been stronger, she would have stood up to her father, told him his plan was wrong, and taken the punishment. Again and again.

"Until he killed you in a fit of rage."

Kel had read her thoughts, but it only startled her a little. Empathy could be that strong. "Without me—"

"The dragon stone would have been useless to him," Kel said. "I know, but he wouldn't be thinking clearly if you kept defying and enraging him. After you were dead and he realized what he'd done, then he'd get it, but that wouldn't do you much good."

"I could have told the Gineal immediately who Shona was and that there were Tàireil here working to take the stone. Your council would have moved to protect her." He'd told her that himself the first night.

She felt his lips press into the top of her head. "You were raised to fear my people; running straight to us wasn't something you were going to do. And besides the council did work to protect Shona; they sent Logan in as soon as they detected a darksider—sorry, Tàireil—near her. It all worked out."

Farran thought of the night her father had made his final, desperate grab for the stone. "It was close. If you, Logan, and Tris hadn't shown up when you had, there's no telling what might have happened."

"You can't beat yourself up over might-have-beens. There's enough real-world stuff to obsess over without adding things that didn't actually occur. Shona's fine, she's happy, she wants to make sure you're fine and happy. No worries."

Her hum was meant to be noncommittal. Maybe he believed that, but she knew better. There was more she could have done, something to prevent Shona from ever being in danger if only she had been smarter or braver or stronger.

Kel put her away from him, looked into her eyes, and sighed. "Aw, hell, sunshine, you're almost as fucked up as I am, aren't you?"

Kel woke slowly. He felt rested, relaxed, and he took a moment to savor the experience. It wasn't something he'd been familiar with for the last thirteen months.

He knew who he had to thank for it. Farran was sprawled beside him in bed, her body warm where it touched his. Kel didn't know why being in contact with her sometimes calmed him, but it did and that had allowed him to sleep.

Turning his head, he checked out the clock. After ten. No wonder he felt so damn good—he'd had more than eight hours of sleep for the first time in who knew how long. Kel looked back at Farran. His cock was hard and it was tempting to roll toward her, cuddle her against him, and coax her into a little morning loving with some kisses, but he wouldn't do it.

Not after last night.

She had self-esteem issues. He'd known that before, of course, but what she'd revealed had driven it home. It was why he'd promised not to try anything when he'd asked her to lie beside him somewhere around 2 A.M. and it was why he'd keep his hands to himself now as well. She was more than her body and the last thing Kel wanted was Farran to believe her only worth to him was sexual. That didn't mean they wouldn't have sex at some point—she got him hot, no doubt about it—but it wasn't going to be while she was vulnerable.

Kel reached over and lightly brushed her hair off her face. He still couldn't figure out what color it was, not exactly. There was a hint of red in it, but it wasn't red and it wasn't a pure brown either. It didn't matter, not really, but he liked answers for everything.

Propping himself up on his elbow, he ran his finger over one of her eyebrows and then her cheek. Damn, she was beautiful; her face was almost flawless. And her mouth . . . Kel traced his thumb across her bottom lip, unable to resist.

Farran stirred and he froze until she quieted again. Since he couldn't keep teasing himself, Kel got out of bed and was careful not to disturb her. He dug some clothes out of the dresser, sliding the drawers as silently as he could, and left the bedroom, closing the door behind him.

He put the coffee on first and then hit the bathroom. Kel had showered and was contemplating a shave when she knocked. "Are you going to be much longer?" Farran asked.

All he had on was a towel tied around his hips, but Kel gathered up his clothes and opened the door. "You can have it now if you need it."

"Thanks." She smiled at him. "How'd your family manage with one small bathroom and seven people?"

"Lots of squabbling, some crossed legs, and an emergency bucket." Her laughter followed her into the bathroom.

Kel went back to the bedroom to get dressed and headed for the coffee. He poured himself a mug, grabbed his notebook and pen, and settled down at the table. While he waited for Farran, he recorded the information Tris had given them at the pizza place. It led to more questions, of course. Like why did the shadow walkers need troubleshooters? If they were imprisoned in a particular dimension, what was the need to travel to others? And the biggest question of all: Why were they targeting Farran?

He was pouring a second cup when she came into the kitchen and he filled a mug for her, too. She took it from him and leaned her hips against the cabinets be-hind her, but he didn't move away. She was wearing her new clothes—jeans and a longsleeve navy shirt with tan stripes—and he was close enough that he could lean down and kiss her. Kel took a swallow of coffee to keep himself from doing it.

"Hmm," Farran hummed as she took a sip. "Thanks."

"No problem. What do you want for breakfast?"

"Waffles?" She smiled up at him, both hands wrapped around her mug, and he forgot to breathe for an instant.

Kel had to clear his throat before he could speak. "If we had toaster waffles, they'd be all yours. How do you feel about leftover pizza?"

"First thing in the morning?"

There'd been a lot of times he'd had pizza for break-fast, but from Farran's question, he guessed she hadn't. "We don't have a lot of choices. It's either pizza or a peanut butter sandwich without jelly."

And they were down to the last of the bread. He was going to have to do something about the food situation. No magic in the cabin, but he could bring the backpack with them to the library, and before they left, call for-ward some stuff to eat. He didn't like the idea of having a pack weighing him down, not when they were wide open between the library and when it was safe to open a transit, but there weren't many options.

"I think it's going to have to be the pizza," Farran said.

"Good choice; I think the bread is stale. You wanna get a couple of plates while I get the pizza?"

Farran put down her mug and crossed the kitchen. Kel missed her proximity immediately, but set aside his own coffee and pulled the box from the refrigerator. Even as hungry as Tris had claimed to be, there were four slices left. Stuffed pizza was filling and there was no way anyone—not even a troubleshooter who'd burned through a lot of power—could eat more than one piece.

"Back to the library today?" Farran asked.

"You know it. Now that Tris unraveled the energy

knot, we might actually learn something that will help."
They were standing in the same position near the microwave that they'd had near the coffeepot, but Kel couldn't
seem to stay away from her this morning. That unnerved
him enough that he forced himself to step to the side.

It seemed to take forever before they finished eating
and were ready to leave the cabin. Kel was definitely
anxious to get out of here. The place was small enough
that it had to be some kind of enforced intimacy thing
plaguing him. Once they were at the tasglann surrounded by books, he'd be back to his old self.

He grabbed the backpack, but hesitated before opening
the transit. Both Seth and the shadow walkers had found
them in the previous location he'd used. It was time to
pick another spot. Kel wanted to use the door they'd entered through before—it was the safest one—but he decided to go north of the building on the same path.

After a quick protection spell, he created the gate.

Kel closed it behind them and signaled Farran to follow him. He'd barely taken half a dozen steps when a
shot hit him in the back, dropping him to his knees.

14
CHAPTER

Farran whirled and squeaked. The two shadow walkers who'd attacked them previously were back. Kel was swaying as he tried to stand and it was daylight; the Tàireil had never had much magic while the sun was up. What was she going to do?

Another shot streaked toward Kel and she moved, trying to put herself in front of him. He yanked her to the ground, covering her with his body, and it sailed over them.

"What the fuck do you think you're doing? They're trying to kill you. Get behind me and stay there."

Before she could do more than growl, Kel was on his feet and returning fire. He made her crazy. What had he expected her to do, let him take another hit when he had yet to recover from the first? Even with the protective barrier around them, those damn shots hurt and he'd taken a huge blast.

She got to her knees. Okay, maybe using her body as a shield wasn't the smartest move ever, but she'd had limited options. It wasn't as if she could call on her strong power and shoot away until they backed off in submission. The protection Kel had around her was solid, but

Farran made sure she was behind him as ordered when she stood.

They weren't in as defensible a position here as they would have been had they crossed in their original spot. There were still plenty of trees, but they were farther from the path and they had thinner trunks, offering less cover if Kel did decide they'd try to reach them. It didn't help that they were at the bottom of an incline and the shadow walkers were on higher ground, shooting down at them.

A cold gust of wind blew through and Farran shivered, hoping it wasn't an omen.

The pair had split apart making themselves two separate targets. Kel shot fire at one, then a lightning bolt at the other, but his focus was splintered and he was getting hit with their blue electricity again and again.

He was shielding her with his body. Farran frowned at his back, but her annoyance disappeared when she realized this was the only way he could protect her—intercepting their shooting angles.

Farran tightened her hands into fists, then relaxed them. The shadow walkers had learned and honed their tactics from the previous encounter and they were working to wear Kel down. It wasn't a bad strategy. Even with sleep, his magic would only last so long, especially two against one. What were the odds Rhyden would show up again?

Probably not great, she decided.

A shot winged by close enough to make the hair on her arm stand up—even underneath her jacket and shirt. "You okay?" Kel asked, not taking his eyes from the enemy.

"Fine."

But she was lightheaded and seeing those tiny colored lights dancing in the air as she had that last time these two had shown up. Breathing deeply got rid of the dizziness, but the lights? Those seemed to be drawn to her.

Raising her arm, Farran closed her hand around one of them and it flowed through her skin. It felt good.

Kel grunted as another shot connected and she sucked in a sharp breath. She had to help him, but how? Last time when he'd asked her to fire, her magic had been weak and useless.

More of the lights sailed toward her and swarmed outside her auric field. What were they waiting for?

That was all they seemed to need and they streamed into her, filling her with an energy Farran had never experienced before. She felt strong, like Hercules and the Terminator rolled into one. Maybe she *could* fight beside Kel.

Before that delusion took hold, Farran reined it in. If she did something stupid, she put Kel at greater risk. Any power she thought she had was a fantasy.

Maybe it was the shadow walkers messing with her head.

The idea that they'd taunt her like this angered Farran. They wanted to kill her, fine, but they should play fair. Making her believe she was powerful . . . that was cruel.

Kel staggered and Farran held up her hands, ready to try and catch him if she had to.

He recovered his balance, but his grimness registered. Farran went up on her toes to see over his shoulder and that brief glimpse told her a lot. Kel had done next to no damage to the shadow walkers and the protective shield he had around him was faltering.

He kept firing, kept fighting, and she could only admire his tenacity.

Time seemed to speed up then, to go into fast forward. Except she wasn't moving at that rate of speed. She went on her toes again and watched a few minutes' worth of battle unfold in seconds. Farran lowered herself back to the ground, confused. Why was she out of sync? And why was everything else moving faster?

The answer to the last question came to her immediately—the shadow walkers. They wanted Kel to run through his magic and do it quickly before they lost their ability to stay in this dimension.

They'd sped up time!

It had to be them.

Okay, it was probably them, but wouldn't this make the pair run through their power more quickly, too? Or did they know something she didn't?

Farran took a deep breath and focused on slowing things down. Why not? It couldn't hurt.

She was doing it.

Somehow, some way, she was returning time to normal.

It couldn't be anyone but her. One of the shadow walkers tried to wrest control away and speed it up again, but Farran thrust her back with no difficulty. It was likely her imagination, it had to be. Things like this didn't happen, but she didn't stop what she was doing. Just in case.

Her energy began to flag, but more bursts of light streamed into her and Farran felt recharged.

Kel fell backward and this time she did have to put her arms around him to keep him from falling. "Kel?"

"Can you open a transit in daylight?"

"Yes."

"I go down, you get to Logan. He'll help you."

Farran didn't like the sound of that and she hated the fact that he was leaning against her and not immediately pushing upright. Kel wouldn't be letting her support him if he had a choice. She willed some of her newfound strength into him until he straightened. And even then, she kept her palm inches from his back to send him more.

The female shadow walker tried to move time faster again and Farran growled low. They already had enough of an advantage, they weren't taking this one, too. Farran blocked her and kept control.

Since Kel seemed steadier, Farran lowered her arm. Electricity crackled in the air, leaving a scent that made her think of scorched linen. The wind kicked up, but her body temperature was running hot enough right now that it felt good. Refreshing.

"We're going to back up," Kel said and that's when Farran noticed the shadow walkers had widened the gap between each other. "Start moving."

Farran matched her pace to his. Their new positions had given their enemy better shooting angles on her and that's what Kel was trying to fix. She sidestepped a burst of blue that was headed for her and kept retreating.

Kel stumbled and Farran immediately reached for him, uncertain if he'd merely tripped on the path or if he'd taken a strong hit. He shook her off.

This couldn't continue. Farran avoided another shot. Kel wasn't going to be able to last much longer—she knew it, he knew it. It was why he'd told her to go to Logan if she needed to. The last time they'd met this pair, he'd said opening a transit was out, that the shadow walkers would simply follow them and take them out in the new location.

He was right, which meant going to Logan just shifted the fight and she wasn't abandoning Kel. She couldn't think of him as just some troubleshooter—not anymore.

She wished she knew if the shadow walkers were fading in and out yet, but she couldn't peer over Kel's shoulder while she was walking backward and she wasn't going to distract him by asking. Please, she thought, let them be running out of time. Let Kel be able to outlast them.

The energy shield around them faltered again. Kel reinforced it, but she didn't think it would last too much longer, and once that fell, he'd tell her to leave.

Like hell.

All these small specks of light seemed to be giving her energy, maybe she could use that. Farran focused on calling them to her, on gathering them inside herself, and amassing them in one spot. Her body felt as if it were giving off enough heat to sear the ground, but it was a good sensation.

And when Kel pulled his arm back to shoot at the enemy again, Farran released the energy and joined it with his shot.

It began the size of a baseball, grew to basketball width, and by the time it slammed into the shadow walker, it was as large as an exercise ball—the kind a person sat on.

The male dropped to the ground and vanished.

For an instant, she stared stupidly and then shook it off. One down, one to go. She peered over Kel's shoulder again, hoping the woman had decided to leave, but she looked determined. Farran began collecting the lights again, but there weren't as many around this time.

Not at first.

And then more came, as if they knew she needed them. Kel was shooting almost continually at the woman and Farran rounded them up faster. *Hang on, Kel. Hang on.*

He groaned softly and swayed. She hurried, pulling the energy into a group as quickly as she could.

"Take another shot," she told Kel.

His hesitation was hardly noticeable and then he did as she asked. He wound up, letting loose with a ball of fire, and Farran released the sphere to unite with Kel's blast. She didn't know how she was doing it and she didn't care. All that mattered was Kel.

The woman tried to dodge the shot, but it was like a heat-seeking missile—it followed her.

Same results. Shadow walker on her butt and then gone.

Kel staggered and Farran wrapped an arm around his waist before he fell. For an instant, he resisted, then he put both his arms around her and held on. He was shaking, breathing hard, and covered with perspiration.

"You're going to have to open the transit back to the cabin; I don't have enough magic left. Do you know the words for the concealment spell?"

Farran tensed. "I don't have enough strength to hide the gate."

"The hell you don't." Kel took a shuddery breath. "You're the one who dropped the shadow walkers, not me. Do whatever you did before you supercharged my shots, only direct it toward this incantation."

It was a short spell, in the language that was nearly identical to Tàireil, and she memorized it easily when Kel shared it. But it required a lot of power, more than she could normally call on even after sundown. Could she really repeat what she'd done before? There were no more lights around anywhere.

"Come on," he growled. "All we need now is for Seth to show up."

"We could go into the library instead of going home."

Kel shook his head. "No, we can't. I won't have enough magic back to fight anyone in five or six hours and Seth is a real threat to be waiting for us when we leave. Just take us back to the cabin."

"But—"

"Don't doubt, just do."

Farran nodded. Closing her eyes, she visualized the lights returning, dancing around the air, and then streaming toward her. She pictured them filling her with power and growing as more and more joined. Concealment spell first, she realized, and whispered the words before closing it. Next she recited the words to open the transit. "And so it is."

"Good job," he said.

She opened her eyes and there was the transit. Wow, she'd done it. Her!

"Let's go," Kel said, and releasing her, he took a step toward the gate. He staggered. Farran caught him again and helped him cross into the cabin, immediately closing the portal behind them.

Kel sighed and said, "Help me to a chair, would you?" He fell onto the love seat rather than sitting down carefully.

"Are you okay?"

He closed his eyes. "Mostly exhausted."

Mostly, but not entirely. She sat in the swivel chair beside him and put a hand on his chest. "You are hurt! Why didn't you say something?"

"Because it's not that bad. A couple of hours and I'll have enough magic to heal myself. Unless you want to do it for me."

Farran nearly told him she didn't have that ability, but stopped. Maybe she'd never do it for a career, but even humans could perform healings and they had no magic. She could at least try, right? And he'd sounded so proud of her when she'd opened the transit. Silly as it was, she wanted to hear that tone from him again. Closing her eyes, she called on the light she had left inside her, and putting her other hand on him, imagined it flowing into Kel, mending whatever needed attention.

Her hands cooled, but Farran didn't pull away immediately. She liked touching Kel even when his winter jacket stood between her palms and his muscles. There was something about it that just made her feel . . . right.

Finally, she had no choice except pull back and she rubbed her fingers over her jeans, trying to get rid of the tingling.

"Thanks, sunshine," Kel said. He didn't open his eyes, but he turned his head toward her and smiled. "You really came through today."

And like an idiot, she teared up at his words.

Kel felt like shit when he woke. Not because Farran hadn't done a good job healing him—she had—but because he'd fallen asleep slouched in the love seat with his jacket on. Not only was he all sweaty, but he was stiff and achy, too. Blowing out a breath, he opened his eyes and looked around. He didn't see Farran anywhere.

That got Kel on his feet faster than he might have moved otherwise. His back protested, but he kept going. Her bedroom door was closed and he knocked softly, not wanting to wake her if she was asleep.

She opened the door.

"Are you all right?" he asked. He should have asked earlier, but he'd been in rough shape and not thinking clearly.

Farran looked quizzical. "Yes, why wouldn't I be?"

"Because you got hit during the fight yourself. I should have asked you right away how you were doing."

"Only a couple of times. You're the one who kept putting himself in their sights." She leaned against the door jamb. "How are you doing? Did the nap help?"

Kel didn't have much magic yet, but his healing talent was innate and he had enough to run his senses over her. She'd been telling the truth—she was fine. He breathed easier. Although he'd done his best to make sure she didn't take strikes, he didn't know how well he'd done, especially toward the end.

"I'm okay," he assured her. "I don't have much power and probably won't until morning. As for the nap, well, it helped and it didn't. The love seat wasn't the most comfortable place to sleep."

She smiled and Kel felt his heart skip a beat. Maybe two. "I'm going to take a shower," he said after clearing his throat, "so if you need the bathroom, you better say something now."

"Go, take a shower."

He nodded, leaned down and brushed a quick kiss over her lips, and turned for the bedroom. Closing the door behind him, Kel unzipped his jacket, hung it in the closet, and dug out clothes that weren't soaked in sweat. He froze as he pulled out a pair of jeans. Hell, he'd dropped the backpack when he took that first salvo and they hadn't picked it up. Nothing he could do about it now, Kel decided, and reached for a sweatshirt.

He tossed the clothes on the foot of the bed, then hesitated. Was Farran still standing there? If she was, would she call him on the kiss? He wasn't sure why he'd done it and he didn't want to face any questions.

No guts, no shower, and he made himself open the

door. Farran wasn't in sight and this time her absence relaxed him.

Getting clean made him feel better, but Kel didn't step out from under the spray until the water turned tepid. He dried off, and after a moment's thought, wiped down the mirror and reached for a razor.

After he returned to the bedroom to dress, Kel collected the wet towels and dirty clothes and dropped them in a hamper. Then he went looking for Farran again. He found her sitting in the swivel chair, facing the windows, and he searched for something to say. "A battle, a nap, a shower, and it all barely took three hours."

"It does feel like it should be longer, doesn't it?" Farran turned from the window. "You look better."

"Thanks." He sat on the edge of the coffee table so he could face her. "You feel like talking about what happened today?"

She immediately appeared nervous. "What's there to talk about?"

Kel swallowed a sigh. "Well," he said trying not to sound brusque, "we could discuss what kind of power you found and how you managed to use it to bolster mine. There was this other freaky thing that happened, too, one I can't even describe, but somehow seemed to involve you. Maybe we could add that to our list of subjects to cover."

"I don't know if I can explain anything."

Farran twisted her fingers in her lap and Kel reached over and covered her hands with one of his. Her skin was warm, smooth, and distracted him for a few seconds. "We'll take it one thing at a time and you just tell me what you can. Why don't we start with the strange thing?"

"Which strange thing?" Her eyes darted around as she asked.

"I'm guessing you know since you can't meet my gaze."

Now she jerked her head up.

"Too late," he said. "Tell me about it."

The blood leached from her face and he nearly scanned her again, but she took a deep breath and some of the color returned. "The shadow walkers—at least one of them—made time speed up." She said that fast, the entire sentence tumbling together until it sounded like one long word instead of a bunch of disparate ones. Farran spoke slower when she added, "They were trying to run you out of power faster—at least that's what I think their plan was."

Kel thought about that for a moment. "So then they're the ones who phased time when Seth showed up the other day and when you were working at the store. But it all went back to normal pretty quickly, didn't it?" He was sure it had and this was when his sense of her grew stronger. "That's where you're tied into this, right?"

"I couldn't have done it, but I think I did. When you were speeded up, I wasn't. Somehow, I might have been able to make time return into its normal rhythm, but I usually don't have that kind of strength."

He opened his mouth, shut it, and decided not to tackle the time issue right now after all. It was one of those things where he needed to be firing on all cylinders and he wasn't, not until he had at least another full night's sleep. And maybe not even then. The paradoxes and anomalies involved made his head hurt even when he was at 100 percent.

"What about the extra power you acquired?" Kel asked, changing the subject. "I know you told the truth about being magically weak, but you weren't earlier today."

She shrugged. "There were these tiny colored lights floating in the air. They were everywhere, hundreds of thousands of them, and when I closed my hand around one of them, it went inside me."

Immediately, Kel scowled. "You didn't know what it was and you let it enter you?"

"I didn't let it do anything, it did it on its own, but it felt positive, and, um, more of them came."

"You mean you wanted more of them and summoned them."

Another shrug. "Kind of. They were some type of energy and they made me feel strong, but I decided that was an illusion and I wondered if maybe the shadow walkers were planting thoughts or something like that."

Had the shadow walkers caused those lights? He hadn't seen anything, but they could have directed it solely at Farran. The Tàireil and Gineal had been one people once upon a time, but so many centuries had passed since their worlds split onto two separate dimensional paths that they'd developed differences. It was feasible the enemy had found those deviations and how to exploit them. "It's possible, but I don't think so," he said.

"I decided that myself when I was able to use that energy to help you against them. It wasn't a delusion, I did have power."

"A hell of a lot of power." His lips curved. "You should have seen the looks on their faces when that first ball grew enormous. I don't know if you've heard the saying *deer in the headlights,* but that fit perfectly."

Farran smiled faintly. "I didn't really know what I was doing, but I felt like I had to try."

"Good thing you did." Kel released her hands and moved from the coffee table to the love seat, propping his leg up on the cushion so that he could continue to look at her. Farran swiveled with him, making eye contact easier. "You called these energy lights to you, they went inside, and what?"

"That's where things get sketchier." She sounded apologetic. "They made me feel powerful, but I didn't believe it and I would have continued to ignore them except you were in trouble. I pictured them forming a ball and then joining your fireball as you threw it and that's it. I don't know how they combined with your power. I wasn't sure they could and I'm not exactly certain how they managed to add strength to your magic."

"Not they, Farran. You. You added *your* power to my

weapon and increased its strength by about a hundred-fold."

She was shaking her head before he finished. "It couldn't have been me—I don't have enough magic to do that—it was the lights."

"Maybe, but you controlled the lights, and that means it is your power." Kel leaned toward her. "Why does that make you uncomfortable? Yes, it does," he said before she could open her mouth. "I can feel it—I'm empathic, remember? Why does the idea of being strong make you uneasy?"

Farran wrung her hands together again, but this time, Kel didn't stop the motion. If she needed it to relieve stress, he wasn't going to interfere.

"I don't know if I can make this clear either. All my life, I've been magically weak. Always. And that's how I see myself. How others see me."

The choppiness of her sentences said how much this topic put her on edge, and even if he couldn't read her emotions as easily as a billboard, he'd know exactly how she felt. Farran stopped there and Kel asked, "It's having your self-image shaken that bothers you?"

"Some." Now she was tapping her heel against the floor, too.

Her feelings were a tangle and Kel wasn't sure which were connected to talking about this and which ones were tied to the subject they were discussing. He tried to sort through the threads, but when he hit a major snarl, he gave up. "Help me out here and explain it to me. Please."

For a long time, Farran stayed silent, but he didn't prod. Sometimes being patient was the most important trait a troubleshooter—hell, a man—could have.

"If I'm powerful," she said, "then people will develop expectations."

He waited again. There was definitely more. Kel might not know what it was, but it was there, as tangible as if it were a solid object.

She looked down at her hands, then squared her

shoulders and met his gaze again. "What if I let those people down?"

Oh, hell. Kel got to his feet and tugged her out of her chair and into his arms. She got to him. Every damn time he talked to her, she said something or did something or even simply felt something that got behind his walls. He didn't want her there, but he couldn't seem to stop it.

Kel rocked her, trying to wordlessly offer her reassurances. Slowly, Farran slipped her arms around his waist and leaned into him. He knew trust didn't come easy to her, but that's exactly what the gesture meant. She *trusted* him not to hurt her.

Not physically. Not emotionally. Not mentally.

"If you do the best you can," he murmured next to her ear, "that's all anyone can ask. That's all you can ask of yourself."

"But—"

"No buts. I've never seen you not give a full effort. You don't have to be perfect. You don't have to meet someone's idea of who or what you should be. Just do your best. That's it."

Farran buried her face against his neck and Kel pulled her nearer. She needed to be held, she needed to be hugged, and sometimes he ached for her. When he thought about the way she'd grown up, how she'd been treated, it tore him up. Part of it was her emotions, but part of it wasn't. No child—no woman—should have to go through what she'd suffered.

She didn't think it had been that bad because her father had mostly ignored her, but that had taken a toll on her as well whether she realized it or not. The miraculous thing was how she'd turned out. Farran was stronger than she knew, brave even if she didn't believe it, and she honestly cared about others.

It said a lot about what kind of person she was. Farran wasn't merely a survivor, she'd gone beyond that. Far beyond.

He felt her shift slightly and then she kissed his throat.

Kel's breath stuttered. It must have been an accident. She did it again and this time she added a small nip, too.

"No," he said, "we're not doing this. I'm not taking advantage of you while you're upset."

"You want me."

"Hell, yeah. I've been all over you twice already, so it's not a secret." She bit his throat again and Kel inhaled sharply. "You're killing me here. I'm trying to do what's right."

Farran leaned back far enough to look him in the eyes. "If we were already lovers, would you be saying no?"

Kel scowled. If they were already lovers, he'd consider taking her to bed as another way to reassure her and make her feel wanted, needed, cherished. "We're not lovers, so it's a moot point."

"We would have been if you hadn't spotted my tattoo." She ran her fingers over his nape as she spoke.

Swallowing hard, he tried to find his willpower. If he made her self-image issues worse, he'd deserve to have someone kick his ass. The problem was Farran had no one who cared about her enough to be that person, which meant it was up to him to look out for her. Even if his cock was starting to get hard and her body felt so damn good against his. She kissed his chin.

"Farran, please."

"Please what? Please touch you?"

Her hand settled over the zipper of his jeans and Kel groaned. He should step back, he should put the length of the room between them, but he didn't. Instead, he stood there and let her stroke him. "I don't want to hurt you," he said thickly. "I don't want you to feel used."

"I won't." She kissed him slowly and his eyes shut. "Maybe I should worry about you feeling used. After all, I am forcing you. Sort of."

Kel nearly choked when he heard that. He looked at her. Her pupils were dilated, her lips were moist from kissing him, and she appeared determined. His own resolve melted away like April snow.

Bending, he swung her up in his arms and headed for the bedroom. Taking her was wrong, he knew that, but he was too selfish to turn her down. All Kel could do was hope that Farran didn't regret it later—and make sure she enjoyed it as much as he did.

15
CHAPTER

Farran held on to Kel as he carried her to the bedroom. She hadn't expected him to lift her into his arms, but there was something about the gesture that made her throat tight.

He set her back on her feet next to the bed, but Kel didn't release her. Instead, he kept both hands at her waist and gathered her close. Afternoon sun streamed through the windows. The ones at normal height had curtains to screen the light, but the triangle-shaped windows near the roof had nothing and the rays glinted off his dark hair. Farran reached up, brushed it off his forehead, and found her attention captured by the intensity in his vivid blue eyes.

She wouldn't be able to conceal anything from him. Not with all the light in the room and not with the sharpness of his gaze. Instead of frightening her, she felt a tingle. Kel wouldn't be able to hide from her either.

When he simply stared, Farran went up on her toes and brushed her lips over his. He returned her kiss, his hold tightening to help her hold her balance. As she sank back to her heels, Kel followed, keeping his mouth on hers. With a soft sigh, she slid her hands around his neck. This was what she wanted. This was *who* she wanted.

Kel coaxed her mouth open for him, and when she did, his tongue dipped inside, there and gone before she could react. He nibbled at her upper lip, nipping and licking and making her insane with the teasing. "Kel," she complained.

He ignored that and turned to her lower lip. Farran tried to take over and hurry him along, but he wouldn't allow that. By the time he lifted his head, she was gasping.

"I can't wait to get you naked," Kel said, running his index finger over her bottom lip. "I'm going to kiss every inch of you like I meant to the other night, but this time I'll finish the job."

Farran lightly bit his finger. "No, you're not."

"What?"

"You heard me. This time I get to do the kissing and touching. You had your turn, now it's mine."

Kel smiled slowly. "The idea of being in charge gets you hot, doesn't it?"

She blushed. It did, but she couldn't quite admit that.

"That's okay, you don't have to say it. I can feel it." He stepped back, breaking her hold easily even though she tried to keep him close. Before she could protest, he went to the dresser, opened the top drawer, and returned to the bedside. Kel dropped a box of condoms on the nightstand and said, "Okay, sunshine, you're the boss." He held out his arms. "Have at me."

Her gulp was audible and her first step toward him was tentative, but her second was more sure. Farran stopped just in front of him and stared. She wanted to see more of him. Now. "Strip," she told him.

"What? No kissing? No coaxing me out of my clothes?"

"Didn't you say I was the boss? Strip, Kel."

With a grin, one that she'd never seen from him before, he reached for the hem of his sweatshirt and yanked it over his head. Kel let it drop to the floor. He got rid of his shoes and socks next, then slowly he toyed with the button of his jeans. It took him forever to slip it through the fabric. She clenched her hands at her sides as he lowered the zipper one tooth at a time. The man should have been a stripper—he had the teasing part of the job down perfectly.

Finally, after an agonizingly long time, it was down. Kel ran a hand over his abdomen, tormenting her by touching himself so close to where she wanted to put her own hand.

And then he turned his back to her and bent a little to lower the jeans. Her gaze, though, wasn't on his rear end—and that was saying something considering how great it was. No, her eyes were locked on the brand he wore.

Until this minute, it hadn't dawned on her how hard giving up control had to be for Kel. He wouldn't have had any say in his life while he was in captivity and she couldn't imagine he'd ever willingly relinquish that again. But he was. For her. Because it excited her to be able to take the lead while they had sex. And because it made her feel safer.

The kind of courage, the amount of *trust,* it took for him to do this floored her. Absolutely stunned her to the very core of her soul. She didn't realize he had that much faith in her.

As he kicked out of his jeans, Farran took a step forward, and after lightly running a hand over his back, she pressed a kiss between his shoulder blades. He stiffened and she understood why. Kel thought she pitied him. "Nice ass, troubleshooter," she drawled, trying to inject lightness into her voice. "Now let's see it bare."

Kel glanced over his shoulder at her, his dark hair falling into his eyes again, and Farran felt her heart crash. She sucked in a sharp breath and tried to get it to start beating again. After a moment, it did, but it throbbed so hard and fast, she was surprised he didn't hear it.

And then Kel reached for the waistband of his briefs and Farran didn't care what her heart was doing. She was about to see him naked. He teased her with this, too, moving as slowly as a glacier, but at last he had the cotton at his thighs.

She couldn't keep her hand from stroking a cheek as he bent to push his last piece of clothing off. His skin was warm, smooth, and his muscles . . . Something seeped into her consciousness. It took her a second to figure it out, but then she realized she was feeling how much Kel was loving this. Her eyes slid half shut as she squeezed him.

"Does my ass meet with your approval?" Kel asked, but he sounded short of breath.

"Oh, yeah, it's nice and hard."

"You know what the response is to that, don't you? That's not the only part of me that's hard."

"How would I know that when you're facing the other way?" Farran was trying to tease him again, but she was too excited to manage the right tone.

"I didn't know I was supposed to turn yet since your hands are still on my butt."

Oops. She dropped her arms and took a step back. He didn't move. Kel was going to make her say it, damn him. "Turn and face me; I want to see you."

"What do you want to see?" he asked, looking over his shoulder again.

"You."

"You can see me like this. What—specifically—do you want to see?"

"Kellan," she growled.

"Say it."

Her cheeks went fiery hot. She wasn't naïve, she knew what he wanted to hear her say, but she'd never actually spoken that word aloud before. "I want to see your front side."

"Chicken," he taunted, but he turned.

Farran gasped. He was hard and he was beautiful and

he already was damp—physical proof that this was turning him on to go along with the feelings she was picking up. Reluctantly, she raised her eyes, letting her gaze skim over his flat belly and his broad chest and shoulders. When she reached his face, she noticed Kel was smiling again and there was something so predatory about it that her muscles clenched.

She might have control, but it was only because he was allowing it. "Thank you," she whispered.

Going to him, Farran rested her hands on his shoulders to keep her balance, and careful to maintain her distance from his erection, brushed her lips across his in the same gentle kiss he'd given her earlier.

"I want you to enjoy this," Kel said when she stepped away.

"I already am. May I touch you?"

His smile broadened. "Didn't I tell you that you're the boss?"

Hands trembling from both nerves and excitement, Farran put her palms on his chest. She ran them over his pecs, across his stomach and abs, and then skipped to his thighs, crouching to caress him there. Kel groaned and she saw his hands fist at his sides. His legs were as heavily muscled as the rest of his body, and the hair tickled her.

As she shifted to play with his other thigh, Farran realized his erection was right at mouth level. She hesitated, then ran the back of her hand across the underside of his shaft.

He jerked at her touch, and when she licked his moisture from her own skin, Kel reached behind him to grip the edge of the dresser. "You taste good," she said, sounding as short of breath as if she'd been running. "I want more." And she ran a finger over his head, getting it nice and wet before putting it in her mouth.

"Farran." Kel's voice sounded choked, as if he could barely get the words out. "My control is only so good. Remember that."

Was he saying he'd take charge again if she kept teasing him? But when she looked up at his face, she realized that wasn't what he meant. He was warning her that he was close to coming.

Getting to her feet, Farran took a step back and pulled her shirt off. Like him, she let it fall to the floor and reached for the snap of her jeans. She had his full attention as she kicked out of them and her shoes and socks. It wasn't quite as easy for her to reach behind herself and unhook her bra. Even with her arousal running high, it was a scary step. She held it to her chest for a moment, and then, taking a deep breath, let it fall. Kel wheezed and the heat in his eyes went inferno hot.

Her nerves disappeared and she turned her back to him, removing her panties with the same taunting slowness that he'd used with her.

When she faced him again, she noticed a muscle ticking in his jaw. Good.

Farran hesitated, unsure what to do next. There were so many possibilities, each impossibly tantalizing, and she couldn't choose. "Tell me what you want," she said. Kel remained silent. "If you could pick what I did to you next, what would it be?"

His eyes narrowed and he measured her for a long moment before he said, "I want you on your knees in front of me and I want your lips wrapped around my cock."

She couldn't breathe.

"You said you liked the way I taste."

Almost like a somnambulist, she went to him, but instead of going to her knees, Farran wrapped her arms around his waist and went up on her toes to kiss him. His mouth met hers hungrily and there was no more teasing. She felt him pressing insistently into her stomach and her desire boiled over.

Rubbing her breasts against his chest, over his stomach, she knelt in front of him and looked up. Kel was watching her, and licking her lips nervously, Farran wrapped her hand around him and began to lean forward.

Only instead of taking him in her mouth, she rubbed his tip over her nipples.

Kel gasped and the groan that escaped him was long and serrated. She grinned, knowing that half his pleasure came from the surprise. "Look, now I'm damp, too." Farran ran the index finger of her free hand across her breasts, just below her nipples.

"Stop teasing."

Farran thought about drawing it out some more because even though he'd sounded harsh, he was still hanging on to the dresser and allowing her to have the reins, but her arousal was running nearly as high as his. She leaned down and pressed a kiss on his head before licking him.

She ran her lips down one side of his shaft to the base and then went back to take him in her mouth and circled her tongue around his head. Farran kept her gaze locked on him and it thrilled her how Kel would look from her mouth to her eyes and back again.

Humming with pleasure and to arouse him, she sucked gently, and then letting him pop from her lips, licked the underside of his shaft. Farran looked up at him again from down there and tried to imagine what he was seeing.

"I'm close," he rasped.

Good. Slipping one hand between her legs, she took him back in her mouth, using her lips, tongue, and other hand to pleasure him.

"Farran, you don't want me to—"

"Yes, I do." She held him against her lips.

"You haven't come yet."

"You're only good for one round?" She gave him another lick to keep him primed.

He cursed, then laughed briefly. "Hell, no. It's been so damn long since I had sex, I might wear you out if you don't tell me to stop."

"Promises, promises," she said with a smile and then slid her mouth down over him again.

Kel hadn't been lying about how close he was. In no time at all, he jerked in her hand and she helped him ride out his orgasm. When he was done, she rubbed his shaft against her cheek, trying to tell him wordlessly how much he meant to her.

"You swallowed," he said, sounding dazed.

"I told you," she gave his head one last lick and stood. "You taste good." Farran kissed his chin. "Now, you were saying something about wearing me out?"

With a grin, he tugged her against him and said, "Don't say I didn't warn you."

He never fully lost his erection and that made Farran feel as beautiful as he'd told her she was. Yanking back the covers on the bed, she hopped in and patted the mattress beside her.

"You're still in charge, huh?" he asked as he sat beside her.

"You know it. Lie back."

"Yes, ma'am."

Kel tucked his hands behind his head and watched her while he waited. She leaned down and kissed him, half expecting him to pull away when she deepened it, but he didn't. Farran liked that. Moving to his chin, she trailed her mouth up his jaw to his ear. She nibbled his lobe lightly and worked her way down his neck, then to his collarbone. His chest beckoned, but instead she ran her mouth over the inside of his right biceps.

"You know," he said conversationally, "you'd probably enjoy this more if you were ordering me to kiss you."

Farran shook her head. "Your pleasure is mine, too."

He froze and appeared startled. "How empathic are you?"

She went on her knees so she could meet his eyes. "With most people, not very much."

"How about with me?"

"It's been growing since we met."

"No chance I'm letting you off with that evasion." Kel sat up. "Give."

"Whatever I have, it's not pure empathic ability—at least not how I understand it. Humans are fairly easy for me to read, but Tàireil and Gineal aren't, although I do get on the same wavelength with some of them."

"Shona?" Kel asked.

"Not much. I could get a little on occasion."

"And me?"

"Nothing at first, but every day it's become easier to read you." She bit her bottom lip, hoping this didn't end their encounter before it was finished.

"I'm wide open to you all the time now?" He sounded appalled.

"Only when we're intimate, otherwise I mostly get a trickle now and then."

His face remained expressionless long enough to make her nervous and then that wonderful crooked grin of his returned. "Damn, I might have found the perfect woman—one who gets off by getting me off." He tucked his hands back behind his head and laid down again. "Go ahead, pleasure yourself."

"Smart aleck," she muttered. "It works the same way for you and don't think I'm unaware of that. *You* get off by getting me off, too."

"Yep, I do, but I never tried to hide that from you."

Since Kel didn't sound angry, Farran quit talking and went back to exploring. She loved his chest. A little hair, a lot of muscle, and all that gorgeous bare skin for her to kiss. Squeezing her thighs together, she edged down to his navel and ran her tongue around it, dipping inside briefly, and then biting the skin just below it. He loved that.

Before she could head any lower, Kel caught her shoulders and pulled her back up. "No, not this time."

"I'm in charge."

He shook his head and turned, putting her under him. "Not anymore."

"Kel—"

"No, you're getting close, I can feel that, and this time

we're coming when I'm inside you." He slid his thigh between hers and rocked into her.

"Then you better hurry." She swore she could feel him probe her emotions and then he sat up and reached for the box of condoms. His hands shook, making the job take longer than it should, but at last he was sheathed and back between her thighs.

He held himself at her entrance and put his hands at her hips to keep her from surging forward. "Nice and slow," Kel said. "Plug into me and feel how much I love entering you. How good it feels when you close around me. Savor it, sunshine, the same way I'm going to savor how it feels for you."

She did as he said and almost came right then. Not only did she have her arousal, she had his as well. It was so intense, it nearly scared her, but then Kel began to slide inside her and pleasure swamped everything else.

By the time he was all the way in, she was crying. They'd echoed everything between each other so many times, it was like a tsunami of sensation. "Kel, Kel, Kel!"

"I know."

And he did. Farran knew he did and his entire body was shaking as he rode the tidal wave with her. If he didn't make them come soon, she was going to shatter into a million pieces. As if reading her mind, Kel began to thrust. She felt him start to climax around the third or fourth stroke and then the world exploded around her.

When she was aware of her surroundings again, Farran realized Kel was prone on top of her and utterly limp. She ran a hand over his side briefly, but it was too much work and she let it fall back to the mattress.

"Well," Kel said thickly, face against her throat, "that wasn't my best idea. Next time we'll have to make sure we partially shield ourselves. I don't think either one of us can survive another orgasm like that one."

He pushed himself up and dropped to her side before wrapping his arms around her. Farran snuggled into

Kel's chest, enjoying the peace that seemed to surround her. If only this serenity, this contentment, could last forever.

Kel sat bolt upright, his heart thundering in his chest. He gasped, straining to take in air. Struggling to figure out where he was. It took him a minute to recognize the bedroom of the cabin. Safe. He was safe.

"Are you okay?" Farran asked softly beside him.

Oh, hell, she'd seen him in the throes. Again. "I thought I told you to get the hell away from me if I had a nightmare. Damn it, what if I'd hurt you while I was thrashing?"

"You didn't thrash. I didn't even know you were having a nightmare until you sat up."

The mildness of her tone underscored how harsh he'd sounded and Kel fought to get control. "Okay, sorry. I was worried, that's all. I don't want to hurt you, not in any way."

"You didn't. You didn't." She touched him for the first time, running her palm down his biceps. He wondered if Farran had known he couldn't handle contact until this moment. Until he'd had a chance to calm down a little.

When he'd fallen asleep, there had still been plenty of daylight streaming through the windows, but it was late enough now to be full dark. At some point, though, while he'd been out, Farran had turned on the lights— everything that could produce illumination was glowing brightly—and it meant the world to him that she'd remembered, that she'd taken care of him. "Thanks," Kel said thickly, ridiculously touched by the gesture. "For the lights," he added when she looked confused.

He leaned forward and her hand moved from his arm to his back. At first, he tensed, but she was on his right side and wasn't touching the brand. Kel didn't want her to feel that ugly, scarred tissue, and he wished she couldn't see it.

His mark of shame.

"Do you want to talk about it?" she asked quietly.

Kel drew in a shuddery breath. Of course he didn't want to talk about it, but somehow he heard himself saying, "You know what made me afraid of the dark? They kept me in a cell with earthen walls and absolutely no light. I sat in there for weeks, hour after hour, day after day, and the only break I had was when they brought me to their altar to torture me."

His hands had clenched into fists, but he couldn't make them relax. Why the fuck was he telling her this?

"It was small. There wasn't room for me to lie down. Four feet by four feet. I paced it off my first day. Sometimes they tortured me right there. I've always hated spiders from the time I was a kid, and they filled my cell with the damn things. Thousands of them. God, I couldn't get them off me—they were everywhere. Everywhere, Farran."

She wrapped her arms around him, but Kel leaned away, breaking her hold. "I can't," he said, "not now, okay?"

"Okay. It's okay."

And he kept going, not looking at her, just staring at the pine wall of the bedroom. "Once, they put a spell on me that prevented me from hearing anything and left me in my cell." His voice was hoarse and Kel cleared his throat. "Pitch black and completely silent. I don't like the quiet either, did I tell you that? I always have music playing or the television on, something to make noise."

"There's no TV or radio here."

"No shit." He smiled to ease any sting from his words. "At least when you're awake, we talk, and while I don't like silence, it isn't a phobia for me. They only did that part for a few days—I think. The dark was nearly constant."

She reached for him and started caressing him again. Kel drew in a deep breath. He'd told her too much—way too much—but at least he hadn't shared the worst part.

That secret was still safe. And then he nearly groaned—he hadn't blocked his emotions. Had she been able to read him? He hoped not. God, he hoped not.

"They loved what they did to you, didn't they?" she asked.

"Yeah, I could feel that. I think they knew I was empathic and I think that's why they targeted me."

"More fun for them knowing you'd feel their pleasure." She sounded disgusted, but he didn't look. "You said you killed them; how'd you manage that without magic?"

Kel drew another breath and wiped his hand over his chin. "They forgot to drain my power. I don't know if they each thought the other had taken care of it or if they simply got careless, but one morning my magic was back. I could have left the dimension and gone home, but I didn't."

He tried to keep his muscles from tensing, but wasn't successful. She needed to know this next part whether it was easy for him to talk about or not.

"I'd like to tell you that I hid my power and let them drag me to the altar before I killed them to protect other Gineal, but that would be a lie. I did it because I wanted revenge. I wanted them to fucking pay for what they'd done to me. My only regret is that I couldn't torture them first before I offed them."

"Why didn't—? Because you'd feel their pain at being tortured," Farran said, answering her own question. "It was hard enough for you to simply kill them."

"Yeah. Being empathic is a bitch sometimes."

"How do you work as a troubleshooter if you're sensitive?"

Kel sighed. "It isn't easy."

Farran pressed a kiss on his shoulder and he finally turned his head and looked at her. The blankets had fallen to her waist, exposing her bare breasts, and her hair was mussed. His body heated as he remembered how it had gotten that way. They'd spent all afternoon in bed, had taken a break for the last of the leftover pizza, and had headed back in here for more. It had definitely been better when they'd kept a partial barrier in place to limit the empathy between them.

One side of his lips quirked up. "Guess you're the one who wore me out."

"I feel oddly smug about that." She grinned at him, following his line of thought easily.

"Are you sore?" She shook her head. "How about a rematch then? This time I think I can outlast you."

"Ha!" Farran gave her hair a little toss and it made her breasts move. "I'm four years younger than you are, that gives me the edge, but you're welcome to try."

Kel threw back the covers and dove for her. "Never," he said against her lips, "challenge a troubleshooter."

"Your egos can't take it?"

He laughed. "Incorrigible," he muttered, but he liked that. She'd made him smile and laugh more in the four days since he'd met her than he had in the previous thirteen months and Kel immersed himself in her teasing, letting her sweetness fill him and blot out his past.

Her lips were soft against his and Kel was growing addicted to her taste. His hand went to the curve of her waist, holding her against him. Damn, he loved touching her.

Taking her hand, he kissed each finger, sucking first one and then another into his mouth and swirling his tongue around it. Kel moved up her forearm to her elbow, licked the bend, and nibbled to her shoulder. Farran's low-grade pleasure reverberated through him.

A nice, slow build, that would be good, he decided. Kel cupped her breast in his hand and ran his thumb over her nipple before bending to take it in his mouth. She liked that—he not only felt it, but she pressed into him, showing him how much. He switched to her other breast, teasing it the same as the first, and licked his way to her belly button.

Kel nipped the skin of her abdomen because she'd enjoyed doing that to him and felt her pleasure spike.

He stored that away for future reference, but he had another goal in mind.

He kissed her inner thigh, then propping her leg up on his shoulder, bent to her. Using his fingers, he opened her and blew out a short puff of air, hitting the center of her pleasure. Kel ran his tongue through her folds, slowly. Carefully. She arched into him, trying to make him hurry, but he refused to be rushed.

Her impatience was part of his problem. Farran's eagerness got him hot enough that he lost his self-command. Not this time. This time he was savoring her.

Sweet. And wet. Damn, he loved how she responded to him. Kel dipped inside, licking in a circle until her hands clenched in his hair, urging him upward. He could take a hint. Drawing her into his mouth, he sucked gently.

That wasn't enough for her and she tightened her hold. He flicked her, loving the way she gasped and pressed upward to meet him. Kel let her feel how much he enjoyed doing this and Farran echoed back her own pleasure, but before long, it became too intense, and regretfully, he put a screen over his empathy. He didn't stop until she was about to come.

Farran moaned a protest when he pulled away, but he'd deliberately left her on the brink, so he ignored it and sat up. He drank in the sight of her flushed and languid. Beautiful. He'd never seen anyone more beautiful.

"Finally," he said, voice foggy, "I get to explore your back. Turn over."

She hesitated, but rolled onto her stomach. Kel started low, nibbling at her calf, teasing the back of her knees with his tongue, stroking her thighs. And then he reached her rear.

He ran his finger over her tattoo, caressing it. For a long moment, he stared at it, letting the turmoil he felt subside, and then Kel leaned forward and pressed his lips to the center of the symbol, showing her that he accepted this part of her just like everything else.

"Kellan." His name was almost a sigh.

Her emotions were making him feel overwhelmed. He eased back and swooped down to bite one of her cheeks. "Damn, I've been wanting to do that for days." He squeezed the other cheek. "You have got a gorgeous ass."

Kel kissed the small of her back and placed his lips against her shoulder before he murmured next to her ear, "You know what I want to do?"

"What?"

Instead of answering, he rubbed his hard-on up and down the crease of her bottom. He knew when she understood.

"Really?"

"Yeah."

"It'll hurt."

"I promise, it won't. You'll love it."

Farran didn't seem real sure about that. "Now?"

He sighed. As much as he wanted to, there was no way. They needed a lot of time and a few things that he didn't have here. "No, we can't, not while there's a threat. I was thinking of when this was over. We could lock ourselves in my bedroom and spend about a week going at each other."

"A week, huh? You haven't even managed a day yet."

Kel kissed her shoulder again, this time in retribution for her teasing. Keeping his weight off her, he continued to run his erection against Farran's body. "So do we have a date?"

"If I don't like it and I ask you to stop, will you?"

"Yes." There was no question about that, but if she agreed, Kel planned to make damn sure she enjoyed it. He was already halfway there because simply talking about it had gotten her more aroused than she'd been a few minutes earlier.

"Okay, if I have your word, I'm willing to try."

Leaning down, he kissed the corner of her mouth. "Thanks." He moved to her side and reached for the rubbers. Discussing it had aroused him, too, and he was ready to move beyond foreplay.

Farran didn't turn over, just watched him roll on the condom. "New position?" he asked.

"Hmm."

He took that as a yes. "Why don't you get up on your hands and knees and we can shift around from there."

When he was settled behind her, Kel slid a hand between her thighs to make certain she was as aroused as he believed. She was and he slowly entered her, letting Farran's slickness draw him deeper. She whimpered when he filled her.

"Screen out some of my emotions," he told her, "or the intensity is going to be as off the charts as it was the first time."

Kel waited until she'd done it and then he thrust. She used her inner muscles to squeeze him and he just about lost it right then. She wanted to play dirty? He could do that. Wrapping his arm around her waist, he found where she was most sensitive and circled his finger there.

"Unfair," she moaned.

"Who started it?"

"You liked it."

"And you like this," he countered.

She attempted to hold off; he could feel her trying to wait. For some reason, Farran wanted him to come first and trigger her orgasm, but this time, she was going over the edge before him. He was damn well making sure of that.

He deliberately sent her impressions—not emotions, physical sensations. Farran tried to counter, but he had a lot more practice at blocking than she did. Kel sat back on his heels, taking her with him and thrust up hard. He sensed her orgasm rumbling through her before he felt it.

Relaxing his control, he let himself follow her.

His ears were still buzzing from the intensity when she complained, "You cheated."

"You know what they say, all's fair."

"You know what else they say?"

"What's that?" he asked, trying to get his breathing back to a normal rate.

"Payback's a bitch."

Kel grinned and hugged her tighter. Damn, Farran might really be his fantasy woman come to life.

16

CHAPTER

Farran smelled coffee as soon as she stepped from the bathroom, and since she knew she'd find Kel in the vicinity of the pot, she headed for the kitchen. She felt deliciously wicked to be wearing nothing except a man's half-buttoned white Oxford shirt, but it was knowing that she was walking toward her lover that made her nipples peak.

Her good feelings weren't only physical. Kel wanted to spend time with her after this was over. It was the last thing Farran had expected. She'd thought that when the situation was resolved, that would be it for them, but they had an official date to lock themselves in his bedroom and experiment.

She slowed as she rounded the corner, hit both by the sight of Kel wearing only a pair of unsnapped, faded blue jeans and by the heat she felt spike off him when he saw her. He put his mug down and stepped forward to meet her partway.

Kel's hands slid under the Oxford to cup her bare bottom and he kissed her slow and long. His lips curved as he lifted his head and gazed down at her. "You know," he said, voice raspy, "I'm not sure what gets me hotter—seeing you wearing my shirt or discovering that you're wearing *nothing* but my shirt."

"I'm glad this is yours. There are so many clothes here that I couldn't be certain." Farran ran her hands over the warm skin of his back, loving the freedom she had to touch him. "Good morning, by the way."

"Morning, sunshine." Kel took her mouth again and this time his hands were busy. "I should have shaved again," he said between kisses. "I'm going to mark you."

"I'll survive," she said, the last syllable coming out as a gasp. He'd hooked her leg around his hip and she could feel him pressing into her. Hanging on to him tightly with one arm, she worked her free hand between their bodies and slipped her fingers behind his zipper. She was able to graze him. "You've gone commando this morning, too."

"Gotta give you some fun, don't I?"

He worked on opening another of her buttons as he bit and licked the pulse point in her throat. Farran closed her eyes and dropped her head back to allow him full access. Kel could do magic with his mouth.

"This is how you stay on guard?"

The voice had her and Kel jerking apart.

"You told me," Tris said from the living room, "that the shadow walkers could bypass our security. It's pretty stupid to lose yourself so completely that I could enter without you having a clue I was here."

Farran yanked her shirt back into place and grabbed the placket near her breasts. Kel had been busier than she'd realized and it was embarrassing to be caught like this by his sister. She tried to unobtrusively redo the buttons.

"Anyone ever tell you it's rude to drop in without advance notice?" Kel asked, scowling fiercely at Tris.

"If you'd answer your damn cell phone, you would have had some warning. Hell, if you'd answer your damn phone, I wouldn't even be here."

"My cell's at home."

Tris headed for the kitchen and Farran sidled behind Kel, trying to use his body as a shield as she buttoned faster.

"You're supposed to have that with you all the time," his sister said.

"Wrong. I got pulled from active duty, remember? I don't have to be tethered to the council anymore." Kel put his hands on his hips. "Would you stand still? You're making Farran edgy."

"Sorry, Farran," Tris apologized, looking past Kel at her. "I didn't mean to embarrass you."

"So if that isn't your aim, why are you here?" he asked.

"I've got news you need to hear. Why don't you two get dressed while I make breakfast? I brought groceries with me." She pointed over her shoulder with her thumb. "I'll fill you in when we eat."

Kel simply stood there and Farran put two fingers in his back and nudged him. "Move," she whispered. "I want more clothes on and you're my screen."

"Got it."

And as easily as that, Kel did what she needed him to do—walk with her and keep his body between her and his sister. Her clothes were in the second bedroom—not that it mattered, since their splitting off and going their separate directions wouldn't fool Tris after what she'd seen, but it made Farran feel slightly less mortified.

"I'm going to take a fast shower," Kel told her quietly when they reached her door. "If you don't feel comfortable alone with Tris, dawdle in here. I'll move as quickly as I can."

"I'll be okay," she assured him.

He nodded, and with a brush of his lips against hers, headed for the other bedroom. She closed the door behind her and was glad she'd showered before finding Kel. That was one less thing to worry about.

Farran dumped her new clothes out of the bags, and after yanking at tags, got dressed. Her shoes were in Kel's room—their room—but she had socks and that was good enough for walking around the cabin. Once she had on her jeans and a brown and beige striped Henley shirt, she felt better.

The shower was still running—she could hear it through the bedroom wall—but Farran didn't feel a need to wait for Kel. Taking a deep breath, she opened the door and returned to the kitchen.

When Farran entered, Tris looked up from the mixing bowl she had on the counter in front of her. "Hey," she said, "I really am sorry about embarrassing you like that. I never expected to interrupt anything."

Not sure what to say to that, Farran made a humming sound, more of an acknowledgment than a comment.

"I hope you like waffles," Tris said, and this time she injected a note of perkiness into her voice. "Real waffles, not the toaster crap that my brother, the anti-Emeril, makes."

Farran laughed, she couldn't help it. "Kel tries."

"He's got you snowed," Tris said with a snort. "He does know how to cook—Mom made sure all of us, even Kel and Logan, can handle basic meals. He's not particularly talented at it, but he can follow a recipe and produce edible food when he wants to. It's just easier for him to nuke something."

"He hasn't had much choice. We've had limited supplies."

His sister grinned. "I brought two bags of real food, so someone is going to have to cook if you guys want to eat after I leave. Make Kel do it. It's good for him."

"We'll probably take turns or something." Farran said, not mentioning that Kel had already cooked for her.

"Ah, man, you're no fun," Tris said jokingly. "But that's okay," she added, face going serious. "Kel's more like his usual self than he's been in a year. For that alone, I like you—despite the fact that you're too easy on him."

"He's had a difficult time." That was an understatement.

"I know—we all know—but he won't let anyone help

him and he won't tell anyone what happened. Not even Logan." Tris hooked her thumbs through the belt loops of her jeans. "Do you know how close those two are? Or I guess it would be more accurate to say how close they once were?"

"Kel's told me."

Tris nodded. "It used to be the bane of my existence, trying to gain admission to their fraternity. Years went by before I understood they had a bond I could never be part of, no matter how hard I tried."

There was something in her tone that tipped Farran off. "Kel respects you, you know. A lot."

With a shrug, Kel's sister reached for the whisk and stirred the batter some more. Farran knew Tris didn't believe her and that there was nothing she could say to change that.

"And he loves you, too."

"I know." Tris gave the batter one last stir before she rinsed the whisk off and laid it in the drainer. "Has Kel told you anything about what happened to him?"

She didn't know what to say to that. There was no way she'd break Kel's trust and tell Tris anything, but if she said that, then the questions would begin. Still, she didn't want to lie. Farran breathed a sigh of relief when she heard a door open. A minute later Kel was there and she smiled at him.

Tris leaned over, plugged in the waffle iron, and said, "Kel, get the toppings out and set the table."

"I can set the table," Farran said and opened the cabinet with the plates.

"Way too easy on him," Tris moaned.

"Stop being such a brat." Kel tugged the ends of his sister's hair as he walked by. "You're going to scare Farran."

"If you haven't frightened her already, no one can." Tris poured batter on the iron. "Everyone knows that you're the evil twin."

"Yep, evil," Kel said and a note in his voice made

Farran stop putting out silverware and look at him closely. He winked at her as he deposited syrup, butter, and jam on the table, but she wasn't fooled. Something was going on beneath the surface.

They were sitting at the table, her and Kel with their backs to the windows and Tris across from them when he asked, "What's the news you have that's so important you had to rush over here?"

"I didn't—" Tris swallowed, took a sip of juice, and with her voice raised said, "I didn't rush right over here. I've been trying to get a hold of you since late last night. How was I supposed to know you'd abandoned your phone?"

"No need to get all worked up over a figure of speech."

His blandness made his sister's face go red. "You called me a brat? You're the brat! And—"

Kel smiled his crooked grin, and with a chuckle, he used the side of his fork to cut off a piece of waffle.

"You laughed." Tris sounded amazed and that told Farran that she wasn't the only one with whom he'd been overly sober.

"Yeah, so?"

"Nothing. I liked hearing it again." Tris's eyes looked misty, but then she glanced down and moved her food around with her fork for a minute or two, and when she lifted her gaze again, the hint of tears was gone. "The council knows there was a battle near the library yesterday. They're trying to find out who was involved and what exactly happened. Word right now is that they're in the dark, but we both know they've got retrocogs on this full time."

"Yeah, shit."

"It gets worse. There was a backpack found near the site of the fight. They have that in their possession, too."

"Can they figure out it was us from your pack?" Farran asked, putting down her fork.

"Yes, but not easily," Kel said.

"Unless Kel wrote his name in it," Tris said, "the

council will have to give it to a monitor to record the energy signature associated with it. Once they have that—and this can be a painstaking process—another monitor with a different set of skills will be called in to track who matches that sig."

"It won't be simple," Kel said, helping himself to a second waffle off the serving plate. "Logan's used that pack almost as many times as I have so the energy should be chaotic."

"Eventually, though, they'll unwind that," Tris told him.

"I know, but I'm betting it takes weeks before that's complete. I'm not worried about it."

"What are you worried about then?" Farran asked.

"The retrocognitive monitors." He looked up from his plate and met her gaze. "They'll be able to replay the battle we had with the shadow walkers—it's only a matter of time."

"And then?"

Kel shrugged, but stayed quiet. It was Tris who replied.

"Kel will be summoned before the council and get chewed out. Definitely for not bringing you to them immediately, but also for not alerting them to the presence of the shadow walkers or Seth. Maybe even for performing troubleshooter duties while he's been suspended, although they might not be too angry about that since Kel was yanked because they were concerned about him, not because he screwed up or got in trouble."

"They'll punish you?" Farran reached beside her and put a hand on Kel's knee.

"Maybe, but it won't be too severe, despite what the doom monster here implied. Probably no more than a slap on the wrist and a lecture about what a troubleshooter's responsibilities are. I'm more worried about how this is going to effect you." He reached under the table and took her hand in his.

"What will they do to me?" Farran linked her fingers

with Kel's. Would they send her back to the Tàireil world? Would they imprison her? Would they question her? Would—

"They'll probably keep you under lock and key until they figure out what the shadow walkers want with you," Tris said.

"That's not going to happen," Kel told her.

"Well, they could assign another troubleshooter to watch over her." Tris put down her fork and pushed her plate aside. "That's a long shot, though, especially once they learn the shadow walkers can break through our protective shields. It's really much more likely that they'll keep her in the most secure location possible, one surrounded by and teeming with enforcers. That means headquarters."

"The council isn't taking Farran."

"How are you going to stop them? You can't fight the ceannards," Tris said with exaggerated patience.

"The hell I can't."

Tris went pale. "Kel, you're not thinking clearly. They can strip you of your magic if they decide the offense is serious enough, and going to battle against the council is treason."

"Then we both better hope that they don't figure out what happened at the tasglann yesterday because no matter what it takes I'm not giving them Farran."

Their room in the library was as quiet as it always was, but Farran couldn't concentrate. After nearly an hour, she was still trying to make it through her first book, but she had to keep reading and rereading. She didn't think Kel could focus either, not when he hadn't turned the page in at least fifteen minutes.

When she couldn't make sense of the paragraph after going over it for a third time, Farran knew she and Kel needed to talk. She pushed the text away from her, but instead of starting with what she really wanted to discuss, she went with a secondary topic instead. "What was up with Tris calling you the evil twin?"

Kel looked at her. "It's supposed to be a joke—you know, Logan's the good twin and I'm the evil one."

"You don't think it's funny."

"Not when anyone except my brother uses it."

Farran turned that over in her head, but didn't come up with a reason. "What's the difference who says it?"

He sat back in his chair and said, "Because when it comes from Logan, it's ironic. He thinks he's the evil twin and I'm the good one, and that the rest of the world has it wrong. When anyone else tosses it out there, they really believe that Logan's the good twin and I'm tired of hearing it."

"As incredibly kind as you are, how can anyone think you're the bad twin?"

Kel snorted. "Have you ever talked to Logan or seen him when he wasn't in warrior mode?"

She shook her head.

"In day-to-day life, he's friendly, outgoing, and when it comes to women—especially our sisters—indulgent. They all go to him when they have a problem, not me. Two of them have never seen him in battle, and while Tris did fight with us once, we were too busy for her to realize what a badass Logan is."

"And you're not indulgent with them? Come on, Kel."

"They don't see it that way. I'm the one who pushes them to be more independent, to handle their own problems, but I want them to be able to take care of themselves no matter what they're faced with."

"And Logan fixes everything for them?" Farran couldn't see it. Granted, she'd only spoken to him once while he was protecting Shona, but she was a good judge of character.

He blew out a long breath. "No, that's more irony for you. Logan makes them handle their own problems, too, but he does it differently than I do. Maybe less obviously.

I don't know. What I do know is that even though I'm the oldest, I'm not the one they seek out when they need a big brother."

Farran felt his hurt and she got out of her chair. Kneeling beside him, she ran her palm over Kel's cheek, and said, "If they're not perceptive enough to know how sweet and gentle you are, that's their loss." He opened his mouth, probably to argue with her, and she kissed him to shut him up. "No, I'm right. I, however, am not that dim—I know how fortunate I am to have you on my side. And to have you as my friend."

This time he kissed her and she leaned into him, savoring his touch. How could anyone miss how sensitive he was? He felt things so damn deeply and he loved with his whole heart. His family meant everything to him and he'd bend over backward for them or walk into hell to protect them. God knew her own brothers hadn't cared what happened to her, and not once in her entire life had Farran ever met another man like Kel.

He eased back, his lips clinging to hers. "Go sit down," Kel told her, "before we get into trouble."

"What?" Farran rubbed her nose against the side of his. "No fantasy about doing it in the library?"

"No condoms. I didn't think we'd need them here."

She kissed his chin. "Maybe you can bring them tomorrow."

His eyes went hot. "Maybe I'll be carrying a few with me everywhere we go from now on."

"Sounds like a good idea to me." And with one last stroke of her hand over his jaw, Farran retreated to her seat across the table. She gave them both a few minutes before she spoke again. "Can we talk—seriously?"

"Sure, what?"

"I don't want you to get in trouble with your council for me."

Kel's body stiffened. "I'm not turning you over to them. That's decided."

"Think about it. You against every troubleshooter in

the world, even your own brother and sister. You can't win with those odds and all you'll do is hurt yourself."

He closed his book, put it aside, and sighed. "You know, Logan and I really do call Tris the doom monster. She can start playing a what-if game and end up thinking Santa Claus is a subversive trying to undermine democracy. You can't let yourself get caught up in her pessimistic imagination."

"If you battle the council—"

"I don't plan to do that. I can keep you away from them without taking on nine former troubleshooters who can probably kick my ass without leaving their conference table."

Realization dawned and Farran gasped. "You were egging Tris on!"

Kel grinned. "It's good for her. She's got to learn to be less emotional and more logical."

"She went right for emotion because she loves you."

He sobered. "I know that, but think about it. I've been a troubleshooter for ten years, I've survived one hell of a lot, and I didn't do it by reacting rashly. She's done the job for six years herself, so she's aware of what it takes. Why would she automatically assume that I'd do something stupid?"

It took a minute for Farran to find the answer. "Because of what you went through."

"Exactly, but I didn't lose any IQ points while I was held captive and she needs to figure that out."

Reaching across the table, Farran put her hand over Kel's. "If you're not going to fight, how do you keep me from being held by the council?"

Kel linked their fingers. "Here's how I see things. The council has to learn what happened yesterday before they take any action and you said the shadow walkers sped up time. I'm betting that messes up the monitors and that it'll take them awhile to sort out what happened."

"Time shifts aren't something we see in our worlds."

"Right. And even once the monitors figure it out and

tell the council, the ceannards are going to contact me before they do anything else. I don't have my cell with me and they know I have a reputation for ignoring all telepathic communication."

He brushed his thumb across her palm and it took Farran a moment to recover. "Won't they just send someone to find you?"

"That'll be the next step, but that gives us a good three to four days depending on how long it takes the monitors to cut through the time shift. And when they do reach that point, I think the odds are pretty good that the ceannards will choose to send Logan after us."

"Treating you with kid gloves?"

"Yep. I was pulled from duty because of my emotional state and they're going to attribute what they consider my bad judgment to that." Kel grimaced and then shrugged. "They'll probably tell Logan to find out what's going on and to convince us to travel to Gineal headquarters, but I don't think they're going to order him to bring us in forcibly."

"Which buys more time," Farran said.

"And an ally. Logan will help any way we need him to. It should be about a week between now and when the council gets pissed enough to send in the big guns. That gives us long enough to learn what we need to about the shadow walkers."

"Even if we defeat the shadow walkers," she said quietly, "the council is still going to want me brought in."

Kel stood, tugged her to her feet, and into his arms. Returning his embrace was automatic. "I promise you, Farran, without a threat against you, the council isn't going to hold you prisoner. All they want to do is talk to you and find out what your thoughts and motives are for staying here."

"They could choose to send me home."

"The ceannards know you went against your father to protect Shona and they know the Tàireil world. They're not going to return you when they understand it's a death sentence."

"But—"

He brushed a kiss over her lips to quiet her. "Trust me. I'm going to be right beside you the entire time you're with them and I won't let anything bad happen to you. You have my word."

Farran nodded, but opted not to argue. She didn't think Kel would be able to stop them. He'd said himself that the nine council members could kick his butt without moving from their table. That left him in trouble and her at the mercy of a furious Gineal tribunal. Maybe they'd even blame her, thinking she'd taken advantage of Kel to incite his insurrection.

"Have some faith," he said, smoothing her hair back.

"I was blocking you!"

"You were trying to block me," Kel corrected.

And she'd hurt him. Leaning into him, she said, "I do have faith in you. Lots of it. It's your council I don't trust." She opened herself almost completely, letting him feel just how much she believed in him.

His pain faded and he held her tighter. "Fair enough since you've never met them, but they're days off in the future. In the meantime, we have more pressing problems."

"Seth and the shadow walkers."

"And the fact that I have to open the transit farther away from the library now."

"I wondered about that."

Kel kissed her forehead and settled back in his chair. "The kids guarding the tasglann would have been instructed to be more vigilant because of the battle yesterday, and since this is probably the most exciting thing to happen at the library in the last two years, you can bet they're wound up."

Farran slowly returned to her side of the table and sat down. They were most vulnerable entering and exiting from this building. "Do we have to keep coming here?"

"Not if we can find out how to fight and defeat the shadow walkers today."

With a nod, she grabbed her book and opened it again. Enough talking, it was time to study and now she had her focus back. The last thing Farran wanted was for Kel to get hurt. It was still more than an hour, though, before she found something new. "Kel, it says here that the shadow walkers were imprisoned in the fourth dimension."

He looked up, a thoughtful frown on his face. "In physics, the fourth dimension is time."

"Kind of fits, huh?"

"Yeah, kind of, although physicists view dimensions differently than— Never mind. See what else that book has to say."

She went back to her text. "Okay, here's more. They can speed up and slow down time, but can't or don't time travel. The word is smudged and I can't make it out."

"Slide it over and let me see," Kel said. Farran did and pointed out the spot in question. After scowling at it for a while, he said, "It is illegible and that word alters the meaning drastically. Can't is a lot different from don't."

"Maybe one of the other books will verify this one."

"I want corroboration on this anyway. It's too big to trust a single source."

"Especially when time reversed around me twice."

Kel nodded and returned her book before bending to work at his own. She read through the rest of the volume without discovering anything else and went on to the next. And the next. And the next.

"They don't draw their power from the planet or the universe like we do, but from an alternate source," Kel said a long time later. "One that can't be blocked."

"Can't be blocked or that the Gineal who wrote the book didn't know how to block?"

"Could be either."

"This is a pain," Farran said. "We're taking so long to find so little and everything is information told from someone's point of view rather than something we know is completely factual."

"That's why we need corroboration."

He went back to his book and with a sigh, Farran did the same. She wanted to find a volume titled *The Complete Guide to the Shadow Walkers and Their World* and she wanted Kel to learn everything he needed to know so they could stay away from here. They were vulnerable at the cabin, she understood that, but the enemy hadn't found them there yet. They had found the library and had attacked here more than once.

"The shadow walkers are cursed to be the guardians," she told him later on.

"Guardians of what?"

"It doesn't say."

Kel must have felt how frustrated she was because this time he was the one who went on his knees beside her chair. "Come on, sunshine, hang tough for me." He took her hands in his. "We knew this wasn't going to be easy."

Farran leaned her forehead to his. "I didn't know it would be this agonizingly slow either. I thought that once your sister undid the energy thing that we'd plow through this stuff."

"It's because there's been so few encounters."

"I know, but Kel, I want you safe and I want me safe, too."

"Definitely should have brought the condoms." He kissed her and straightened away from her.

"What?" She didn't get his train of thought at all.

He stretched and leaned his hip against the table beside her. "Think about it. You're feeling kind of hopeless right now and what gets endorphins flowing better than sex?"

"Considering my mood today, we'd be going through condoms a lot faster than books."

Kel grinned. "I don't have a problem with that."

"I do."

His smile faded, and before she could guess what he

was going to do, Kel probed her emotions. She frowned, but it was far too late to block him.

"I get it now," he said. Kel held out a hand, not saying another word until she put hers in it. "Here's the thing, I'm a troubleshooter. I'm used to facing danger—it goes with the job description—but you're smart enough to know that simply living is a risk."

"Not like this. The shad—"

"When I was captured," he interrupted, "I wasn't on a mission, and as far as I knew, there was no threat. It was an ordinary day with nothing much going on. Just being in the wrong place at the wrong time and having someone decide that you'd make a good victim is a risk."

"I know, but—"

"We all take our chances every fucking day. The only difference is that you know we're vulnerable around the library. That doesn't mean we're not vulnerable at the cabin or inside the tasglann or even in downtown Chicago. I appreciate that you're worried about me, but don't be. I survived the worst thing I'll ever face in my life. This doesn't even come close."

She tightened her hold on his hand. "I just—"

"I know. I know, but now I have you to help boost my power. Together we can kick shadow-walker ass." He tried to smile, but it didn't quite make it. "Come on, let's leave, have some dinner, and make that bed rock. Not necessarily in that order," Kel added with a wink.

Farran let him assist her to her feet, but they both knew whether or not she could help him a second time was a crapshoot. She didn't know exactly what she'd done and wasn't totally sure she could repeat it.

"It's early yet," she said. "Maybe we should stay a little longer and see what else we can learn."

"I want to vary our routine as much as we can and it's not that early, maybe forty-five minutes ahead of schedule."

"If we stayed later—"

"We'd be leaving in the dark."

And Farran had her answer. Kel couldn't handle the dark and she wouldn't force him to do so because of her fear. She could. She knew if she pushed him, he'd agree to stay to soothe her nerves. But she wouldn't be a coward, not when he needed her to be strong. "Are we taking books home?"

He shook his head. "I don't want either of us impeded."

She waited while he returned all the texts and then followed him through the library to the door. Her heart was already pounding hard and fast, but she breathed deeply and tried to keep her senses clear. They were leaving through a different exit than they'd used to enter, an exit they hadn't used on any other day. What were the odds someone was waiting out there for them? Even supernatural beings with powers beyond what the Gineal or Tàireil thought of as normal?

Kel wasn't careless. He had strong protection around them both before he opened the door. Farran tensed, but nothing happened.

Her nerves pulled tighter as they put more distance between themselves and the building, and when they rounded the bend and entered a small wooded area, she had her heart in her throat. This was a perfect location for an assault.

It stayed quiet.

As they cleared the trees, she breathed a sigh of relief. And that was when the attack came.

A fireball as big as a Frisbee hit Kel's shield.

He was shooting back before the glow faded.

The truly ridiculous thing was that she was glad to see the demon. Kel said he could handle him. That meant she didn't have to try to replicate the power-boost thing—probably.

Seth shifted and Kel moved with him. She didn't understand shooting angles, but they were both maneuvering for them.

Kel thrust aside one of the demon's shots and it

exploded as it hit the ground, sending earth shooting everywhere. Farran backed up and turned her face away from the spray.

An arm went around her waist at the same time a hand covered her mouth. She tried to scream anyway, but it couldn't be heard over the sounds of the battle. Farran twisted and writhed, but the grip was too tight. Whoever it was, he was taking her away from Kel and she fought harder.

Farran saw the little flecks of light surrounding her and she knew for certain who it was. She'd been captured by the shadow walkers.

17
CHAPTER

Farran nearly sent out a silent plea for Kel. He'd pick up her call even if he did block out everything when he was in battle, but it might distract him and she didn't want to do anything that got him hurt. Or killed.

She fought harder.

Kel believed she was tough. She wasn't, but for him, she would be. She had to be because if something happened to her, he'd spend the rest of his life blaming himself.

"Be still," a male voice ordered near her ear.

Right. Be a good little girl and obey the command of someone who was trying to kill her. Like hell. If it took every ounce of energy she had, she wasn't giving up. She couldn't. Farran wasn't only fighting for herself, she was fighting for Kel, too.

There were more sparks of light around her and Farran tried to draw them in. The man's arms tightened around her and he muttered in his language. It took a minute before she realized it was a spell and she tried to pull the energy in faster.

She wasn't in time.

Not only did he obstruct the flow of the lights, he also

locked her major muscles. Farran couldn't move her arms or legs, and when she tried to mentally reach for Kel, she discovered he'd jammed her there, as well. Her scream was barely above a squeak. The bastard had shut down every avenue she could think of trying.

There had to be a way out of this. There had to be—cause Kel carried too big a burden already.

The shadow walker released her and Farran feared she'd fall, but a cushion of air supported her. Why had he bothered? Some code about not shooting an opponent who was on the ground?

At least they were in the copse of trees and out of view. Kel wouldn't see her die. He'd find her body—there was nothing she could do to keep that from occurring—but thankfully he wouldn't have to replay her actual death in his nightmares.

Farran blinked back the tears. She wouldn't cry. It was weak and stupid, but she couldn't stop the jaggedness of her breathing or slow her pounding heart.

She braced herself as the shadow walker came around to stand in front of her. Farran had expected it to be the man who'd fought with a partner, but it was the one she thought of as Rhyden. The one she'd thought might be on their side. Kel had warned her about this man's motives and he'd been right.

"I will not hurt you," he said calmly.

He spoke English today. She nearly commented on that, but decided it didn't matter. "Then why did you grab me? Why did you shoot at Kel when we were in his house? He had to fight you to protect me."

"I had no understanding that he was your protector." Rhyden spoke with an accent, but it was light. "I believed he was same as the demon. A threat to you. When he defended you from Arawn and Erzsi, I learned the truth and fought with him to keep you safe. You know this is so."

Call her skeptical, but she wasn't ready to blindly trust anything he told her. "And you grabbed me today because?"

There was a few seconds' delay while Rhyden seemed to sort out what she meant and then he said, "We had need to talk. Your man is fierce in your defense and would battle first, ask why later. I haven't energy for war and conversation."

That would fit with the information they had about how much strength it took for the shadow walkers to leave their dimension even for a short time. A skirmish would burn through power faster than merely standing around, but this whole thing was bizarre. She wanted to ask, *what the hell is going on?* But Farran didn't want to agitate him and the longer she could keep Rhyden talking, the better. "What do you need to say to me?"

"You wonder why much centers around you, no?"

Farran could move her head and she nodded.

"Five days ago you altered time."

"I did not! I'm not powerful enough to do anything like that." Belatedly, Farran realized that vehemently arguing with him probably wasn't in her best interest and she shut up.

"You did and you are that powerful. That was your first instance. The second took place four days ago and that raised more alarm."

At the store and when the demon attacked—Kel had notes on possible causes for those two events. Rhyden's timing matched, but her as the source? If she wasn't the weakest Tàireil, she was close. But she had helped Kel in his fight with the other two shadow walkers—she didn't know how, but she'd done it. Was that tied in somehow?

"My people," Rhyden said quietly, "are required to be the guardians of time. It is our task to ensure that no one alters the flow, but you did."

"I didn't, I swear. And if I somehow did do that, it was an accident."

His lips curved. "We know it was not your intent, but your ignorance of your powers risks our people. That is why I was dispatched after the first incident."

"To kill me."

"No! To speak with you, to bring you to our world in order that you might be trained and not inadvertently cause the sentence to begin anew. But I arrived to find you being stalked by a demon. He knows your power, too, sa māsi, and no doubt hopes to use it for his own ends."

Something about the words in his language made a shiver go down her spine, but Farran ignored it. What he'd said seemed to fit what had happened with Seth—the demon had wanted her to come to him voluntarily. She'd assumed it was to torture and kill her, but what if that hadn't been his aim? Still, that didn't explain the other two shadow walkers and their actions. "If you don't want me dead, then why are the other two of your kind shooting to kill?"

"Those in power do not wish to end your life. That is why they sent me; they knew I would not harm you in any manner. There is a faction, however, that believes the sole way to eliminate the threat you pose to us is to eliminate you. They assigned Arawn and Erzsi to do that after the second incident."

"Once was a fluke, twice is a pattern," she said, repeating what Kel had told her.

Rhyden inclined his head. "Your actions were small enough not to restart our term, but we couldn't be certain a third or fourth incident would not do so."

"Seriously, Rhyden—your name is Rhyden, right?"

He nodded.

"Here's the thing: you keep saying I'm powerful enough to alter time, but I know I'm not. Even the strongest of the Tàireil don't have that ability and I'm not among them. Really. So no matter what it looks like, it was someone else who changed the flow, not me."

The shadow walker stared at her so long, Farran feared she should have kept quiet. Maybe she should have let him believe she was strong. Maybe now that he knew she wasn't the one who'd messed with time, he could kill her and find the true person who'd done it, take him or her back to his world to be trained. He hadn't said there was any need to keep a fake alive.

"You are only half Tàireil."

"What?"

"Your father was Kādunesen."

Farran gaped. Her brain had frozen along with her limbs or maybe she was unconscious. Yeah, that made more sense. She'd been hit by one of the demon's shots, had fallen and hit her head. When she woke up, Kel would be bending over her, sending her healing energy, and then she'd tell him about her wild hallucination and they could laugh over it.

"Did you not hear me, you are half Kādunesen."

"I heard you, I just don't believe this. Any of this."

"It is true." Now he looked angry.

"I'm not calling you a liar. I just think I'm asleep and this is some strange dream."

His face cleared and Rhyden's lips curved. "This is no dream. Perhaps a nightmare, no?"

She smiled back. He had a sense of humor and she liked that—even if he was a figment. "Who are the Kādunesen?" Farran said the word carefully, breaking it into syllables to make sure she pronounced it right.

"My people. What do you call us?" Rhyden asked.

"Shadow walkers or the neach-faileas."

Again there was a slight pause and then his smile broadened. "I like this." Then he sobered. "Our time, though, is short and there are things you must know. Things you must trust. This is no dream, sa māsi. You are only half Tàireil, you must understand this."

Farran nodded because he was waiting for a response, but she didn't believe him. It was some mind game, a trick, and she wasn't falling for it.

"Your mother's people pull their power from the planet first, the universe second, and naturally you strove to emulate this. That is why you think you are weak. You can only take slight energy from these sources because your magic is much more oriented toward the Kādunesen's and we draw our power from a different supply."

"The flecks of light?"

"Yes and no," Rhyden said putting his hands on his hips. "The lights you see are a result, not the source itself. Here, I show you."

Before she knew what he was up to, Rhyden was in her head and in control. Farran knew it was useless to try and pull free, but she made the attempt anyway—and failed.

"Shush, sa māsi, all is well. Believe."

Like she had a choice. He led her on a path she'd never known existed, and when they reached their destination, she realized this was the home of the lights.

Not the lights. This is your energy source, Rhyden sent. *When you require power, draw from here and put it behind your spells and magic. You've done it unconsciously on several occasions, now you know in your head and your heart where to go.*

He brought her back and released her mind. Not her body. That he still kept locked up tight, but maybe he knew that if he relaxed his hold on her physically, she'd run for Kel.

"Now you can believe everything I say to you."

Yeah, right. Just because the power part felt absolutely true didn't mean anything else was. People lied to achieve their aims and they'd use others if they had to—she'd watched the master at work enough times to know this. "If I really am half Kādunesen," she still had to say it slowly, "and if I am capable of altering time—something your people are supposed to prevent—why didn't you come for me years ago and avert any mistakes?"

Rhyden frowned. "Because we did not know of your existence. We only discovered you five days ago when the first incident occurred. Study was given and your bloodline identified. Until that moment, many would have claimed a . . . hybrid child was impossible. That is the word?"

"Close enough. And the man who you say fathered me had no idea?" He'd at least known there was a possibility she'd been conceived—if any of this had really happened.

"He died before your birth. If he told anyone of his liaison with your mother, we are unaware of it. Had we known, there would have been searches to find any progeny."

"Why? Simply to make sure no one messed up time?"

The shadow walker began to reach for her, and although Farran couldn't move, she mentally shrank from him. Rhyden stopped abruptly.

"Trust must be earned, this I know." He gathered his long hair in both hands at the back of his head and then released it with a sigh. "That fear would have been part of it, but only a small part. You see, sa māsi, you can do things that the Kādunesen cannot and no one would have dreamed your Tàireil blood would cause such differences. No, the central reason you would have been sought is our . . . devoutness . . . no, *devotion* to family. There would have been a welcoming upon your arrival."

"I don't feel too welcome right now," Farran told him.

Rhyden scowled. "That should not be the case and it will not be if you accompany me to our world. You will be trained how to use your magic and that will take care of any threat to you."

"You hope it takes care of any threat to me," Farran countered. "Even with training, there'd be those among your people who wouldn't trust me not to alter time again and the only way to be absolutely certain I didn't is to kill me. What is the big deal anyway? I mean, yeah, we shouldn't mess with time because of the paradoxes and all that, but why are your people the guardians and so rabid to ensure nothing happens?"

His frown grew more and more fierce as she spoke. "Long ago, or so the legends say, the Kādunesen selfishly and repeatedly affected time in outrageous manners. In response, we were imprisoned in a dimension that was not ours and sentenced to stay there until we could last ten thousand years without doing such things. Again and again, our punishment began anew because someone violated the rules. Now we are close to the end, closer than we have ever before been, but you are considered one of us."

"And if I violate the rules, even inadvertently, your people start another ten thousand years."

He nodded.

"Educating me isn't going to quiet the fear."

"The faction in favor of your death is small. Once you are taught, their numbers would decline. You would be safe in our world, you have my word on this."

The lightbulb went off. "I'd be safe in your world because I'd be imprisoned in there with you, wouldn't I?"

Rhyden looked away without replying.

"I would! Hardly anyone can leave your world, even for short periods, before being sucked back and I'd be stuck, too. I wouldn't be able to return to this dimension no matter how much I wanted to—I'm right, aren't I?"

"It is likely, sa māsi," he admitted quietly.

"When were you going to tell me this? After I was trapped? And why do you keep calling me sa māsi? What the hell does it mean, anyway?"

"It translates to *my sister*."

Farran shook her head, her neck muscles seeming to grasp what he was telling her a few seconds before her mind caught up.

"It is true. We share the same father and—"

"Farran!" Kel sounded frantic.

She tried to shout his name, but her voice stayed soft.

"Farran!" He was closer now and she could hear him running.

Kel, help! I need you.

He moved faster and she knew he'd picked up her call— Rhyden's block must have weakened. Kel would be here in seconds.

"You ask too much of me," she told Rhyden. "I'm not leaving my world."

"This isn't your world."

And then Kel burst around the bend, drawing his hand back as soon as he saw the shadow walker. Rhyden disappeared immediately and the spells around her disintegrated, including the cushion of air she was leaning against. She fell to the ground, unable to catch her balance quickly enough.

"Are you okay?" Kel demanded, dropping to one knee beside her, but he only glanced at her briefly before he resumed scanning the area.

"Yes. Let's get out of here, Kel. Let's go home."

Kel didn't know which of them was more rattled—him or Farran. That bastard shadow walker had grabbed her right in the middle of a battle and Kel hadn't had a clue she was gone, not until after the demon had bugged out.

Seth had known, damn him. He'd probably watched it happen. Kel pivoted when he reached the wall near the front door and paced back toward the table. It explained why the demon had fought the way he had. He'd wanted to get to where Farran was being held and take her from the shadow walker himself.

Scowling, Kel struggled to regain command. He could have lost her today. He could have fucking lost her. God, his hands wouldn't stop shaking.

The son of a bitch could have dragged Farran back to his world and Kel wouldn't have known anything beyond the fact that she was gone. He made the turn into the living room and looked at the bathroom door. Still shut.

She'd filled him in, answered a few questions, and then told him she had to take a shower. Kel eyed the door a few seconds longer, but resumed his pacing. She needed space, time to regroup—he understood that—and even though he hated to have her out of his sight, he could give that to her.

Kel stopped at the back door, decided a fire would help relax both of them, and took the flannel jacket off the hook. Grabbing the first armload of wood, he thought about why the shadow walker hadn't simply taken her away. There had to be a reason because standing around and talking had been idiotic. He might not have spoken to Rhyden himself, but the man hadn't struck him as stupid.

Holding a second bundle of logs, Kel ran through the options and eliminated some, but they didn't know enough about the shadow walkers for him to guess which of his ideas—if any—was right. He filled the wood box before locking the door, removing the jacket, and starting the fire.

As he put the screen back into place, he heard the door open, then another close. Getting dressed? Damn, he hoped she was putting on clothes and not planning to hide in the bedroom.

He went to the kitchen sink and washed his hands. When Farran came out—she had to—he wanted to take her into his arms without getting her dirty. And damn it, he needed to wrap himself around her, to reassure himself that she was okay—that she wasn't going to disappear.

The door opened again and Kel tossed down the towel he was using and rounded the counter. Her hand was on her cheek and he nearly growled. She only did that when she was feeling uncertain about herself. He drew up, and opening his arms, said, "Let me hold you."

Farran half ran to him and Kel drew her against him, swaying slowly from side to side to comfort her. It took all his willpower to keep from squeezing her too tightly, but he managed.

Her hair was slightly damp and he picked up the scents of soap, shampoo, and woman. His woman.

"I'm scared, Kel," she admitted, voice muffled against his throat.

"Me, too, sunshine. Me, too." He was more terrified by this than when he'd been held captive. Then he'd been powerless, but it had been happening to him. With this he could find himself powerless again, but it was Farran at risk.

"I keep thinking what if he hadn't decided to talk first? What if he'd taken me right to his world? I'm more frightened now than I was while it took place."

He rocked her some more and said, "When he was talking to you, you had to pay attention, you needed to react to him, to deal with what he told you. There wasn't time for you to think about what the possibilities were. With it over, there's nothing else to do except replay it. What if you'd said this? What if you'd done that? What if he'd done this? It's natural."

"While the conversation was going on, I should have been thinking of what-ifs, thinking if he does this, I'll try that. I should have had a plan for the most likely scenarios and I didn't."

"He had you boxed in. You told me how he'd taken away your options. The only thing you might have been able to do is come up with how you'd respond if he said a particular thing, but I think you would have been hard-pressed to imagine he'd claim kinship with you."

Farran leaned back to meet his eyes and her lashes were wet. There were no other signs that she'd been crying, but he felt a clutching sensation in the center of his chest and Kel leaned down to kiss her. Slow, gentle, careful. She was fragile and he treated her as if she might break.

He eased away reluctantly. "I built a fire. Do you feel up to sitting down, watching it burn, and discussing today's event?"

"Of course." Farran clutched him tighter. "I want your opinion on a few of the things he said."

In a more perfect world, Kel thought, the fire would be atmosphere for foreplay. Instead of snuggling in front of it, though, he led her to the love seat facing the fireplace, and while he put his arm around her, it was for support rather than a loverlike embrace.

"Do you think he's really my brother?" Farran asked almost the instant they were settled.

That told him what was uppermost in her mind. Kel thought about it for a moment, and then said, "I doubt it. It's much more likely that he told you that to get you to trust him and maybe convince you to go with him to his dimension."

"It was a miscalculation on his part then, because I'm far less likely to trust a relative than a stranger."

Her hand touched her cheek again and Kel hugged her closer to his side. "Maybe he didn't know the way you'd grown up. Most people would feel a connection to family."

"True, but I keep wondering what if he was telling the truth about my father being a shadow walker? It would explain why the man I believed to be my father had no interest in me. Why would he when I wasn't his daughter? And if he did murder my mother, it could have been because he'd discovered she'd been unfaithful."

Kel kissed the top of Farran's head. "It's possible that the shadow walker *was* aware of how you'd grown up and tried to use it. Maybe his miscalculation was that he thought you'd leap at the opportunity to have a different set of relatives, ones that would love you sight unseen."

"He did say his people had a devotion to family and it would be a natural weakness to exploit. I'm not gullible, though. I watched my father and brothers maneuver others to achieve what they wanted—and I wasn't about to blindly trust Rhyden about this or anything else."

Listening to her made Kel think of his family. He'd been surrounded by their love and had never doubted for a minute that he could trust them with almost anything. Leaving for troubleshooter training hadn't changed that and when he went home, it was as if he'd never left. Juxtaposing that with what Farran had been subjected to made Kel's heart feel heavy. How had she managed to stay normal living in that world?

She turned and wrapped an arm around his waist. "You know what bothers me?"

"What's that?" he prompted when she didn't speak.

"Why did he talk with me for such a long time? If the shadow walker wanted me in his world, why not just take me there?"

"I've been giving that some thought because it was such a boneheaded move. The thing that makes the most sense is if he couldn't. It takes a lot of power for them just to leave their dimension, right? How much more would it take to bring you back kicking and screaming?"

Farran nodded. "So he would use too much of his magic to force me."

"Right. Instead he talks, tries to persuade you to go with him. That way he isn't wasting his energy fighting you and maybe he even convinces you to travel under your own steam."

She rested her hand on his thigh and Kel relaxed at her touch. "The demon tried to get me to go to him willingly, too."

"That ties into my second thought. What if they need you to do something for them? You're not going to do a favor for anyone you're angry with, right? And if you can alter time like he suggested, it becomes clear what they're after."

"That part you believe?" She shifted until their eyes met. "I can't change it, you know that."

"You're the common denominator between the incidents."

"There could be another one that we don't know yet. Besides, you said you don't think I'm part shadow walker."

"I don't, but you don't have to be—all you need is enough power. If you found an alternate source to draw from, it might contain more energy than what the rest of us use. That could bump you up enough."

Farran shook her head. "It's not me."

"Okay," Kel said easily. She was becoming upset and

there was no reason. "Keep in mind that it doesn't matter what you can or can't do if Seth and the shadow walker *believe* that you have the ability. But the first possibility is the most likely anyway—that Rhyden doesn't have the amount of magic it would take to force you to travel with him."

But if Farran did reverse time, everything made a lot more sense. It explained the demon's interest in her and the shadow walker's sudden appearance. This even fit in neatly with the sequence of events that she'd laid out for him. One minute her life was ordinary, but a few hours later she'd been pursued by Seth and then had a battle unfold in front of her. It was a sure thing that she hadn't caught their attention by stocking toothpaste.

Kel watched the flames dance. The whys didn't mean anything—the only thing that counted was that she was being hunted—but having a reason that felt concrete left him more at ease.

Farran was warm against his side and he took a deep breath, letting her presence help him take it down a few notches. Despite his screwup, she wasn't gone and he'd move heaven and Earth to make sure she stayed safe. "I'm sorry," he told her.

She lifted her head to meet his eyes. "For what?"

"I didn't know the shadow walker was there today until I rounded the curve and saw him. I should have been able to sense him, if not his energy then his emotions, and there was nothing."

He thought he'd blocked her, but Farran must have gotten something. Sitting up, she knelt beside him and her lips were soft against his. "It's not your fault. I didn't know he was there either until he grabbed me."

"I closed you out when the demon attacked. I should have kept a line on you."

"You couldn't, not without losing some of your focus."

Kel shrugged. True, but his first priority was to keep Farran safe. He'd been a fool to think the shadow walkers wouldn't take advantage of Seth if the opportunity arose and that should have been part of his contingency planning from the start. Should have been, but wasn't. He hoped to hell that the six months off active duty hadn't dulled his instincts.

"You're too hard on yourself," she said.

"I should have known."

"Has anyone ever told you that you're stubborn?"

"It's been mentioned."

"I don't doubt it." Farran huffed out a long breath. "I'm not blaming you, so give yourself a break, okay?"

He nodded, but he didn't mean it. It was enough, though, to get Farran to settle beside him and put her head back on his chest. Kel wrapped his arm around her again. This felt right. In a while, he'd have to see about feeding her and they'd have to come up with a strategy to make sure the shadow walker couldn't surprise them again, but for now, he could simply hold her.

"Kel," she said after a few minutes, "have you ever known a Tàireil to be able to use any real power when the sun was up?"

"No." He knew where she was going with this and her circling back wasn't a surprise. Kel didn't like this particular line of thought, but he wasn't going to brush her off.

"I can do almost everything during the day that I can at night. That's unusual."

"Very," he agreed easily, but his muscles had tensed up once more. Farran didn't reply, but she was thinking and there'd be more on the way when she was ready to say it. Kel couldn't blame her, but he wished she could shrug off what that shadow walker had told her and not pick at it. When he noticed that she'd tensed, too, he braced himself. It was coming.

"You've got a lot of healing talent, don't you?"

Hell. He knew what was next. "Yes."

"You could scan me for genetic makeup, right? Then I'd know if what he said was the truth or not."

Kel wanted to tell her he couldn't, but that was a lie. Maybe he hadn't been formally trained as a healer, but he'd learned a lot on his own as well as from watching his mother, and what Farran had asked him to do wasn't outside his range. He thought about telling her that he didn't know the shadow walkers' genetics, but that would be a lie, too. It was second nature to check them out using all his abilities, looking for a weakness he might be able to use in battle.

"Are you sure you want to know?"

Farran sat on the edge of the love seat and turned to face him. "I have to know. Have to, Kel."

"Okay." Kel felt that ache in his chest intensify as her emotions washed over him. She couldn't live with the uncertainty and he could eliminate that for her. "I'll need to put one hand on your head, the other over your heart, and it could take awhile to get a good read, so I'll need you to stay patient and still for me. Remember, I'm not a professional healer."

She smiled tremulously. "Maybe not, but you're the only person I'd trust to do this."

Damn, he had to kiss her for that. "You want to lie on the coffee table or the floor? Neither one is comfortable, but it'll be easier than on the bed."

"Coffee table."

When Farran was in place, Kel knelt beside her, and taking a deep breath, lowered his hands. He closed his eyes, established the connection, and began to scan. It was a slow process, and it took more than half an hour before he had the answer, but he kept going anyway. Maybe it was overkill, but she needed him to be sure. After another twenty minutes, there was no doubt left and it explained why her vibration felt a little off for a Tàireil.

Kel brought his energy back and then lifted his hands. By the time he opened his eyes again, Farran was sitting up and staring at him, waiting expectantly.

Taking a deep breath, he reached for her, and linking their fingers, gave it to her straight out. "He didn't lie about everything. You are half shadow walker."

For a moment, there was nothing and then Kel felt emotion slam into her. He tugged her into his arms and held her tightly while she navigated the maelstrom. Farran clung to him and she took shuddery breaths. Crying. God. He circled a hand on her back, trying to give her what comfort he could, trying to let her know he was here for her no matter what.

His knees began to hurt and he moved them, sitting on the love seat and settling Farran on his lap so that she straddled him. She kept her face buried against his throat and Kel felt her tears moisten his skin.

Farran cried for a long time and he rode out the waves with her, not blocking anything she was experiencing. It didn't all make sense to him, but then emotions often didn't. What mattered was that he understood her turmoil. Kel stroked his fingers through her hair, hugged her closer when she tightened her hold, and made soothing sounds when it got rougher for her. By the time the worst of it passed, he felt as exhausted as she did.

"I'm sorry," she said, not lifting her head. "I don't know why this hit me so hard."

"There's nothing to apologize for."

After a pause, she said, "I got you wet."

"That's okay, I'll get you wet later."

She sucked in a surprised breath as she raised her head. He winked at her and she smiled. "You're incorrigible."

Maybe, but she'd needed something to lighten the mood and this had done the trick. "Are you all right?" he asked, growing serious again.

"Yeah, I guess. It's going to take some getting used to."

Nodding, he smoothed the hair back from her face and used his thumbs to wipe the tears off her cheeks. There was nothing he could do to fix this for Farran, but Kel could hold her and be here for her.

Out of the blue, she said, "Rhyden told me that this isn't my world."

"It is now," Kel growled.

"Not really." She looked away from him. "Your council could tell me to leave at any time."

"They won't." He had no doubts on that score.

"But they could," Farran insisted. "I'm half shadow walker. Maybe I should go with Rhyden."

18
CHAPTER

A few hours and a couple of orgasms later, Kel was still agitated. They were naked in bed, Farran asleep beside him, but he couldn't relax. Talking to her had gotten him nowhere—all she'd kept saying was some bullshit about how maybe she belonged in the shadow walker dimension. He tightened his embrace slightly. She was exactly where she belonged. Why the hell couldn't she see it?

Kel forced himself to loosen his hold. He didn't want to wake her and she needed rest after what she'd been through. She *had* been off balance since the shadow walker showed up. Maybe when she got up tomorrow, Farran would have her feet back under her and understand that the Gineal world was hers.

Yeah, it would be better in the morning. Had to be.

His eyes drifted shut and Kel forced them open again. He was physically exhausted, but his mind wouldn't slow down and that was a dangerous combination. One of his nightmares could be back there, somewhere, just waiting to spring itself on him, and the last place he should be was in bed. It would be better to get up, pace a little, anything except lie here, but Kel didn't want to leave Farran. He'd come too close to losing her today and now he had to worry she might leave tomorrow or the next day.

She sighed in her sleep and shifted away from him. It took a lot of control to let her go, but he did it. Her brow was scrunched, probably because of the light filling the room, but she never complained about that. Until he could learn to tolerate the dark again, he'd have to get her one of those masks to wear.

Kel rotated the arm Farran had been lying on, trying to get some feeling back in it, and let his eyes close. It was okay since he was moving. He wouldn't fall asleep.

He started to unwind as soon as he went still. Kel sighed and knew he needed to get up and walk around.

But did he really have to? Yeah, the ingredients were in place for a flashback, but he didn't feel it barreling down on him like he sometimes did and he didn't always have one simply because his mind and body were out of sync. In his experience, this same mix was more likely to bring insomnia.

Maybe he'd just lie here for a while.

Tasglann again tomorrow, but damn he didn't want to go back there, especially if Farran was still talking about that other world as a possibility. There was no choice, though; he had to keep researching until he found some tactic that would work against the shadow walkers. It wasn't as if the cabin was safe. He knew that. But it was tempting to fall into the illusion, to think if he holed up here with her, that everything would be okay.

It wouldn't be.

One day, maybe while they were in bed, the shadow walkers would show up, and the cabin was too damn small. There was no room to maneuver, nothing to use for cover. When it came right down to it, he would rather face the enemy outside the library.

Kel yawned and pulled the blankets closer to his chin. What was he thinking about?

Oh, yeah, the library. Which path would they use tomorrow? There was only one left that they hadn't been attacked on yet, but would that be the natural place for his adversaries to stake out? Maybe. Might be better to choose the walkway with the most cover.

The big boulder.

Put Farran's back to that rock and . . . fight in front of her. No way anyone could come up from behind, not without taking the stone out first, and . . . they'd both notice that.

Of course, the way his luck had been running for the last year or so, they'd be nowhere near that boulder . . . when the attack rolled out.

What if . . .

Hmm.

He could . . .

Absolute darkness.

It pressed in on him. Smothered him.

Kel knew he was breathing too fast, knew he had to slow it down. He couldn't lose control, he couldn't hyperventilate. They weren't going to kill him by cutting off his oxygen—that was too quick, too easy. No, when he died, they'd make it hurt.

That day wasn't here. Not yet. He shuddered, made himself inhale slowly. They wanted him to fear that any moment could be his last, but Kel didn't.

He could read them too clearly and he knew they hadn't finished playing with him. Right now, he was still giving them enough sport to keep them entertained. How long that would last was anyone's guess, but for the moment, his life was safe.

His body throbbed, every inch sore and aching, but it was being alone in the dark that got to him.

Breathe. Count it out. Get control, man, get control.

Gineal troubleshooters were trained to hold on to their self-command. It was supposed to keep the dark forces at bay, but Kel had lost his center days—weeks—ago and they hadn't shown up to entice him. Only he could find himself in such a bad situation that even the forces of evil had forsaken him.

And you think I'm the doom monster? You're no better than I am. Forsaken by the dark forces? You wish.

Tris? *But there was no answer.*

The dankness of the earthen walls made it harder to breathe, but Kel forced himself to inhale and exhale for a count of eight. He wasn't going to lose it; it would give them too much pleasure.

He wouldn't be here much longer. The Gineal were looking for him and the monitors were good at their jobs. And even if they couldn't find him, his brother would. Logan could scry, and while he only saw the present, that would be enough for him to locate Kel. Enough to launch a rescue mission.

They haven't found you yet, have they, Gineal?

They will.

Laughter rang through his cell and it was worse than the sound of his breathing.

Weak, helpless. Selfish.

No.

Yes, you are. You'd consign someone else to this place you call hell simply to have a companion.

No.

It's true, Gineal. You don't want to be alone in the dark. We can arrange that for you. Would you like company?

No.

Liar. We can feel the surge of hope the idea brings you, think that we can not?

Kel was breathing fast again and he fought it. He needed control. Needed it now.

Good news, Gineal. We've decided to grant your wish.

He felt them coming and Kel struggled to his feet. Couldn't be in a weakened position—just in case. Just in case.

They were right outside his cell, but there weren't only

two. He could feel the emotions of three. Three, and one was confused. Scared. His only other clue was that the feelings seemed feminine.

The door opened, but there was no light, no lessening of the dark, and Kel strained to see who was with them.

Here's your cell mate, Gineal.

They must have pushed her into the room because she stumbled into his arms. Kel grabbed her, tried to keep her from falling. Her breasts pressed into his chest.

Kel?

Farran?

It was Farran; he recognized her feel, her scent. No, it couldn't be. He hadn't known her when he'd been held.

She's here because you don't want to be alone.

No! She doesn't belong here. She doesn't fucking belong here.

You wanted her, Gineal. You sentenced her to share your hell. Enjoy your time with her.

The cell door closed and he felt his captors leave.

Kel, help me.

I will. Whatever it takes, I will.

Kel made himself inhale. It's not real. It's not real. It's not real. *Farran hadn't been imprisoned. This was a nightmare not a memory. This hadn't happened.*

He had control of his dreams and he wasn't letting this happen. Kel wrested his mind away.

And Farran was gone. Safe.

His sigh of relief was short-lived. He went from dream to flashback and there wasn't anything he could do to get away from this ghost. Kel knew. It was the one that he never wanted to remember. Never wanted to replay. And the one he'd never been able to stop until the bitter end.

The altar was wet, sticky beneath his stomach from the rivulets of blood and sweat that had run off his body.

No sleep. No food. Little water and then mostly thrown in his face or on the stone in front of him. They laughed when he lapped it up, when he tasted his diluted blood along with the water, but he'd stopped caring.

His pain was constant, incessant, and it had been for days. There were no peaks, no valleys, only this unchanging line near the top of the scale.

There was never any relief. If they'd make it more painful and then bring it down to this level, it would be easier to bear. It would feel like a break. But they never did.

Monotonous, ceaseless, unrelenting.

Four days? More? Less? Did it matter? The pain kept flowing through him second after second, minute after minute, hour after hour. Day after day.

He'd screamed.

Prayed.

Begged.

Cried like a girl. More than once.

And it still didn't end.

His captors were right. No one was going to save him. They'd told him it had been a month since they'd taken him and if someone had cared enough to rescue him, it would have happened by now.

No one had come.

No one.

He didn't want to cry again, God he didn't want to, but he wasn't sure how much longer he could hold out. Wasn't sure how much longer he could endure this. His body shook and trembled, but he'd lost control over it days ago.

The pain is unbearable, isn't it, Gineal?

Kel wanted to be defiant, but they'd drained that out of him. All he managed was a whimper.

Do you want it to end?

Of course he did. He'd do anything to make it stop.

Anything? Really?

His moan lacked energy.

There's one thing that will end your imprisonment. Give us a name.

No.

Okay, Gineal, be stubborn. We'll talk later.

It felt as if an eternity passed before they returned to his side. He knew they'd deliberately picked a time when he was crying, but it didn't change anything. The pain had to stop, he couldn't bear it any longer.

He'd lost everything. His dignity, his resolve, his stubbornness, and he was about to lose more. He knew he was.

Are you ready now, Gineal? Tell us who we should take in your place. Give us that name and you're free.

His lips were chapped, his tongue swollen, and his entire body shuddered uncontrollably. It was difficult to form any word, but Kel fought to do that. Three tries, that was how long it took to throw away his soul—and give them a name.

Kel shot upright.

"Noooooooooooooooooooo!" The scream was torn from him, and frantic, he looked around. Had to get out of here. The blankets were smothering him, imprisoning him, and Kel fought his way free, scrambled off the foot of the bed.

He fell flat on his face.

"Kel!"

Ignoring her, he struggled to stand, and then fled.

The main rooms of the cabin were dark, but he didn't deserve the light. He belonged in hell. He belonged there.

Kel sank to the floor between the love seat and the chair, wrapped his arms around his legs, and put his head down on his knees. Why hadn't he willed himself to die? He should have died. It would have been a just punishment.

He felt her come into the hall and turned his head. The glow from the bedroom silhouetted her and he could see her hand reaching for the light switch. "No lights," he ordered, his voice harsh, thick.

"Kel?"

She still had her hand on the switch. "Don't turn on the fucking lights."

If he wasn't such a selfish bastard, he'd tell her to go

away and leave him alone—the same way he'd told his family—but he was weak and he needed her too much. She couldn't see him like this, though. He didn't want that. Was his shame written all over him? It had to be. It had to be.

He'd given them a name. Like the basest of cowards, he'd been willing to consign someone else to hell to save himself.

His captors told him they'd do it. They'd been right. They'd broken him.

Farran hesitated, unsure what was going on with Kel. No lights? He was afraid of the dark.

She'd grabbed his sweatshirt off the floor and thrown it on. It was big enough to hit her right above the knees, but she tugged at the hem anyway as she gave herself time to adjust to the darkness. Once she could see—kind of—Farran looked for Kel. There was moonlight streaming in through the triangular windows and his voice had come from the area by the love seat, but it took her a couple of sweeps to find him.

He was huddled on the floor, naked.

Her heart leapt into her throat and Farran didn't wait any longer. As she neared, he turned his face away from her. God, what was wrong with him?

"Kel?" No reply. "Kellan, talk to me."

Still no answer, but he hadn't told her to get the hell away from him and he would have if he didn't want her here. Farran knelt beside him, started to put her hand on his shoulder, but pulled back. He hadn't flinched, but he might as well have and then she remembered—with the last nightmare he hadn't wanted to be touched right away and that dream had seemed to be a lot less severe than this one.

Making sure the sweatshirt was tucked under her bottom, Farran sat on the floor. Kel had his back against the arm, facing the kitchen table and she sat on a ninety-degree angle from him with her back against the front of the love seat, facing the fireplace. She was close enough to feel the heat of his body, close enough to touch him if he needed her. His breathing was loud, jagged in the quiet of the cabin, and she hurt for him.

She didn't say another word. He'd talk when he was ready—if he decided to share anything at all—but Farran wouldn't push him. That would close Kel down and she could be patient. She could be here for him, the way he'd been there for her.

As the silence lengthened, Farran grew cold, but she didn't move. Kel had less on than she did and if he could stand it, so could she. But it was too bad he'd extinguished the fire before they'd gone to bed and too bad she hadn't grabbed a pair of pants and some socks when she'd left the room.

His breathing began to even out. It remained rough, but better, and when he slowly sat up, something inside her eased. Kel wasn't blocking his emotions from her, but she was unable to read him. Everything was all twisted up together like a bowl of spaghetti and she couldn't find any single strand to follow. But maybe his emotions did have to be viewed as this messed-up tangle.

"I should have died," he said. His voice was quiet—and emotionless.

He couldn't mean . . . "You want to die?" Farran held her breath, terrified of his answer.

"No. I don't want to die, I wish I *had* died."

"Kel—"

"I could have, you know. I wasn't just fucked up mentally and emotionally, I was fucked up physically, too. Bad enough that I almost didn't make it even with teams of healers working on me around the clock."

Farran's throat was tight and she couldn't speak, but she put her right hand down on the floor, palm up. Kel didn't take her up on the invitation.

"Survival instinct sucks," he said and he sounded flat. "They were growing bored with me when I got my magic back. If I hadn't done anything, they would have killed me in a day or so, but the need for revenge was too strong. After I took care of them, I could have laid down and let other darksiders find me and they probably would have killed me. Instead I opened a transit and appeared inside the Gineal healing temple. Stupid. If I'd gone home, I could have died there."

She couldn't stop the tears, she didn't even try. "I'm glad you lived. I'm glad you're here."

"Even with the best healers working on me, I was unconscious for more than a week. My family was with me nearly the entire time—or so I was told—but when I opened my eyes, only one person was there. No one knew I was coming around and the rest of them had gone to get dinner. Except Logan. They tell me he never left my side, that he wouldn't have bothered to eat at all if someone didn't bring food for him."

"He's your twin, of course he wanted to be with you."

"Yeah. Our special bond."

Farran froze. Kel didn't sound emotionless anymore, but she couldn't label what he was feeling.

"I had flashbacks from the beginning and after about five months of it, I found a spell that I thought I could change and it would take these replays and send them out to the universe."

"But it didn't work."

"Not the way it was supposed to, but I didn't know that, not at first. For six weeks, my mind didn't ambush me. Sure, I'd remember what happened and think about it, but it's not the same as the damn thing repeating itself as if it were real. I was able to sleep most nights. And then I found out the truth."

She froze, afraid to even blink, but he didn't continue. "What truth?" she prompted.

"Instead of sending my nightmares to the universe, I'd sent them to my brother. Whenever he used too much magic, he'd have something he referred to as a seizure. He hid it from me, he hid it from the council, he hid it from everyone. Logan could have died. If he'd had one of my flashbacks during a battle, he could have died and it would have been my fault."

"It would have been an accident. That's not the same as if you intentionally did something to hurt him."

Kel made a noise Farran couldn't identify and she turned to look at him. She couldn't see anything. He was staring straight ahead and all she could view was part of his face.

"After I undid the spell," he said awhile later, "and my replays returned, it was worse. Maybe because I'd had a break and had gotten used to them not being there. Or maybe they intensified for other reasons. Who knows? But at the end of September, the council had enough and yanked me from my job."

"There's more to it than your flashbacks." Farran wasn't sure how she knew that, but she did. Kel had left something out.

"Yeah, I did," he said, reading her thoughts. "They pulled me because—according to them—I was taking outlandish risks and they weren't going to enable my death wish."

"Were you gambling with your life?" she choked out.

"Maybe."

He had been. Oh, God, he had been. Farran wiped impatiently at the tears rolling down her cheeks. What if the council hadn't found out what he was doing? What if they hadn't relieved him of duty? What if Kel had died before she'd ever had a chance to talk to him, a chance to get to know him?

"Damn you, Kel."

"It would have been the best thing."

"Best? For who? For your family? For your brother? For me? If it wasn't for you, I would have died the night my father tried to get the dragon stone from Shona."

"No, you wouldn't have. Another Gineal would have been there in time to save you. Even if it was just Tris or Logan pouring unfocused healing energy into you, it would have been enough to keep you alive until an actual healer arrived."

"Then I would have died last Friday night. Or at least been captured either by Seth or by the shadow walkers."

"No."

"Yes and you know it as well as I do. I'd gone to Logan's home and neither he nor Shona were there. If you hadn't answered the door, what do you think I would have done? Do you think I would have sought out another Gineal to ask for help?"

"Probably not," he admitted reluctantly.

"Definitely not. I would have sat on their doorstep for a few hours, and when they didn't return, I would have wandered around Seattle, trying to hide. How long do you think I would have made it before being found? A day? Two, if I kept moving? It didn't take Rhyden long to track me down at your house."

She reached for him then, wrapped her hand around his biceps. "Don't be cavalier with your life. You're important to a lot of people, and if you can't believe that, then at least understand how important you are to me." And not only because he was protecting her.

His muscle flexed beneath her hand, but Kel didn't pull away and Farran took a deep breath. He was allowing her to touch him. Good. They had to be making progress. Time to rip off the scab and try to cleanse the wound.

"What was your nightmare about tonight?"

He went rigid, but she'd been expecting that. "There were two," Kel said with a mildness she knew was false. "Which one are you asking about?"

"The one that sent you screaming from our bedroom."

She felt him recoil, but he didn't shake her off. He needed to talk, maybe even wanted to talk, and he trusted her enough to share things he hadn't told anyone else. Farran bit her lip and sent up a silent prayer that she didn't mess up—she couldn't because too much depended on her doing this right. *Kel* needed her to handle this right.

The room grew silent again, their breathing the only sound. She slid her palm down his arm, found his hand, and linked their fingers. Kel held on tightly and she returned his grip.

"It's funny the things I remember. Some parts of my captivity are nothing but a blur, while other parts are so crystalline that I know I'll remember every word, every sight until I die."

"The flashbacks—"

"Are only some of it," Kel interrupted. "There are memories that I never get in my dreams, but they still eat at me. Like the first time they dragged me to their altar." His voice lost its inflection again. "I was fighting them even though I had no magic and knew it was pointless. I'm a troubleshooter—that's what I was supposed to do, fight, right? They strapped me down on that slab and the tall one leaned over and he said, 'We'll break you, Gineal.' I told him to go fuck himself. They weren't going to break me, I was a trained enforcer for my people."

Farran had a sick feeling descend to the pit of her stomach. She knew how this was going to end, but she squeezed Kel's hand and waited.

"I didn't expect to be there long. I'm not the most sociable guy around, but it wouldn't take more than a day or so before I was missed—sooner if the council needed me for a call-out—and then the search would start. The Gineal have monitors that can remote see, trackers who can hunt down anyone anywhere at any time. How long could it take?"

"Too long," she said quietly.

"Yeah. I lost track of time because I never saw daylight. If I wasn't in the blackness of my cell, I was in their altar room and there were no windows there, just candles and bowls of fire. And when the rescue didn't seem to come fast enough, I assumed that less time had passed than I believed."

"But after a while, you'd have to wonder." Had he felt forgotten? Unimportant? Had it helped weaken his determination to hold out? Farran kept quiet, though, and let Kel tell the story his way.

"They constantly worked on me. I told you some of what they did, but their every action was designed to undermine me. I lost my sense of self, my sense of the world, and I lost my faith in the Gineal. They weren't coming—after a while even the biggest idiot had to accept that."

"You're not an idiot," Farran said fiercely.

Kel laughed, but it was bitter, not humorous. "Wrong. I was the biggest damn fool around. Too confident, too cocky." He shrugged. "I learned."

Scooting over more, she pressed her lips to his shoulder. She still couldn't see most of Kel's face, but he wanted it that way, she was certain of that.

"By the time we entered the final stretch, I was battered. It wasn't the physical things, although those were pretty bad by then. I'm talking more mentally, psychologically. I'd been starved, sleep deprived, had largely been kept in solitary confinement, and tortured for sport. I'd given up, Farran, and I didn't care if I died, not if I could take those bastards out first. That was all I wanted."

She was crying again and couldn't talk, so she made a humming sound to let him know she was listening.

"But they weren't finished with me yet. I'd realized they'd played this game before, but what they chose to do to me felt random. It wasn't. They had a sequence and they identified when it was time to go for the jugular."

Kel took a deep breath and she knew he was girding himself. "They brought me to the altar. There wasn't any fight left in me by then and they only strapped down my arms and legs, not my neck. I thought that would make it easier. It didn't. I'm not going to go into what they did to me, there's no point, but they kept my pain level high and even. If it had been graphed on a chart it would have been a straight line across the top."

He was trying to block her out now, but Farran could

feel enough of his emotions that she couldn't stifle a sob.

"Don't cry for me," he said thickly. "I don't deserve your tears." He didn't give her a chance to argue. "They'd taken me down until I was more animal than man. Dignity, honor, pride—those were long gone. All I had left was stubbornness and determination and they took those from me, too. I didn't think they could, but I was wrong."

Kel drew another deep breath and let his head fall back to the arm of the love seat. "Normally, with pain there are times when it's excruciating and times that it's less so, but I didn't have that. It was steady and unending and it wore me down. I swore I'd never beg them, but I did. I begged and pleaded and promised them anything if they'd make it stop."

"But they didn't." She raised her free hand to wipe at her face again.

"No, they wanted more. You see, they hadn't broken me yet and that's what the goal was. While I was beseeching them one of my captors told me what I needed to do to make this session end. I refused and the pain continued unabated. And then he asked again, and again, and again, but I stayed silent."

Farran slid over farther until she was shoulder to shoulder with Kel, took his hand between both of hers, and held on tightly. She wasn't letting go of him no matter what he said next and she wanted him to know this.

"Until the final time." Kel's breathing was ragged once more and his voice had lost all its distance when he said, "They wanted my soul and I handed it to them. But I handed them more than that, more than I can ever get back."

He had to stop for a minute, but Kel didn't sound any better when he said, "They promised to free me if I gave them someone to take my place. They made sure I understood that this person would suffer the same tortures I had, that there'd be no leniency. How could I give them what they wanted? How could I subject another person to my hell?"

Oh, God. Farran was sobbing now and there was no way to stop it, no way to conceal it from him.

"But I did. I offered them the person I loved most in this world. I told them to take Logan."

19

CHAPTER

He'd said it. There was no relief, no lessening of the burden, no absolution. Kel had known there wouldn't be.

What he'd done was unforgivable.

Farran was still holding his hand, but he couldn't figure out why. Maybe the horror of what he'd told her hadn't sunk in yet. That made sense. Who would believe that a man would sell out his own brother in such a way?

He closed his eyes, knowing that he'd see the moment he'd been broken replay over and over. Kel didn't give a damn. He'd earned this torture. Hell, he'd earned worse.

"How long did you hold out?" she asked.

"What difference does that make?"

"I want to know. How long did you lie strapped on the altar that final time, enduring the pain and degradation they put you through before you cracked?"

His breath rasped and he swallowed hard. "Six days. At least that's what I overheard them say."

The bastards had been gleeful, excited because he'd set some kind of record. Yeah, what a laugh. He'd crumbled like a cookie under a sledgehammer and it had been for nothing. Everything they'd said had been untrue. They hadn't stopped the pain and they wouldn't, not until they were ready. And as he'd lain there, hating himself and trying not to scream or cry, Kel had realized his life was measured in days. Maybe hours. With him broken, the game was over. He hadn't cared at that moment, but—

"Six days!" Her voice yanked him from his memories. "How long do you think you should have held out against the agony?"

"Forever."

"You don't expect much from yourself, do you?"

Kel took another harsh breath, but didn't comment. Didn't she get it? He should have died instead of giving up his brother.

"This is why you pushed your family away and closed them out," Farran said. Her voice was thick, choked with tears. "I'd wondered why you didn't lean on them, let them help you, especially when it's obvious how much you love them."

"This is why," he confirmed, struggling to sound somewhere close to normal. "I could never tell them what I did." He opened his eyes again, but kept staring at the ceiling. "It's cowardly, but I can't bear the thought of them hating me."

"They wouldn't. They love you!"

"They love Logan, too, and he never betrayed anyone." His breathing was coming too fast again and Kel tried to make it slow, but he couldn't seem to do it, not with the darkness closing in on him.

"It wasn't a betrayal. You were tortured for weeks even before that last stint; no one could blame you for caving in."

"I blame me." He tugged his hand loose. "This is *my brother* we're talking about here. Not just my brother, my twin. We came from the same egg, we shared the same womb, we were born within minutes of each other and spent most of our time together after that. What I did is as low as it gets."

"Oh, Kel."

"You know what makes it worse? He's trying so damn hard to help me. Every time I turn around, he's there. Logan hasn't stopped since I opened my eyes in the healing temple and saw him leaning over me. God, Farran, I don't deserve him."

She reached for him again, her hand landing on his arm, but Kel couldn't make himself pull away.

"Do you think he'd love you this much if you didn't deserve it? His feelings are based on a lifetime together, not only one incident."

He finally turned his head, not enough to meet her eyes, but enough so he could see her face. "And do you think that if I told him how I betrayed him that it wouldn't change how he looked at me? What he felt for me?"

"I don't know, but how much longer can you go on keeping him and the rest of your family at arm's length?"

Kel swallowed hard and said, "With a little luck, the rest of my life. Maybe my relationship with Logan isn't what it used to be, but it's better than having nothing."

"Is it?" She gripped him more tightly. "Every time you push him away, you're hurting him. When does the pain you're inflicting become more than it's worth to try and help you? To try and maintain a relationship? And how about your guilt? How long until that drives you to sever your ties to him completely? Don't shake your head at me. I know you and you can't tell me it doesn't agonize you every time you see your brother."

Farran did know him too well and it became harder and harder to be around Logan every time Kel saw him. Emotional exhaustion washed over him then, but physically he was wired.

"You've never told anyone anything about your time in captivity, have you?"

"No. I could probably talk about the rest of it, not easily, but I could manage. The problem is that once I started, Logan or my parents or whoever would keep at me until I told them everything and I can't do that."

She reclaimed his hand, her fingers linking with his again, and Kel started to get hard. Adrenaline looking for another outlet, but realizing that didn't make the blood disperse.

"Why'd you share it with me?" Farran asked at last.

Good question. He wished to hell he had an answer. It would be easy to lie and tell her she'd simply been in the right place at the wrong time, but he knew that wasn't it. She wasn't the first person to catch him on the ragged edge and he'd never discussed his past with anyone else.

"I don't know," Kel admitted. "Maybe because I knew you'd make me feel better and I needed that too much to resist. Maybe because you had to learn what kind of man I am. Maybe because I knew I could trust you with it."

More silence, and even with the moonlight casting a glow into the room, it was too damn dark. He could feel the churning inside him getting stronger.

"Kel, wha—"

He brought her hand to his lips and kissed it. "I can't do this anymore. Not tonight. I just can't."

"It's okay, I understand. Let's go back to bed."

"I probably should stay out here."

She stiffened. "Why?"

"Because I want to fuck you."

"What's the problem?" she teased.

Farran didn't get it, that was obvious, and Kel sighed. "There's a difference between that and making love—they're on opposite sides of the spectrum. Everything we've done so far falls on the making-love end of things. That's foreplay and tenderness and caring. Fucking is hard, it's fast, and it's raw. It's about nothing but coming."

Just talking about it made his cock ache and it didn't help that she stared at him, mouth slightly open—likely in shock. "Go to bed," he said, "and close the door behind you."

"You won't be able to sleep out here."

"I won't sleep anyway." He never did after replaying this one. Usually not for a couple of days.

She squeezed his hand. "Come with me, Kel."

He didn't offer her any more warnings, simply followed her down the hall. When they reached the bedroom, Kel turned off the overhead light and tipped the shades on the lamps away from the bed. If he could stand it, he'd turn off the lights entirely—he didn't want her to see his face—but he'd had as much of the dark as he could take.

Farran stripped out of Kel's sweatshirt, tugged the covers out of the way, and got into bed. As he put on the condom, Kel sent up a silent thank-you to the universe for sending this woman to him.

And it was her selflessness that kept him from just falling on top of her. They weren't going to make love, he hadn't lied about that, but Kel took a minute to use his mouth on her. His goal was to heat Farran up as fast as possible, and as soon as he had her wet enough, he was on his knees.

Using his thighs to move her legs farther apart, Kel pushed her knees up to her chest, and held on to her. Farran was wide open now and he watched himself enter her with one solid thrust.

He pumped her hard enough to make the bed bang into the wall, but he didn't slow. That sound—along with the others—added to his arousal.

Not much longer.

Gritting his teeth to hang on for a few more strokes, Kel opened their empathic bond and flooded her with his need. And then it didn't matter, he was coming.

He had no idea how much time passed when Farran said, "You worried me for nothing. I liked this and I'd do it again."

Kel lifted his head and looked down at her. "You would?"

"Not all the time," she said, smiling up at him, "but now and then, yes."

"I don't even know if you came."

"I did. Are we going to repeat it tonight?"

Since he was still hard, the question wasn't out of left field. "Yeah, and I think I can go slower this time. Still not nice and pretty, but better."

Farran's smile widened. "I'm ready when you are."

Her hands stroked down his sides and he immersed himself in her caress. Damn, he really had found his perfect woman and it pissed him off to know that Farran deserved better than him—the evil twin.

Farran leaned back in her chair and eyed the stacks of books on the table. They seemed unending and she was tired of the library. She understood why they were here, but she was growing frustrated again.

Shifting her gaze, she checked out Kel. He looked as bad as he had first thing this morning, but then he hadn't lied about not being able to sleep. Every time she'd woken up throughout the night and checked on him, he'd been lying with his hands behind his head, staring at the ceiling.

She ached for him, but she hid it. Kel would get all defensive and withdraw if he thought she felt sorry for him. She didn't pity him. Yes, she was sorry he'd been captured, sorry he'd had to go through hell, and even sorrier that he was putting himself through even more hell since he'd escaped, but there was nothing pitiable about the man. After more than three weeks in captivity, he'd held out for another six days on the altar against incredible odds. The strength of character that took . . .

And it wasn't good enough for him. He expected more from himself.

Kel looked up. "Did you find something?"

"No, I'm getting that hopeless feeling like I had yesterday." She leaned toward him. "Are you going to help me release some endorphins?"

"Right. You were sore enough this morning to be walking stiffly, remember?"

"And you healed that. I feel fine now—except for low endorphin levels, of course." She winked at him and watched Kel reluctantly smile.

"Study," he ordered, but he sounded amused. "I want to find some way to fight these guys before they corner us again and we don't have that much time left before we leave."

Farran gave him a small salute and went back to the book in front of her. The spidery handwriting was tough to read and the Gineal language was slightly different than the Tàireil, which sometimes made it difficult to work out what the author was trying to say. Not that it would be fun reading anyway.

Kel never complained, though, and she wouldn't either. At least not too much. And she'd try to do a better job at keeping her emotions under wraps.

Running her thumb across the corner of the page, Farran frowned. Last night, Kel's nightmare had distracted her, but now there was too much time to think. She was half shadow walker and she didn't know how she felt about that.

It would make sense if she was happy. After all, that would explain her fath—her mother's husband and his attitude toward her. But there was no joy in the knowledge.

Feeling unhappy or betrayed would be every bit as logical. She'd lived a lie for twenty-five years and no one had thought to fill her in on the truth. But how could Farran feel deceived? Her mother had died when she'd been a very small child, far too young to understand affairs or illegitimacy. And considering how violent Hammond Monroe could be, her mother wouldn't have risked Farran inadvertently saying the wrong thing.

Would she have told Farran when she'd gotten older? It was a question without answer because her mother hadn't lived long enough.

She could blame Hammond for not telling her and she liked that option, but there was no proof that he'd known he wasn't her father. Farran had his family symbol tattooed on her bottom and he wouldn't have allowed it to happen if he'd believed she wasn't his. What he'd learned later was anyone's guess, of course, but at her birth, he'd claimed her as his daughter.

Farran turned to the next section of the book and frowned. So she wasn't happy, she wasn't unhappy, she wasn't mad, she wasn't excited. What was she then? Apathetic?

That wasn't right either. There was definitely emotion, she just couldn't label it.

Ambivalent. That was better. She felt ambivalent about the whole thing. Maybe if she knew Rhyden or the shadow walkers better, it would be different, but she didn't. And maybe that was another reason to go to their world.

Except if she went there, she'd be stuck and she didn't know for how long. It could easily be for the rest of her life. What if she hated the shadow walker's dimension? What if she didn't fit in there any better than she had with the Tàireil? And what if she did belong in the Gineal world? She felt the most comfortable here and—she glanced briefly at the man across the table from her—it was where Kel lived.

Did she really want to leave him?

He talked about how messed up he was and it was true—to an extent. There was no doubting he had issues to work through, but Farran knew he could do it. Kellan Andrews had strength way deep down where it counted. He also had his family and his upbringing on his side.

It wouldn't be fast, and God knew it wouldn't be easy for him, but he could heal. No, he'd probably never get rid of the nightmares entirely, but he could live a mostly normal life again. If he was willing to tackle the work it would take.

And it said a lot that it was easier for her to concentrate on Kel's problems than on her own.

Farran sighed. At least thinking about her situation,

however briefly, had given her one answer—she wasn't making any decisions about traveling to the shadow walker world until the ambivalence passed and she had her head on straight. This wasn't something she could rush into, not when it likely was permanent.

With another sigh, she resumed reading. There wasn't anything they didn't already know and she moved on to the next book. This one was older, but the writing was firmer, the lines thicker, and that made it easier for her.

She was about to call this one a waste of time, too, when something caught her eye.

The book was written by a former troubleshooter and she was talking about the difference between the energy the Gineal used and what the shadow walkers used. Farran's interest piqued when she realized the woman had actually *fought* a shadow walker. Most of what she read was pure speculation and some of it felt so wrong that Farran decided to go with her own instincts on the data.

Stopping short, she backed up and reread the last paragraph, the one where the troubleshooter talked about what had happened when the two different energies had hit head-on. Not just crossed each other, but an actual power-to-power collision.

According to the woman, the streams had been incompatible, and when they'd crashed into each other, a huge mushroom cloud had gone up. Farran closed her eyes and tried to remember what she'd done when she'd boosted Kel's shots.

She had to have unconsciously drawn from the shadow walker power source because she didn't have that kind of strength without it. And that made this information more interesting.

Why had things been different for her and Kel?

Because she was half Tàireil? Or was it something else? Farran reread the information again and something else clicked—the shadow walkers channeled the energy differently. Oh, the troubleshooter didn't come right out and say that, but her description of the battle reminded Farran of the encounters they'd had with the Kādunesen and she knew it wasn't the same.

"Hey, sunshine, let's pack it up for the afternoon."

"Kel, you have to read this." She shoved the book across the table, but before he could glance at it, she said, "I think the reason the shadow walkers can hit so hard is because of how they hold energy. The Tàireil and the Gineal have to bring it through our—their—bodies and channel it outward. The shadow walkers don't. They only have to bring it into their auric fields to fire it. That means they can handle more energy and use it faster."

"And because there's no cells or body tissue in the way, it's purer energy."

"Stronger?"

"Has to be. Rhyden didn't mention this when he took you to the source of your power?"

"No and that begs the question of how much trust I can put in him. Is he really my half brother? Do you know?"

Kel shook his head. "To find out that level of detail, I'd have to scan him by touch. It wouldn't take as long as it took with you, but I don't think he's going to sit still for it anyhow."

"Me either." Farran frowned.

"With the Gineal and Tàireil, family members often have similar energy patterns. It's probably the same with the shadow walkers, but everything is different enough that I wouldn't trust that kind of evidence alone."

She realized he was talking and not looking at the book. "Read that." Kel started to bend his head and Farran added, "The woman who wrote it was a troubleshooter and fought a shadow walker."

He looked back up again and asked, "Do you want me to read or do you want to tell me everything it says?"

Farran opened her mouth, and then realized what he was pointing out. "Sorry. I'd rather have you look at it yourself and form your own impressions."

It almost made her crazy to sit quietly for so long, but

she gripped the table and waited until Kel lifted his head again. "Well?" she demanded.

"Well what? She got her ass kicked the same way I did and nearly every word here is conjecture."

"The mushroom cloud thing. That didn't happen with us."

Kel knew exactly what she was saying. "You weren't shooting *at* me, you were shooting *with* me."

"You think that's the difference?"

Standing, he starting sending the books back to their shelves. "That or the fact you're half Tàireil or about a thousand other possibilities. What's your theory?"

"The half-Tàireil one."

"Good enough for me." Kel grabbed his jacket and put it on.

"Why aren't you excited about the book?"

He picked up her jacket and held it until she slipped her arms into the sleeves. "I'm more interested in what you're telling me than what that troubleshooter had to say." Farran stopped midzip and looked at him. "Whatever she wrote," Kel said, "triggered something for you. I trust your instincts and my guess is the longer we discuss this, the more you'll know."

"And we're going to talk at home?"

"Yep. Come on, let's get out of here. Quietly."

Farran guessed she was beaming as they walked through the library. No one—not ever—had trusted her instincts. That meant a lot to her and she was nearly giddy with the fact that Kel was more enthused about what she had to say than what a fellow troubleshooter wrote in her journal.

They hit the outside door and she felt him reinforce the protection spells around them. That took her elation down a few rungs. She hated this part when they had to leave the library and walk far enough away that Kel felt it was safe to create a transit.

"I hate it, too," he murmured softly, and then taking a deep breath, Kel opened the door.

Her pulse was throbbing before she took a step outside, and by the time they were out of sight of the tasglann, her nerves were strung tight. She fought to get her emotions under control, afraid they'd distract Kel.

It wasn't easy living with an empath, but then she guessed it wasn't easy to be an—

Kel fell to the ground. There wasn't time to check on him. Farran turned frantically, trying to find the enemy. She had to locate him and put herself between him and Kel, had to make sure he didn't take a second hit.

The instant she picked up motion, she moved, ready to defend Kel.

It was the demon strolling toward her.

"How nice to have you to myself at last," Seth said in the same tone of voice he might use at a dinner party.

"Stay where you are."

"Or what?" Seth smiled. "Your troubleshooter has bigger worries right now than attempting to defend you."

Farran started to shake. What had he done to Kel? She took a deep breath and grabbed hold of her control. It was up to her to protect both of them now and she wouldn't let him down.

The demon kept walking.

It was natural to try to draw energy from the Earth, but then she remembered. That wasn't her source. Farran pulled from that place with the colored lights. Don't take it in your body, she reminded herself. Hold it in the aura.

She felt it surround her and kept it ready. It wasn't time to let loose yet. Seth needed to be closer.

"You and I will get along famously. When I think of what we can accomplish together . . . Ah, well, you'll soon see for yourself." He held out a hand as he neared.

Wait. Just another second. Just another— Farran fired, letting loose with everything she had.

Seth flew backward, his body a good five feet in the air.

Her shot didn't emerge as lines of crackly blue electricity; it was a bright green and it came out like a cannonball. And even after expending that energy, Farran still had plenty at hand. Without her doing anything—nothing at all—her power had refilled. It felt like a miracle and she might need it.

The demon stayed down, but Farran didn't move, not even to check on Kel. She'd been fooled by Seth once before and she couldn't risk it now.

Sure enough, he got back to his feet and he no longer looked genial. "And here I thought you were a reasonable woman."

Farran didn't wait this time. She blasted away and Seth sailed even farther. "Come near me again," she told him when he started to move, "and my next shot will be to kill."

He stared at her, measuring her resolve.

"I should kill you anyway for hurting Kel," she said with a snarl as she took a couple of steps his direction. "If he dies, you die, demon. I'll hunt you down to the ends of the Earth if that's what I need to do to take care of you."

She closed ground on Seth, and without another word, he disappeared. Farran scanned, but didn't feel him in the area. Had she really gotten rid of the demon?

And if she had, for how long?

There was a noise behind her, near Kel's position, and she spun around, ready to fire, but he was alone. She rushed over to help him sit up. "Are you okay?"

"Yeah, just dazed. It was a spell, not a shot—something that paralyzed me. Little prick," he grumbled as he stood.

Kel was steady and Farran lowered her arms. He didn't need her to keep him upright.

"Nice shooting," Kel said, "but let's move. We need more distance from the library before I open a transit and I want to get out of here before the shadow walkers trace your magic."

"Sounds good to me."

They made it two steps and then Kel muttered, "Fuck."

Farran backed up before she could stop herself. Arawn and Erzsi blocked the path ahead and they looked determined.

20

CHAPTER

Farran watched Kel raise both hands and start firing, but the shadow walkers were already separating, fragmenting his attention. She knew their position was bad. Low ground again, no cover, and Kel was tired.

Tentacles of electric blue headed for her, but Kel sent a wall of flames at them. They receded.

"Can you fire more of that green stuff?" he asked.

"Yes, but—"

"Then fight with me, sunshine. I need you."

Using all her strength, Farran sent three green balls screaming toward male shadow walker. Casually, calmly, the man shot a bolt of blue. It broke into strands, hit her blasts, and the energy turned to a mist, falling harmlessly to the ground.

She kept firing, putting more power behind it. This was the same stuff that had sent the demon flying, but it caused no damage to the Kādunesen.

But it did keep him busy. And wasting time dispersing her shots. If she could keep it up until he began to phase out . . .

He made an adjustment. Instead of firing at her orbs,

he erected some kind of wall. As each shot hit, it splatted like a water balloon against the sidewalk.

The shadow walker shot at her again, the tendrils snaking everywhere. Farran dodged one and nearly backed into another.

Damn, she hated those things.

Kel stiffened beside her and smothered a curse. He'd been hit.

She sent her energy at the enemy's blue bolt, but instead of stopping his shot, hers disintegrated. Damn it, she was weak compared with other shadow walkers the same way she was weak compared with other Tàireil. Why couldn't she be average in at least one group?

Why did she always have to be worthless?

A bolt slammed into the shield around her. Her knees sagged and she fought to stay on her feet.

And then Kel was in her head. It was startling because he rarely used telepathy with her and this was more than sending thoughts. It was closer to a merge and it was incredibly intimate.

It was also faster than mere telepathy. In a microsecond, Farran knew he was going to open a transit to a more defensible position. She knew that he was going to cover her while she crossed and she was aware of where he wanted her to go once they were there. He had her acknowledgment without her forming words.

The transit opened. Farran leaped across and immediately moved near the boulders that Kel wanted her to use as cover. He was right behind her.

"Try to connect with Rhyden," Kel said. "We need help."

Farran didn't have time to nod before the shadow walkers were there and Kel was sending ropes of fire at them again.

She wasn't sure she could do it, not when she'd never linked with him before, but she'd try. If Rhyden hadn't been lying and he really was her brother, she'd have a better chance of reaching him in another dimension than Kel did. Maybe.

The blue energy hit the boulders around them. Rock flew as it was chipped off and scorch marks covered the cream stone. Farran ducked and tried to stay focused on Rhyden.

Kel was protecting both of them again while she stayed out of the way. Her heart pounded hard and fast. She didn't want anything to happen to him; he meant too much to her to lose.

And then Rhyden was there. At least she'd done one thing to help. He looked battered, but he took up a position on her right and she was between the two men, shielded by their bodies and their magic.

"You look like shit," Kel said as he fired at the shadow walkers. "How long you got here?"

"Short time," Rhyden replied, sending blue out at the enemy. "Fought their allies in our world."

And had been beaten.

How long did they have before Rhyden was pulled back to his dimension and she and Kel were on their own again? Her stomach twisted at the thought.

They had some small advantages. Now they had the high ground and were shooting down at the shadow walkers. The rock garden provided decent cover, although it wouldn't last indefinitely, and they had the sun at their backs.

Maybe they could outlast the—

Kel and Rhyden both took hits at the same time. Rhyden phased out for almost twenty seconds and Kel was gasping as he leaned against a boulder.

She had to do something. She had to. Farran couldn't stand around while her lover and her maybe-brother fought for her.

There was a chance she could combine her power with Kel's again. That had worked well the one time she'd managed. And it should be easier because now she knew how Kādunesen magic functioned—sort of.

Gathering herself, Farran watched, and as Kel let a fireball go, she added her green light to his shot.

Instead of boosting his blast, it seemed to weigh it down, and by the time it reached the female shadow walker, it was almost nothing. Farran frowned. That must not have been the way she'd done it. Why didn't magic come with an instruction book?

It does, Kel sent as he continued to fire. *Millions of them. You saw them in the Gineal library.*

That's no help now.

There was no answer, but then Kel was busy. Rhyden vanished again, gone for nearly a minute, and they wouldn't have him much longer. When he reappeared, he was shaking.

"Shit," Kel swore. "Here come the kids."

They weren't children. There were four of them— three men and a woman—and Kel was immediately talking to them mentally. Farran was still connected to him; she heard him explaining the situation to the young troubleshooters and she felt his frustration when they dismissed his instructions. He obviously was losing and they believed they knew better.

Stupid to ignore a veteran troubleshooter.

Some people have to learn the hard way. "Besides, they'll buy us time and keep the dynamic duo occupied." Kel looked past her to Rhyden. "You need some healing work done while we have a chance?"

"If it's possible, it would be an assistance," Rhyden said.

Kel! You can't afford to give up that energy.

Rhyden has a better chance of beating the shadow walkers than I do. We can't afford to lose him and he's already phasing in and out. If I don't heal him, he's gone before the kids get their asses handed to them.

His arm went behind her and Kel put his hand on Rhyden's shoulder. She couldn't see the energy flow, but with her ties to Kel, she felt it.

Farran turned her attention to the battle and hoped

Kel was wrong, that those newcomers really could defeat the enemy. The four young troubleshooters had flanked the two shadow walkers and were firing continually. And they were taking far more hits from the pair than they landed themselves. Kel was right, those kids were going to lose and they wouldn't even last long enough to wear down the shadow walkers.

And then something occurred to her. If Kel could heal Rhyden, why couldn't she send pure energy to Kel? After all, she had access to incredible power now and—

"No," Kel said. "It's incompatible with mine. I can heal Rhyden because that's a different kind of vibration." He pulled his arm back. "But if you try to channel the stuff you're using into me, you'll probably drop me to the ground."

"But—"

Kel pressed a kiss to her forehead and looked past her to Rhyden. "Ready to rejoin the battle? Maybe we can make some progress while the kids pester them like a bunch of gnats."

Rhyden inclined his head and the two men added their firepower to the fight.

One young troubleshooter took a hit from the female shadow walker and went down. A second had a blue tendril hit him and he staggered. He wasn't going to last much longer either. It wouldn't take long before the three of them were on their own again—unless the kids called in more help.

Farran half expected Kel to answer, but he didn't.

She took in the grim set of his mouth, the slight shaking in his hands, and realized he didn't have the energy to spare. Damn it, she'd known doing a healing was a bad idea. And she was scared. If anything happened to Kel, it would destroy her.

Rhyden appeared as grim as Kel and he phased out again. He was gone less than five seconds, but if he wasn't steady now, he didn't have that long with them despite Kel's energy work.

When she looked back to the fight, only the young female troubleshooter remained on her feet, but even as Farran watched, a bolt hit her and she was out, too. For a moment, she wondered how badly the kids were injured, but only for a moment. Kel got blasted and fell back against a boulder.

The rock and sheer dint of will were the only things keeping him from falling.

Terror morphed to fury. Damn it, why was she helpless? It was unfair, she was half Kādunesen and half Tàireil, she should be able to—

Farran stopped short. She'd tried to fight using only shadow walker energy, but she was half Tàireil. Rhyden had said something about her magic being oriented more toward the Kādunesen. *More toward.* But not completely.

Kel was standing again, but leaning against one of the stones as he fired.

If she discounted Seth, the greatest successes she'd had were when she'd attempted to use Tàireil energy and had unconsciously drawn from the lights. What if she tried to do that consciously? Would that create a mushroom cloud inside her or a formidable weapon?

Rhyden disappeared again and Kel was shooting infrequently, trying to conserve magic. She had no choice but to try. Not if she wanted the three of them to live through this.

The Kādunesen power filled her aura and Farran pulled from the Earth like the Tàireil. She let that energy fill her body.

"I've but minutes," Rhyden warned Kel when he returned.

Slowly, carefully, she allowed the two to mingle. No implosion and she felt fine. With a deep breath, she opened the door wider. Energy flowed, intermingled.

It was dizzying, but in a good way.

The men were gasping, sweating, weakened, and she trickled the energy to both of them. Neither one dropped unconscious and Kel straightened, looked at her. "What are you doing?"

"Are you okay?"

"Yeah, it's replenishing me, but what—"

A shot winged him and with a curse, Kel returned fire.

Farran let her power flow faster. Rhyden began to phase out, but solidified midvanish. Kel's fireballs were bigger and brighter again. She was having an effect. She was doing something. She was helping!

"Rhyden," Kel called, "show her how the hell to fire that shit you guys use."

Without hesitation he opened his mind to her and ran through how he manipulated energy as a weapon. Farran tried it out immediately.

Another green ball that disappeared with one blast of blue.

Half Tàireil. She was half Tàireil. How could she mix styles? She slipped deeper into Kel's head and experienced the way he used his power.

As she ran through the two styles, she figured out how to mesh them into one that took elements of both. Kel suffered another hit, and furious that he'd been hurt again, Farran collected her power and shot it out using her new method.

This ball wasn't green. It was a mixture of the blue color of the Kādunesen and a purple that she knew instinctively came from her Tàireil side.

It was big, it was bright, and it traveled fast.

And when it slammed into the female shadow walker, she went down and stayed down.

"Get the other one, sunshine."

Farran did as he asked, dropping the male every bit as quickly. She stood there, staring, not quite able to believe the fight had ended this easily. Kel's arm went around her waist and he hugged her to his side. "Not easily. Rhyden and I are both pretty wasted, right partner?"

"This is so."

"Are you going to take the bodies back with you or leave them here?" Kel asked.

"Bodies? I killed them?"

Kel's hold tightened. "You did what you had to do, what we needed you to do."

She had and she'd do it again to save Kel.

"How safe is Farran with them gone?" he asked Rhyden.

"The opposition has no other warriors capable of leaving our world. This should end the threat."

"Good."

Rhyden addressed her. "Will you return with me to our world? You must be shown the extent of your power and how to ensure you do not manipulate time."

"You can train her here," Kel said. His muscles had gone rigid and she slipped her arm around his waist, trying to relax him. "An hour a day or every other day—you can travel that often, right?"

"It would be best—"

"Would it?" Kel interrupted and he sounded belligerent. "For her or for you shadow walkers?"

Farran stepped in before this escalated. "Rhyden, I'm not making any decisions about going to your world until I decide how I feel about being half Kādunesen. I need time."

"Time is the problem, sa māsi."

"If you can come to this world like Kel said, you can show me right away how to be careful, can't you?"

He inclined his head. "You have family waiting for you in our world, not only me, but cousins, aunts, uncles, grandparents. All want to meet you and none have the strength to leave."

"Sounds an awful lot like emotional blackmail to me," Kel growled.

"Kellan," Farran warned. "I'm sorry, Rhyden, but I'm simply not ready to make a decision."

"I will talk to the rulers, see if they will agree that I should train you here. They might be obliging with the deaths." He gestured to the downed shadow walkers. "Their bodies do need to return with me and I'd best go before I haven't the strength to travel with them."

Rhyden headed toward the downed Kādunesen before stopping short and turning to her. "I will return with an answer when I have one, but it will be at least a few days."

Farran nodded.

"Using family to impel you to do as I desire was not my intent. I only wished you to know that you would not be alone." Rhyden didn't wait for a reply. That was a good thing, since Farran didn't know what to say and any response from Kel was likely to be inflammatory.

When the three shadow walkers were gone, Kel's body went slack. And almost immediately went taut again. Farran followed his gaze and saw that a contingent of Gineal had appeared behind her.

"Kellan Andrews," the woman snapped, "do you have any idea how much trouble you're in?"

"I think I have a good idea, Council Leader."

Council leader? Farran went rigid herself.

There was an instant where the woman appeared angry and then she calmed and nodded. "You always were smart; you just might. What happened here?"

"It's a long story, Ceannard. I think you better request some healers for the kids before I begin."

She nodded, and within seconds, people appeared near the fallen troubleshooters. "We'll do this in chambers. Both of you," the woman's gaze settled on Farran, "report to headquarters. I'll be there shortly." She began to walk away.

"Ceannard?" Kel called.

Turning back to them, she said, "Yes?"

"Can I get the information on that healer you told me about a year ago. The one I could talk to about what happened to me?"

"I'll have it for you before you leave the council room." The council leader's lips were curved as she left.

* * *

Seth stopped at the area near the cabin only long enough to retrieve a few possessions and put them in his pack. He could still transport himself magically, but at the moment, his power was low enough that he was unable to call his own things to him.

It angered him, but he didn't have the energy to rant or curse the fates. The Tàireil woman had defeated him. Roundly.

After working tirelessly on his plan, after locating the perfect spell and discovering how to dispatch it through the protection of the Gineal to take the man out of the equation, Seth had been thwarted. Thwarted!

Leaning back against a tree trunk, he stared down at the lodge. He longed to hurl a bolt of lightning at it and set the wooden structure ablaze to show his displeasure, but the shield that surrounded it wouldn't allow any damage. And as much as it pained Seth to admit, he hadn't the magic to spare.

This had been his best chance to reclaim his lost power and it was gone. All he'd needed was for the Tàireil female to take him back to the time before he'd met Maia. With foreknowledge, he'd stay far away from her, and because that meant he wouldn't have lost the first sliver of magic, the second incident—the one where Maia had stripped him down to mere Gineal strength—would never have happened.

Greed had cost him and his attempts to fix things had only made it worse. His sole desire now was to return to his previous level of power and even that had been denied to him. If he'd merely been defeated by the troubleshooter, Seth wouldn't surrender the field. Eventually, the woman would be alone and he'd reach her.

But it hadn't been the Gineal who'd trounced him.

She'd learned how strong she was, and in his current state, he was no match for her.

If he approached her again, she'd shoot first and ask

questions later. She might even kill him on sight. It was a sad day when a demon of his stature worried about a Tàireil mongrel.

With a sigh, he hefted his pack and took a final look around. Seth refused to spend the rest of his days hiding from Horus, but for the moment, there was no choice. He had no desire to return to Seattle, but he needed a city with a lot of water to confuse his hunters. Venice? He hadn't been there for quite a number of years. That could be enjoyable.

He might be on the run again, but Seth wasn't losing hope. So he could no longer use the woman to achieve his goal; it mattered not. There was some method to regain his lost power, he was certain of it, and he wouldn't stop trying until he was successful.

Kel took Farran back to the cabin. It was night and he used magic to turn on every light in the place the instant they crossed the transit. They had food, clothes, and she'd probably feel more comfortable here than at his home since this was more familiar. "I told you the council wasn't scary," he said. At least they hadn't been today. He used another bit of magic to close the drapes.

"Then why am I still shaking?"

"Nerves. You were sure they were going to send you back to the Tàireil world."

The ceannards had figured out quickly that she was frightened of them and had treated Farran with incredible gentleness. Not that she realized it, but Kel appreciated their care. They hadn't even been that angry with him over his unauthorized activities, although when they heard the way the kids had ignored his advice on how to fight the shadow walkers, Nessia, the council leader, had bristled. He had a feeling some young troubleshooters were headed back for more training.

"I didn't think they were ever going to let us go." Farran sank onto the love seat and leaned back.

"We had a lot of ground to cover. Not only what's been going on for the past week, but they also wanted your take on what happened during the dragon stone situation."

Farran didn't say anything for long enough to worry him and then she met his eyes. "They actually welcomed me here and some of them smiled. I didn't expect that. And I definitely didn't expect them to talk about integrating me into your society. They meant that in a good way, right?"

Kel grinned at her. "They did unless you don't want to find yourself working for the Gineal."

"I don't mind and I should pull my weight while I'm here."

That wiped the smile off his face. Damn it, she was still thinking about going to the shadow walker world. He'd been hoping to do a little wooing first—a nice dinner, a romantic fire, some hot lovemaking—before talking about this, but after hearing her say *while I'm here* he couldn't stand to wait that long.

He sat on the coffee table in front of her, his feet on either side of hers, and tried to figure out how to start. There were probably a dozen options, but what came out of his mouth, wasn't what he meant to open with. "I love you, Farran."

She stared at him and that made Kel uneasy. He didn't dare read her emotions, and instead, cleared his throat. "I know, I'm a mess and you'd be foolish to hang around someone like me. I have nightmares, flashbacks, insomnia, you'd be stuck sleeping with the lights on for who knows how long, and listening to me blast the music when I couldn't handle the silence anymore or the chanting I sometimes hear in my head." He shrugged. "But you've seen me at my worst—believe me, it doesn't get much worse than last night—and if you can handle it, I'd like it if you'd stay with me."

Farran still didn't say anything and Kel felt his stomach cramp up. Well, what had he expected? Really?

"If you don't feel like you want to live with me, maybe you could at least remain in this world and we could, I don't know, keep seeing each other or something. That way you'd be spared most of the downside about me. Although, maybe there isn't much upside."

Here was this beautiful, sweet, loving woman and he thought she was going to settle for him? He was an idiot, no doubt about it, but Kel kept talking, unable to stop himself. "I'm aware that I don't deserve someone like you, not after what I've done, and we both know you can do better than me, but I'm too selfish to let you go—at least not without telling you how I feel first. And I promise you, if you stay with me, I'll work every day to show you I can change, I can become a better person—a whole person—again."

She stared some more and Kel cracked. "Please, say something. If you're trying to find some way to let me down gently, I promise you, it's better to just spit it out."

"You love me?" Farran sounded stunned and that gave Kel a spark of hope.

"I love you," he assured her, leaning forward and resting his hands on the sofa cushions beside her knees. "I know I'm not an easy man to be with, but I promise you, I'll love you for the rest of my life and into the next one if you give me a chance."

"You love me." She didn't sound dazed this time, but Kel wasn't sure how to take it.

"Yeah, I do. Here, feel how much." And he opened the gate between them, letting her experience his emotions. He knew she was getting his anxiety and stress along with how deep his feelings for her ran, but he couldn't hold anything back, not if he wanted her to believe him.

"You love me!" Farran smiled as she said it and something inside him eased. It was going to be okay.

"With everything I am, sunshine."

Her arms went around his neck. "The way you were talking yourself down, I wondered if you felt you had to say you wanted me around, but were really hoping I'd walk away."

"What?" Kel couldn't even grasp that line of thought.

"Keep in mind, troubleshooter, that you're not the only one who's got a few issues. Living with me won't be a picnic for you either. You think I'm tough, and I can be, but not always. I get bouts of insecurity, times when I wonder if I'm completely unlovable. My family . . . well, you know enough about how I grew up to understand the scars that were left behind—and I'm not talking about the one I had on my face."

"I understand scars, probably better than anyone."

Farran nodded. "Yeah, I guess you do. The thing is, all I've ever wanted was to belong somewhere and I never have."

"You're wrong," he said, drawing her nearer. "You belong with me. The only question is if you want to."

She kissed him, a slow, tender meeting of their mouths that made him close his eyes to savor every nuance. Farran eased back and their gazes met. "Oh, I want. I love you, too, Kel."

And she opened herself up the same way he had, letting him feel her love for him. It humbled him, made Kel realize just how damn lucky he'd really been the night he'd answered the door at his brother's house. This time he kissed her, holding Farran as close as he could given their positions.

Reluctantly, he broke away and straightened. "I guess I better tell you one more thing—it wouldn't be fair to you if I didn't." He took a deep breath. "Rhyden really is your brother. I checked it out while I was sending him energy this afternoon."

"I thought he might be. It felt right."

Kel tensed up again. "Does this change things? For us, I mean. You'll still stay in this world?"

"I'm not going anywhere. Are you serious about my moving in with you or was that just talk?"

She'd remained open for him and he picked up her vulnerability. "We are a pair, aren't we?" He shifted to sit beside her on the love seat and pulled her on his lap. "Yeah, I want you to live with me. If you don't like my house, we'll go shopping for a new one, something that's ours and—"

Farran put two fingers on his lips. "You're kidding, right? I love that house. It's beautiful and it's got a good vibe to it, but the kitchen needs a little work."

He smiled and leaned back, wrapping both arms around her. "Thirty seconds and you'll never know a battle took place inside it." Kel sobered. "I'm glad, though, about the house. Change isn't easy for me and I feel comfortable there with nature all around me." He sighed. "I wish I'd started dealing with my problems a year ago. Maybe by now, I'd be normal enough that—"

"Stop it, Kel. Just stop, okay? We love each other, we're going to have a future together. Let's leave it there."

"You're right."

"That's what I like to hear."

Kel laughed, not because what Farran had said was funny, but because he felt so damn good. For the first time in a long, long time, he had a life that was worth living.

Epilogue

FIVE MONTHS LATER

Everyone else had congregated in the den and kitchen, but Kel stood alone on the back porch. He felt awkward, uncomfortable, and he wanted to get out of here, but he and Farran couldn't leave. Not yet. Not until after they brought out his dad's birthday cake and presents were opened. But the family celebration was taking place at Logan and Shona's house and Kel was having a hell of a time staying out of his brother's way.

After months of daily sessions to work through his time in captivity, his healer had suggested that Kel needed to tell Logan what had happened. He'd argued, balked, dug in his heels, and finally, two weeks ago, Kel had invited his brother to one of his appointments and confessed.

Logan had stared at him without speaking for an eternity and then he'd said, "I need some time." He'd walked out and Kel hadn't seen his brother since. Until today.

Farran came up to him and slipped her hand in his. "How are you doing? Okay?"

"No. I never should have let you convince me to come."

Immediately she began sending him soothing waves

and Kel let her help him. "We had to be at the party," Farran said quietly. "It would have ruined your dad's day if you weren't here."

"Yeah." And instead he was ruining Logan's day. Probably Shona's, too, since it was hard to imagine his brother keeping secrets from his fiancée. "I wish this would end, though. It's been a long afternoon."

And getting longer, Kel thought when Logan came outside and headed toward them. "Hey," his brother said, "why don't you and I take a walk by the lake?"

Kel gripped Farran's hand tightly for a moment, but he collected his courage and said, "Sure."

Reluctantly he went down the stairs. If Logan was ready to tell Kel he was a no-good asshole and that he didn't want him to come here again, his brother had the right.

But Logan didn't say anything as they walked and Kel grew more tense with every step. They were out of sight of the house when his brother finally stopped and hopped up to sit on a retaining wall facing the water. Kel leaned against the stone blocks near him, but not too close, and waited. Still nothing.

The anticipation became excruciating and Kel decided someone had to say something. "Look, I'm sorry. You don't want me here, but I couldn't find a way to get out of it without hurting Dad, not after Farran and I already promised to come. You don't have to worry about it happening again, though. I'll turn down all future invitations."

"What?"

Logan was looking at him now, but Kel didn't turn away from the lake. It took him a second to get control back. "I know you hate me, and if I could change one thing, it would be that moment, but I can't. I betrayed you and I'll have to live with that—and the consequences— for the rest of my life."

"You think I hate you?"

Kel nodded. His throat was tight, but he said, "You getting up and walking out made that obvious. I want you to know that I'm not making any excuses for my actions. I realize it seemed like that, but the healer insisted I tell you the whole story, not just the part where I sold you out. She claimed you needed context."

His brother's eyes seemed to bore into him and Kel struggled harder to hang on to his self-command.

"You're a moron," Logan said.

"And a bastard, a prick, a coward, a—"

"Be quiet," Logan said, dropping from the wall to his feet.

Kel shut up. His hands were fisted at his sides as he fought to remain steady. Logan deserved to be able to tell Kel what he thought of him and he'd survive this. Somehow.

"I don't hate you. I'd never hate you—for heaven's sake, you're my brother." Logan muttered a curse and from the corner of his eye, Kel saw him shake his head. "I can't even believe you'd think I'd hate you. I was at that healing temple within minutes of your arrival that day. I saw what kind of shape you were in and I know we almost lost you. How the hell can you think I'd blame you for saying or doing whatever you needed to in order to make it out of your prison alive?"

"It wasn't a matter of survival."

"Bullshit." Logan came around in front of him and Kel had to force himself to meet his eyes. "You thought they'd stop torturing you if you offered them what they wanted. You couldn't have taken much more so you did what you had to."

Kel scowled. "I shouldn't have given them your name."

"Whose name were you going to give them? Dad's? Mom's? One of the girls'? Subconsciously, you had to realize those darksiders were never going to put anyone else in your place, but on the off chance they did, you picked me because you knew I had the best odds of coming through it."

"I never should have given them *any* name," Kel insisted.

"They would have killed you trying to get one."

He shrugged. "Probably."

Logan swore again and spun away, pacing in a circle before he stopped in front of Kel once more. "You'd rather have died, wouldn't you? That's too bad because I'd rather have you alive. Do you have any idea what the hell it would do to me to lose you? Damn it, Kel, we're connected in ways I can't even begin to explain, but I feel them here." He tapped his chest.

Kel knew that. He felt those bonds, too, he always had and that was what made his betrayal harder to bear.

His brother tipped his head back, closed his eyes for a moment, and then said more calmly, "When I sat beside your bed in the temple and the healers honest to God didn't know if you were going to make it, one of the things I kept thinking over and over was that I wished it had been me instead of you."

"No."

"Yes. I would have willingly taken your place on that damn perverted altar. Just like we both know that if I'd been captured, you would have traded places with me. So how can I hate you for mentioning my name when I would have volunteered anyway?"

"But when I told you—"

"I walked out. I know." Logan looked away for a minute. "You know why? Because it ripped me up to find out what you'd endured and to know it was partly my fault . . ."

"How the hell do you figure that?"

"I can scry and we have a connection. I should have found you. I should have been able to fucking find you."

"Logan—"

"I knew you'd been badly hurt back then—that was hard enough to live with—but I didn't know how systematic the abuse had been or how much psychological torture was involved and hearing it two weeks ago—it's taken me time to work through it, to accept that I failed you when you needed me most. I never thought you'd take my leaving wrong. You always seem to read me accurately and I guess I just assumed you'd know what my problem was without my saying anything." His brother looked rueful. "I was too focused on me to think about what my actions would do to you."

"I . . . I couldn't imagine you not hating me. Why wouldn't you when I hate myself so much?"

Logan moved and leaned against the wall, close enough to Kel that their shoulders brushed. "You're too hard on yourself, but then you usually are. You're my brother and I love you—I'll always love you." He cleared his throat. "Now that we have that straight, you think you'll get back to normal?"

"No. I'm never going to be who I was before, but maybe in a while, I can find a new version of normal."

"Works for me. I think I should come to a few more of your sessions with the healer, you know, so we can talk this out with a neutral party to keep us from misunderstanding each other."

Kel unclenched his hands. "Might be a good idea." He had to clear his own throat. "Logan? I'm not the only one being hard on himself—you didn't fail me. And I love you, too, little brother."

Farran leaned off the porch, trying to see if Kel was coming back yet. She'd felt his anxiety, bubbling and spiking before he'd shut down and she'd gotten nothing. That worried her. What the hell was Logan saying to him?

Please, she prayed, *don't let Logan hurt Kel. He's already been hurt so much. Please.*

"Why don't you come in the house?" Shona invited and Farran jumped. She hadn't heard her friend come up beside her.

"I'm waiting for Kel."

"He and Logan might be awhile; they need to talk."

"I know. That's what has me worried."

Shona put an arm around her shoulders and Farran took a minute to be grateful they'd picked up their friendship again so easily after talking about what had happened with the dragon stone.

"They'll work it out," Shona said.

"Sure." They had to because it would destroy Kel if they didn't.

It hadn't been easy, but both she and Kel had been making progress dealing with the scars from their pasts. Hers were tough because they'd been there since she was a toddler, but his were much worse, and if Logan didn't forgive him the way she believed he would, Kel would lose most of the ground he'd gained.

Farran reached out mentally for him, but he remained closed off. She changed the subject hoping that it would lessen her nerves. "How are plans going for the wedding?"

Shona huffed out a breath. "My mom is second guessing every choice I make and Logan! He keeps saying, *if you're happy, I'm happy.* I'm going to kill him if he doesn't make some of the decisions with me."

Her friend's obvious frustration made Farran smile in spite of herself. "I'd guess he doesn't care, he just wants to marry you."

"You have it exactly right, but it's still aggravating and he knows it."

"Your best bet would be to tell him, verbally, that you want him to take some of the burden off you. Guys need things spelled out someti— They're coming." Farran broke away from Shona and tried not to look obvious as she stared at the men, but as they grew closer, she couldn't pretend. "Oh, God, they're smiling." She turned to her friend, tears in her eyes. "Kel's smiling!"

It was all she could do to stand still as they neared and finally, as they started up the steps, Farran rushed over to meet him. He stopped and pulled her into a hug. She felt Logan brush past her, but she rested her head against Kel's chest, wrapped her arms around him, and hung on.

"It's okay," Kel said next to her ear.

"Logan, wha—" Shona began.

"I'll explain later, let's go inside," Logan told her.

"What happened?" Farran asked as soon as she heard the door to the house close.

"My brother doesn't hate me." Kel pulled back far enough to smile down at her. "It never even occurred to him to hate me."

Farran threw her head back and laughed in sheer joy. She'd told him over and over that Logan wouldn't feel that way, but Kel had been adamant. *Thank you, God. Thank you!* "It's going to be okay?"

"Yeah, I think so. I know I've been making slow progress for a while now, but this was a big move forward. And it helps me. A lot."

It had to. Nothing ate at Kel more than the guilt over giving his captors his brother's name. Logan not hating him was huge for Kel, but her hyperresponsible trouble-shooter needed to work on not hating himself. That would be the hardest part and he'd still have to tell his family what had happened, but that was later. Now it was time to enjoy his good news.

Kel brushed her hair off her face and gazed down at her for a moment before he said, "Let's talk." He settled them on the top step of the porch and took her hand in his. "I love you, Farran."

She tried to speak, but Kel gave her a small squeeze and she subsided.

"You're special," he continued, "and you deserve someone who isn't dragging half a cargo bin of baggage with him, but I'm glad you've stayed with me. Every night when we go to bed, I realize I've fallen a little deeper in love with you and every morning when I wake up with you beside me, I thank God that you've stayed with me one more day."

"Oh, Kel, I love you, too." Farran pressed her lips to his chin, but he wasn't finished yet.

He kissed her, stood up, and fished a ring out of the tiny pocket in his jeans before sitting beside her again.

"It was important to me to wait until I knew I could offer you someone half worth marrying. I think I'm there." He smiled his crooked grin and her heart turned over. "I chose a ruby because one of its properties is that it lights a person's darkness and since you're my sunshine . . ." Kel shrugged. "It seemed more appropriate than a diamond."

"It's perfect." And it was because he hadn't just bought what was expected; Kel had given it some thought and chosen a ring that had meaning for them.

He slid the band down her finger and she wasn't surprised that it was an exact fit. That was Kel—he paid attention.

"If you don't like it, we can pick out something else."

"It's beautiful and I love it." It was more than beautiful and much bigger than anything she would have chosen for herself, but she wasn't telling him that, not when he was already wondering if she'd prefer something else. "You know where I want to get married?"

Kel put his arm around her shoulders and hugged her close. "Where?"

"Up at the cabin, in the clearing by the lake. Maybe we could even stay there for our honeymoon, go for walks, throw a blanket on the grass and have wild sex."

"You don't want all the hoopla like Shona's having?"

"No, definitely not." The thought of getting married in front of that many people made her stomach knot up. "And I don't want to wait that long to claim you as mine. Do you think we can set a date soon enough that it'll still be warm outside? I'd hate to throw a blanket down on the snow."

"Probably. I'll go online when we get home and check out the requirements for that county in Wisconsin. We'll have to make sure we pick a time Rhyden will be able to come to our dimension; you're going to want him to be there."

"Yes. He is the only family I really have."

He hugged her again. "Wrong. I don't know if you realize it, but when you took me on, you gained three bratty sisters, another new brother, and a couple of parents. My family is yours."

"Yeah," she said slowly, "they are." It was true. They'd accepted her and had never made her feel like an outsider. She made Kel happy and that was all they'd needed to know.

"You told me once that you just wanted somewhere to belong," Kel said softly. "Do you feel like you have that yet?"

She went still. Farran hadn't thought about not belonging anywhere in a while—maybe because she hadn't felt lost in such a long time. Not only did she have a place among the Gineal, she had a brother who came to visit whenever he could, a best friend who'd forgiven her in minutes for her past sins, and a new family that accepted her.

But most important, she had a man who loved her unconditionally. He didn't care whether or not she was powerful, all he cared about was her. "I have it, Kel. I am exactly where I belong. With you."